I0584471

ASCENSION

OF THE

SEVEN

BAILEY BLACK

Copyright © 2025 by Bailey Black

All rights reserved. No portion of this book may be reproduced in any form without written permission from the publisher or author, except as permitted by U.S. copyright law.

IBSN: 979-8-9996882-0-0 (paperback)
IBSN: 979-8-9996882-1-7 (EBook)

No part of this publication may be reproduced, stored or transmitted in any form or by any means, electronic, mechanical, photocopying, recording, scanning, or otherwise without written permission from the publisher. It is illegal to copy this book, post it to a website, or distribute it by any other means without permission.

This novel is entirely a work of fiction. The names, characters and incidents portrayed in it are the work of the author's imagination. Any resemblance to actual persons, living or dead, events or localities is entirely coincidental.

Bailey Black asserts the moral right to be identified as the author of this work.

Designations used by companies to distinguish their products are often claimed as trademarks. All brand names and product names used in this book and on its cover are trade names, service marks, trademarks and registered trademarks of their respective owners. The publishers and the book are not associated with any product or vendor mentioned in this book. None of the companies referenced within the book have endorsed the book.

NO AI TRAINING: Without in any way limiting the author's exclusive rights under copyright, any use of this publication to "train" generative artificial intelligence (AI) technologies to generate text is expressly prohibited. The author reserves all rights to license uses of this work for generative AI training and development of machine learning language models.

Editor: Mallory Day, www.mallorydayediting.com
Cover Design: LilyTea Art, lilytea.art
Formatted by: Lorna Reid

For the one's who've learned to survive in silence, who watch everything and trust nothing—but still crave a love that feels safe enough to fall into. You are worthy of that love.

CHAPTER 1

OUT OF SERVICE

12 Years Ago

Willow stared at her older brother's lifeless corpse. Her eyes stung as she tried her hardest to keep the tears from falling, failing miserably. *She told herself she wouldn't cry.* Peace drifted across Kai's features. His walnut curls cascaded in soft waves along his neck, lying loose at his shoulders. He had been growing out his hair, which was both against law enforcement protocol and how they were raised, but Mr. Rhodes wouldn't dare scold his perfect son. Willow's eyebrows furrowed as she took it all in, knowing that under the pristine white button down they put him in, his torso lay obliterated–ripped to shreds.

To her left, her parents huddled together in grief. Her father's arms engulfed her mother completely, while his face remained painfully vacant. As the Chief of Police, he had to keep it all together, so her mother wept for the two of them as the entire town of Misty Pines watched them in the darkest moment of their lives. Every ounce of love they planted into their son, uprooted. They lost the most precious thing in their existence.

Willow's bicep stiffened, fingernails scraping the inside of the snowy velvet lining of the onyx coffin. Her nose scrunched and her mouth turned downward as her tears silently fell. Alone. He had left her all alone. She wanted to wail in his face that she would never forgive him. But that would be a lie.

A uniformed officer approached her father from behind, placing a firm hand on his shoulder. "Sir, whenever you're ready, the service can begin."

Her father nodded, releasing Willow's mother from his embrace. He straightened his posture, rearing his shoulders back and aligned his head as he took in Willow. He motioned in the direction of the wooden pews, holding her gaze. *Sit the hell down, he means.* She took a long inhale, sniffing her runny nose as she gave her brother one last glance. Teardrops littered his suit jacket.

The townspeople that awkwardly lingered started to fill in the pews, the old wood creaking as they sat down. The room swelled with bodies as more and more people arrived. Some even stood along the back of the old stone church. Did any of them even know Kai? That his favorite snack was mint chocolate chip ice cream with pretzels? *She doubted it.* What little sun Misty Pines had shone through the multicolored stained-glass windows, causing fragments of vermillion, gold, and sapphire to shimmer off the stone walls.

Kai's coffin sat centered in the arched altar at the front of the room. Willow took a seat front and center, opposite of her parents who sat with the rest of the officers. She could feel the weight of everyone's stare burrowing into the back of her head. Physically, Willow was there, but mentally she had disconnected from the room long ago. She'd say she didn't care what anyone thought—but that'd be another lie. The officer from earlier made his way to the altar and stepped up to the podium.

"Today we are here to honor the tragic death of our fellow Officer, Kai Rhodes. Officer Rhodes was loved by many across the station and our town. I was lucky enough to be trained by him. The bravery he showed during this investigation will never be forgotten. Today, Officer Rhodes would want us…"

Willow tuned out the rest. The emptiness in her chest caused deafness, the spoken words mutter into white noise. Static scratched the air as she stared past the officer speaking, attention resting on Kai.

Other selected officers, the mayor, and an Oregon State Official came up to the podium to speak. Only when Willow's father finally appeared at the podium was she able to pull herself back into reality. Chief Rhodes grasped the podium, as if he were trying to steady himself, and he cleared his throat. "Thank you everyone for coming. I am Chief of Police, Rhodes." He paused, gathering himself to speak again, knuckles white as they clutched the wood.

"Kai was an excellent officer. He gave everything he had to his job. Every day he would wake up, put on his uniform, and fight for the good in the world. There is evil in this world, and it was Kai's mission to find it. Some may say evil won the day he died, but not me. I am hopeful we will find the culprit behind this attack and serve them justice. Kai will forever be remembered as a hero. He was the best officer, and the best child a father could ask for." Chief Rhodes choked on his tears, while Willow winced at his words. He wasn't wrong, Kai was the guy you could always count on. He had always listened to their parents, always did well in school, always willing to lend a hand to those in need. There wouldn't be anymore "always".

Muttered whispers filtered toward the front from the townspeople in the back of the sanctuary. Sniffles from almost every pew echoed through the cavernous building. Once Chief Rhodes rejoined his wife, an officer began to project a slideshow of Kai's photographed memories—from his first year on duty as a patrol officer, baby photos of him beginning to walk, high school football action shots, and then pictures of Kai and Willow. Tears welled up behind her eyes once again as she watched the highlights of his life, reliving the wonderful memories Kai had made with those around him.

He was so extroverted, it hurt. He actively forced Willow to be the same, despite her more reserved nature. He was kind-hearted, so sincere that it was almost suspicious, and the guy you'd call randomly at two in the morning to help you move a couch with no questions asked. Seriously, that happened. No questioning it, he showed up ready to assist. Goodness lived in the small things he did when no one was watching. But Willow always was watching. She gripped her necklace, a sterling silver cross that Kai had given her months before his death. Under her touch, the metal hummed, creating a slight indent in her hand as she squeezed it.

Instrumental piano covers played as the pictures continued until eventually the slideshow restarted from the beginning. A new officer stepped up beside Kai's coffin, clearing his throat to speak.

"Thank you to all who submitted the wonderful photo memories of Officer Rhodes. At this time, can all the designated pallbearers, flag team, and firing staff please come to the front to assist in moving to the burial site around back." He nodded his head as he began to close the casket and drape the American flag over the top. Willow stood without thinking, watching the officers line up on either side of Kai.

"Come. Let's go before they move him," Chief Rhodes approached Willow, still holding Mrs. Rhodes firm within his grasp.

Willow twisted out of reach, side stepping the two of them completely and walked alone down the center aisle of the church toward the exit. The beige and white checkered floor clicked beneath her black heels. As she pushed the wooden church doors, the wind carried them open for her the rest of the way. Rain sprinkled soft kisses, landing on the exposed skin of her shoulders. She didn't bother using an umbrella, allowing the rain to rinse away the stifling air of the sanctuary, continuing around the back of the building toward the cemetery.

Rows of tombstones cluttered the ground. Every step Willow took toward Kai's empty plot, she couldn't help but think of the people buried underneath her heavy tread. Who were they? What had they been like? What did they do to end up here? She'll end up there one day. The caws from a murder of crows broke her from her rambling thoughts as they passed overhead.

The rest of the mourners filed in behind what remained of the Rhodes family. By the time the pallbearers made it down the steps and around the back of the church, only one narrow path remained for them to take to Kai's burial spot.

The rest of the procession melted into a blur. Bagpipes played "Amazing Grace" as two officers lowered the casket into the ground. Chief Rhodes picked up his radio, making the last call for Kai.

"Radio 1623 Rhodes. Radio 1623 Rhodes," Mrs. Rhodes's wailing sobs grew louder in the silence of the call. "No answer 1623 Rhodes. Rhodes out of service. Gone, but never forgotten," Chief Rhodes bit through as he completed the end of watch call. The murder of crows gathered on the top of tombstones furthest from the church, their caws mimicked the sadness in the air. Each squawk pierced her brain, jabbing her nerves like tiny needles.

One by one, close family and friends who had acquired a rose from the funeral director dropped it onto the casket in the ground as a last goodbye. Hesitant steps prolonged her arrival as long as she could until she forced herself to finally peer down into the hollow earth below. She fidgeted, twirling the thorned rose stem in her fingers until at last, letting go. The crimson rose plopped atop the coffin. That's it.

"I will make them pay," she muttered under her breath, through gritted teeth. Justice will be served, one way or another. Black wings thundered above. A single raven feather plummeted, skimming the air before settling at Willow's feet.

CHAPTER 2

THE SECRET CITY

Present Day

The bulletin board hanging on the accent wall isn't nearly as full as Willow wishes. Several mugshots are thumbtacked, a single red yarn thread hangs, the end whipping with every rotation of her overhead fan. The trail is cold. For *years*. Over a decade, to be precise. Her fingertips press against her eyes so hard colored dots glitter behind her eyelids. A yawn stretches her mouth. She stands up from her small wood and ivory kitchen table, stretching her arms overhead. The pitter-patter of rain fills her silent home. The sky gradually lightens from a dark wall of gray to overcast with tiny beams of sunshine peeking through the clouds.

Water pours from Willow's brass watering can to the various plants dispersed throughout the house, from her bookshelves, kitchen counter, and windowsills. She may not take care of herself, but her plants? They might as well be her children.

The face of her digital watch flickers to life in the darkness of the cabinet under the sink. The watering pitcher lives there after its use to not be such an eyesore. Eight-thirty in the morning. Since she's currently off duty, it's the perfect time to get her training in. For twelve years now, Willow has dedicated her life to two things: becoming the best detective the town could ever have and finding her brother's murderer. It wasn't a goal to be better than Kai—as that could never be achieved. But if she could reach even close to his level, it'd really rub salt in their father's wound. Petty? Yes. Does she care? No.

The city of Misty Pines hasn't changed much at all in the last few years. Everyone knows everyone, since living in a secluded town doesn't give others the option not to. Unless, that is, you don't mind being called an arrogant asshole who doesn't care about the community. Willow, unfortunately, *has* to care to succeed in her career. It isn't like she doesn't care about people, but it'd be a dream to live in a cabin in the woods and have everyone forget about her. Typically, there's encouragement to move out of small hometowns. To get out in the world and explore, experience life. But Willow's world perished twelve years ago.

The rain falls in a soft drizzle as Willow makes her way out of the house to head for the local gym. Patchy fog hovers outside her home. Luckily, even though her home is shrouded by nature—keeping her privacy intact, the main square is within walking distance from her. She lucked out finding this cozy starter home. The only downside is the proximity to her family home, but it's not as though they try speaking to her. It's been years since their paths crossed.

The wooded, shortcut path to town is encircled by Coastal Redwoods in every direction– earning the town's nickname of the "Secret City" of Oregon. Not to mention the inconsistent fog covering them like a blanket. Rows of trees act like a barrier, keeping the rest of humanity out as the town operates in a world of its own. Beneath Willow's feet the uneven ground becomes smooth pavement. History of witches plague the town; the founder is known for the slaughtering of more than seventy women–all of whom he claimed were witches who would curse the town. It's ludicrous, but an excellent selling point for tourists. Especially for Halloween.

In the center of Misty Pines, locally owned shops, cafes, and restaurants nestle within historical buildings. The aromatic delight of fresh baked bread permeates through the air. The golden scent of the Rustic Roll bakery causes saliva to pool in her mouth, even if it's just walking by the building. The town has less life to it this early in the morning. The tranquil atmosphere allows for its natural beauty to shine through without the bustling crowds that walk the streets in the afternoon and night, thanks to the newly found tourists visiting the new casino.

The gym comes into view, and with each step closer, Willow's eagerness grows. Opening the door, Willow finds faces that are only familiar because of their similar routine. The scent of sweat hangs faintly in the air, mixing with the smell of the rubber mats and exercise equipment.

A steady rhythm of treadmills fills the room, along with the clank of weights and heavy breaths. Mirrors adorn the left and back walls, offering one's reflection in what's supposed to be motivation but has always made her uncomfortable. Why would anyone want to see the veins popping from their forehead in the middle of a heavy lift? In the center of the room, treadmills, ellipticals, and stationary bikes spread out in rows. A hum of conversation buzzes in the back right corner of the gym near the group fitness auxiliary room.

The owner at the front desk welcomes Willow with a warm smile. The crow's feet lines deepen the more teeth she flashes.

"Good morning, Detective Rhodes!" she beams. Her curly auburn hair gathers in a ponytail flowing halfway down her back.

"Hi, Donna–" Willow's response cuts off, her eyes meeting the man standing directly behind the owner.

Towering above Donna's petite frame, his tall stature rests against the back wall. The playful twitch of his mouth causes her pulse to jump, leaving Willow uncharacteristically flustered. She averts her gaze back to Donna.

"Detective?" The man's interest piques as he beams.

"Oh, Gideon! Let me introduce you! She's just wonderful," Donna exclaims, pulling Gideon around the front desk by his arm.

Self-consciousness washes over Willow. Her fingers fidget to adjust her workout top, smoothing out the creases across her stomach so skin doesn't show.

"Willow, dear, this is the new personal trainer I was telling you about a couple weeks ago! This is Gideon." Donna's hand gestures to the blonde. She blocks out most things Donna tells her, usually responding to her with a nod and friendly smile then carrying on her way.

His icy blue irises match the shade of hers. He has an undeniable allure—several other women who hop off their treadmills swivel their heads in his direction to eavesdrop.

"He specializes in yoga but will teach our Saturday and Sunday HITT classes as well!"

Gideon extends his hand to Willow. Her hand warms as his fingers curl around hers. Her lips arc into a tight, unnatural curve. "Nice to meet you," she responds curtly.

Donna chuckles. "Detective Rhodes here isn't much of a talker, but she does a wonderful job protecting our growing town and frequents here. You've got to stay in shape to protect and serve! So, you'll see her often," she chimes, her smile lifting from ear to ear as she winks.

Willow groans internally. Donna has a bad habit of trying to play matchmaker, and she is *awful* at it. The first being a man by the name Luke, who had an aversion to brushing his teeth. The last told her how much he hated law enforcement. That *obviously* didn't go well.

The corners of Gideon's mouth lift in quiet amusement. She waits for his grip to ease, but he prolongs the handshake and shows no sign of letting go. A jolt shoots through her chest, and she wrenches her hand free.

"I look forward to getting to know you, Detective. Thank you for your service," he adds, each word flowing effortlessly from his lips.

"Uh–I–yes. I'll see you around," Willow stammers, turning on her heels, tucking her light brown hair behind her right ear and picking up the pace.

Donna briefs Gideon about some other regular patrons, her commentary growing further away. Willow takes deep breaths to regulate her heart rate, heading to the treadmill section in the center of the gym. Out of the corner of her eye, she meets Gideon's gaze once more, but this time he snaps his stare aside. The attention makes her squirm. If she could fly completely under the radar, she would. Running recalibrates herself. The thought alone eases her racing heart and mind.

She approaches every part of her job with unwavering seriousness–physical fitness is one of those priorities. Everything she does is for her career. Her legs glide with ease atop the treadmill, each stride pushing herself further than the last. Her limbs move with fluid grace, muscles flexing in perfect harmony with the rest of her body, propelling herself forward, driven by the always present memory of Kai. After the rawness of grieving passed, his death now acts as her sole motivator.

Nearly forty minutes of running numbs Willow's thoughts. Beads of sweat glisten, dripping off her dark brows. The jarring ringtone from her phone buzzes inside the cup holder of the treadmill, snatching her out of her trance.

Willow grins at the screensaver. Her fist pounds against the emergency stop, halting her movement.

"Do we have something?" Willow blurts out, answering within seconds of the sound ringing.

"Oh, Will. It's bad. I'm in Misty, and we have a crime scene." The palpable sense of unease colors Nadia's voice.

"Text me the address. I'm on the way."

CHAPTER 3

THE FIRST MURDER

B ranches snap under Willow's footsteps as she ventures further into the dense wooded area in the outskirts of town. "Nadia's location says it should be near here," she whispers to herself.

Directions aren't her strong suit. Willow's stomach knots as the neon yellow crime scene tape comes into view, securing the scene from further contamination. There have been deaths in town since Kai's, sure. But not murders. It's not confirmed, but she's almost certain this call is a homicide given her trek through the woods. Moss and leaves cling to her boots as she makes it to the blocked off area.

Additional investigators are on the scene, moving their kits from each section of the blocked off area. Flashes from cameras strobe in waves. Like a marionette losing its strings, she slows—locking onto the form that death claimed. The pads of her fingers heat as she grips her bag strap. Nadia stands over the corpse in observation, the pen in her hand scribbling viciously against her yellow notepad. A sterile white crime scene suit consumes her from head to toe, her olive skin only visible through the protective visor.

Nadia hesitates. "It's been a while since Misty has seen something like this." Her pitch carries a quiet gravity and flashbacks of Kai's shredded torso crash into Willow's mind.

Moving her focus from Nadia to the deceased, Willow holds back a gag, the corners of her mouth turned down and drawn together. She holds her white knuckled fist in front of her mouth, hoping it'll prevent her from puking.

A male's distorted corpse lays prone— directly into a puddle of rainwater, mixed with what is presumably his own bodily fluid. Deep lacerations, both ragged and irregular in shape, stretch from the base of the man's neck, down to his lower back in every direction. Broken exposed pieces of bone jut out of each individual limb, each extremity folds in a different direction than the other. Blood soaks the ground under his mangled vessel.

Willow's nose scrunches. "*Damn*," she mutters under her breath, attempting to not inhale any more than necessary. The one day she forgets to pack her Vicks VapoRub, of course a dead body is discovered. She circles the figure from a distance, taking note of each angle of destruction. What kind of monster did this? The violence speaks for itself; whoever did this acted with pure rage. *Would she have this level of rage the day she comes face to face with Kai's killer?* She shakes her head, ignoring the nagging question.

Nadia nods, dabbing the contents on the forest floor with an elongated cotton swab. "We won't know the cause of death until we ship him to the examiner, but this guy definitely suffered an immense amount of pain before dying, there's no doubt about that." Her profile steels, unphased by the gruesome scene in front of her. Nadia gets outsourced to busier counties nearby all the time to analyze crime scenes, whereas Willow works solely for Misty Pines. On a busy day, Willow solves cases on carjackings or drug busts. The memory presses in before she can stop it. She's only ever worked with Nadia once on a crime scene—a teenage boy who struggled against bullies, both at school and home. He couldn't take it anymore and chose to end his own life. Neither of them walked away from that day untouched.

"In all my years of doing this, I've never seen this kind of damage. Such…brutality. All his bones are broken. That takes a tremendous amount of force. This may be the case of the year for you, Will." Nadia glances back to Willow.

"I told you, don't call me that while we're working. I'd rather you not call me that at all, but especially not at work," Willow deadpans.

Nadia beams, her pristine teeth sparkling. "Oh, I know. I'm going to keep doing it, though." Her breath fogs her visor.

Willow drags her gaze heavenward in exasperation, a small smile tugging at the corner of her mouth before disappearing as she assesses the environment around the crime scene. The thick scent of damp earth and decaying life rots throughout the air. The Coastal Redwoods tower, looming overhead and the tree branches obscure what little sun is present on this overcast day. Branches, twigs, and dying foliage litter the ground while the victim lies in the center of a small break of trees. Flashes shoot like fireworks as other agents photograph the scene.

"Any footprints? Trace evidence of any kind?"

A frown pulls at Nadia's lips. "That's what's bizarre. Nothing. The rain could have washed anything that was left away? *Maybe.* Without the full autopsy, there's no way to tell at this moment what the estimated time of death is. That's beyond what I do. We need a little more time, and to get him out of the elements. Wild animals could have rummaged through it between his death and now. Who knows?"

Willow's eyebrows furrow, teeth gnawing the inside of her cheek.

Nadia studies her friend's exterior, weighing her next words. "These gashes–"

"I know. I thought the same thing." The silver necklace twists between Willow's right index finger and thumb. "This may be enough to reopen Kai's case."

*

The police station greets Willow with its bland, monotonous interior. Various shades of grey that practically scream *purgatory*. Not an ounce of comfort lives within the walls. Luckily for Willow, discomfort's all she's ever known. A small hum of conversation thrums as Willow enters the double doors. A familiar face welcomes her—Sunshine "Sunny" Anderson, the station's front desk receptionist and administrator. Sunny handles all the complaints and makes sure the team gets paid, which everyone appreciates. Ironically, Sunny's appearance is the opposite of what comes to mind when hearing Sunshine. Her jet-black locks sharpen the ghostly pallor of her porcelain skin, each strand finger curled, the attention to how well she takes care of her hair shows. A *"It's a beautiful day to leave me alone"* plaque stands in front of her computer where all who approach her can see.

"Afternoon, Willow!" Sunny greets, her facial features expressionless.

"Hey, Sunny. Boring day as usual?" Willow mimics Sunny's lack of expressions.

"Shoot, you say that as if we didn't have our first *murder* in years today. I told everyone that once the city started building that casino, we would get a whole lot busier with crimes. And now look at what happened today! No one believed me." As her frustration grew, the southern drawl in her accent intensifies.

Growth eventually catches up in smaller towns, so it's only a matter of time before Misty Pines starts booming with other businesses. When the idea of the casino was pitched, everyone cried in outrage. Very soon after it opened, the locals changed their mind, embracing the additional jobs and entertainment. She nods in response to Sunny, passing the front desk to reach the door to the detectives' offices.

"You're always right Sunny, when will someone finally listen?"

"That's what I've been saying!" Sunny's pitch rises to make sure Willow heard her before disappearing in the distance.

The gunmetal gray walls of the station match the weather in Misty Pines and the dullness of the building doesn't help anyone's seasonal depression. After passing the interrogation room on the right, the bullpen opens up to six desks, each with their own nook and corner for work. Willow's sits the furthest from the entrance, selected purposefully. Several other detectives huddle by the coffee maker on one of the side tables, all conversing as Willow walks in.

"We haven't had anything like this in over a decade."

"That guy's body was annihilated."

Irritation bristles in the back of her mind. Willow chimes in, "How would any of you know? You weren't there."

Milo turns toward Willow. None of the other detectives hear her come in, but they follow Milo's gaze.

"We may have not been there, but we heard the call on the scanner. Also, don't act like words don't travel fast in this town." He winks. His light brown, wavy hair is lightly tossed, as if he recently ran his fingers through it.

Willow ignores him, plopping down at her desk to compile notes from her assessment of the crime scene. This needs to be wrapped up before the witness who discovered the victim comes in. There's no time for Milo's advancements. He saunters behind her, peering over her shoulder as he leans forward. Willow clicks her pen over and over, fingers restless as she feels him breathing down her neck.

"Do you mind?" she questions.

"Not at all, go ahead."

"You do know you have your own desk, right?"

Milo's head turns toward his desk at the opposite end of the room. "Yeah, but you're not at that desk, you're at this one. I feel like I already know the answer, but do you need any help?"

"No. I've got it," she snaps. Bringing others in will only slow her down. As her father always said, *"If you want something done right, do it yourself."*

"Well Willow, I'll have you know I am this close to busting this meth lab on the outskirts of town, and I don't want any of your help!" Leo butts in, pinching his index finger and thumb an inch apart.

Willow clutches her chest with theatrical flair. "My heart is broken, Leo."

He grins. "Aren't you in a chipper mood?" He beams back at her.

Milo studies Willow while he sits on the corner of her desk and she leans back, processing his words. She didn't think she was acting any different. It's the closest she's been to any sort of progress in Kai's case. For the first time in a decade, hope lifts her weary heart from dragging her down.

"I guess." Willow pauses before speaking. "Days like this remind me of why I chose this career."

She reciprocates a grin back to Leo. Kindness shines from his soft features. Leo is the youngest out of the office, so he usually gets the brunt of the grunt work and Willow has a soft spot for him. He's also never tried making a move on her, which is much appreciated.

"I, for one, think Willow's always this pleasant." Milo raises his eyebrows at her.

"Such a kiss ass." Willow shakes her head, hiding a smirk.

Leo rubs his thumb across his own nose as he stares at Milo. "You got a little something brown on your nose, Mil."

"Oh, shut up," Milo grunts as he hops off Willow's desk and heads toward his own.

"We need more estrogen in this office," Willow mutters under her breath.

"Detective Rhodes," the Chief booms.

Willow whips her head in the direction of his office, standing from her chair. Her spine elongates, straightening like a ruler. Milo and Leo jolt, stiffening their posture as well.

"Please come to my office." He motions for her to follow.

He reclines in his jumbo brown leather chair that faces the entrance of his office. The current Chief is nothing like Willow's father. He's a kinder man, a gentle giant, one could say. He has thick salt and pepper hair and a beard that's kept nicely–only due to having to keep a clean appearance for his position. His skin is soft but aged from everything he's seen during his tenure in law enforcement.

"Something wrong, Chief Hastings?" Willow's eyebrows raise, claiming the seat across from him.

"I need you to be honest with me, you got it? I picked you specifically for this new murder case. I know your friend, Nadia, works for CSI but I was the one that gave the clearance for you to be summoned. Are you ready for something like this?" His eyes narrow on her.

"Yes, Sir! Of course. I want to make sure justice is served and we catch whoever did this," she states. Her posture stiffens as she holds his gaze.

"And you're going to be a team player with this, right?"

The question stings her pride. She doesn't need help. Just like everything else she's accomplished in her life, working alone has always gotten her far. Willow crosses her arms. "Of course, Sir."

Seconds pass before he continues. "Good. I picked you for a reason, and I know you can close this case. I wouldn't be doing you any service if I didn't check in with you after knowing your background."

Willow attempts to hold in her wince, knowing he's alluding to Kai without using his name. *Speaking of.*

"Actually, Sir. Can I make a request?" Willow's confidence wavers. Her index finger mindlessly scratches the skin around her thumbnail.

"Let me hear it." He leans further back in his seat, crossing one ankle over his leg and resting it on the opposite knee.

"I'd like to request the reopening of Kai's case." A sudden flick of surprise flashes across his expression, brow raising.

"On what grounds? Do you have evidence that would point to the case being able to be reopened?"

"Well, not exactly. Not until I get more evidence. I have a gut feeling that this case is related. Somehow." Regret pools in her chest the second the question leaves her mouth. She inspects the ground.

"Request denied. I need physical proof. Once you have that, then come ask again," he adds, craning his head down to grab Willow's attention.

She straightens back up, searching his soft brown orbs. She knows he wants her to find the proof, he would love nothing more than to help her solve Kai's case. Chief Hastings replaced Willow's father. He often, unintentionally, finds himself taking her under his wing. She's the daughter he always wanted, and he's the kind of man she wished her father could have been to her. They both have boundaries set in place to remain professional, but there's an unspoken level of protection for her.

"You got it, Chief." She stands up wearing a practiced expression, polished and empty. "Am I dismissed?"

"Yes. Oh wait, that reminds me," he shuffles through some papers on his desk, "the examiner received the body. I got the message a little while ago. Typically, the autopsy takes some time but seeing that we have a new examiner–and I've heard some choice words circulating about him, it may be best for you to go ahead and go over. Introduce yourself and help establish our new working relationship. We need to be on his good side," he directs, shifting in his seat as his work phone rings.

"Absolutely. After the witness interview, I'll go right there."

"Take Dunn with you to interrogation. Especially if it's a female witness," the Chief directs.

Willow's head turns, hiding her disdain.

"Yes sir," she winces.

The blinds tap the glass as the office door shuts behind her. The second the door clicks back into place, all her colleagues' attention scrambles back to whatever task they had in front of them. Trembling fingers adjust her blazer, keeping one hand in her jacket pocket.

"Willow, your witness has arrived. I put them in interview room one for you," Sunny calls from the entryway of the door to their offices.

"Thanks. I'll get with her shortly." She turns toward Milo, his face buried within another file. "Dunn, can you assist me with this interrogation? I need it to be speedy."

"You need *my* help?" His thick brows shoot up and her jaw tightens. "You don't have to say another word." He grins, hopping to his feet.

Interrogation rooms are supposed to be warm and inviting to help make the witness feel comfortable. The more comfortable someone is, the more they'll speak freely. However, the gray walls and sterile stainless-steel table and chairs radiate the ambiance of a prison. Not sure there's too many individuals in prison willing to confess details. Interrogation is one of her least favorite parts of the process. Milo, on the other hand, is a natural. Women being interrogated usually feel more at ease speaking with another female, but Willow doesn't quite have the approachable sentiment. It didn't bother her…most of the time. Somehow, to her shock, Milo always did well with getting women to talk to him. She could moderately see the appeal with his 'boy next door' charm. His smooth talking helps him get by more often than not which is probably why he keeps seeking attention from Willow–she doesn't give him any.

A woman in her early thirties sits across the table from Willow and Milo. She's dressed in athletic wear, and her amber hair pulls into a slick back ponytail. A sleeping child is strapped to her chest in a baby carrier as she sways and bounces up and down to soothe the infant's cooing.

"Good morning, Miss—" Willow glances at the paperwork. "Miss Taylor. We really appreciate you coming down to speak with us."

The woman shifts at an odd angle and the steel chair scoots back, creating an ear-piercing screech against the floor. They all wince.

"I know you've had a really awful day. Today you experienced something you'll probably never forget. I've never forgotten the first scene I visited." Milo puts a bottle of water in front of her, which she grabs immediately.

"How do you do this? Day in and out?" she asks Milo, her puppy dog eyes gloss over. The bottle in her hand shakes, stirring the water.

"Luckily, we don't get these kinds of tragedies often. But when they do happen, it hits the town hard. That being said, that's why it's so important for us to get any and all details from you, since you were the first one to locate the victim. We need to identify him and bring peace to his family. You can potentially help us with this."

Miss Taylor visibly relaxes, her shoulders slouching in a normal resting position, no longer rigid like she's sitting on a block of ice.

"Please tell us what you were doing that led up to your discovery." With precision, Willow times her addition to the conversation.

The woman swallows deeply, staring at her water on the table. Tiny ripples spread throughout the bottle with every little movement. One hand rests behind her child, patting their back in a gentle motion. "I was out for my morning run. I typically run around town for five miles. I'm trying to get back to my pre-pregnancy time," she adds.

Willow nods, jotting down notes. The conversation is recorded, but it helps her memory if she writes them down. "There aren't many trails out where the victim was found. Was there a reason you strayed from a path?"

The young mom's leer shifts to Milo.

"We have to ask hard questions. Please answer them fully and to the best of your ability," he reassures her, lips curving and offering quiet compassion.

"The weather wasn't awful today. I thought it'd be nice to take a hike through the wooded area, let my baby see the beauty of the trees. But I came across a snake," she pauses, "I hate snakes. I made a run for it, but it chased me...until I stumbled upon—*him*."

"A snake? What happened to the snake once you arrived at the scene?" Willow follows up.

Something about this feels off. She's more than likely not a killer, but there's something here that doesn't sit right.

"The snake just– slithered past me. The creepy, slimy thing," she shudders, "I may have scared it off with my screams. That's when I called 911 and laid by the largest tree nearby until someone else arrived."

"It's a good thing you scared it away. Some of the snakes in these woods are venomous." Milo always assumes the role of the good cop. Which, even against Willow's wishes, does benefit her.

"I honestly didn't stay near long, I just couldn't. I know my daughter is young, but I didn't want her around any of that." She picks at the cuticle of her nail, frame swaying back and forth. "I don't know if I'm much help."

"What time of day did you start running, and what time roughly did you arrive on the scene?" Willow asks, tapping the pen against the folder.

"She woke up early today, absolutely screaming," she peers down, weary, at the sleeping child on her chest, "I thought the fresh air would help so we started our run around seven forty-five. I think I found him probably around eight-thirty this morning? That's the time I think I heard other officers say. I wasn't exactly paying attention to the time."

Milo nods. "After the initial shock, did you notice anyone else around the area? Or any animals?"

Willow's pen scratches against her paper, filling the silence and Miss Taylor sits in thought for a few seconds.

"Not that I could tell. Not other than that snake, but I came across it way before the body. And snakes don't do that kind of damage." She frowns, as if she's reimagining the scene. So, she *did* get a good enough look him to at least remember the condition of the remains.

Willow peeks at Milo. "I believe at this point in the case I don't have any further questions. As always, evidence or additional questions may come up, so we ask you not to leave the county without giving us notice."

She stands to her feet, Milo follows suit. "Thank you for your cooperation with this investigation. If you think of anything or come across anything that may be useful to us , please don't hesitate to give me a call." He slides his business card along the table. The witness picks it up, holding it between manicured nails.

"I'll make sure to do that, thank you." Her mouth pulls into a stiff line as they exit the room. The baby begins to shriek from her chest wrap as they leave the building.

"Well, that wasn't helpful," Willow exhales. Gathering paperwork into a protective binder, she places it within her bag before taking out her phone, dashing to text Nadia.

Milo shrugs. "I've had worse. Are you out of here already?"

"I've got a date with a John Doe."

CHAPTER 4

MISTY PINES MORGUE

"Will, are you sure we should show up here so soon? I mean they *just* received the remains. It does take time–" Nadia twirls her thick, highlighted hair around her finger as she scans the empty funeral home lobby.

Willow leans to the left, scoping out the hallway. The funeral home stands among the first buildings built in Misty Pines. The morgue supposedly rests in the basement. Behind the funeral home, the local church stands strong despite being built in the 1930s. Both buildings have had renovations, but the essence of their original structure remains.

The soft lighting inside casts a gentle glow on the polished wooden furnishings, creating warmth amid the somber ambiance of the space. In the main lobby, claret curtains drape elegantly along the walls. Rows of cushioned chairs, staged plush couches, and benches fill the empty space adorned with spots for arrangements and family photographs.

"I'm just doing what the Chief said. I agree it's pretty soon. Maybe this guy will walk us through his process and let us watch? I'm supposed to introduce myself," Willow's reply carries a fragile optimism.

Nadia whips her head toward her. "Wow! Look at you being positive!" She grins.

"Don't get used to it," she teases. "The Chief mentioned in passing he's heard some choice words on the new guy. I didn't get any details though. If I had to guess, he's probably just a dick."

"I'm not sure I exactly need to be here. I can't really do much more than

I already have on the scene," Nadia blurts, flipping through the pages of a guestbook on the entryway table.

If Willow's being honest, Nadia is the only person in her life she's even somewhat comfortable asking for help. But this isn't really help. It's more for support to bridge the gap of Willow's lack of understanding in certain areas. *Not to mention that Nadia's bubbly personality works better on men than Willow's indifference.*

"You'll understand their lingo better than I can. You're also an unbiased person to Kai's case. I briefly spoke with the Chief earlier, and he said I need more evidence if he's ever going to reopen it." Silence passes between them for a minute, broken up by the clicking of Willow's pacing heels against the floor. It also helps that Nadia knows of Kai's history as well. She forced herself upon Willow right before his passing, starting their *mostly* one-sided friendship off with Nadia risking her own health to save Willow from the pit of her despair.

"I'll do my best to help you with this, Will. Have you talked to your parents about this at all?" Nadia hesitates to ask.

Willow's forehead creases. "What do you think? *No.* I don't even remember the last time we spoke."

From around the corner, a figure floats with grace down the hall, moving as though he walks on air.

His androgynous features catch Willow's gaze—his countenance harsh yet tender, while his caramel hair parts off the side, shorter on the sides but slightly longer on the top. He's tall and slender but his frame projects strength.

"Good evening, how may I assist you?"

"Hi, I'm Detective Rhodes and this is CSI Valentine." Willow motions to Nadia as she moves to Willow's side and they each flash their credentials. "I believe the new examiner has received a new corpse that we need information on. Are you the examiner?"

"No, but I'm the Medical Examiner Assistant. My name is Samuel, but you may call me Sam. I can take you to the victim, but I will warn you that Dr. Blackwood hasn't started his examination yet."

The warmth in Willow's eyes spread to the rest of her features. "It's nice to meet you. I don't believe I've heard your name before. Are you also new?"

His dimples pinch, making them more prominent. "Yes, that's right. This town doesn't get a lot of bodies needing to have their cause of death confirmed, so I suppose you wouldn't have a reason to meet me unless someone close to you passed away recently. Please, follow me." Sam turns, gesturing for the women to follow. Sam's black button up tugs within his waistband, stiff as a board as he walks. His black dress shoes clack against the concrete flooring, leading them to the stairway.

Compared to the warm ambiance that the upstairs carries, the basement leading to the examiner's area is stark in comparison. A lightbulb flickers at the bottom of the stairs and the halls possess a clinical and sterile energy, devoid of any sentimentality. There's only so much happiness that can surround death, she supposes. The fluorescent lights overhead illuminate the walkway as Sam leads Willow and Nadia forward.

"These lights give me a headache," Willow complains, rubbing the side of her temple.

"*This place is depressing,*" Nadia whispers to Willow.

"You're a Crime Scene Investigator, yes? You must also be surrounded by the deceased often. I imagine that takes an emotional toll on you as well?" Sam asks, catching them from the corner of his chocolate eyes.

"Yeah, I see a lot of bodies, but something about this place gives me the creeps. It's just not right," Nadia rambles, her arms motioning the sign of the cross on her chest and forehead. Willow's fingers brush against the gun holstered on her hip for reassurance before grasping Kai's cross around her neck. Nadia's anxiety brushes against Willow, asking for her to take its hand. The chill of the silver against her fingertips soothes her.

As the group approaches an isolated door at the end of the hall, Sam asks, "Did the two of you get here earlier than expected to meet with Dr. Blackwood?"

The heavy metal doors swing open and a low mechanical hum rings through the space. They are greeted by the back of a white coat towering over the remains on the stainless-steel table. The man rubs his stubbled jaw, adjusting his coat as he turns toward them.

"No, I didn't get the pleasure of being alerted I would have guests."

CHAPTER 5

FIRST IMPRESSIONS AND DEAD BODIES

His imposing stature draws the attention of both Willow and Nadia and the latter's mouth hangs ajar before slamming shut. The perpetually dark five o'clock shadow along his jaw accentuates his pale complexion. A striking single white strip of hair frames his sharp features, standing out against his raven locks that cascade past his shoulders. Under his white examiner coat, he wears earthy tones—a pristine white button up tucked into high waisted trousers, with a wool brown sweater vest and darker taupe tie hanging around the neck. A quick observation tells Willow he tries to hide his frame under the layers of clothes. His piercing hazel eyes lock onto Willow as she enters the room.

"And to whom do I owe the pleasure?" the man grunts, his posture reclines against the table and tilting his head to the side, keeping his challenging gaze on Willow.

"Detective Rhodes and CSI Valentine," Willow responds. "You must be the new examiner. Our Chief gave orders to go ahead and introduce ourselves and get whatever information you have." Her lips curve with forced intensity.

"Warren, I'm sorry I didn't give you a heads up, I was under the assumption they had at least called–" Sam trails off, pointing a frustrated glare through the women.

Nadia squirms under the awkward confrontation. *This is a great start.*

"Our intentions weren't to deceive, just merely following orders from our Chief," Willow states as a matter of fact. Over the years she's learned to never be the first one to break eye contact, it indicates lack of confidence.

Warren breaks the staring contest first, glancing at Sam, then back to the two women.

Uncertainty dances on his features. "Next time, I would appreciate a heads up."

"Of course. It's nice to meet you." Willow extends her hand to Warren.

His focus lingers on her necklace then travels back up her neck as their hands clasp one another's. "The pleasure is all mine." Sarcasm drips from his voice.

"I'm Nadia!" She peeks from behind Willow, asserting herself into the conversation with the rugged man. Hesitation holds their grip as Warren's handshake lingers, before releasing to greet Nadia. "I've heard you're new to town. How do you like Misty Pines?" Nadia blurts. *Really, Nadia? At least Willow doesn't have to force a conversation this way.*

Warren adjusts his stance, pushing off against the table and letting out an exaggerated sigh. "You've heard about me? I haven't been here long, but so far, I'm very much enjoying myself." He looks from Nadia to Willow, adjusting the cinnamon leather watch band around his left wrist. A faint smirk ghosts the corner of his lips. *What's up with that?*

"It's a pretty small town, so better get used to everyone trying to know everything here." Nadia giggles.

A sigh escapes Willow's lips. "Anyway, we were hoping to see if you had anything you could give us regarding the case?"

"I don't have any information yet, seeing as I just received the deceased. It could take weeks to properly do the internal and external examinations. With Sam's help, I can potentially finish sooner. This body," Warren fixes his stare on the corpse, "isn't exactly a one-day examination, I'm afraid."

"Definitely not," Sam agrees, investigating the scalp of the victim.

"Of course! We were sort of hoping that you would maybe let the two of us watch your process? We are both eager to start working on any leads for this case we can find." Nadia's warm grin lights up anyone she meets. But not Warren.

He shakes his head. "It's against policy to do that. You will have to follow protocol and wait for us to call you to let you know when we have made our conclusions. You would have known that if you would've called before showing up at our workplace." He shoots Sam a sideways glance.

"Once again, I apologize for the misunderstanding. We will follow protocol and will wait for your alert that it's done. Sorry to have interrupted your work. Nadia and I will see ourselves out." Willow's lips tighten. On the way out of the metal doors, Willow removes a business card out of her jacket pocket and extends it to Sam. *He's at least pleasant to speak with.*

"Please call me as soon as it's complete. Thank you."

*

"That man sure is a tree I'd like to climb." Nadia brings a straw to her mouth, sipping a frozen margarita with a sugar-coated rim.

Willow's attention drifts around their local Mexican restaurant, El Pino Loco. A fluorescent beer sign hangs above the bar in the center of the building, the blue and white neon lights bounce off the tables. Hums of conversation and loud music emanate from every corner of the room and the aroma of grilled chicken and queso makes her stomach growl. Fresh fajitas sizzle, distracting her as they pass by the table while Nadia's speaking.

"What?" Willow asks.

"That examiner. Warren? He's stunning. In like a—rugged, sleep deprived, and maybe a little twisty kind of way?" Nadia fans herself with her hand, and a dusty rose blush tints her cheeks. A result from either the alcohol, or from not getting laid in a while–Willow can't be sure.

Willow grimaces, taking a drink of her crisp Sprite. She's not wrong. Willow's always been drawn to the twisty, *bad boy* types. However, those always ended poorly. She's sworn off relationships to devote her time to justice for Kai. *And she will deliver it by hand.* The blaring scream of a toddler catches her attention at a nearby table where a mother attempts to console her son as tears stream down his red face and he shakes between cries. On the other side of the table, an older child shows his father the baseball cards he pulled out of his brand-new pack.

The gentle breeze carries the scent of blooming flowers and children sprint past the wooden park table the Rhodes family sits at. Ants scurry across the surface of the uneven wood, collecting microscopic crumbs as they march off the table, out of sight. She hates family picnics.

"Willow, you need to eat your hot dog. It's getting cold." Her mother's speech is muffled by the chewing of her own food.

"I'm not hungry, I just want to play!" Willow whines, slumping her shoulders.

"Are you really going to do this? We're having such a nice day!" Her delivery becomes sharp as her fury buries into Willow. Willow's eyes never leave the table.

"I'm not hungry. I'm allergic to the corn and I don't even like hot dogs—"

Her mother's nostrils flare, jaw tightening before she speaks. "Why can't you just do what I tell you to? Look at how well Kai has done with eating his food. You'll never get big and strong like him if you don't eat."

Families passing by turn to stare in their direction, attention focused on Willow.

Kai nibbles his food beside his mother across from Willow, his mouth drawing downward into a frown. He doesn't like hot dogs either. Willow can barely see the table through her glassy vision as she shoves away from it, springing toward the playground, finding shelter under the slide. Silent tears flood her skin as she holds her cries in, trying not to draw attention to herself and holding her face in both hands. A gentle warmth embraces her.

"Hey, are you okay?" Kai's soft voice asks.

"Hey, are you okay?" Nadia's hand waves in front of Willow's vacant stare.

Willow's focus flickers back on Nadia, who has nothing left in her drink and concern written on her features.

"I'm fine."

Her eyes squint as they search Willow's face. "Is it about the case? Is it too much for you?"

Willow exhales, the cracks in her neck audible as the muscles in her shoulders tighten.

"No, Nadia. It's not too much for me. I just– I hate relying on others for me to continue doing my job. But alas, here I am, forced to do nothing and wait all while stuffing my face with chips and guac." Her arms open, motioning to the three empty chip baskets littered across the table.

"Are you sure? There's a lot to process. Have you thought about reaching out to your parents? I know it's been a while, but your dad was so good at what he did back in the day—" That's as far as Nadia gets before the slam of Willow's fists against the table catches her off guard. The silverware rattles against the force and the chatter of conversations lull, drawing attention to their table in the newfound silence.

"*That's enough.* You know my answer." She places a twenty-dollar bill on the table and slides it to Nadia. "Take that and pay for our food. I'll text Leo. He's patrolling and going to make sure you make it home safely. See you later."

She stands, and without a second glance to her friend she sticks her hands in her jacket and weaves through waiters balancing stacks of dishes on their trays, exiting the restaurant. Nadia slumps against the booth picking at what crumbs remain in the last chip basket.

*

"Have you seen the new trainer?"

"He's a well-known social media influencer for his fitness stuff!"

"Marissa gave him her number and he never called her. I guess he's too nice to say no."

Whispers in the auxiliary gym room mingle together, all gossiping about Gideon. Willow adjusts the tongue of her tennis shoes, pulling them snug. Not surprising, the intermediate yoga class this evening is booked full, with barely any room for the patrons already inside. Most of the attendees are packed like sardines near the front platform where the instructor teaches, leaving the back corner free for Willow to take. The recent stress of the murder makes her muscles ache so she's hopeful this class will help alleviate her issues. It's unlikely, but maybe it'll be a fleeting relief.

The lights in the room dim, shifting to a soft orange glow. Willow's thighs deepen the more she stretches. The faint rustling of mats and occasional creak of the wooden floor replaces the whispers; heads turn to the clicking of the entry door shutting within its frame. Gideon beams in delight as he nods and squeezes by each patron, careful not to step on their mats, to make it to his stage.

"Good afternoon, everyone," his words soothe the room, "thank you all for coming to one of my first few classes. I'm excited for the opportunity to help each of you achieve your fitness goals and follow along in your journey." He pauses, scanning the room, smiling at the crowd.

Willow can't be sure, but she feels like his gaze lingers on her before flickering to the next.

"As a reminder, this is an intermediate class. If you aren't intermediate level, that's okay! I'm prepared to help all levels of expertise. Make sure to listen to your body and take breaks when needed."

The class's energy hums with excitement, the entire front row swoons at his every word. Their big doe eyes ogle Gideon, waiting for his instructions. The way the light catches his profile projects an angelic glow across his features. Willow doesn't mind letting herself watch him. *He's the instructor after all? I'm learning.*

"Now, let's begin, shall we? Everyone, find your place on your mat, and let's move into Warrior III," he instructs, demonstrating the pose without breaking a sweat. "Go into a lunge, hinge forward at the hips, bringing your weight onto your front leg. Keep your core engaged, arms reaching forward or alongside your body. Imagine your form as one long line, from fingertips to the lifted heel."

The class follows, and a few students wobble and lose balance, their faces hung in disappointment.

"If you fall out of the pose, that's okay," he encourages. "Balance isn't about perfection–it's finding your center again. Breathe into it and try again. And hold."

Willow's legs shake. *Geez.* After holding the pose for a few breaths, he leads them back to standing.

"Shake it out if you need to. Next, we'll be going into the half-moon pose. Plant your front hand on the mat or a block, if you grabbed one," he says, moving into position. "Lift your back leg, open your chest to the side, and extend your top arm toward the sky. Focus on one point of the ceiling to help steady yourself."

A couple women glance his way, their uncertainty in the pose begs him for assistance. Gideon approaches a woman continuing to lose her balance.

"Try shifting your gaze to the floor instead," he whispers. "Also try picturing pushing through the heel of your lifted leg. With a strong foundation, use a soft breath."

Willow overhears this and uses it to help her own unsteadiness. She definitely overestimated her own athleticism, thinking she can hop into an intermediate class, and it'd be easy. His instructions, luckily, make it easy to follow.

Willow takes a few breaks in between poses for water, making sure to catch her breath when her muscles cry for help.

"You're all doing amazing," he purrs. "To wrap things up we're going to go into pigeon pose. From downward dog, bring your right knee toward your right wrist. Slide your left leg back, keeping your hips square. You should feel a deep stretch in your hip–don't force it though. Let gravity do the work."

He wanders the room, pushing toward the back, observing postures as he passes. "Remember, this isn't about pushing past your limits. It's about listening to your body and honoring that." His voice carries, growing closer to Willow's corner. Her eyelids close, focusing on the pull of her muscles. Tension pulls at her muscles, but the pose offers no relief. Does she need to readjust?

"It's incredible the amount of tension our bodies store in the hips. Really let yourself deepen the stretch, allowing your emotions to flood to the surface. Yoga is healing in that way," he says in a whisper. "May I?"

Willow opens her eyes to find Gideon beside her, offering a hand.

"Uh, sure," she stumbles. She didn't think she was doing *that* poorly.

"Lean forward some," he instructs. "Do you feel like you aren't getting a good enough stretch in your hips?"

Her eyebrows raise. "Yeah, I feel like I should feel it more?"

He nods. "Here, I'm going to press down on your hips to hold them in place while you lean your torso forward– try all the way to the ground if you can." Warm hands splay across her lower back, putting pressure on her hips. The compression alone aids her muscles, discovering the pull that they were craving to release tension.

A groan escapes her lips as her hip flexors lengthen. *That was too loud.*

"I'm guessing it worked?" His low voice sends goosebumps up her back.

"Yes," she breathes. "Ouch."

He stifles a chuckle behind her, his thumb grazes against her exposed skin as he pulls away, moving his attention to someone else for help.

Gideon guides the class into resting in the last pose. "Lay on your back, arms by your side, but palms up," he murmurs. "Let go of any lingering tension. Breathe into the sense of release. You've earned it."

Willow lays flat, staring at the ceiling. The rise and fall of her chest soothes her.

"Beside your mats I've put towels for you to use. It'll help cool you down and relax into your breathing," he adds.

She lolls her head to the side, finding Gideon procuring her towel. "Let me help," with delicate fingers he brushes the flyaway strands of hair from her forehead.

Willow doesn't know how to react; her mouth opens before slamming shut. His touch is light, draping the cold towel on her forehead, a coy grin playing on his lips before the cloth covers her vision. Orange and honey tickle her nose and another deep inhale clears her sinuses.

"Whenever you feel ready, you may stand, *slowly* rise to your feet and leave. Thank you everyone, you did great. I look forward to seeing you next time." His lilt is steady, but more energetic than the calmness he radiated during the workout.

She could fall asleep right here, but the call of work beckons her so she resentfully sits up, catching the hand towel that falls in her lap.

Several women have left, but most of the class lingers as clusters of cliques wait for their turn to speak with Gideon. He's in conversation with another woman; her icy blonde hair almost matches the shade of his. Her two friends on either side belly laugh at whatever Gideon said. Willow directs her attention back to her yoga mat where sweat outlines an impression of her back and butt.

Her mouth furls into a grimace. "So gross," she mutters.

"I wouldn't say it's gross, it's just a sign of how hard you worked," Gideon comments, approaching her.

"Oh, well that's embarrassing– I didn't think I said that loud enough for anyone to hear."

He grins. "Nothing to be embarrassed about. You did great! Not surprising, coming from the town's best detective known to man?"

She scoffs, her ears heat as she turns to roll the mat up for travel. "Don't let Donna fill your head with nonsense."

"She had a lot of wonderful things to say about you."

"Like I said, nonsense," she retorts, almost snorting.

Gideon laughs. "Listen, this may be too forward of me," he pushes the platinum hair off his forehead, "but I was wondering if I could have your number?" His chest puffs forward, his head tilting to observe her reaction.

Her eyes widen. "I–uh, I don't date?"

"Oh, don't worry, when I make a move you'll know," he grins, "I haven't lived here long, and I don't have many people to talk to. Plus, it's always nice to say I have a detective's phone number ready on speed dial, right?" he jokes.

Her mouth twists. It can't hurt, right? It's not like she must respond to him. Displays of jealousy from across the room light her on fire as she takes Gideon's phone from his extended hand, punching in her contact information. *Hopefully these crazed, infatuated women don't attack her as she leaves.* She doesn't dare to make eye contact with any of them.

"Thanks! Don't worry, I won't bother you too much. But I do hope to see you around." He winks. "Don't forget to drink plenty of water."

CHAPTER 6
LATE NIGHT CALL

Over a week has come and gone, with no updates on the remains. The days are filled with mundane traffic stops, helping the elderly cross the street, and stopping local teenagers from spray painting graffiti on the brick walls of the school. She must admit she's impressed by the intricate design of the lavender and bubblegum pink skull they painted. Somehow, the week stretched and blinked past in the same breath. It's not often she allows herself to rest, but when she does– it's fully immersing herself in a book.

Under the somber brilliance of the thrifted standing lamp, Willow nestles in the corner of her cozy living room, her fingers dance between the pages of her romance novel. The pale light casts shadows across her room, highlighting the homemade case file notes sprawled out on the coffee table. Outside, the stars twinkle through the clouds that try to block them from shining. The pitter patter of rain knocks into the dragonfly wind chime on her front porch, the melody whispering into the late night against the sound of the elements.

The silver necklace pats against her chest as she sways. The anti-hero, male lead in her book confesses his love for his servant. Just as their lips are about to touch, a shrill ring from Willow's side screams. She jolts, her heart throbbing, only to exhale at the sight of her illuminated phone screen on the ledge of the coffee table. She folds the corner of her page and sets the book down, trading it for her phone. *Unknown number*. A call this late signals it's work related.

"Detective Rhodes," she answers.

"Good evening, Detective, or I guess I should say night. I didn't expect you to be up this late, I planned to leave a message but since you answered," he rasps, "I have completed my examinations, tomorrow you can–"

Willow shoots up from her chair, the book tumbling to the ground from her quick movement. "Mr. Blackwood? Are you still there? I can be there in ten minutes!" she jumps with a response.

"It's *doctor*. I was just about to leave. This case has been extensive for me too–"

Willow cuts him off again. "I'm already heading out the door, I'll see you in ten!"

"Detec–" Click. She ends the call.

Willow floats around her living room, shimmying back into her black sweatpants and throwing a reflective rain jacket over her sports bra. Her thumb helps wiggle her heels into her sneakers as she jogs out the front door with her bag. The love confession can wait.

Chilly water droplets pelt her exposed midriff. Standing pools of water sink into the divots of the ground; she weaves around them, attempting to keep her shoes clean. Damp dirt and pine weigh down the air and the mist swirls lazily around the tops of the trees through the small breaks of moonlight through the clouds. Willow jogs to the main roads, continuing her journey across town. Streetlamps alone illuminate the way for her. Despite the surrounding darkness and approaching storm, stillness hums beneath her skin.

The newly built Golden Wolf Casino looms ahead, and with it, the once foggy path to the funeral home clears. Outside the casino, the neon lights cast a vibrant radiance on the pavement and surrounding trees, painting hues of gold, acid green, and white. On top of the building, a saffron wolf statue with a viridian stare peers down, preying on each patron that enters. As daylight fades, residents flock to this area of town.

Patrons pack within the parking lot; some are local residents and the others, travelers passing through. The odor of cigarettes invades her nose, seeping into her pores as she passes the building. A cough forces from her throat; she shakes her head, pushing forward. Her parents were always heavily judgmental of smokers when she was growing up. She can recall several instances where they would exaggerate their cough and snarl in their face.

Midnight cloaks the funeral home. The windows are black, the only light visible radiates from a wall sconce adhered to the brick beside the door. The balls of her feet hop up the brick stairs. No doorbell. Her hands cup around her eyes, pressing against the windowpane, as the door opens. She jumps back, jerking the rain jacket hood off her head.

The white frame door holds open, held by Warren's extended arm. Clacking echoes from his foot, the sporadic tempo beating against the floor. He reaches for the nearest indoor lamp, turning it on to cast a low light over the space.

"I really appreciate you staying until I got here."

He nods, checking his watch as he closes the door with his other hand. "You didn't exactly give me an option," he retorts.

Exposed skin hits the cold air as she shrugs off her raincoat. Her brows raise, yanking the coat back in place. It didn't cross her mind to put a shirt on over her sports bra before she left. Her eagerness betrayed her. Warren pushes his round-rimmed glasses up the bridge of his nose. "Aren't you going to put your rain jacket up to dry?" He cocks his head. A challenge.

"I left in a hurry, alright? I'm keeping this on." Her eyes narrow, adjusting the jacket over her shoulders. "Anyway, you didn't have to stay, you could have left. But you didn't. So, thank you for that," she adds, holding her words firm. This is her trying her hardest to show civility and not ruin the working relationship between him and the rest of the police force.

He scratches the scruff on his chin, gazing toward the ceiling. "I suppose I could have. I guess next time I won't be so nice."

What an asshole. "Well, I'm here either way so can you show me the victim and your findings?" She forces a close-lipped smile, tilting her head.

A smirk creeps up his lips, pushing the sleeves of his navy turtleneck sweatshirt up past the bend of his elbow. "Of course. Follow me."

Willow catches a glimpse of a red ink snake tattoo on his right forearm.

"Do you normally work this late?" Willow inquires, holding onto the rail leading downstairs. The frigid air of the basement mixes with her wet skin, raising goosebumps along her arms and neck and her abs tighten from the cold.

"Not this late. However, a few weeks was the deadline I gave you, so it called for a few additional late hours for it to happen." Multitasking, he ties his long hair in a half up half down bun while walking. He's much more casual in this encounter, compared to the first, she notes. Perhaps it's because he wasn't ambushed this time. Well, *maybe* he was a little, but this time it was by invitation.

"Is Sam here too? I thought I'd be hearing from him since I'd given him my card." She peers through the passing open doors, searching for other signs of life.

"You won't find anyone living, other than myself and you, present. Sam's attendance is spotty. His wife is in another state tending to her parents, so he travels often. Not like it's busy in this town, anyway. I took your card off his desk."

Warren pushes the doors, leading into his examination room. The emptiness allows Willow to observe her surroundings clearer. Along the walls, cabinets and shelves house an array of medical tools and other stainless-steel equipment. Each section is organized for specific use. A constant hum in the background fills what would be silence in this small space.

The victim rests upon the stainless-steel table, supine, while a white blanket drapes across his lower half. A bluish pale tint glazes the spots of skin that avoided being warped from the attack and laying in standing water. Willow pushes a strand of his auburn hair off his forehead, revealing a scar along his temple that stops as it gets to his eyebrow. The skin around the other eyebrow distends, mimicking the rest of the remains. His hollow shell operated as sponge, absorbing and expanding as it soaked in all the water.

Warren opens a filing cabinet to retrieve his documents. "Please refrain from touching the deceased." He peers at Willow from behind the paperwork.

"Right, sorry." She studies the victim's face. He couldn't be much older than Willow. The laugh lines set deep into his skin, even with his figure bloated and frozen. He must have lived a happy life, until this, that is. The farmers tan clings to him like a permanent white t-shirt burned into his skin. *Could he be from a construction background?*

"Dental records match male, Jonathan Davies. Thirty-five." He turns over the case notes in a beige manilla folder. "Approximate time of death is roughly a week and two days ago."

Willow's brow arches, fingers scrambling to open the folder. "He had only been dead two days before he was found? The assailant could still be in the area! Or completely out of town by now…" *There's so many possibilities.*

"Potentially, I suppose," he responds, a touch of optimism in his tone.

"And the cause of death?" She scavenges the papers, searching for the answer.

"The cause of death is cardiac arrest due to massive internal bleeding. As you can see," Warren pulls the victim's shoulder, careful to move him to lay on the side to expose his wounded back, "these lacerations penetrated all the way to his heart, puncturing it."

"Punctured his heart through the back? What could do that kind of damage?" She leans down to get a closer observation of the lacerations, tucking her hair behind her ears.

Warren studies her from above. "When the heart is punctured, blood leaks into the pericardial sac surrounding it which can quickly lead to cardiac tamponade, which essentially means the heart's chambers are compressed by the accumulating blood, therefore causing the heart to stop. As far as the weapon goes, the edges of these lacerations are jagged and irregular so it's hard to determine for certain. My best guess would be an older butcher's knife, or another sharp household item potentially. But I cannot say without a doubt that either of those are what caused these cuts." What a horrific way to die.

He lays the victim down to rest and a chill runs down her back. Willow straightens her posture, grabbing her arms and rubbing them to calm her shivers.

Warren takes note of her movement. "Are you finished with me? It is getting late, and it appears it's too cold for you down here."

Self-consciousness takes over as she keeps her arms crossed and frowns. "I'm fine. Tell me about his bones. They appeared broken when I arrived on the scene." She changes the subject, studying the victim's exposed wrists.

His eyes narrow as he looks from her to his watch. "Very well. Yes, each extremity suffered a compound fracture. This kind of damage is often seen in suicide victims that jump from high distances, but this is not the case for him since the rest of the body is intact other than his organs and back. Based on my findings, his arms and legs were broken after he died."

"Dealing with a monster. *Great.*" Willow forces a small laugh. Discoloration travels up and down his arms, into his palms. The tops of the victim's knuckles are calloused. *He definitely works a job that's labor intensive.* There's a sliver of an open wound between the victim's index and middle finger and a ring of dried blood encircles the digit. She directs her attention back at the documentation in her grasp, noticing that it isn't on the report, nor circled on the injury mapping chart.

"Where did this come from? It's not in your notes." Her brows furrow.

His attention flickers between Willow and the remains. "Oh, that. Let me get a closer look." He moves shoulder to shoulder with her to observe the hand. "That's where the pressure of the broken arm came forced back into his hands, causing the skin to split. I must have missed that. I'll put it in the notes that I'll submit on the computer."

Willow's chin lifts, hugging herself tighter with one arm, the other twirling her necklace. *An interesting response. It may be possible he's missed something else.*

"Where did you get that necklace?" he questions.

She steps back, surprised by the inquiry, and hesitates before answering. "It was a gift from my brother."

"Didn't mean to pry. It seems familiar, so I was curious." He scratches his beard then rubs his neck.

"I mean it's a cross—It's kinda everywhere. Don't worry about it," she responds curtly. "That's all I need for now. Can I take these?" Her hand holds up the manilla folder full of documents.

"That's your copy. You may keep them." He nods.

"Then I'm done here. Thanks for going over this with me past your work hours. Sorry to keep you up, I'm sure you'd rather be asleep," she jokes, turning toward the door with a grin that didn't match the tension in her shoulders.

"I'm sure you could use the sleep too, Detective. You know, sleep is important to remain healthy," he adds.

"I'll sleep when this monster is dead." Bitterness spews after each word.

"Right, of course. Safe travels in this rain." He lifts his chin as he speaks, opening the door for her to exit. A sarcastic asshole who still has a sense of chivalry? If he gets the job done and gives her the information she needs, she doesn't care what anyone has to say about him. He can be as rude as he'd like.

The fresh air awakens her senses the second her foot steps out the door. The lock of the door clicks. Warren leans against the building, lighting a cigarette under the cover of the porch as he fades into the distance. His stare buries into her as she catches a glance over her shoulder.

"Gross," she mutters under her breath. The storm surrounds her, swirling around each limb that takes stride. A low reverberating thud of thunder rolls in the distance, chasing her all the way home.

CHAPTER 7

DREAM TEAM, ASSEMBLE

Just as Willow succumbs to the call of sleep, her phone pierces the air with its insistent ring. Groaning, she fumbles for it, patting the couch without a sense of direction. The base of her skull throbs. *This is what she gets for falling asleep in the living room.* The sun stretches just over the horizon, letting rays shine through the windows, brightening the living room. She squints at Nadia's name on the display screen.

"Not now," she mumbles, her voice thick with exhaustion, answering the call.

"Will, I didn't wake up this early for nothing. We're running, remember?"

With a heavy sigh, Willow rubs her under eyes, the weight of the day settling upon her shoulders. "Fine. But I'm making coffee first. Meet you at our spot," she grumbles as she stands. She shouldn't have stayed up reviewing Warren's notes. Nothing beats an invigorating hour-long power nap to start the day. She yawns, her movements sluggish as she stumbles into the kitchen.

Her weary hand reaches for the coffee pot, the familiar aroma of toasted hazelnut with hints of cocoa comforts her as she fills her cup with the unused batch from the previous night. Nothing the microwave can't fix. The steam from the coffee rises as it spins, offering promises of wakefulness in the middle of her fatigue. With the ding of the timer, she opens the door, lifting the cup to her lips. The warmth seeps into her bones, asking them to wake. "Hm," escapes her lips. Not too bad for reheated coffee.

The cool morning air greets her, a contrast to the internal warmth from her coffee. Birds chirp from above, not a cloud in sight. Days like these are few and far between. With each step forward, the heaviness of sleep disappears. Adjusting her pace to match her awakened energy, she sets off toward the meeting point.

She slips between the trees enclosing her home, footing steady on the uneven ground, cutting through the woods toward the park where Nadia waits for their weekly runs. When she arrives, Nadia's legs flail, swaying on the rickety swing set.

"I hope you've had your tetanus shot." Willow's jog comes to a halt, her fingernail scrapes against the rusted foundation of the swing set.

"If I die by swing set, so be it. At least I die happy!" Nadia teases, a grin spreading across her face. She adjusts her ponytail, tucking more of her blonde highlighted strands back into the hair tie.

Willow stretches, wearing the same sports bra and sweatpants from last night and her ashy brown hair wraps into a disheveled ponytail on top of her head.

"Ready?" Nadia asks Willow.

Willow nods, starting forward and picking up the pace as Nadia joins her side. Willow inhales, the sunshine soaks into her already sweating skin. The air is so crisp she can taste the upcoming transition from summer to fall. A symphony of nature echoes in between the reverberations of their feet pounding against the ground. It's her favorite time to get out of the house. She uses running as both a way to decompress from work and time to internally process updates with cases. There's something about the new mortician that isn't sitting right with her. And it's not that he's just an asshole. They pick up their pace as they pass the boundaries of the park, trudging along past the downtown shopping areas. They turn the corner to make a loop, passing the coffee shop.

Willow's lids close in response to the aroma of the coffee beans, reminding herself that even though her heart beats against her chest, mentally she's still exhausted. As she opens her eyes, Nadia yells, "Watch out!"

Willow plows into another runner, shoulder checking them–which almost knocks her over, like she rammed herself directly into a giant boulder. She sticks out her arms to balance, barely catching herself. For a moment, time slows as her vision meets the runner's.

"I'm so sorry I wasn't paying attention!" Gideon stands before her, leaning down with his hands stretched, as if he was going to help stabilize her balance himself.

Willow attempts to not stare at his shirtless and muscular torso. Nadia, however, makes no such attempt. His exposed build is cut from lean muscle, which isn't surprising given his profession. Nadia gawks at the man before her.

"Oh, Willow, it's you!" His brows raise. "Are you okay?"

"I—sorry. I wasn't watching where I was going either. It's fine," she stammers, a silent plea for Nadia to rescue her out of the situation.

Gideon looks between the two girls, then beams at Nadia.

"Will, don't be rude. Introduce me to your friend here." Nadia nudges her and bats her thick eyelashes.

Willow tries to hide her subtle eye roll. "We've only met briefly, but this is Gideon. He's the new trainer at our gym."

Gideon wraps Nadia's hand within his. "It's a pleasure to meet you. I hope I can continue to see you around the gym more, both of you I mean." He smiles, eyes gleaming, and runs a hand through his hair, pushing it off his forehead and adjusting the headphones in his ears.

"Oh, you'll be seeing me. If you're lucky that is." Nadia winks at him.

"Well, I do consider myself a pretty lucky guy," he laughs.

Oh, brother. Willow squirms, groaning internally at the interaction. "Well, the two of you can continue this. I need to finish my run. See you later, Nadia. Nice running into you Gideon, literally," Willow jokes, waving at the two of them.

Her heart rate pounds the further she runs and the harder she pushes herself. There's complete effortlessness after the first thirty minutes of a run—the sensation after the first few miles almost euphoric.

Running alone, it's easy to let her mind drift back to the case. So far with this investigation, there are no leads. Identifying the victim was step one. Thankfully, it'll open a whole new leg in the investigation. The biggest question now, who did he piss off enough to warrant the kind of damage they did to him? Someone with a personal vendetta against him? Have gangs finally started making their way into Misty?

She approaches her front porch where the rays from the sun catch her wind chime, casting different shades of greens and blues across the side of the home. *Home.* A spark of happiness touches her features as she slows her run, finally arriving at her house. As she catches her breath on the front step, a slithering tail dashes under the porch. *Oh no. Maybe Miss Taylor wasn't lying? Is there a snake infestation in the woods she's unaware about?* Unwanted creatures are a downside to living in the woods. Willow pulls out her phone to find a text from Nadia.

Nadia:

You've been holding out on me!! I have SO MUCH TO TELL YOU! Dinner soon?

Willow lets out a heavy sigh.

Willow:

I'll let you know what it looks like for work.

The green wooden door creaks as she pulls it open. The case files greet her from the coffee table, ready to be picked up once again.

*

The steady ringing of phones and rhythmic clacking of keyboards greet Willow upon entering the station.

"Another day, Willow," Sunny groans behind the computer. Not quite a welcome most would expect, but it's on brand for Sunny.

She nods, acknowledging the familiar faces along the way but never makes eye contact. As she lowers herself into a chair, Warren's notes in hand, the Chief steps out of his office.

"Attention!" He barks, demanding the attention of everyone in the space. Without hesitation, Willow hops up to her feet.

"As most of us, and now the whole town it seems, are aware, we have a murder case. After reviewing the autopsy notes from the medical examiner, I'm now assigning half of you to this case effective immediately, joining Rhodes as lead. This is more than a one-person job," he adds in response to Willow's frown.

She asked Milo to assist in the witness interview just as he asked. Isn't that enough help? Hushed whispers scatter among the small group of detectives.

"Rhodes, Dunn, Bennett, Brooks. You're on the case." The Chief connects with each as they offer sharp, confident nods. Each person has a different set of skills to make a well-rounded team. There's no denying their masteries— even if working as a team irritates her.

"Get to work. You all have a killer to catch. For the rest of you, keep working on the cases you're on. If anyone gets any leads, make sure to give it to the team on the case. Keep up the good work," the Chief adds. Pride and admiration boasts within his praise, returning to the seclusion of his private office.

Milo grins as he approaches Willow, more than eager to get the chance to crack the case and work closely with her. A short ping of resentment pulses within her. Anger comes as easy to Willow as breathing, being one of the first emotions she experiences—she is her father's daughter after all. *She should probably mention this in therapy. But someone must start therapy first before they can have their issues solved. Maybe one day.* The thought of anyone else but her solving this sets her on fire.

Behind Milo, Leo Bennett follows. Leo epitomizes the archetype of the moralistic nice guy within the ranks of the unit with his unwavering commitment to justice and integrity and his kindness and empathy towards others. He's been in the department for only nine months so far, but that speaks volumes to his work ethic.

Trailing last behind them all, is the meek Jasmine Brooks. Jasmine has a gentle demeanor and thoughtful presence, allowing her to seamlessly blend into the background—and that's exactly what she wants any criminal to think of her. Her unassuming nature hides her sharp intellect and proficiency in the information technology department. But Willow knows better—and the Chief sees it too. Whether it's unlocking encrypted files, tracing digital footprints, or hacking into systems, Jasmine's expertise in the cyber realm goes unmatched. It's really a dream team from any outsider looking in. The three of them huddle around her.

"Alright, Rhodes. What's the game plan?" Jealousy tinges Milo's voice and the spiteful part of her enjoys that.

"Milo and Leo, you two will investigate the life of our victim. We have his name and location thanks to a dental record match, Jonathan Davies. I'll send over the copies from the notes I took from the new examiner. Go visit his home. We need to let his family know of his passing if they don't already. Talk to his significant other if he has one, his work, and any leads you get while you're there." She turns to Jasmine, voice steady and sure.

Jasmine pulls the sleeves of her royal blue cardigan over her hands; the color forms a striking contrast against her ebony skin.

"Jasmine, I'll need you to do the digging on the victim digitally. Find out all there's to know about him. Is he registered for dating apps? Has he been having an affair? Who has he been talking to on his phone records? Is anything out of the ordinary going on with his money? Where was his last purchase around the time of his death? Those are good places to start."

Jasmine nods, glancing down as if trying to remember everything as a mental note.

"Oh! Also, after you gather the intel about Jonathan, can you see what information you can find on the new medical examiner, Warren Blackwood?" Willow adds. She isn't sure she should air her suspicions so soon, but the words came before she could stop them.

Milo and Leo both tilt their heads. "The examiner? Why?" Milo questions.

Willow weighs her words. "He's only been in town for six months. It may just be a coincidence, but I'd rather not leave it to chance and make sure we properly investigate everyone. Trust no one."

The men nod as if that answer is good enough. *Phew.*

"You think the mayor will cancel this year's Halloween Bash?" Leo asks. "I know the town as a whole is concerned, but it's also the biggest community event we have each year." He inspects his shoes, staring at the ground.

"I'd be shocked if it's cancelled. We get a lot of our funding through it. Plus, the mayor loves a good costume party." Milo grins.

Each year for the last six years, Misty Pines hosts a Halloween Bash. The sole goal of the party is to help fundraise for different sectors of the town; the police station included. Each year different departments are instructed to attend, either for fun, or to work the event. Willow finds the costume aspect pointless, but Mayor Caldwell loves going all out and turning heads each year.

"Let's get this monster off the streets so we don't have to worry about that. I'm going to investigate Warren and expand the search around Davies crime scene. Report back any findings that are worth noting as soon as you get them, got it?" Willow commands.

The group agrees in unison and disperses. Leo and Milo fist bump each other as they walk away, discussing which gas station they should stop at for road trip snacks.

Jasmine is already back to her desk by the time Willow looks up. Willow settles at her desk and adjusts her framed childhood photo. The day Kai sworn in to become an officer. A solemn smile ghosts her lips before she hurries to grab her keys and case files.

CHAPTER 8
ICED COFFEE AND MAGGOTS

I ced coffee chills her lips as the cubes crash against the mouth of the cup. The driver's seat of Willow's beat up, four-door silver Toyota Corolla leans as far back as it allows. The piece of junk is one of the only other items of Kai's she was allowed to take. *She adores the mobile hunk of trash.* Kai's case documents are scattered in an organized mess among the passenger seat and floorboard. Chaotically dispersed—but in an orderly way only Willow understands. Pops of vibrant colored crushed energy drink cans break up the monotonous tan shades of the car's interior.

In her hands, she flips through the walk-through notes of Kai's crime scene. In moments of self-reflection, she finds herself searching the old notes. She will never admit how many times she's combed through them throughout the years, but she almost always has them on her person. The words transport her to the day of his death. The detective that signed off on the report notes that there were signs of an injury prior to the immediate scene and a blood trail leading to where Kai's body was discovered. These records are another unspoken gesture of favoritism between Chief Hastings and Willow. A major violation of policy and procedures, scattered in her rundown car.

A flicker of movement shuffles freshly fallen leaves on the ground outside of her car door, bringing her back to the present-day crime scene. She lurches forward, hand flying to hover over the firearm holstered to her right hip. A black, reddish, and off colored yellow striped snake coils its body, slithering from the leaves up the rough bark of the tree beside Willow's car, its length easily as long as her car bumper. Her heart rate rests as the snake ascends further, curling around a jagged branch, until it disappears within the tree itself.

Her muscles ease. *Right*. Time to go back through the crime scene. It's not necessarily protocol to return for a second sweep after the scene has been searched and documented, but she doesn't quite have faith in the others' attention to detail. She shuffles the documents within her organized chaos. Kai's walkthrough notes join the statement of the witness, crime scene photographs, and documentation. The mossy earth gives beneath her feet.

Willow's head swivels, analyzing the path leading to the crime scene, and comparing the notes of the outer perimeter documented. Thick woods cut this area off, while only being a football field distance from town, the trees and wildlife aid in covering things that are meant to stay hidden. Tree crickets fill the space with their chirps, muffling the sounds of civilization. This area is far enough from prying eyes, but close enough that someone could return to town unnoticed with ease. Broken tree limbs scatter amongst the ground. It's hard to tell whether they were broken by the fall, an animal snapping them, or human footsteps.

Bright caution tape still encloses the perimeter, though it waves in the breeze, tattered and faded from attempting to withstand over a week of Misty Pines weather. Reviewing a scene without the victim is equally as off putting. It's less emotionally draining, but there are always traces of the brutality. Fragments of the violence linger in the air, casting fleeting shadows of the murder. A cluster of white, blood-stained lilies sit at the base of a nearby tree. The photograph in her hand captured a more vibrant red, whereas now the stains are an oxidized deep crimson. The crimson essence travels higher up the base of the tree, matching the exact height of the victim's back. The results of the DNA swab haven't returned, but her instinct tells her it will match Davies. It's a low chance that the assailant suffered any sort of injury. Jonathan didn't stand a chance. Willow's current hypothesis is the victim backed against this tree for rest, then fell over, face first, before succumbing to his exhaustion and wounds.

Maggots squirm beneath the soil, wriggling in search of sustenance from where the remains once laid. Her nose scrunches, fighting the itch coming from within her nostril. The maggots weren't present after the immediate removal of the body. She should collect them to give to Warren or Nadia to have as extra confirmation for the time of death. *Which is also a good excuse to get near the morgue.* She removes an empty vial filled with preservative fluid from her backpack. Thanks to Nadia, she has some insight on the proper way to handle collecting living evidence like these disgusting insects.

Her features crinkle as she scoops a few maggots into the container, attempting to use the ground instead of having to use her fingers. Even though she has gloves, she doesn't do bugs. Once a few are collected, she swiftly places the vial back in a secure pouch of her backpack. Nothing else appears different from the original photographs, minus the environmental changes from rain. The peaceful sanctuary of the forest. Towering trees block what little visible sun remains of the day. Willow glances down to her watch. It's best to get to the morgue before it's too late.

The tangerine glow of the sunset peeks through the small breaks in the tree and leaves rustle against the gentle breeze, sending a chill through her core. A forceful hiss pierces the air and she freezes. *Oh no.* Her hand hovers over her holster. She's not above shooting a snake. It would cause a ton of paperwork, explanations, and probably a write up for misusing her weapon, but in her opinion, it's justifiable. Deliberate, slow turns of her head search for any sign of danger. There's not a snake in sight. *The tree.*

"Shit," she breathes, darting to her car.

The car door rips open, slamming behind her. Her head slumps forward, resting on the steering wheel as she exhales a sigh of relief. She reaches for her backpack halfway thrown over her shoulders, struggling before she's able to pull it to rest in her lap. The cool glass of the vial clasps within her fingers, holding it up to the setting sun. When bugs are preserved within fluid, it's much more manageable to view. She tilts the glass. The curvature of the vial magnifies the insect's mouth, exposing its hook-like features. Her mouth pulls into a deep frown, placing the vial back inside the safety of her backpack. *Nevermind.*

*

Small-town life offers many perks, including the quick drive to the funeral home. Typically, she travels by foot to most places, but it's been a while since she ran her car. The premise of funeral homes and morgues should be saddening, and they are, but Willow can't help but admire the Victorian architecture of the building. The siding fades from sun exposure, but the elaborate trim and carvings are etchings of history.

Two Corinthian columns frame the entrance to the funeral home, and it looks much less ominous in the daylight. A muted echo trails behind her steps in the hushed atmosphere of the lobby—the parlor and entryway are devoid of people. She bites her lower lip, pressing further into the building instead of waiting for another staff member to greet her. Navigating the somber surroundings comes with ease after her recent visits.

The instant her foot connects with the basement floor, icy, dry air blasts her cheeks. Will she ever adjust to the drastic temperature down here? Hopefully there isn't a reason to have to visit this place much longer. Her shaky fingers zip up her black MPPD embroidered jacket and her steps soften as she nears the autopsy room. Her heels lift from the floor as she peers into the small window of the door. Warren sits on a rollable stool, his torso hovering over the table, his face mere inches from the corpse's head. Her fingers drift to rub the sterling necklace against her chest. A comforting warmth washes over her skin, encouraging her to push through the doors.

"Oh, hello Detective. Yes, please, come in without knocking or waiting on an escort here." His sarcasm cuts through her like a knife while he remains focused on his work. "The badge allows you to have free reign everywhere, I'm sure."

Willow's face is stone, expressing no level of amusement.

A color matching pallet is gripped within his left hand, intentionally taking into consideration the colors–mixing hues of yellow, red, and blue together to create the perfect match for the deceased skin tone. An older woman, maybe in her eighties, lays on the table. No visible wounds. She wears an expression of peace, complete rest.

"Bold statement coming from someone who doesn't know me. I collected a maggot from the crime scene. I assumed you would need it to confirm your estimated time of death. These *things* weren't present when we first collected evidence," she states, holding up the vial. It swirls, the pest circulating the small space as if sucked into a tornado. How disorienting that must feel. "Why would you assume no one told me to come down?" she challenges.

He huffs. His feet extend, pushing his stool out, swiveling in her direction. "I'm aware you came down here on your own accord simply because I am the only one in today. *And I did not ask for a visit.*" His words slice through the air with an edge of impatience. "It seems as though you're searching for an excuse to see me again," he adds, his voice laced with teasing venom.

She wavers, searching for a response. "I have a killer on the loose and every day that passes gives them another opportunity to strike again." A scowl creeps along her flushed face, and she crosses her arms.

He leans in, resting his forearms on his knees while continuing to sit on the stool. "Listen, I assume it's just your lack of sleep, because I don't take you for an idiot. If you would have called your CSI friend and let her know of your discovery, she would be of more help to you than I. Furthermore, if you don't trust my expert opinion then don't ask me for help." His brows furrow.

She avoids eye contact, finding her focus on the vial that grows cooler with every minute that passes in this icebox of a room. Sure, she could have called Nadia. *But Nadia isn't a murder suspect.* "My sleep schedule is none of your concern. And there's no need for your condescending tone," she snips. Her conscience twists, ringing her stomach. The sharpness in her speech slashed further than intended. "I'm sorry for interrupting. I guess I just wanted answers quickly and assumed–"

Warren cuts her off. "Assumed that I would know about entomology and be of use to you," he finishes her statement, his words clear that they're more valuable than hers.

Her conscience loosens its grip as she bristles with anger. "Maybe if you had other employees working here, I wouldn't have had to escort myself down here," she seethes.

"I barely need an assistant. It's a waste of money when I can complete everything myself. I'm saving the funeral home money by being the only one they need. If it was truly up to me, I *would* be the only one working here."

"Wow, you're such a saint!" she exclaims. Her cadence mimics his dry tone.

A micro expression of amusement pulls at his lips, almost too fast for Willow to notice. "If you are done berating me in front of someone's dead grandmother, you can take your leave. I don't have anything for you." With that, he swivels on his stool, turning his back on her.

Her eye twitches. For a fleeting moment, she attempts to come up with a retort. In the end, she decides not to give him the satisfaction of continuing his irritating banter.

She cracks her knuckles, the popping rebounding off the walls of the empty hallway as she exits the morgue. Beneath the irritation lies a small sense of satisfaction at having been able to rile him up. Though he wasn't forthcoming or willing to assess the maggot, the interaction helped gain more insight to his work. Everyone has a pattern of behavior. This is step one of discovering his system. The brisk air hits her as she steps outside, her breath becoming hazily visible with her exhales. A digital ring breaks the insects' late evening chirps. Her hand circles her pocket, fishing for the phone. A welcomed distraction.

"Jasmine, what do you have for me?" she jumps in with her question, not bothering with pleasantries.

Jasmine typically offers few words anyway, with a dry, but calming personality. Her voice is like a warm blanket.

"I've found a little about the examiner. Warren Blackwood, age thirty-seven. His medical examiner license is active. It looks like he may live off the grid, as I've had a difficult time finding any information about his personal life. He's well established in his profession and has been called as an expert witness for several homicides where he's testified in court in other states spanning across the last eight years," Jasmine's words ring an octave above her environment, computer keys clicking in the background.

"Great work. Can you look more into the cases he testified on and get me those files? I need everything. The crime scene photos, his autopsy notes, the court reporter notes, everything," Willow asks. "If possible."

"I'll keep working on it."

"Also, keep trying to find anything about his personal life. He must have a digital footprint somewhere," she adds to Jasmine's growing list of tasks.

"Already ahead of you. I'll call when I have more information." Jasmine hangs up.

CHAPTER 9
THE STAKE OUT

Another day drags, as Willow inhales her fifth cup of coffee. She sinks within her seat, surveying Warren locking the door to the funeral home. The music fades to a hush with the twist of the radio dial. Darkness envelops the sky like a thick blanket and the clouds hug the moon, casting partial moonlight onto the earth below. The whites of her eyes barely peer over the side of her car door; Warren disappears behind the building.

A fleeting question enters her mind as fast as it leaves it. When did she sleep last? Her foot eases on the gas, trailing his blacked-out Lexus exiting the parking lot. Back roads curve like a snake the further they exit the main town. The brake lights on Warren's car illuminate, a warning for her to slow even more. He hangs a right, taking a steep paved path that feels out of place among the sea of trees. To avoid suspicion, she passes the driveway until his brake lights disappear from her rearview mirror. The car slows, jolting forward as Willow hits a pothole to make a turn on the side of the road. She shuts off the headlights the second her tires hit the driveway.

The woodland opens, revealing a secluded home nestled amidst the dense thicket of forest. The trees act as a wall, providing a hidden fortress. *Complete privacy in the woods? Perfect for a serial killer.* To keep a low noise profile, she parks halfway up the driveway, approaching the home by foot. The slightest sound of her gasp escapes her throat. A striking multitude of glass windows adorn the exterior, allowing most of the interior to be seen from outside. *It's stunning.*

Shadows consume her– her figure mere inches from the perimeter of light shining from the windows. Her gaze pulls to the most prominently lit room: a spacious library bathed in a warm glow. Rows upon rows of books line the entire room and a ladder leans against one of the shelves. A cozy setup of a sectional and coffee table sits in the center of the room. The room alone is almost as big as her entire home. *What a dream. She could live in that room and be content for the rest of her life.* With swift movements, she tiptoes to a tree nearby to view the adjacent room where Warren stirs. The kitchen. Warren searches the area with his brows drawn together, then disappears down a hall.

Minutes feel like hours as she waits. Animals scurry and scratch, the sound of crunching earth rattling within the dense part of the trees. Warren's silhouette reappears in the kitchen, wearing one less layer of clothing than before. His back muscles flex as he opens the refrigerator, black hair cascading past his shoulders, forming a curtain obscuring the upper parts of his sculpted back. A crimson drink swirls within the wine glass he pulls from the fridge and his back leans against the marble countertop as the cup touches his lips.

Intrusion creeps within her mind. Guilt gnaws at her as she realizes the intimacy of her scrutiny. She's no better than the Peeping Toms she arrested back in her patrol days. This is for an investigation though, it's different. There's no pleasure from this. If anything, it's causing more irritation. Why does he have to look like…*that?* The leads have been slow, so it's easy for her to worry she may be wasting her time. She exhales all the breath from her lungs, kicking the stick she stands on.

The air circulating around her tightens and the hair on the back of her neck stands. She shudders. Her gaze lifts— and he's watching her. She sinks backward as her heart rate skyrockets, survival instincts kick in, forcing her to retreat into the shadows of the wilderness. He searches the darkness beyond the window and panic overwhelms her for a fleeting moment until she believes she's moved far enough out of sight. A cluster of five, broad trees keep her hidden while she bends over, taking deep breaths—four seconds of inhaling, holding, then eight seconds exhaling until the sinking pit in her stomach evaporates.

There's no way he saw her, she rationalizes. Still, it's difficult for her to shake the uneasiness sitting in the pit of her stomach. This is too close for comfort. At this distance she's as far away as possible, while still having vision on the crystal home. Vibrations of her phone send into flight mode as she jumps to her feet, her pulse rising. She settles, seeing Milo's name on caller ID. With a heavy sigh she peeks around the trees to redirect her attention back to Warren's house, bringing the phone to her ear.

"*You better have good news for me,*" she hisses in a whisper.

"Damn, woman. What crawled up your ass?" He fakes his offense.

"*I'm hanging up.*"

"Wait! I called to give you an update!"

"I'm here too, Willow!" Leo beams, his call distant. A hazy conversation from a television fills the background silence.

"*I'm only staying on because Leo's there. Now hurry, I'm busy and you're distracting me,*" she whispers, trying not to draw any more attention to herself.

The overhead interior lights shut off. Soft glows of light flicker in the room, but there's no visible sign of Warren.

"Whatever," Milo huffs. "We were able to find more about our victim, Jonathan. Nyssa resident, blue collar construction worker with a wife and two kids. We spoke with his boss and apparently, they sent him out to work on a project just outside Misty. That's the last they heard from him." *She was right! Construction worker. Noted.*

Willow dazes off, her forehead scrunching in place. "*That's great and all, but that doesn't explain why he was found dead in our city.*"

"That's where the wonderful Jasmine has come in. She called me about half an hour ago to tell us that she accessed his bank account, and his last purchase was made at the Golden Wolf Casino," he adds with self-satisfaction.

A tinge of jealousy nips at her. Why didn't she call Willow first?

Despite her underlying irritation, she pumps her fist. Nothing but the darkness of the night sees her reaction. "*I could kiss her face!*" she whispers, but with a subtle rise in pitch.

"I'm sure Milo would love to see that," Leo mutters in the background loud enough for her to hear. The sound of a slap echoes on the other end of the phone.

"*We'll regroup when you two get back in town. Looks like we're going gambling.*" Willow ignores them, too focused on the scent of a new lead.

"We'll be back late tomorrow. Leo and I are going to try to speak with the victim's wife to see if we can obtain any other information that may be useful."

The lack of movement in Warren's home makes her weary and her cornea burns from refusing to blink. "*That's great. Find something good for us and we'll touch base tomorrow.*"

She hangs up, not wanting to drag a conversation out with Milo any longer than she must. If you give him an inch, he runs a mile with it. The last thing she needs is him misreading her intentions. *Again.*

The night stains his home, blackening any details within. She sighs in frustration, listening to her own breath and the creatures scurrying across the forest floor, their pattering echoing through the still night. Reluctantly, it's time to leave. Unanswered questions and unease buzz within her mind. With one last glance toward the shadow house, she turns away to trek back to her abandoned car.

CHAPTER 10

SUBPOENA?

"Will, I've been trying to call you all day!" Nadia screeches, her fist rains down on Willow's front door.

Willow jolts upright in bed, disoriented and groggy. Case files are scattered across her mattress and floor. She presses her fingers against her eyelids and groans. Stumbling out of bed, she scoops the files on the bed into somewhat organized piles, so they won't fall. To avoid the heaps on the floor, she plays hopscotch to make it out of her bedroom. Nadia's fist swings down on the door harder, the thumping echoing in Willow's head, ringing her ears.

"I'm coming!" Willow yells, unlocking the door to greet Nadia's wrath.

The door swings open and Nadia scowls at Willow, whose disheveled hair veils the exhaustion lining her face. Willow crosses her arms, partially as a reaction of being defensive and other part to cover herself, as she didn't bother putting on her bra before answering the door.

Nadia pushes past Willow, skipping into the entrance of her home. Willow's eyebrows raise.

"You never texted me," Nadia pouts.

It slipped her mind. "I'm sorry. I've been so caught up," Willow starts.

"In this case? *I know*. Willow, it's not healthy." Nadia states.

Willow blinks at her. "Nadia, it's literally my job?" Willow shifts, taken aback by her forwardness.

"Yeah, Will, it's your job. But you aren't taking care of yourself. You did this with Kai too, even before you got into law enforcement. I just don't want you to get bad again—" she trails off.

Willow won't let herself get bad again. Her clenched fists heat.

"I'm taking care of myself just fine. You don't need to keep trying to take care of me like high school. As you can tell, I literally just finished sleeping. It could've been longer, but I thought SWAT was busting in." *Most people prefer to wake over gradual time, on their own accord.* Somehow, emergencies or interruptions always find her when she does allow herself to sleep. Must be a sign she doesn't need sleep.

Nadia's shoulders shrink. "You know I'd do anything for you, right?" She squeaks in almost a whisper.

"Yes, Nadia. But please. I'm okay! I can take care of myself. I'm almost *thirty* for crying out loud."

Nadia sighs and nods, giving in. "Okay, Will. Whatever you say. I'm still keeping an eye on you."

Willow rolls her eyes. The couch gives under her weight as she sits, adjusting a blanket to cover her. "Is that why you came over? To drill me about self-care?"

"Oh, no! I wanted to update you about that God of a man, *Gideon*. The one you didn't tell me about!" Nadia drools.

Willow's eyebrows raise. "That's an interesting statement coming from a devout Catholic," she says, struggling with the comparison.

Willow grew up in religion but fell away from the church after Kai's incident. Even now, comments related to it make her uneasy, unsure of where she stands. Nadia, on the other hand, always stands firm in her beliefs and makes sure everyone knows that she doesn't care what they think. It's admirable.

"Okay, he's obviously not God, but you know what I mean. Why didn't you mention him before?" Her voice strains.

"I've met him like, twice. I know nothing about him," she adds, uninterested in the conversation.

"Well, after you left to finish the run, we stood there a while talking, and boy did he want to know more about you!" Jealousy seeps into her words, tainting its usual warmth with a sharp edge of resentment.

Willow pulls her hands up, palms facing out to Nadia. "Listen, I'm not interested. He's all yours."

"I told him as much. But he's such a smooth talker. I bet if you'd give him just a minute of your day you'd swoon." She grins from ear to ear. "He seemed really *really* interested in you. He asked about if you live locally, what you like to do for fun, or if there were any tips I could give him to get on your good side."

"Did you tell him I'm boring and again, not interested?" Willow deadpans, hoping that Nadia didn't give him any words of wisdom.

"All I told him is if he wants a challenge, then he's in for a treat." She giggles.

"*Nadia*," Willow groans.

"When's the last time you've been on a date? Or hell, gotten laid?" Nadia prods.

Willow fake gasps, her hand over her chest. "What vulgar language you have, Ms. Purity Ring."

Nadia's cheeks redden. "Oh, shut up and stop deflecting my questions!"

"Listen, all I need is me, myself, and I. My career doesn't allow for a stable relationship, nor is it a priority for me. You can focus on winning him over yourself and don't worry about me, alright?" Her head tilts toward Nadia, making sure she knows she's serious. "Speaking of, I need to eat and stop by the office before my afternoon starts." Willow stands, hoping Nadia gets the hint to leave.

"One of these days you will listen to me. Also, if you don't answer me within two business days again, I will continue to show up here. That's not a threat, it's a promise," she adds, walking toward the front door.

"Yeah, yeah. I'm shaking in my slippers," Willow teases. "We'll talk soon. Let me know how everything goes."

"You know I will." She winks as she closes the door.

*

As the night falls, she finds herself going against Chief Hastings orders–sitting at the Golden Wolf Casino. *"Rhodes. Take the day off. You look awful. We'll have a debriefing on everyone's findings tomorrow when Dunn and Bennett return. They're running late. I'd like to receive an update on where we are with this,"* he commands before shooing Willow out the door of the station.

Maybe she wants to start gambling as a hobby? Her head shakes at the ridiculous excuse. *Like she has money to even gamble with.* A cacophony of sounds engulf her—the clinking of slot machines, chatter amongst the patrons, and melodies of music drifting from a lounge. Technicolor of flashing lights glitter off the solid black interior of the walls, tables, and chairs.

To most everyone's surprise, Willow has never visited a casino. Growing up, Willow's parents warned of the dangers of gambling and how it's a gimmick to waste money. It's all rigged. Had there been a nearby casino growing up, she would've gone–simply to piss them off. Luckily for them, she outgrew the rebellious phase early due to Kai's death. Nothing ages a person quite like losing a loved one. A protector.

Typically, the night shift patrol officers are the ones dispatched to the casino in instances of disturbances. From time to time, several officers stay posted in their cars and sit in the parking lot talking to each other. The calls that come in from the Golden Wolf, in most cases, revolve around a drunk patron who loses their temper after losing their money. Patrol days suck.

Willow's crystal blue eyes roam the room, a flicker of recognition pulling her in the direction of a far game table. A telling silver streak against raven hair, all pulled into a loose bun at the base of the neck. Warren sits at the burgundy and black table with three other individuals. Poker cards fan out between his fingers, the dealer being his sole focus. Willow's shoulders hunch forward, shrinking behind the closest group of patrons. Is luck on her side? With subtle motion, she sneaks a few photos from her phone of Warren mid-game. The new mortician just so happens to gamble at the same place the victim had his last purchase? Very unlikely that it's a coincidence.

He doesn't present himself as a gambling man. Perhaps that's how he affords the crystal mansion he inhabits. This further proves how little she knows about him. To her knowledge, Jasmine has yet to discover anything from his personal life.

"Excuse me, ma'am. Can I help you?"

Her head swivels, meeting a man in a boxy black suit with a scowl plastered on his face. On the bridge of his bulbous nose, a pair of silver, thin rimmed glasses rest. Charcoal hair sticks to his head like two wet curtains framing his oblong head. On his jacket pocket, a crooked nametag reads: *Brian–Floor Supervisor.*

"Oh, hello– Just looking at all the different games," she responds.

His gaze sharpens. She sighs.

"Fine. I came in here to look, but then I found someone I recognize. Can you tell me if he comes here often? Or provide me with any video footage? Maybe from the last two weeks?" she asks Brian, flashing her badge from her pocket.

Two weeks would cover the timeline of Jonathan's visit. Brian's lips flash a snarl before he returns them to a neutral position.

"You have a subpoena?" He tilts his head, eying her.

"Obviously I don't. I didn't have any intentions of that when I first came in, like I told you." Without realizing, she mimics his body language, tilting her head and crossing her arms.

"No subpoena means you don't get anything from me," he answers with clipped words. "Now either go play one of the games, pay to get entrance to the lounge, or get out of here."

"Yeah, I'll see you soon *Brian*." She squints, with the tilt in her mouth offering no kindness. With one final glance toward her main suspect, she finds Warren's seat, cold and empty. Her fingers have a mind of their own, picking at the nails on her opposite hand. Brian has made it to her shit list.

CHAPTER 11

DRINK FOR TWO

Once again, Willow finds herself submerged in the shadows of the towering trees surrounding Warren's home. Spotting him at the Golden Wolf solidified his spot as the number one suspect. Tonight, she's nestled against a tree located behind the front windowpane looking directly into the kitchen. Black leggings and a charcoal workout jacket aid her stealth. She's positioned much closer to the window tonight, hopeful the closer proximity will lead to more evidence. However, she won't risk leaving the shadows. Her stomach flutters with nerves.

Everyone has a routine. Even individuals who will call themselves spontaneous. If someone pays close enough attention, a routine can be discovered. Warren's a creature of habit, dimming the main light, and then disappearing further into the home out of the line of sight from her perch below the window. Music inside the home echoes, but with no sign of movement. The bark of the tree Willow leans against pokes through her clothes, making her shift. A yawn escapes her mouth, only to stiffen as Warren's frame glides into the kitchen.

He pushes his black, round rimmed glasses up his nose and rubs the back of his neck, tossing his hair off his shoulder to fall against his back, obscuring the logo of a vintage rock band t-shirt. Like clockwork, he pulls a wine glass out of the fridge, already filled to the brim with a deep red refreshment. Instead of drinking it right after the pour, he sets the glass on the marble island and reaches for a second empty wine glass from a cabinet above. He pulls a new bottle of wine from below the island and fills the second glass with the same burgundy wine.

Is he preparing for company? Maybe he's had an accomplice with his crime. Willow's leg bounces. If she nails this, the Chief will certainly overlook the trespassing, she convinces herself as she picks at the skin on her bottom lip. The two glasses sit on the counter as Warren pulls his phone from his olive-green lounge pants–bringing it to his ears. The conversation is brief, or perhaps he left them a voicemail, and he lays his phone back on the island, picking the two glasses back up.

Warren moves with grace to the front door; her breath catches in her throat and stomach twists as she shimmies behind the tree away from the window. *The guest must almost be here.* There's a spark of excitement charging her. She remains submerged in the dark, but this way she's obscured by the tree itself, not just the shadow. He steps outside with both drinks, one in each hand. The door closes behind him. He sits one wine glass on the railing of his porch as he leans to the side of the door frame, sipping his glass before clearing his throat.

"Care to join me for a drink?" His voice is smooth and playful, like a cat playing with a mouse.

Willow's heart skips a beat as any words she can come up with fall into her stomach. How could he possibly know that someone was outside? This is terminatable. Her career will be over. Her fingers twirl her necklace, sitting in the sharp silence, hoping that if she remains quiet enough, she can fool him into thinking he's imagining things.

"Detective, you and the shadows are not one in the same. Come. I assume there's a reason you're trespassing on my property. Let's discuss this *civilly* over a drink," he adds. *He knows it's her. Damn it, damn it, damn it!* There's no malice in his delivery, but almost curiosity. "Unless you enjoy sitting outside by trees on a cold night."

Willow shifts through different scenarios that could play out, most of which end in her expulsion after Warren complains to the Chief. None offer the outcome she hoped for. She sighs, side stepping around the base of the tree into the dim light, letting it illuminate parts of her face and make her presence known–as if he wasn't aware already.

A surge of heat bubbles in her chest, sharp and sudden. *What a rookie mistake.* She's better than this. Warren's chin tilts up, peering down at her, flaunting his triumph like a weapon. Tension coils through her every fiber of her being, ready to erupt at any moment. Warren grins, pushing off the door frame and steps closer to her, idling on the porch.

She breaks the silent battle between them, throwing in the white flag. "I would love to talk more about your findings about the victim, Jonathan Davies." She fakes, trying to play the situation cool while controlling her building disappointment in herself.

He smirks, taking a drink from his glass. "You've caught me in a good mood. Let's talk. Come inside."

Willow's eyelid twitches, mumbling as she follows him across the threshold, *"Must be my lucky day."*

The interior of his home takes her breath away. Smoky fragrances of vetiver and tobacco fill the air and every inch of the residence exudes a refined, masculine touch. He must not be married. That makes it easier for him to commit murder without raising suspicion, but on the same coin, he's less likely to have an alibi.

"We can chat in the library. Follow me," he states, leading Willow toward the left side of the home.

The walls are painted in deep charcoal greys and muted blacks. His style is minimalistic, with very little excess but several stand out pieces, such as a brass sculpture and several potted plants, giving the room a little life and pop of color against all the neutral tones. The library showcases the same color pattern and the atmosphere is even more inviting than how she viewed it from the window. Several candles are lit on the coffee table, and a knitted grey blanket drapes over the brown leather couch.

"It's beautiful," Willow whispers to herself.

Warren claims a seat on the single leather chair opposite of the couch. His gaze softens, noticing her admiring the area, before she takes a seat across from him.

"It's my favorite room in the house, besides my bedroom." he adds, lifting his drink to his lips.

She gives a flat expression. There's no time for this.

"So, I came here to talk," she says with hesitation.

"Right, the case. I'm sure it's so important that a call couldn't work?" he questions, handing Willow the wine he poured her from before.

"How certain are you of Jonathan's cause of death?" She takes the glass, swirling it in a smooth motion.

His eyes meet the ceiling, taking a moment to formulate a response. "We've had this conversation already. I am not perfect, but I am very good at my job. I had to study for quite a while. So, I'd say I'm certain."

"How long have you been a medical examiner? Are you used to many homicide cases? Or do you typically work in the funeral home industry—

helping to prepare bodies for burial?" She hammers out several questions all at once.

"This has been my career for quite a while, but when it's that long, sometimes you lose count. I have dealt with it all. Homicide, suicide, death by natural causes, you name it. Typically, I would operate as the examiner for the city, but with Misty Pines being as small as it is, I took on the role of both mortician and funeral director." He observes her with focused attention.

Willow nods. "What made you choose to move to Misty Pines? What do you think of it so far?" She glances down, peering into the crimson liquid, waiting for his response. Small bubbles float to the top.

"I can pour you another glass if you don't trust the one I poured before. But you should know I didn't do anything to it *since* you watched me pour it."

Her skin heats. She takes a large gulp of the wine, then crosses her legs as she leans further into the couch.

"Very well. I needed a change, I suppose. I felt called to the area. I enjoy it. It's secluded but large enough to not feel like a ghost town. You sure are asking a lot of personal questions," he adds.

"You felt 'called' to the area?" Willow's eyebrows raise, challenging his statement.

"Yes, a calling. Have you not experienced a calling of your own?"

"Can't say that I have." She takes another sip of wine. It's raw bitterness, makes her mouth pucker.

Warren's gaze drifts to the delicate necklace around her throat. He studies the silver cross, his face impassive but a flicker of recognition dances within his eyes. "You wouldn't call your career a calling?"

"It wasn't something I intended to do from a young age, but I guess you could say outside circumstances made it my calling." She considers this for the first time. Did she feel called to her position? Or was it forced upon her?

"Were your father and brother the environmental circumstances you speak of?" he asks with casual ease as he finishes his drink and sets the glass on the side table. Red stains the crystal of his glass.

Color drains from her face. He's been investigating her history. There's no reason he should know about them unless he's been poking around. Unease washes over her, her mind racing and unable to form a sentence. With a forced calmness masking her rising panic, she struggles to find the right words, her voice catching in her throat with the realization that he knows far more than he should. "How–" The necklace heats under her touch.

"I assumed with your family history of law enforcement that would be what inspired you to your 'calling'."

She's unable to read his intentions, which makes her shift in her seat. *He's the killer.*

"You've been doing your research on me, I see."

"I do research on all things that catch my interest, Detective." He crosses his legs, resting his chin in his hand. A faint smirk plays on his lips as he awaits her response.

Rage sizzles beneath her skin. Her knuckles are white from how hard her fists clench around her glass. "Well, it's a good thing that I'm a person and not a *thing*, isn't it?"

He ignores her question and the sharpness of her retort. "Did you grow up in a religious household?"

"What does that have to do with anything?" she snaps, not bothering to hold back her irritation.

"I'm simply trying to get to know you. I presumed you would be willing to speak with me, considering you are on my property illegally, without a search warrant or subpoena, and this is private property. Is it not?" he snaps back, matching her energy.

"Is that a threat?" Willow shifts forward, resting her forearms on her knees, her volume low.

He scratches the side of his stubbled cheek. "I would never threaten an officer of the law. I'm trying to make small talk and would appreciate some banter. Especially after being grilled about my own personal life, wouldn't you think?" He sneers.

The implications of his expression are easy to understand. She's furious, but not an idiot. If it will keep her out of trouble at work, she'll oblige.

"Fine. Yes, I grew up in a Christian household," she states flatly.

"Still practicing?" He appears genuinely curious.

"No. Not really. I have other things preoccupying my time." She finishes the rest of her wine.

His mouth purses. "I see. Well, depending on who you ask, eternal life isn't something to gamble with."

"I thought you liked gambling?" she bites back, smiling to herself with the jab she landed.

His gaze darkens and he grins enough to show his teeth. "You'll have to do more than follow me around for a couple days to get to know me, *Detective.*"

"I plan on it," she responds, calling his bluff.

"I do look forward to it," he hesitates. His gaze is unfixed and his head tilts a few inches to the right before his posture stiffens. Is someone here? His accomplice?

Willow shifts in her seat, glancing behind her chair.

"Perhaps it's time you take your leave."

Her stomach tightens at the change in demeanor. "I'd love nothing more. I'll see myself out." Her feet extend, hopping to action at the first chance she's gotten to bolt. The erratic pounding of her heart betrays her calm exterior as she navigates to the exit.

"And next time remember, I do have a doorbell!" he shouts as the dark door slams behind her.

CHAPTER 12

RESPITE

The conference table feels like a stranded island. She's lost at sea and isolated, her gaze unfocused, consumed in thought while she waits for the meeting to start. The chatter of her colleagues fades into the background as she replays last night's conversation with Warren in her mind. Her brow furrows. *What's his game here?* He's got her in a gambit. She grapples with the implications of her getting caught. To her knowledge, the Chief doesn't know about last night's impromptu interrogation. She didn't even have the chance to record the conversation. Her thumbnail bends under the pressure of her canines.

"Will-O." Milo saunters to the chair next to hers, grinning ear to ear.

"What's the look on your face for?"

"Just some good old fashion detective work and glad to see you." His brow wiggles.

Willow ignores his flirting. "What did you find?"

"Tsk tsk," he wags his index finger, "that's what this meeting is for. You'll find out when everyone else does."

"The last time I checked, I was leading this investigation." Her jaw ticks.

Sunny plops identical folders in front of each chair, prepping for their upcoming meeting. She glances around the room. "Dang, she got you, Dunn." Her mouth forms a circle, whistling. "You've grown mighty comfortable teasing your boss." Her eyebrows raise. Like a matador taunting a bull, she waits for his charge.

"Yeah, well, she may be my boss– but when my boss's boss tells me to wait to present our findings in our meeting, that's what you do," he retorts, his mouth forming a straight line while he shifts in his seat.

Sunny huffs, disregarding him completely and exiting the room. At the last second, she gives Willow one last glance, rolling her eyes and holding her smile.

Leo and Jasmine join them at the table and Willow's shoulders loosen. More company means she's less likely to have to strain to hold a conversation with Milo. Or at least, it's less likely the conversation will go sideways with more witnesses around. Warmth spreads across Leo's expression as he sits down and Jasmine nods in Willow's direction. The group sits in silence; heavy footsteps of Chief Hastings thunder into the conference room.

The Chief greets the group with a warm, worn-down smile. "Afternoon everyone. Rhodes, please start with the latest updates in the case." He plops in the office chair at the head of the table, waiting for her to present.

Willow clears her throat as she stands, walking in front of the bulletin board covered in photos from the scene, map of the town, and any information on the victim the team hustled to piece together. "Thanks to Milo and Leo, we received more information on our victim, Jonathan Davies."

She moves to the side of the board, directing their attention to the photo taken from his driver's license, a much happier and lively expression than the one she found at the crime scene.

"He was a blue-collar construction worker. According to his supervisor, he was on his way to Vale to do business and never returned. Jasmine discovered his last known purchase before his estimated time of death was betting chips at the Golden Wolf Casino." Willow nods in Milo's direction, acknowledging his turn to share.

Milo clears his throat, shuffling through the notes in front of him. "I spoke to his wife. Turns out, Jonathan has a history of a gambling addiction. When I confirmed the location of his death, she broke down into tears, practically falling on the floor. It seems that he had been in serious debt before the two of them met. She helped him get clean, even with the money he owed to an underground money shark in Nyssa."

Willow rubs her hands; that's very useful information. What connection does Warren have to the casino?

The Chief offers an approving nod, a glint of excitement in his eye. Willow takes a quick exhale before speaking again. "I examined and revisited the crime scene, not finding much more information. I did find maggots after reassessing the crime scene. I took a sample and brought it back to the examiner, hoping to get more information out of him and observe him more." She pauses, selecting her next words with intention. "I'm not entirely certain about him yet. Regardless, he proved unhelpful, so I got Nadia to analyze the sample for me, and she corroborates Warren's estimated time of death."

The Chief studies the bulletin board. "Why are you 'unsure' about our new examiner?"

"A gut feeling. I don't have anything other than that, but I'm keeping it in the back of my mind as we continue the investigation." She's careful to not reveal more information than needed.

"Don't let him get you sidetracked from considering other suspects. It sounds like we need to dive more into the Casino. We need concrete evidence, not wild theories," the Chief responds straight to the point. She can't wait to prove them wrong.

Willow cracks her knuckles. "After Milo gave me the update he received from Jasmine about Jonathan's last purchase, I took a walk to the casino. Incidentally, I ran into a floor manager who's a total *dick* and unwilling to let us view the video footage without a warrant." She sighs; replaying the interaction reignites her anger. She leaves out the fact that she spotted Warren there, for the time being. "It's not surprising, and of course that's the proper protocol, but still."

"There's more than enough probable cause to get a warrant. Jasmine, work on drafting the affidavit to send so we can get that footage as soon as possible." He adds to Jasmine's list. She nods, writing down her tasks on her scribbled memo notepad.

"While you all have downtime, don't forget there are other petty crimes to attend to. Rhodes is taking the lead so this is her main priority, and the rest of you will follow. If there's any in-between while we wait for footage or tracking down suspects, make sure the other cases are handled as well. I don't want a call from Susan Michaels down the street that the vandalism on her mailbox isn't being taken care of. We assist the other departments here, right?"

"We need this case closed quickly. The public is getting antsy and the more time that passes, the worse it'll be. Not to mention the Halloween Bash. As it stands, there's no way it's getting canceled," the Chief adds, standing from the table with a wave of his hand, ending the conversation and returning to his office.

"I'm assuming I'm back on drug busts for the time being?" Leo leans forward with his elbows propped on the table, staring at Willow.

"Just for the time being. I think there's too many tasked on this already. Once we have some more leads you'll need to jump back in, I'm sure." A flicker of light touches Willow's features.

"What about me, Willow? Need me to shmooze the dickhead at the casino? Or keep an eye on the examiner?" Milo smirks, running his hand through his brown, tousled hair.

Her throat tightens. "I don't need your help with Warren. The *dickhead* can't be dealt with until Jasmine confirms we have the search warrant to obtain the footage. But once we get that, I will need you to lead the interrogations of the employees that worked the night of the victim's death. Until then, wait for my command." Willow's inflection rings with authority.

Milo crosses his arms and leans back in the seat, "Fine. I guess I'm chopped liver then."

Willow and Jasmine sigh in tandem. "You're an asset to the team, Dunn. Like the Chief said, we need to make sure the other things in the town are taken care of too. Trust that I've got this and your back." Willow searches for his approval. Even with her higher-ranking power, the younger version of herself peeks through, needing validation from others.

He nods, uncrossing his arms. "Well, duh." He stands, pushing off from his knees, then uses a firm grip to clamp his hands down on Leo's shoulders before shaking him. "Alright, man. Let's get back to it."

*

The aroma of coffee grounds smacks Willow in the mouth as she opens the door to the Misty Mugs coffee shop. There's a momentary respite from the chaos that the rest of her day has been as she files in line behind other customers, gazing over the menu mounted to the wall over the cashier's head. She twirls her necklace in her mouth, nibbling the warm metal between her lips. A familiar voice breaks through the ambient chatter, she turns. Gideon approaches her with a wave.

He leans in toward Willow, a playful sparkle lighting up his expression as he flashes her a boyish grin.

"Well, well, if it isn't the most captivating detective in town." His velvety lilt caresses her skin, causing her to tense under the proximity.

"May I?" he asks the woman behind Willow, gesturing to see if it's okay for him to cut in line.

She grins ear to ear. "Of course, I'm in no rush."

"I—wouldn't quite say that," Willow fumbles with her words. She drops her necklace from her mouth and crosses her arms in front of her, unsure what to do with them.

"I couldn't help but notice you were here as I passed on the way to the gym, so I just had to stop by."

"Good to see you. I've been told your conversation with Nadia went well? She seemed excited."

He appears pleasantly surprised by Willow's question. "Why, yes, yes, I did! I always enjoy making new friends. It seems to be a wonderful community. She said you two will try to come to one of my yoga classes together. I promise to take it easy on you both."

"That does sound like her—volunteering me for more events," her head shakes, "though, it's hard not to like Nadia," Willow adds, inching forward in line.

"I'm sure everyone says the same about you, Willow." There's tenderness in the look he gives her.

She laughs out of discomfort. "I've literally never heard that in my life."

"Care to join me for a coffee? It'll be the most stimulating conversation you will have all day." His words drop with innuendo and he closes the gap between them, their shoulders now touching.

She stammers, not forming words. Warmth presses against her opposite side, pulling her focus away from Gideon. Willow's scowl turns into a slack jaw as she finds Warren at her side, his shoulder pressing against her other side. He doesn't look at her—he's too busy scrutinizing Gideon.

"Sorry I'm late, Will. Dead bodies don't just embalm themselves." He postures, caging Willow in between the two men. "She won't be joining you this afternoon, she's having something a little stronger than coffee with me." He leaves no room for argument. A possessive arm snakes around her shoulder, pulling her closer to his side.

She somehow feels safer, which annoys her, but she remains silent to observe the two men's pissing contest.

Gideon's confident demeanor never falters as he tips his chin upward, straightening his posture and glaring at Warren. "What a shame. Looks like I'll have to sweep you off your feet another afternoon. Looking forward to seeing you in class." He winks as he waves, swiveling away to exit the shop.

Her face flushes and she pulls away from Warren's embrace, pushing him with both hands. He doesn't budge. "What the literal fuck was that?

And '*Will*'? You don't call me that." The apples of her cheeks burn with heat.

"I think you mean 'Thank you, Warren, for saving me'." He imbues his words with irritation.

"I didn't need *saving*," she hisses as she scoots up to order her latte from the barista.

The two of them pause their arguing and Warren orders a black coffee. Together, they wait for their drinks to be called before he follows her to a table that she sits her bag down on. Willow's gaze shifts from table to table. Why is he following her?

"Your awkward stance could have fooled me," he continues. The salt and pepper haired barista calls Willow's name first, then Warren's seconds later. Willow stands, but Warren rises faster, leaving to grab both drinks. The table shakes as Willow's leg bounces under the surface. The bouncing slows as Warren approaches, sitting both of their drinks down.

"What was that even about? Are you following me now?" she asks, studying his reaction.

Warren brings the coffee cup to his lips. Steam rises, fogging the bottom portion of his glasses and a fleeting grimace pops onto his expression. "Hypocritical to ask that, don't you think?" His head tilts as his shoulders rest against the back of the chair. "I was around the area."

Her nostrils flare as she drinks her iced latte, knowing that he's right. "I can handle myself. Besides, what if I was about to say yes? You just ruined a potential date." She avoids his stare, changing the subject.

He deadpans as he raises a brow. "Oh? Were you about to say yes?"

She pauses. "...No. Maybe? It's none of your business." She isn't sure why she feels inclined to tell him anything.

He smirks and the coffee mug clinks against the table as he sets it down. "That's what I thought."

A cough tickles at the back of her throat, causing her to swallow her drink down her airway and the heat returns to her cheeks. Regaining her composure, she clears her throat. "My personal life is none of your concern. But back to my question, what was that about?"

"As I said, I was around the area. I noticed you in line. The blonde clung suffocatingly close to you and I perceived discomfort in your voice, so I intervened on your behalf. I won't help moving forward, so don't worry."

"I don't believe you, just so you know. And I sure as hell trust him more than I trust you." She sips her coffee again. Her sound holds no malice, just a matter-of-fact statement. There's no way she's going to let a *killer* try to act like a hero. His time is running out, and Willow is right on his tail.

"You don't have to believe me. But you're welcome either way. I also figured that this would be easier for you, watching me here, rather than from the bushes." He stands up from the seat. "Next time you visit, the key is under the mat. I may not hear the doorbell, plus it'll save me from having to open the door myself."

CHAPTER 13

GIRL'S DAY

The justice system stands riddled with flaws. The steps for obtaining and requesting evidence is understandable, but the timeline it takes to get things moving is criminally slow. Willow curls up in the corner of her reading nook, thumbing through old case files she shouldn't be in possession of. The sun rises through the clouds, waking up the rest of the world. Through the window, thick fog creeps through the trees. It wafts through the air, draping over the flora and fauna like a mother tucking her child into bed.

THUD THUD THUD

A heavy bang jumpstarts her heart, and the noise echoes throughout the home. Willow's sigh is audible as her hand hovers over the doorknob. The dread pushes her to open the front door to Nadia, who breezes into the house in a tornado of enthusiasm.

"Surprise! Girl's afternoon!" Nadia announces, her high pony swishing behind her with every step, dropping an assortment of snacks on Willow's coffee table.

Salt and vinegar chip bags crinkle, bouncing off each other, then resting in place next to a cardboard box of Hot Tamales. Willow's protest dies on her lips as Nadia drags her into the living room, her plans of diving into the case files now obsolete. She chews the inside of her cheek.

As the afternoon unfolds, Willow finds herself enjoying the company, despite her initial resistance. Nadia's infectious energy and nonstop chatter provides a welcome distraction from the investigation looming over her. Yet, even as they laugh and reminisce, she can't shake the nagging guilt for neglecting the duties she's placed upon herself. She makes a mental note to carve out some time later to revisit the files, specifically the witness statements so that her focus doesn't waver too long. For years she's analyzed these files, but she knows in her gut there's something she's missing. She will find it.

"So have you gone out with Gideon yet?" Willow asks, popping open the bag of barbeque chips.

Nadia giggles, rocking side to side. "Actually, I've met someone better!" She flips through the entertainment magazine she brought and sips on carbonated water. The term *magazine* is used loosely— since it's a tabloid with numerous conspiracy theories conglomerated on each page.

Willow leans forward, interest piqued in the lack of Nadia's words. "Give me details?"

Nadia grins ear to ear, browsing the magazine, flipping each page with flare to add dramatic effect. "His name is Adalric, and man oh man Will. He is tall, dark, and *handsome*." She fans herself, a light blush dusting her amber cheeks. "I thought Gideon was the prettiest man I'd ever laid my eyes on, but Adalric is up there. He took me to Portland, and we had a night out on the town."

Willow's eyebrow raises. "Night out on the town? What does that mean?"

Nadia laughs. "You need to get out more. He told me to wear cocktail attire, so I wore the nicest dress I own, and he took me to an extravagant restaurant where we had a three-course meal and wine. We visited other bars, and he ended the night walking me to my doorstep, kissed my hand, and that's it."

"That's it? Any talk of another date?" Willow interrogates her.

She nods in rapid movement. "Oh yes. We've talked on the phone each afternoon since our date. He's planning another one soon, he's just busy with work right now."

Willow stands to stretch, raising her arms over her head. "What does he do for work?"

Nadia pauses. "I think he said something about finance management? It sounded boring, so I didn't pay attention."

Willow shrugs. "Understandable."

"But he lives right outside of town so it's kinda nice I can get out and see more than Misty Pines. Outside of death, I mean."

Is it nice? The thought never occurred to Willow that she should leave her hometown. Perhaps if she didn't have unfinished business here then maybe she would've left?

"Well, he better treat you right. Don't let him treat you like garbage just because he's hot." Willow's words dance between playful teasing and a sharp warning.

Even though Nadia forced Willow into friendship growing up, Willow found herself protective over Nadia. Probably in the same way Nadia feels about Willow, except Nadia's concern has always been Willow's mental state. Willow would need three hands to count all the times a pretty boy tried taking advantage of Nadia.

"Yes, *mother*." Nadia mocks, switching magazines from conspiracies to this year's fall fashion. Above knee plaid skirts, solid-colored turtlenecks, paired with ankle high booties are the go-to business casual attire.

Willow checks her watch, keeping an eye on the ticking time. Half the day wasted away on snacks with deadly amounts of sodium and small talk. Nadia acknowledges her distraction with a sigh.

"Well, I'm proud of you for attempting to at least enjoy my presence for half the day before thinking about work," she states, gathering the remaining snacks and magazines she brought.

"I—"

"I'm just giving you a hard time, before you come at me," She holds her hands up as if to shield herself from Willow's scolding. "Just know that I care about you, and you need to take care of yourself. That's what I want you to get out of today. But I'll leave you to whatever's itching at you. I'll enjoy the rest of my off day at home. Drink your water." Nadia hugs her friend against her will.

Willow stiffens but allows her to wrap her arms around her. A weight lifts from her shoulders as the door closes behind Nadia.

In her reading corner, Kai's files remain in the precise location she left them. The manila folders fade along the spine, cracking from constant flipping and harsh handling. She palms through them, as if each touch of the wrapping would reveal a new discovery. Years of wear and tear apparent in each crack rippling through the witness statement folder. The first witness interviewed surrounding Kai's death was a man who went by the name Chester. Stringy brass hair stood from the side of his head. His mugshot *far* from being magazine ready. He never would provide his last name, and the officer interrogating him didn't believe Chester was his government name. Chester's criminal history of multiple charges of possession, public intoxication, and intent to distribute pulls immediately when searching his name in the database. The officer wrote his statement off soon after this discovery. Chester was never called into the station for further questioning, which given his history is understandable.

Witness 1: "Chester"

Noting: Scent of alcohol on witness's breath.

Transcribed notes from interview:

Chester: "Well–well–well–I can't tell you what I really saw. You won't believe me. I don't believe me."

Officer: "I'd like to think I'd believe you. Please tell me what you saw regarding the deceased.

Chester: "He. He was tearing his shirt off."

Officer: "That's it? You saw him taking his shirt off?"

Chester: "No!! You're not listening! Tearing it–like ripping his skin off. He started clawing himself! So–much blood."

*

Burnt orange and fuchsia hues sway across the sky, closing like a curtain after the performers bow at the finale of a play. Standing pools of water in the pavement reflect the colors, the ripples breaking them up with every car that passes down the road. A chilling breeze sends goosebumps racing up her arms, even through her suede peacoat jacket. Warren's car isn't present, she notes as she scans the parking lot. It's a Sunday afternoon. Many of the church members are parked in the same lot, lingering by the doors for their evening worship service to begin. The light to the front of the funeral home flickers on. It's unlikely anyone is working, but it's worth a shot.

She ambles up the front steps, pushing forward into the building. She scans the low-lit interior, searching for any sign of presence. As she suspected, nothing. If he's anywhere, he's downstairs. As she ventures further inside, Sam turns the corner, heading up the stairs and bumping into her. A jolt of static shocks the two of them from the contact and her necklace prickles from the electricity.

She gasps. "Jesus, Sam. I didn't even hear you coming."

Sam's smile brightens, placing a firm hand on her shoulder. She's stunned by the heaviness of it, compared to his size.

"Apologies, Detective Rhodes. I didn't mean to startle you. I heard the door alarm ring and didn't want to have anyone wait. Are you here to meet with Warren? If so, I'm sorry to tell you but he's off today. Events are slow, thankfully." He speaks in a measured cadence.

She steps out of his grasp. "Actually, I was in the area and thought I would stop by. We didn't get off on the right foot the first time we met. I wanted to come and apologize," she adds, recalling how she omitted some of the truth the first time she arrived, which ended with Sam being scolded by his supervisor for letting two strangers in.

Sam nods. "That's water under the bridge. But I appreciate the thought."

Willow coughs. "Well, as you know, I am currently investigating the murder of the victim that the two of you autopsied. I hoped I could ask you some questions." She phrases it not as a question but more of a hopeful statement.

Sam shifts, leaning against the wall beside the stairs to the basement. "Am I a suspect?" His stance becomes guarded.

"No, no," she affirms. "I wanted to know a little bit more about you. I've yet to work with either of you and I always like to get the background of my potential expert witnesses if you ever get called into court." *A half-truth.* She adjusts the chain of her necklace where the latch brushes against her chest; the irritation has caused a prickly patch to itch beneath it.

"Oh, of course." His lips curve in understanding. "I moved here not too long ago. I'm originally from North Dakota. I grew up on a farm, that's probably hard to tell." He chuckles.

Willow's nods. "I definitely wouldn't have guessed that. That must have been a great way to be raised." The thought of living on a farm crossed her mind every now and then. Escaping the world to live like the Amish.

"It had its perks. However, I longed to see more of the world and an opportunity opened here shortly after I received my mortician assistant license, so I packed it all up and moved. I've enjoyed it here so far." He straightens, no longer leaning against the wall. "What about you? Have you always been here?"

Willow's stare draws downward. "I have. Maybe one day I'll leave the town. When the time is right." *Maybe the more she says it, she'll believe it.*

"It's hard to leave family behind," he says. "My wife hopes to arrive within the next year, once her parents' health stabilizes."

"Oh, I don't really have any family. I mean, I do, but none that I'm on speaking terms with." *That's more than she should have shared.* "But this town holds a lot of great memories and there are good people here. It's good you get to experience it too, even if we're growing quicker than the amount of space we have." She laughs, attempting to break the thick air.

"It's good to be here finally. I'm very interested to see how everything changes and unfolds."

"Well, I don't want to take you away from work if you're the only one here. I hope it stays slow for you. The next time Warren's in, please tell him I have some questions for him as well." She's growing tired of playing cat and mouse with him.

"Of course. Have a good night, Detective. Be careful out there." The wooden stairs creak as he descends, until the growing distance shushes the sound.

CHAPTER 14

DEAD WEIGHT

The familiar buzz of activity envelopes her senses as she steps inside the Golden Wolf Casino. The flashing lights and ringing bells add to the excitement as a winner cheers. A dull casino concierge bores her glare through Willow as she vexedly waits for her to retrieve a crumbled five-dollar bill from her wallet. Without a word, the woman trades Willow for coins to use, clinking against each other as she places them in her palm. The slot machines call her name.

She swivels left to right, her body fidgeting on the round red stool in front of her claimed slot machine. She surveys the profiles of the crowd, none recognizable. Inserting the coins, she pulls the lever. The reels spins with great force before coming to a stop with a satisfying chime.

No win. She's not surprised; she's never been lucky. To be fair, she has no clue what she's doing. Willow pulls out her phone. By now Jasmine should have an update on the subpoena. It would be an easy grab while she's already here.

The phone rings a few beeps before Jasmine answers. "Hey, Rhodes."

"Hey, Jasmine. Just wanted to see if there were any updates on that warrant for the footage from the Golden Wolf? I'm here now so it came to mind to ask."

"I wondered where you were. It sounds like a fire station with all those bells. But no, nothing yet. I sent the affidavit off, but the access is still pending. It could be another day or so, but I hope they will get back to us soon."

"Got it. Well, keep me posted if you learn anything sooner. Any updates on the examiner's background?" Willow probes.

Jasmine sighs. "No, I've been preoccupied working on getting the warrant, checking more on the victim's banking, and then the rest of the cases I'm on. Like I said before, he's pretty off the grid. I will have to delegate serious focus time to try to find more on him."

Willow winces, hearing the irritation in Jasmine's timbre. Jasmine's being stretched thin. "You're right. You've got a lot going on. For the time being, don't worry about him. It may just be a wild goose chase because I'm paranoid. Thanks for all your hard work. Get some sleep tonight and sorry again for calling so late."

"It's fine. I signed up for this. Murder puts everything in a spin, doesn't it? And it's interesting hearing you tell someone to get some sleep," she pauses, "but I will, trust me. Good night."

She clicks the phone and the screen goes dark. No matter how good Jasmine is, Willow doesn't trust that Jasmine will ever find the information she's searching for. Killers often leave at least some sort of evidence behind, but when they are morticians–they know exactly how to manipulate bodies or what to look for at crime scenes that could implicate them. It's apparent Warren knows what he's doing, but Willow will be the one to catch him.

After multiple lever pulls and losing all her coins, she grows tired of sitting at the machine. An upscale bar sits in the center of the casino, providing drinks to already intoxicated patrons. A drink wouldn't hurt. Plus, it would give her something to keep her hands busy and hide her discomfort. She's acutely aware of her surroundings despite her casual demeanor. In her mind she makes mental notes of individuals with odd behaviors or identifying markers. Large man with three lip rings, a thin male server with a red mohawk, a petite woman who's without a doubt on coke and may still have it on the tip of her nose, *noted*.

At the bar, she pulls her arms through the gray cardigan she carries, letting it relax down her back and covering the stool she sits upon. Most of the patrons are at the card tables scattered within the building. There are a few tables on the first level. Peering up from the bar, she observes a second story level that contains more tables, slot machines, and several other auxiliary mystery rooms.

A welcoming toothy grin greets Willow from behind the counter while she's distracted by her observations. "What can I get for you?" the bartender asks. A stark difference from the greeting she received from Brian the Floor Manager, previously.

Willow glances up, meeting her gaze. She notes the woman's swarthy skin, cloaked behind the black dress shirt and pants that all employees appear to wear. Her shoulder-length, wavy hair tucks behind both ears, revealing a dozen piercings.

"Just a vodka soda, please. Thanks," Willow replies, her mouth twisting upward, more performance than pleasure.

The bartender nods and turns to pour Willow's drink. The ice clinks as she haphazardly plops several pieces into the glass. The bar stands freely like an island in the middle of the room. In the center stands a tall wall, filled with shelving for various liquors and wines. On the opposite side of the bar, Willow notices two employees slumped over the smooth wooden bar top in conversation. Must be on break.

"Man, I told you. Ace has like fifty shipments coming in. I've been in the game a while, but that's nothing compared to the shit I've seen Ace get." The thinner, balding man whispers, but the depth of his voice carries loud enough for Willow to piece together a few phrases.

Her curiosity piques with the mention of shipments. She pulls out her phone to make note of the nickname, Ace, to run by Jasmine. Could Jonathan's death be the result of a good deal gone bad?

"Here's your drink. Cash or card? Or would you like to start a tab?" the bartender asks.

Willow pulls out her wallet, placing her card in the woman's hand. "Just card, no tab please."

"I'll be right back with the receipt," the bartender adds, taking the card to a terminal further down the bar.

Willow shifts to look back at the two men but they're nowhere to be seen. *Damn.* The bartender slides the card and receipts back to Willow, setting a pen down beside her.

"Have a safe night," she adds, before turning away to service other patrons waiting on the other side of the table.

Willow nurses her drink, taking casual sips and people watching as they come and go.

Employees in their black-tie attire are stationed at tables, some roaming the floor, and others watch over the banister from the second story as they keep an eye on the bottom floor. The dull lights of the casino seem to cast longer shadows. She flips her wrist to check the time; it's almost midnight. The alcohol rushes down her throat as she slams the rest of her drink, leaving her glass at the edge of a table with other discarded cups and plates. Her shoulders slouch with disappointment at the turnout of her evening. Ace seems like an interesting character.

Maybe the night isn't a total waste. The brisk air cuts through her clothes like a knife. She wraps herself within the cardigan like a cocoon, quickening her pace. The warmth of her cottage home whispers *comfort awaits*. A shout rings out from a nearby alley, rough and jagged. She can't make out the words, but the tone cuts through—sharp and aggressive. Violent. She turns toward the source of the commotion, tip toeing into the side alley of the casino.

Her heart races as she rounds the corner into the back alley. The chilling of the brick slashes into her back as she presses against it, moving her torso forward to peer around the corner. In the distance, two figures are locked in place, every muscle taut, the space between them charged like a drawn wire. The details of their facial features are unclear due to the lack of light in the alley but the taller of the two men appears to have the advantage, cornering the other against the back brick wall of the casino.

"I told you man, I'm not telling you shit!" the shorter man yells, shoving the other's broad chest, he doesn't budge an inch.

"And I think you will," a familiar gruff voice echoes through the alley, though who it belongs to escapes her.

She inches closer. The taller figure shoves the man against the wall and grips his throat, lifting him along the wall. Realization strikes her like a match and she lurches forward. She runs, pulling her concealed firearm out of the holster on her right hip.

"That's enough!" Willow yells as she approaches.

Warren's stare burns with barely restrained fury—his composed demeanor replaced by rage, poised for confrontation. In Warren's grasp, a thin man with frail hair dangles inches off the ground, gasping for air while struggling to reach Warren. It's one of the workers from the bar who discussed the shipments. His legs flail erratically, desperate to hit his opponent. Warren's attention shifts to her.

"For fuck's sake, Detective. *Leave.* There's nothing that concerns you here," Warren barks, cutting the air with sharpness.

"I think this whole situation concerns me! Step away from him and we can talk in the station, both of you!" she threatens, lifting her gun toward them.

Before she can, another set of arms wraps around her shoulders, immobilizing her. She stiffens. Time moves in slow motion as she's shoved to the ground in a blink of an eye. Her face smashes against the wet concrete, her gun clinking against the ground. The instant force rattles her senses.

"A detective? In our neck of the woods? Well, that's not good, is it Ryan?" an eerie purr rasps from behind her.

She regains focus, flipping around on her back to stand, only to be met by a towering figure. His thick torso blocks her vision from anything else as the heaviness of his foot comes down on top of her like a hammer, pinning her to the pavement. The man has incredible strength, despite Willow's wiggling and pushing, he remains steady and unbothered. Warren's look hardens, nostrils flaring at the new individual standing above Willow. His grip tightens around the smaller man's throat.

"I know plenty of places to dump a body. It'll be the talk of the town! I can see the headlines now, 'another detective murdered in Misty Pines'." The man cackles a hoarse laugh and the end of each breath wheezes.

"Ryan, Ace didn't give you a gift for nothing, stop wasting it." The burly man straddles Willow, a thick tree trunk of a leg on each side of her torso, as he pins each of her arms under his legs.

He pulls out a long, black bladed pocketknife from his jacket pocket. The blade reflects the moonlight, the smallest sliver visible through the clouds. She continues to struggle, exhausting her energy as she shifts left and right, the pure weight of the man presses on her chest like a truck. She's immobile.

"Now beautiful, are you a good cop or bad cop?" he teases with a smirk, his golden front tooth shining in the moonlight.

She grimaces and her jaw tightens as she takes the saliva pooled in her mouth and spits in his face. "*Fuck you,*" she bites.

He wipes the spit off his upper lip, features bending with a sick sense of joy.

"Oh, I will sweetie. And I'll enjoy cutting you into pieces too," he threatens as he brings the blade to Willow's neck.

The knife slices into the tender flesh and blood trickles down her neck, the sharp pain stealing her breath. The warmth of the fluid chills as soon as it meets the surface of her skin.

In an instant, Ryan lets out a guttural choke, followed by the sound of a lifeless form hitting the ground with a sickening thud. It could be the blood loss, but seconds feel like hours. In the time it takes the beefy man straddling Willow to turn his head the slightest, she watches through struggling consciousness as his head twists 180 degrees and his body falls limp to the side. The sound of bones snapping cracks through her ears. The weight from her arms releases, but an even heavier dead weight sits on her legs.

Warren glares down at her, his shadow covering her entirely and his chest heaves. Willow shakes her head with disbelief, her vision swimming with confusion and pain radiating from her neck. Her hand rushes to her throat and scarlet coats her fingers as she pulls it away.

Her heart thumps, bewildered as she blinks, catching a glimpse of Warren—sharpened facial features and all. His stare cuts through her like a knife, his irises glowing as if illuminated by a single lightbulb in each iris— radiant blues and greens making the whites of his eyes seem dull in comparison. His shoulders rock back and forth while he stands in place, his mouth agape as he breathes heavily. The angles of his cheekbones are sharper than before, matching his sharper than knives, elongated canines. Fear grips her and the inside of her head swims with dizziness from the pain and confusion as she battles consciousness. She's drowning in it. The world around her blurs. Each breath comes in shallow gasps, her heartbeat pounds in her ears, keeping any other sound from being heard.

Warren kicks the dead weight lying on top of Willow with ease, as if it were a soccer ball. The sudden removal of the weight allows her to catch her breath, but her air is shallow, a panic attack in the making. Warren gives an angry sigh as he kneels beside her. His arms tremble with pent-up energy as he hovers over her injured body.

"Detective, can you hear me?" His voice strains.

She's unable to move. Her shallow breaths are her focus; every gasp plunges a knife of air into her chest. As she attempts to focus harder on staying awake, her peripheral vision blackens and she goes limp.

"Very well." He takes her up in his arms, her feet dangling lifelessly in the air. "You just don't know when to quit, do you?"

CHAPTER 15

SUTURES

She writhes, sinking deeper into the soft surface beneath her. An uncomfortable pressure bears down on her neck, a rhythmic throb of pain pulses, radiating into her shoulder. Her eyelids, though closed, squeeze tighter as she groans. Another press into her neck causes her vision to rip open, and her head turns in response to the touch. Warren moves his hand away from her neck with caution, a handful of blood-soaked cotton pads pinched between his fingers. Her senses reel as she tries to piece together the disjointed fragments of her memory. The unfamiliar surroundings envelop her and a surge of panic washes over her as her eyes meet Warren's. He studies her face, his presence resting with leisure in a leather chair pulled beside the bed. She recoils, her heart thrums into tachycardia once more.

"Get away from me!" she demands, her cry laced with fear and accusation as flashes of Warren's devilish features from after he snapped a man's neck infiltrate her mind. "What did you do to me?" Her mind races as she scoots back. *Whose bed is this?* The veins in her forearms bulge from how hard her fists grasp the sheet below and her neck burns red hot.

Warren stands and takes a cautious step back.

"Get the hell away from me!" She dashes off the bed, throwing the sheets to the side and making a run for the closest door. The stabbing pain hacks through her neck, traveling down her back, and shoots into her leg, making her hobble. She ignores it. She's got to get out of here. Only silence creeps at her back.

Until there's more.

A blur darts past her. There's no time to stop as she collides into

Warren's chest as he stands still as a statue. His arms extend on either side of her, but he doesn't touch her.

"You don't need to do that." His tone mirrors that of a zoo handler—calm, practiced, coaxing something wild without letting it bolt. But he's not a zoo handler, he's the predator. And Willow's the prey.

"I'm going to ensure you're arrested for the murders you've committed!" she screams, her sounds cutting in and out, growing hoarse as she turns once more to run the way she came. *There's got to be another way out of here.*

She's back in the bedroom she started in, frantically searching for alternate methods of escape. There's no windows. Warren strolls into the room behind her. The extravagantly carved wooden dresser against the wall homes a vase, white roses bloom inside. Without hesitation, she bolts to the dresser, clutches the vase in her fist and pitches it as hard as she can at him. Standing in place, he twists his torso, dodging with ease.

"Are you finished?" he demands.

"What do you want from me? Why am I here? What are you?" Her voice croaks, hands swinging in wild, exaggerated motions.

"Don't make any more sudden movements or you could tear a suture," he asserts.

Her fingertips trace over five small stitches along the side of her neck. "You stitched me up?" Her eyebrows draw together. *Why?*

"Yes." His reply unfolds softly.

"What else did you do to me? Where am I?" Rage cascades within her, shifting to fear. Like a volcano flowing and transitioning into a glacier, freezing her body in place.

"Without my help, you would have eventually bled out. Don't worry, I know you're not good with giving thanks, so you're most welcome," he jokes, but his expression remains stoic. The tension stretches across the room, holding her fast within its embrace. "I've taken you far away from the scene. You may not recognize this room, but you're in my home."

A muscle ticks in her jaw. "What does it matter if I bled out? You snapped a guy's neck, if I recall correctly?" she hisses, panic and confusion coloring her words. "You should have let me die. I'm a witness, right?"

Warren offers a thoughtful nod. "Two, actually. But I wouldn't quite call them your typical *guy*." He adjusts his stance. "And it was in self-defense. There's no reason for you to die, you have no real intention of arresting me."

The muscle in her jaw quirks. *Oh? Is that so?* Willow's mouth opens, just to slam shut as she catches a glimpse of her bare leg below. There's a rock in her throat. "What did you do to me?" Rage surges through her at the implication of being taken advantage of.

"I simply tended to your wounds, nothing else."

"I'm in different clothes! What did you do to me?" she demands.

"Yes, I removed your shirt to examine the rest of your torso for more injuries. If you remember, a giant delinquent was crushing you. I found none, so instead of putting you back in your blood-stained clothes from before, I gave you a shirt of mine. No need to act so coy, it's not like I haven't seen a naked woman before." A soft grin pulls on his mouth before fading.

Heat pours into her cheeks. Willow searches beside the bed, scrambling for her gun or anything else that she could use as a weapon.

Warren steps forward. "Your gun is in the kitchen on the table. You won't need it here, if you can just calm down and listen."

"Don't move!" she yells as she pushes backward more, finding herself pressed against the dresser. "I have questions, and you *will* answer them," she hisses, her words like blades.

Warren leans against his bedroom wall, his body language relaxed for the most part. His fists are stiff, hinting at either anger or discomfort, more than likely both.

"Why did you kill Jonathan Davies?" she accuses.

Warren scoffs, "What do you take me for? An amateur? I didn't kill that man. The first time I saw him was when he was brought to my morgue."

"What were you doing arguing with that man in the alley? And also—self-defense, my ass! You were the one about to attack him! And by the looks of it, he didn't have a chance!"

"You cannot begin to fathom the capabilities he could have had. He was just inexperienced," he strains. The blues of his eyes rock like waves, the green in them floating atop the water like lily pads. He seems genuine.

"What does that even mean? Inexperienced at fighting? Yeah, most normal people are, I'd say!"

"Inexperienced in wielding powers, Detective. Not just fighting." His brow arches.

A million thoughts race through her mind—so many she can't make out one in particular. She shakes her head, hoping the movement would help them flow in a straight line. "Did you—did you break out of a penitentiary somewhere and wind up here? Do you need help?" A frown pulls at the corner of her lips. "There's resources I can find to help you," she pauses. "But you're still going to have to face the trial for the murders you've committed.

Warren's fingers pinch the bridge of his nose. "There's plenty of help I could probably use, but not for the reason you're thinking. You're processing a lot of information. You need to lie down and rest."

"You're going to give me my cell phone, I'm going to call the police, and I will leave."

"I will do no such thing." The icy aqua of his iris's flashes with a brief pulse of red.

The windpipes in her throat tighten. "Am I dead?" she whispers.

"You are an intelligent woman, Detective. Do you think you're dead?" His figure coils, as though preparing for a bomb to go off. His arms cross, each hand grabbing a bicep.

Willow bites at the skin on her bottom lip. "Being dead would be easier than what I think you are– what I think I saw," she admits.

"Yeah, I feel the same way most of the time." His expression mirrors her pain, softened only by the shared understanding.

Willow brings her knees to her chest. "I've been reading too many fantasy novels. It's just a bad dream. I'll wake up, slumped over my couch because I haven't slept for days and needed the rest," she starts muttering, convincing herself.

The sound of Warren clearing his throat breaks her rambling. "You're getting a lot of life altering information right now. I assure you, unfortunately, this is real and not a dream. If you do not take deep, calming breaths, you will have a panic attack." Long strands of hair fall in front of his face. He tucks the white strand behind his ear with a quiet touch, then pushes his round rimmed glasses back up the bridge of his nose.

"There's no way," she draws a long breath, attempting to regain some form of composure. She pulls the comforter further up to rest at her chest, her expression stretches tight. Caught in between dread and doubt. "What am I even doing here," she whispers to herself.

Warren takes hesitant steps forward toward the bed, his palms face out. "Whatever it is you're thinking, it's not as bad as it seems," he tells her. "One thing at a time. You're alive and safe. I am not a threat," he tells her.

"Not a threat?" she rasps. "How can you look at me and tell me you aren't a threat? You're not–I'm not sure what you even are?" she says with uncertainty. This is lunacy. Every word that comes out of her mouth furthers the proof of her insanity.

"Fine. Let me clarify, I'm not a threat to *you*. I have no ill intentions of harming you. If I did, I could have killed you the moment we met. You're alive because I chose to keep you that way." His brow quirks.

"Is that supposed to make me feel better?" Her features pucker as though she swallowed something sour.

"It should. There are plenty of creatures like me in the world that are way worse. I at least have some empathy."

The word *creature* leaving his mouth solidifies what she's most afraid of. She doesn't speak—only stares at him, willing she would wake up from this nightmare already. Her chest heaves as her breath quickens.

"You're in shock. You need to sit down now," he steps back, motioning to the bed.

She can't do anything but shake her head, her vacant stare drilling a hole in the floor. With an exasperated sigh, Warren takes a few steps toward her and before she can blink, he picks her up and tosses her onto the bed.

It all happens within a blink of an eye. Willow lifts her hand and, as hard as she can, slaps herself against the cheek. The contact her palm makes with her face stings, and warmth floods the area. "This–is real," she rasps. "What–are you?"

"There are many legends with different names for what I am. But the most common is *vampire* I suppose." His words are laced with disdain.

Willow swallows, feeling the gravity of that statement. "Great. Wonderful." She falls on her back, the softness of the bed catching her. Whatever her fate may be, she must accept it at this point.

"I understand your distrust," he admits. "And this is a lot to take in. But rest assured that I am not too keen on *humans* knowing about me either. You don't have to believe everything right now, but please try to keep an open mind and hear me out."

"Why am I still alive? I have this valuable information and could tell anyone. Why keep me alive?" She glances at him from her peripheral vision. A part of her maybe wishes this could be her end.

"Why keep you alive?" he repeats her question, looking away from her and considering his response. "I see– potential. You're a skilled detective, resourceful, and determined in whatever your cause may be. These are qualities that can be very useful in my world."

Willow sits up, her stomach twisting in knots as she bends. "And what does that mean? Your world?" she presses.

Warren sits on the edge of the bed, making sure not to touch her. "It means that we can help each other. I have my own reasons, and you have yours, but you may find it beneficial to work with me too. Our interests may align more than you think." His words are cryptic.

"Work–together? On the murder cases? Why? Why on *earth* would I do that?" Her eyebrows knit together.

"By bringing my knowledge in, it gives you an advantage to solving your case. Do you really not think knowing about a whole new world wouldn't open your options up for the suspect you're searching for?"

"You know more than you're letting on." Finally, she turns her head to look at him and squints.

"I know more than you at this moment, yes. However, if you agree to work with me, both of our goals can be fulfilled. Once that happens, I will leave town, and you never have to see me again." His words hang in the air.

Thoughts swirl in her mind. Vampires are real. What other things are real? The characters from her books? Are they real? She doesn't trust Warren. She would be stupid to believe anything he says. For all she knows, he has his own agenda for finding the killer, and if Willow somehow solves it, she'll wind up dead the next day. *Or he's the killer, as she originally hypothesized.* However– this could speed up her investigation exponentially. She could finally catch Kai's killer.

Warren's mouth twitches, just barely. "We can discuss this further, but for now you should rest. When you're ready, we'll talk about how we can help each other." He hesitates, leaving room for another conversation in the future as he stands from the bed to leave the room.

"Wait–I can't just stay here? Where are my things? I need to work. This is just a flesh wound." The comforter bunches as she attempts to stand. Before she can turn her head, Warren stands in front of her, blocking her from leaving the bed. The fast movement startles her, a small shriek escaping her mouth.

"Sit," he demands, his command raspy and firm.

"Are we helping each other or are you going to kill me? I have a job that protects a lot of people's lives. I need to leave." She frowns, his commanding presence stirs her irritation, but she isn't dumb enough to poke an angry bear that can maul her in seconds.

"I told you; you need to rest. Even without the gash on your throat you were already sleep deprived. That is helpful to no one. Sleep. Your work has already been taken care of." He doesn't move an inch.

"What? How? I can't–"

"I have a friend in the office. They are relaying a message on your behalf.

You have the max amount of PTO so there's plenty of sick time to use. That's what's happening. Now sit and rest before I make you."

"Asshole," she spits. There's nothing more aggravating to her than being kept from something she wants to do.

He offers a lazy shrug, a faint smirk playing on his lips as he adjusts his glasses. "Maybe I am," he agrees, unfazed by her insult and rage. "But you will thank me later. Now, rest."

"Can this not be done in my home? Why do I need to be here? I can rest better without a *blood sucker* watching me. This is kidnapping." For a brief second, she swears he winces.

"You are good at what you do, but when you deal with the supernatural, you aren't as stealthy or clever as you have hoped. Making enemies at the casino wasn't the smartest decision when you're investigating them for Davies's murder, is it?" He lifts his chin.

The comment makes her jaw tick. "How long have you been watching me?"

"Since the second you stepped into my workplace unannounced. Take that as a lesson learned." He turns to leave.

"I'm leaving. You can't make me stay here."

His barely glances back over his shoulder. "You're staying under my watch until I know you won't try to turn me in or kill me. Keyword, *try*. You will not succeed. Now, rest. I'm tired of bickering with you. If you step outside this bedroom door without me being present, I will *kill* you."

The bedroom light blinks out and the door locks in place behind him. Though she struggles against it, the lull of the darkness sings her to sleep. Her restless eyes grow heavier and heavier, until she exhausts herself from trying to stay awake.

The light of the early morning creeps through the windows. At the first sign of light, her body has been trained to come alive, however this morning, she stills. Fatigue and pain sit heavy on her shoulders. The only thing Willow can muster is to swivel her head around the room now that she's able to get a better observation of her surroundings.

Like the rest of the glass window exterior in the front of the home, this bedroom also has several large windowpanes. These windows, however, have automatic curtains that pull down to cover them, dimming the natural light I n the room. The bedroom matches the minimalistic and modern design of the rest of the house. The space is sleek and understated, with dark neutral colors dominating the color palette. The furniture is clean-lined and contemporary, blending in seamlessly with the subdued color scheme.

Maybe he should decorate her house. Somber serenity casts throughout the room. Though her stomach twists in knots, a wave of exhaustion washes over her. A sharp twinge of pain pulses from her neck, heating under the gauze. Despite her irritation and the uncertainty of the situation she finds herself in, she can't help but feel comfort laying in this bed alone. Her eyes bore holes in the speckled ceiling, counting each groove until they fall closed and she drifts into another peaceful sleep.

CHAPTER 16

ANNUAL HALLOWEEN BASH

Creaking wood followed by silence causes Willow to stir. Her eyelids flutter open, finding herself lying in a comfortable bed. A comfortable, but unfamiliar bed. Conflicting senses of rest and disorientation fight within her body. The room is quiet with a dusky ambiance. The only light comes from the hallway. It's real. She's in Warren's home.

Warren steps into the doorway, watching as she stirs awake. "Good evening," he greets in a gravelly welcome. "Take your time, no rush."

Willow flinches hearing his voice, then blinks. "Evening? How long have I been asleep?" she asks.

"Two nights," his shoulder braced against the doorframe.

Willow jolts forward, sucking in a gasp. "Two nights?" This is the most amount of work she's missed in her tenure. She doesn't count the year she caught the flu, came into work anyway, and was kicked out.

"You needed the rest it seems." He gestures for her to follow him as he leaves, disappearing out of sight.

The palm of Willow's hand rubs into her eye sockets vigorously, moving to her cheeks, dragging the skin of her face downward. She stands for the first time in days. Pressure surges to her head, stumbling as her balance tilts. She hasn't trained in a few days either, and her muscles will make her pay for it. Warren's shirt extends to her mid-thigh, tickling her skin. A frown pulls her lips, accompanied by a heavy sigh. Her attention lands on the silk top sheet of the bedding. The corners of her mouth quirk.

Upon entering the kitchen, she acknowledges the warm atmosphere. The marble counters are spotless, void of anything on them other than a plate of steaming food. Warren leans against the counter across from her. A playful glint flickers in the sparkle of his stare. "Well, that's a fashion statement." His lingering look trails to her waist, recognizing his torn bed sheets wrapped around her midsection. "That's Mulberry silk, you know."

"I wasn't left with many options," she bites. "Where are my things?"

A low chuckle escapes his mouth, startling her. "Don't fret, everything is in the bathroom, clean and ready for wear. Have a seat. I made some food."

She grimaces. "I'm not hungry."

He deadpans back at her, his lips tighten. "Eat. It wasn't a question."

Willow tilts her head at him with a glare. A part of her always enjoyed playing with fire. "*No.*"

"How many times do I have to tell you I have no plans to kill you? It's not poisoned. Now, *eat.*" The last word a whisper.

Fear holds her heart hostage. There's no other choice. An herb crusted chicken sits on top of a pile of rice. Steam rises from an additional side of broccoli. The gas in her stomach gurgles, begging for food. The aroma wafts into her nostrils and it smells damn good. Willow uses the available fork to poke around the food, inspecting for any signs of tampering.

"You owe me a new bed sheet."

"I should've had my clothes to put on. I don't owe you anything." She stabs the food with her fork. If she can keep from having any prolonged conversations, she can make short work of the meal. The lemon zest on the chicken makes her mouth water.

Warren exits the kitchen without a response, leaving Willow alone to finish the food in peace. The knot in her stomach loosens. The sustenance helps, but him leaving her presence helps even more. The mouthwatering flavors of the food take her by surprise. Garlic and thyme dance on her tongue, the savory taste of the chicken filling her stomach easily. When did she eat last? Nadia would kill her if she could hear the questions Willow asks herself.

Warren times his return right as she finishes the plate. His attention is distracted, checking the smoke-grey watch on his wrist. *Wait.*

"What's todays date?" Her chest tightens.

"Happy Halloween."

"Shit!" Panic consumes her as she pushes off the chair to run out the room. The Halloween Bash is tonight. Has that much time passed? "Have you heard any word of the Bash being cancelled?" she yells, scrambling to gather her belongings from the bathroom.

"Still happening," he yells in the distance, disinterested in the conversation.

Good. Then he won't care if she—*BANG*. With a slam, she bolts out the front door of his home without another word.

If she could live the rest of her life without seeing his face, she'd be happy. But, based on the latest series of unfortunate events–it doesn't seem like she can get away from him that easily. He made that apparent enough. Out of all the times to miss work, being smack dab in the middle of a murder case and the Halloween Bash is not something she can afford to miss. What if she had continued to sleep? Rage simmers within her core.

The walk to the station is long. Much longer than she realized, but doable. By the time she reaches the building, a slight sweat breaks across her forehead. Most of the teams are gone, readying themselves at home for the party. Others prepare and get dressed at the station, wanting to walk in together for their group costumes to make more of a statement. *Costume.* She wonders if there's a chance she can get away with attending without wearing one.

The first thing Willow sees upon entering is black, curly hair standing straight up, almost touching the low bearing ceiling of the office.

She blinks in quick succession. "Hello?"

Sunny's head raises from the computer, the hair following suit, brushing the ceiling. A lopsided grin finds Sunny's mouth. "What do you think?" As Sunny turns, Willow notes a white lightning bolt streak in the extended hair.

Willow squints. "Bride of Frankenstein?"

"You know it!" she squeals. It's Sunny's favorite day of the year. And probably the only day at work she truly seems happy. "I'm forcing Malcolm to dress as the Doctor with me."

Willow has met Sunny's husband, Malcolm, a handful of times–each of those times being at the Bash. Between the two of them, they've shared maybe five sentences together.

"You did an incredible job with your hair! I imagine it'll take a while to get your hair back to its normal state." Willow's pessimism seeps through the conversation unintentionally.

With a shrug, Sunny responds, "Worth it. Oh! Your friend is here looking for you by the way. I think she's been at your desk most of the day?"

"Friend?" Arms wrap around Willow's waist, tackling her into a side hug as Willow enters the detective's offices. Adrenaline pumps through Willow's veins, catching herself from falling over. Her muscles tighten, pulling at the sutures in her neck, and her senses reel with pain.

"Don't you dare think you're getting away without a costume!" Nadia practically screams. "Oh my gosh, Will–what happened to your neck? Are you okay?"

"Nadia, we are at my *work*," she hisses in a whisper. "Be quiet! I'm fine. Just a little scratch I had to get fixed."

"Are you sure about that?" Nadia scrutinizes.

"Yes, now drop it," Willow whispers in response.

"*Fine.* But I mean what I said. Come with me, we're getting ready for this thing." Nadia pulls Willow by the sleeve, dragging her to the bathroom.

*

This cannot be real life.

Willow wants to die. The dread of walking into the community center pools in her legs, making her drag her feet.

"Willow *Roseabella,* stop your pouting! You're acting like a child," Nadia scolds, gripping Willow's arm as though she would bolt at any moment.

Oh, she's using middle names.

"I look ridiculous!" Willow hisses. "I am *so* mad at you," she mutters under her breath.

Nadia had to ensure Willow didn't have a repeat of the last two bashes where she came dressed as a detective. Which just means Willow dressed for work. Out of all the options for costumes, of course Nadia selected this one. Willow's skin flush as she walks hand in hand with Nadia through the orange and black balloon arch. A DJ poses front and center of the community stage, dressed in an inflatable dinosaur suit. Indoor fog machines spray in each corner of the unlit room, matching the mist that encases Misty Pines most of the early mornings and nights.

Most of the town gathers in the room, small awkward pockets of empty space scattered among the cliques. Various costumes occupy the room— mummies, pop culture icons, cops, prisoners, cartoon characters, ghosts. Goosebumps rise along her arms. *Could—any of these be real monsters?* A group from the station greets members of the community who enter. She discovers Leo first, followed by Milo. Both of their jaws fall slack. She purses her lips, continuing to allow Nadia to drag her. The Barbie wig Nadia wears bounces as she skips into the entrance. Classic Halloween songs blast through the speakers.

"I know there's no way you did this on your own accord," Milo cackles over the music, greeting the two women. All attention focuses on Willow.

"What's that supposed to mean?" Willow snaps.

"I think what Milo meant to say is, wow Willow, you look great. Happy Halloween. I'm glad you're feeling better. We thought you were dead." Leo's hand grasps Milo's shoulders, his grin so wide, it seems painful.

Her posture stiffens. *Right.* She coughs. The group takes a subconscious step back. "Sorry, yes, I'm fine. Don't worry I'm not contagious," she gestures to herself and Nadia, "I'm obviously fine." She scans the room, catching a glimpse of the punch bowls without a line. *Perfect.* "I just need a drink. I'll be back."

The tension in her shoulders fades as she breaks from the group, making a beeline for the drinks.

Three large punch bowls sit on the table. One holds a lime green, foamy drink, labeled *The Bubbling Cauldron.* The next is bright crimson, *Blood Orange Vampire Punch.* She winces. The last is apple cider. Cider sounds safe. The drink sloshes in her plastic crystal cup.

"They say imitation is the best form of flattery," a honeyed voice calls behind her.

Willow spins, flinching as she finds Gideon dressed in all black, his blonde hair styled back. Fangs flash in his smile, a streak of red trails from the corner of his lip.

"Woah, sorry! It's just me. Gideon." He digs the fangs out of his mouth and squishes them, making the fake teeth clamp down. *A vampire.* The outfit compliments her own vampire costume well, the red corset laced around her long lace black dress accentuates the red lipstick and colored contacts she wears. If someone looked at the two of them next to each other, it would look like a couple's costume.

A forced exhale escapes her lips. "Sorry. Just a little jumpy tonight. Nice to see you. Uh–Great minds think alike I suppose?" She swallows a gulp of cider. The music shifts from a techno beat to a lulling melody. Groups break apart, some couples pull into a slow dance.

"Care to dance?" His long fingers extend forward.

This is the worst day she's had in a while–and she's had *a lot* of bad days. Willow doesn't dance.

"Actually I'm–"

"She'd love to!" Nadia swings from behind Willow, pushing her forward into Gideon's grasp. Willow shoots daggers with her stare into her. "Sorry, pardon me. Just need to grab myself a drink. Will, when you're done, I want to introduce you to someone!" She winks.

"I won't bite," Gideon assures, a wave of concern falters through his grin.

"I know that." She frowns, allowing him to pull them to the dance floor. "I'm sorry. I've just had a lot going on and didn't want to be here to begin with. Dancing isn't–my thing."

"I'll lead. And if you can't take it anymore, we can stop."

She nods. When she works up the courage to make eye contact with Gideon, she's stuck there. He leads, moving with fluid grace to the beat, while pulling her closer into his chest. Neither of them speak.

Left, left, right, left. Right, right, left, right. The warmth from his touch encircles her, calming her racing heart—only for it to quicken again as he peers down at her. He watches her like he's savoring the view. The song edges toward its final note, the melody trailing off and Willow averts her gaze, attempting to distract her body's reaction. The mayor makes her way through the throngs of people, shaking hands and laughing at whatever conversation she's having. Past her, Warren leans against the wall watching with a wolfish, piercing glare as Willow dances.

For a second, she forgets where she is, freezing in place.

"Everything okay?" Gideon let's go, surveying the area.

She shakes her head. "Ah, I–Uh yes, sorry the song was over I thought." When her gaze returns, Warren is gone.

"Was I that bad?" His hand rubs the back of his neck.

"No!" she yells, reaching out to Gideon. "Sorry," she corrects her octave. "No, you were great. I–thanks. I think–I think that sometimes I can forget I'm a person outside of work." *Why did she say that out loud?*

He beams. "Good. I'm glad I can do that for you." He glances down at Willow's hand that wraps around his. For some reason, Willow squeezes it before letting it fall.

"I have to go find Nadia, but I'll see you around?" The faux fog swirls heavier around them, making her eyes strain in the dim light.

Gideon smirks. "You absolutely will."

The muscles in Willow's legs burn. *Note to herself, don't dance ever again.* Nadia twists strands of her blonde wig between her fingers, swaying her hips while chatting with a stunning man. Willow draws near to the pair at a steady pace, attempting not to interrupt in the middle of a conversation. The plan fails— Nadia spies Willow from her peripheral and clenches her teeth in a wide grin. "Will! Come, come! I wanted to introduce you to Aldaric."

A Rolex adding to the weight of his grip drags Willow's arm down in a handshake. His white teeth shine bright against his olive skin. Even in the dark, his green and gold flecked orbs shine. He's the Ken to Nadia's Barbie. She didn't lie, he's gorgeous. Nadia's enamored, googly eyes and all.

"It's a pleasure to meet you." Willow beams.

"The pleasure's all mine. Nadia speaks very highly of you." Longing dilates his pupils every glance they share.

"What brings you into Misty Pines?"

"I'm an entrepreneur from Vale. I've been interested in investing in some property and other businesses here in Misty Pines because of how quickly it's becoming a tourist attraction." He reveals an authentic warmth in his expression. "I got approval from Mayor Caldwell to introduce myself. I come from a line of philanthropists, so I've loved being able to meet the teams I can financially contribute to."

"Oh, well we appreciate your donation. The town can use some updates."

Willow's social battery runs low—her attempt to live as a wallflower this evening proved unsuccessful.

"It's getting late. I'm going to say goodbye to my team and head out."

"It's great meeting you! I'm sure I'll see you around." Aldaric waves.

Nadia gives an expression of protest, but it falls when Aldaric continues a previous conversation.

Phew.

Sunny and Malcolm linger by the exit, drinks in hand. "Hey Bride and Doc," Willow greets unenthusiastically, unable to hide her exhaustion.

Malcolm's dressed in a long, black cloak, a white, high stiff collar tugged tightly around his neck. His dreads are pulled back from his face.

"Evening, Willow. Hope you're doing well." Malcolm nods.

A man of few words. She appreciates that.

"Heading out already?" Sunny frowns.

"Yeah, I'm still getting over whatever sickness I had and don't want to push it. So, I'm going to go home, wipe this ridiculous makeup I was forced to wear off, and go to bed."

"Do you need someone to walk you to your car?" Malcolm asks, shifting in place.

"No, thanks. I appreciate the thought. I'm not too far away. I'll see you guys soon."

The crisp fall air cuts through her corset the second the door opens. An owl hoots deep into the woods and crickets sing a beautiful melody. All the children that went trick-or-treating should be in bed, fast asleep. The idea of sleep pushes Willow forward, craving the feeling of her own mattress.

CHAPTER 17

THE SECOND MURDER

A heavy bang against Willow's door rips all sense of peace as the violent thuds echo in her home. Why can't Nadia just leave her be? The doorknob is cold against her warm hands as she pulls the door open.

"Nadia, please–" She halts.

"Willow." Warren stands on her porch. His hair is pulled back into a half up, half down topknot. "Another victim is about to be discovered, and this time it's closer to home."

Her heart sinks, jumping back at the sight of him. "What? Where? How do you know? Where's my phone?" she fires question after question, not allowing a pause for him to answer. She backs away, grabbing her phone off the ledge of the couch. No notifications of a new homicide investigation.

"Our partnership with this is going to have to start sooner than anticipated. Do you understand? This is going to keep happening until we can solve it, and no offense to your team, but we are the only ones that can discover what we are looking for."

Her shoulders sink, the reality hitting her quicker than she can process.

"It hasn't been reported yet, but unfortunately it is near the school, on the other side of the playground. If we head that way now, we can beat everyone there to get a fresh look."

She nods, her mind racing with possible connections and leads. She doesn't want to do this. But what would happen if the rest of her team found out about this new world? Everyone would die. She grabs her necklace, thinking of Kai. Whatever she must do to bring them to justice, she'll do it.

"Stay focused. This is important." His attention moves from her trembling hand wrapped around the necklace back up to her eyes.

She sneers, "I am focused! It's a lot to take in!"

His forehead softens, just for a moment, before returning to stone. "I understand. I am not particularly thrilled at the situation either. Now, let's help each other on this?"

"What do you get out of all of this? What is it about this case that involves you?" she asks. Her right hand grips her left shoulder, massaging her triceps.

"I have–" he glances up for a brief moment, "my own personal answers I'm needing. I'm searching for someone. I've been following a trail, which brought me here six months ago. I'm not sure how it's all tied together just yet, but I do know you are the person to help me find it."

"Are you suggesting this is the work of a serial killer?"

He bites his bottom lip in thought. "Perhaps, in a way. There are a few things that this clouded town will be able to reveal in time, which I hope can give me the answers I'm searching for, or if not–point me in the direction of where I need to go next."

Air fills her lungs as she inhales a long breath. "If this will help me close this case and get the answers *I'm* looking for, you have a deal. But don't think for a second if you steer me away from solving this for your own issues, or try to backstab me, that I won't try to kill you. I would rather *die* trying than let you have an easy kill."

He grins at the challenge, the tips of visible fangs poking against his lips. "I would expect nothing less. Let's go."

*

Silence fills the first half of the drive. Clean leather permeates the air of Warren's pristine Lexus. Willow pivots toward the window, watching the orange and rust trees flash in a blur. Warren insisted on driving to remain inconspicuous. Her fingers swipe through pages of missed calls and texts–most of which are updates on other cases and requesting to meet to discuss how to move further on the homicide. It's about to get more complicated if this new victim is related. *Which it more than likely is.* A text from Jasmine states they have a warrant to serve the Golden Wolf Casino. Willow's toothy smile pulls across her cheeks. Among the calls, she finds one from Nadia. She glances at Warren driving before hitting the call button under Nadia's name. Warren shoots her a glare, his head shifting from the road back to Willow.

"Hey Nadia, it's me," Willow says as the call connects.

Warren grimaces, obvious disapproval. She shrugs in response.

"Will, are you okay?" Nadia jumps to the question.

"I've got a favor to ask," Willow replies, trying to keep the conversation brief.

Warren clears his throat loud enough for Nadia to hear. Willow's nostrils flare, sneering at Warren. He shrugs.

"Will—are you with—a *man*?" Nadia asks in shock.

Willow's lip twitches. *No, not exactly.*

"Yes…but not for the reason you think. Also, I don't appreciate your tone."

Warren bites back a smirk.

"Listen, something urgent has come up. I'm on my way to the park near the school. There's been another murder," Willow continues.

"Hold up, at the park? How did you hear about this before I did?"

Warren's eyebrows quirk, as though saying *I told you so.* Willow hesitates, considering her response.

"I'll fill you in later, but can you meet us there? I'd like your expertise on this before we get other first responders."

"Oh, yeah? Who is *us*?" Nadia asks.

Willow can hear her grin from behind the phone. With a groan of defeat, Willow responds, "I'm with Warren. We're driving to the scene now. Please meet us there?"

"You're with the examiner?" her pitch shoots up an octave.

"Nadia, focus! Meet us there?" Willow begs.

"Are you safe? Say our word and I'll call backup."

Willow bites her lip. Is she okay? No, not remotely. But putting on a brave act is what she's always been good at. "It's fine. No safe word needed. But I do need *you* to do this!"

"We have so much to discuss, Willow Rhodes. I'll be there in ten." Nadia hangs up.

"You should have consulted with me before bringing another person in on this."

"Nadia is the only trustworthy person in town and extremely talented with what she does. If anything, she's the only one we should consult with," she explains, gazing out the passenger window. She doesn't regret calling Nadia. "Also, if you really didn't want me calling her, you could have stopped me, right? So—" she trails off, testing the boundary of his limits.

"I understand that you feel that way about your friend, but as you recently have discovered, this is much more than murder. I am only one person, and you're putting her life at risk. I cannot afford to protect everyone." His lips tighten as he scratches his stubble with his left hand, the right gripping the steering wheel. "We will have to handle this situation carefully."

"I don't need your protection," she huffs.

"We will see about that."

Willow finds herself watching him from the corner of her eyes. From this angle, she can't help but notice his striking features. The mixture of sharp angles and smooth lines on his profile captivates her. He's rugged, but his style of fashion forward clothing makes him appear very neat and tidy. His tied back hair allows the top of his ear to peek through and she notices for the first time that the tips are slightly pointed at the top. An intensity presses into his features; intensity mixed with deep thought. It's like animals in the wild. A masterful creation, captivating beauty–all to attract their prey and that's when they strike. Her posture straightens at the thought.

"I'm not a shapeshifter, no need to stare," he quips, a teasing lilt in his words.

Pink dusts her cheekbones; she averts her gaze back to the window. "I spaced out," she murmurs.

"Just admiring the view, I'm sure," a dismissive chuckle leaves his throat.

"Don't flatter yourself," she mutters under her breath, mentally taking back every positive comment she thought about him just moments ago.

"I don't need to," he says, carrying an edge of confidence. "But if you insist on staring, I'll allow it. Just don't get too distracted from the mission at hand."

CHAPTER 18

JANE DOE

Gravel crackles beneath their feet, trekking through the eerie stillness surrounding the playground. Trained senses sharpen as Willow examines the environment leading to the crime scene ahead of them. They could already be contaminating clues for all they knew. The fog of the morning lifts, hovering inches above the ground. Warren squares his shoulders, his spine rigid. *The body.*

Willow's hand flies to cover her mouth as the pit of her stomach flips. A female victim, stripped of all her clothes except a bright cherry red lingerie piece. The lace curves over her hips, crisscrossing on her back and wraps around to cover less than a quarter of her exposed breasts. *The most unsettling aspect about this murder— the pose.* The Jane Doe is staged on her hands and knees, arms extended outward with her palms pressing together. It's a familiar position that Willow saw often at church—praying at an altar. Her dark hair lays neatly over her left shoulder, draping onto the mulch below. *It even looks recently styled.*

Warren frowns as he circles the deceased. He doesn't touch her, but crouches near, studying different areas of the victim's remains. Branches and leaves crunch behind Willow as Nadia strides up to the scene, clothed in her crime scene gear. In each fist, Nadia carries a container with a camera dangling from her neck. Her purposeful steps falter as she takes in the sight before her.

"Jesus, be with me," Nadia whispers to herself. She glances back and forth from Willow, to Warren, to the cadaver. "This is—unbelievable. Two only a few weeks apart? *And* in Misty Pines?"

Willow nods grimly. Nadia sprints around the crime scene, placing markers down around the evidence, then moves to set tape around the entire perimeter of the playground, unsure of where the crime scene would begin or end. The camera flashes with every press of the shutter button. Close ups, distance shots, various angles, Nadia captures them all.

"How did you two find out about this?" Nadia pulls the camera away from her sight, approaching Warren.

Willow tries to speak as Warren cuts her off, "A friend of mine passed by and saw them, they thought to call me first since they know I examine the bodies. Willow and I were together at the time, and she thought it would be best that you arrive first. A very lucky scenario, I'd say."

Nadia scoffs, "Yeah, not so lucky for her, I'm afraid." Her lips tighten and draw into a frown. "Have you guys called in for backup yet?"

Willow swallows. "Not yet, I wanted to get your thoughts first. Do we have a serial killer? Two murders so close can't be a coincidence, but this one," she pauses. "There's a different motivation for this kill."

Nadia nods in agreement. "If it is, this kill is worse than the first. I can't outright see the cause of death, but that's what you're for." She motions to Warren.

The gears in Willow's mind keep turning. "How fast can you get me all the photographs and evidence you're collecting?"

"I have to follow the chain of command. I can't give you a time for sure, it depends on the rest of the team's findings and evidence with it."

"I was hoping that this could just be—my case file for me to use, while I call in backup and they get the rest. You weren't scheduled today, right? So maybe you could just pretend you were never here?" It's a huge ask and goes against everything Willow and Nadia stand for. Or at least, everything the badge stands for. She knows Nadia would wrestle with the idea of it. Hell, she's having a hard time asking her.

"I don't know Will," she replies, her hesitation seeps with doubt. "This feels…wrong."

Nadia's diamond shaped face scrunches in discomfort. It's putting both of their jobs at risk, and Willow knows this. She can't help but press. "I understand." Calm steadies her speech, yet every syllable lands with quiet authority. "Please trust me when I say that I wouldn't ask you to do this, if I wasn't sure of the importance."

Nadia takes a deep breath and after a long moment of inner struggle, nods reluctantly. "Fine," she whispers. "I'll do this, but you owe me so many explanations later."

She directs her gaze to Warren, then squints at Willow. *Yeah, yeah. Hint taken.*

Warren watches the exchange, his expression impassive. "We need to move the body. This positioning could hide more evidence that you need to photograph."

Anxiety takes hold over Nadia. "I don't know if that's a good idea." Nadia strains. "This scene has already been compromised enough as it is, don't you think? Moving it would completely change the analysis of the scene for the team that comes in after us." Nadia directs to Willow for backup.

"You're not wrong, but I'll take the lead on this one. I will have these originals, and I plan on cracking this. I'm with Warren on this." Willow's speech is low, as if she's trying not to scare a small animal away, or maybe even to convince herself. "If this is too much and making you uncomfortable then just pretend I didn't call you and delete everything and leave. I can call backup." Guilt swims in her stomach. Nadia wouldn't leave her. Since the day the two of them met, Nadia has imposed herself on Willow, aiming to be her healer. It's a rare occasion for Willow to ask for help.

"No, you called me. It's obvious you need my help, even if you are being super shady about this." Her words sting. "We just need to be careful. Move her body and I will document it all, but Warren needs to place her as close to how you found it, okay?" Nadia throws in the towel, crowning Willow victorious.

Typically, Willow would revel in her win, but there's no true win in this.

"Here put these on." Nadia tosses Warren blue rubber gloves from her bag. Together the two of them shift the woman's still figure onto her side.

"The victim is at least in livor mortis. Her limbs have not fully stiffened yet. Time of death could range anywhere between six to twelve hours, maybe more. I will need to get her on the table in my morgue," Warren notes.

That puts her death during the Halloween Bash. That would knock out most of the town as suspects since they have an alibi.

"Oh, no," Willow whispers, the words catch in her throat. "She's a teacher at Wood Grove. She goes to my gym."

An unspoken rule of the gym is not to talk to someone if they have headphones on, but she always smiled at Willow, acknowledging her presence.

Nadia's countenance opens with compassion, as if carrying part of the pain herself. "Will, I'm so sorry."

Willow shakes her head. "We weren't friends or anything like that. I've just run beside her a handful of times. I can't say that I even know her name. It's just– sad," she pauses, gathering her next words, "it's different when it's someone you know. I guess it makes them more…human when you've seen them outside of death." Despair lingers in her breath as the image of Kai sears into her mind. The term *human* also means more than she realized it would.

"I can only imagine," Nadia says, a doleful expression adorning her preppy features. "This never gets easy. No matter how many I see. I love what I do, but boy does it take a toll on you." The camera light strobes while Nadia photographs Jane Doe's front side.

Purple discoloration pools at the victim's knees and elbows, like mini galaxies of purples and red swirls. Warren uses gentle movements to roll her back to her starting position.

"You should probably leave now. Send over everything you have to mine and Willow's email and then delete it. Any physical evidence you found, feel free to analyze it, document that, send it over and then burn it. Try to remove any proof of your presence." Warren urges.

"You owe me big, don't forget that." Nadia's finger presses against Willow's chest. "And I'll have some interrogation questions for you later." Nadia trudges to her car, throwing her hand in the air as a last-minute wave.

"I hope getting your friend involved was worth it." His attention shifts to Willow's, his voice dry.

"She's the best. It's worth it." *Is it, though?*

"Right, well if this was any other ordinary murder she would be the best. Unfortunately, that's not the case."

Willow's mouth twists. "How do you just know that this isn't a human related crime?"

Warren stands tall, her doubt visibly angering him. "You've recently discovered what I am. Has the thought crossed your mind on how old I could be?" He snaps.

The thought hadn't even crossed her mind. Now that she reflects, there are a lot of questions she should probably ask him. Has she been too scared to know? To ask? Or has she just been blinded by the recent death? She breaks eye contact.

"As I thought. I assure you that I have been alive longer than most of your living and dead relatives. I've experienced a multitude of supernatural beings. I don't need to prove this to you. However, this," he gestures to the remains, "is something I have not come across. An unfamiliar aura of magic surrounds these bodies. This is what we need to find out." He continues, not missing a beat. "I will work on the autopsy once the deceased is back to my morgue. Let's get out of here."

Willow's head tilts. "We can't just leave. We need to call this in."

"We are leaving, and I will have her arrive at the morgue within the hour."

She pinches the bridge of her nose, a headache forming behind her brow bone. "How will–"

"Everything will be taken care of. Some adjustments need to be made to protect your friends, if you *must* involve them. That's what you want, right Detective?"

It's hard for Willow to not take his words as a threat. She stifles the fight she wishes she could let out. "Fine," she grits through her teeth. "I'm going to the casino. I have a subpoena to serve." Right back into work mode. There's no time to waste arguing with him. "If you need me— *don't*."

"Try not to piss off the Floor Manager again when you go." His head cocks to the side.

A quiet chill slips through her. "Stop using your freaky little vampire tricks to spy on me! That guy is an asshole." She turns on her heels. From behind, a low stifled laugh breaks through. Willow's middle finger hangs in the air until she disappears out of Warren's sight. It'll be a good hike to the casino on foot, but she could use the fresh air.

CHAPTER 19

IT'S "DETECTIVE"

"Y ou must have been really sick to not come in. How're you feeling?"
Jasmine's calming presence radiates through the phone.

Willow's legs move as fast as her mind, pedaling almost quicker than she can keep up with. How can she quantify her true feelings? A never-ending apprehension of impending doom? That vampires, werewolves, and zombies run the world and it's only a matter of seconds before everyone's massacred and sucked dry? The heaviness of the situation is suffocating and an audible sigh escapes her mouth. Willow stuffs the thoughts into a box, compartmentalizing it deep within her mind.

Lights from the casino flash in the distance.

"I'll be fine. I'm back up and running as we speak, heading toward Golden Wolf. I'm sure you were sad to not attend the Bash," she teases. "I saw your texts come through and I appreciate you keeping me updated. So– I'm clear to get that footage?"

"So, so sad." Willow can practically see Jasmine grinning on the other end of the phone. "Yes, the subpoena was approved. You have an emailed copy and then I've also sent it to the casino itself, so either way they know we are about to knock on their door." There's a noticeable glimmer of satisfaction in her voice.

A surge of relief spreads through Willow. "That's great. Thanks, Jasmine. I don't know what we would do without you." The corners of her lips lift with ease and sincerity, even though no one's there to see it.

Jasmine connects all their skewed pieces together, creating one aggressive puzzle–minus Jasmine that is.

"Things would definitely move slower," she laughs in a whisper, as though trying not to draw attention to herself.

"Very true. I'll bring it in this evening, so get the popcorn ready," Willow says, halfway joking.

A twist in her stomach pulls her back to the reality of her situation. Forced to work with a *vampire* on this case, a supernatural killer—while also playing the other side, forced to work with her team when all she wanted to do was fly solo. Throwing them all into the mix complicates things. She couldn't live with herself if any of them were to get caught in the middle of it all. There's no one she can trust or rely on in this.

"See ya," Jasmine says before hanging up.

*

An undercurrent of tension crashes upon her shoulders as she inches closer to the casino. The golden neon lights flash above in the afternoon sun and she exhales a deep breath as her foot enters the threshold of the building. The familiar sound of slot machines and dice hitting tables fills the air. *There's something addictive in the sounds.*

To her surprise, there are plenty of patrons milling about the machines. It's not as crowded as it grows at night, but the numbers this early in the afternoon are shocking. Is gambling this enjoyable? It must be, considering there are probably thousands of people addicted to the act all around the world. It doesn't appeal to her, *thankfully*. Her parents always told her to ride the straight and narrow since addiction runs in the family. Her perception drifts without focus across the tables as she approaches the front desk. As long as she gets anyone other than the first guy, it would be an easy trip. She shakes her busy mind, meeting the gaze of the manager behind the front desk. Her nose flares. *Just her luck.*

"Can I help you?" Brian asks, his words oozing with a superiority complex. *What she would give to take him down a peg.*

"Golden Wolf Casino has been sent a subpoena to release the video footage from the night of Jonathan Davies's murder. But if that doesn't suffice, I have the digital PDF on my phone." She pulls out her phone and clicks the subpoena to view in full on her screen.

His beady orbs narrow at her. "And why should I help you?" he sneers, not attempting to hide his disdain.

"Because it's part of an ongoing *murder* case and if you don't, I will arrest you for impeding on an investigation," she snaps, her stance rigid as she holds onto any professionalism she has left. "But feel free to fight me on this, I'd love nothing more than a reason to put you in handcuffs."

"Everything okay?" A smooth, familiar voice sings.

Gideon peers from behind the nearest game to the front desk. His table appears to have drawn a small crowd of onlookers, as they move out of his way. Gideon's shoulder brushes against Willow's, taking a place beside her. The rigidness in Brian's shoulders falter, but his face levels with lack of amusement.

"Oh," Gideon squints to read the name badge on Brian's wrinkled black dress shirt. "*Brian*. I'd hope a Floor Manager at this fine establishment isn't arguing with a woman of the law, are you? Detective Rhodes here is the best of the best, you would do well not to cause her any grief." Though his words could be taken as a threat, his cadence is smooth as butter, helping to not escalate the situation.

"*Fine. Whatever.* I'll be right back with that, Officer," Brian bites back.

"It's *Detective*," she grits through her teeth.

"I get to see you two days in a row? It's my lucky week," Gideon whispers as Brian's back turns away to fetch the required footage. "That guy's the worst, right?" His lips pinch.

"Are you famous here or something to have that effect on him?" She scans him, suspicion tightens her features. Maybe Brian doesn't like women in authority. *Weak man.*

"Luckily for me, I have a mutual friend of the owner! So, I have a little bit of pull here. I try not to use it often though." He winks as his hand brushes against hers.

She moves back a few steps to reclaim her personal space. A wash of pink rims the whites of his cornea, setting his irises aglow with an unsettling blue.

"Are you winning big this evening?" Willow's focus drift to the table Gideon came from. Cards are placed downward in front of the empty chair and the game attendant scowls while his fingers drum against his crossed arms.

"That depends, will you allow me to take you to dinner?" he flirts, his eyes half-lidded. He has his trademark charm, and a smolder plastered on his face. *He's definitely drunk.*

She hesitates, caught off guard by the invitation. "I'm flattered, but I have a lot I'm working on—" she trails off. It's not like he isn't attractive, but there's no time for leisure. Yet, a part of her yearns to know more about him. There's something in the way he looks at her, something terrifying yet thrilling. The feeling of being perceived makes her squirm. She felt it all last night. But Gideon seems–different.

"I take it as not a yes, but not a no to dinner then?"

"It's a maybe. I'll have to think about it," she responds. It isn't a lie; it would have to be a decision she thinks through with care. *When she has time to consider it, that is.*

He grins while pulling away from her. "I'll hold you to that. I look forward to the night you let me take you away," he says before he turns to leave, his presence lingering in the air like a subtle, intoxicating fragrance. A small part of her deep down wishes he would stay.

The small crowd parts at Gideon's return. Many of them appear already drunk, as a man and woman sloppily grope one another, and another couple whispers sweet nothings in each other's ears before they stand from the table and head toward the ascending stairs. They stumble past several employees posted at the top of the stairs and outside additional doors with sloshing movement. She notes to scope out the upper floor the next visit she has.

An aggressive, forced cough breaks Willow from her observations. Brian stands back behind the desk with a flash drive in hand.

"Here." He drops the flash drive into her palm. "That's all I got." His scowl rakes her with frozen contempt.

Willow clutches the flash drive in her fist. "Thanks." She begins to walk away but stops in her tracks. "If there's anything missing, I'll be back. I suggest you and all the other employees stay in town for the foreseeable future, *Brian.*" She can feel Brian's eyes burning holes into the back of her head, which makes her laugh internally in victory.

CHAPTER 20

BASILISK

The flash drive weighs heavy in her pocket. This has been weeks in the waiting, a next step in finding the sinister individual or individuals behind the murders. It won't be the last either, unless she does something about it. She isn't convinced Warren isn't somehow involved behind all of this, but for now, working with him is the only choice she has, at least until she can find leverage against him. How is a vampire killed? Does garlic really scare them away? This gives her something else to research. Her focus glazes over the passing scenery. The vibration of her phone keeps her hands busy, pulling it out of her back pocket. Warren's name flashes across the screen.

A mix of irritation and uncertainty swirl through her and her thumb hovers over the answer button before reluctantly clicking.

"What is it? Surely you aren't done with the examination yet?" She isn't in the mood for distractions, or to even speak to him.

"Charming as ever, I see. I thought you would like to be informed that you're being followed." He states without a hint of concern.

Her throat tightens and she coughs. "Is that so? And how do you know this?"

The standing water in the grooves of the pavement splashes with each step she takes, keeping her pace normal to avoid suspicion.

"No need for the condescension, Sherlock. I am everywhere; I told you I'm always around even if you can't see. He lurks in the shadows behind you."

That's not ominous.

"I do love good news." Her inflection raises, to an outside listener it would appear enthusiastic, but her response couldn't be far from it.

"From the size you can take him, however I suspect we are getting closer to the people we are attempting to locate, so he may not be human," he states. "It's hard for me to tell how powerful he is without being there myself. Go to the funeral home. You can return to whatever you were on the way to do after a short detour."

"This is super inconvenient," she groans.

The sidewalk turns to foliage as she takes a sharp cut in between the trees to bypass the police station. The most direct path to the morgue requires her to cut through the trees.

"Can you still see me?" she whispers.

"Would you like to broadcast that to the person following you a bit louder?"

She could feel his eyes roll from behind the call.

"Just stop talking at this rate and meet me at the back of the building." He ends the call with no warning.

"Asshole," she mutters under her breath.

Heavy clouds roll in above her, obscuring the sun. *Rain is on the way.* Her pace quickens as the Victorian building comes into view. A flash of shadow surges forward, pausing in the darkness of the trees lining the back of the property. Piercing red orbs peer back at her. Her fists uncurl marginally at the sight of a white stripe within the penumbra, but it disappears.

Heavy footsteps approach her from behind—no longer attempting to hide themselves.

She turns, taking in the soft features of an unfamiliar man reaching for her pocket. *The pocket that contains the flash drive from the casino.* Willow drives his hand away in a swift movement, pushing backward to put distance between them. In rapid motion, she draws her gun and aims straight at the man. His appearance is that of a humanized mouse, petite with small round features and a protruding nose. All he's missing is whiskers and fur. "At this rate, you people are really pissing me off. Who are you? Lay on the ground and put your hands behind your back."

The man's eye twitches, followed by his hands. His fingers move robotically, as though he's relearning how to be human. "I–I've been waiting for this." His expression carries an unexpected depth and rasp. His fingers twitch again, except this time a droplet of water forms. It floats in midair, growing into the shape of a large water balloon–but without the balloon.

"What–whatever you're doing stop, or I'll shoot!" she stammers, unable to believe her own eyes.

"I must, I must. You don't understand. This will only save you from further pain in the end." Tears fill his lower lash line, lip quivering. Until something within him snaps, and a twisted grin stretches into his cheeks. "*You're welcome.*"

Willow's jaw drops. Before she can think, her entire head is encased with water. Her gun falls from her hand. Liquid rushes into her throat, closing off her airways. The roar of water fills her ears, nose, and mouth. It's deafening. She strains to open her eyes, though the encircling water blurs the limited sight she has. It's useless, her arms flail, clawing at the water. Her fingers run through the water sphere, but nothing happens. She can't win. She collapses against the ground, shaking her head as she gasps for air, until her sight grows splotchy. Each inhale includes another gulp of water.

A muffled growl breaks through the watery sound barrier. Right as her vision darkens, the water falls, splashing against the pavement. Sweet air fills her nostrils, leaving her mouth open to inhale a sharp breath as she coughs, choking on the water that settles in her airways. Her chest heaves, as her vision returns. Willow holds back a scream, finding a goliath of a serpent constricting around the mouse man. *How fitting, but absolutely terrifying.* Warren stands unbothered next to it.

Out of breath, Willow forces herself to grab her handgun that fell into a divot of water in the concrete. Her aim bobbles from both being worn down from being drowned, and unable to truly tell who's the villain here.

The fifteen foot snake coils, tightening until the man's breath escapes in a choked gasp. His skin burns red, then violet. Warren steps forward, his gaze cold and unyielding.

"I'm afraid you picked the wrong person to follow, my friend. It's a shame I couldn't get any useful information out of you."

Life drains from the man's eyes as Warren watches, running his tongue across the tip of his fangs. With a flick of his hand, the creature uncoils and the carcass thumps lifelessly against the pavement. Willow's heart jumps into her throat and she keeps her shaky arms pointed at the snake.

"Holster your weapon. The enemy is dead," Warren states without hesitation.

"Is it? What in God's name is *that*?" she yells in a whisper, scared that any loud noise would cause it to attack.

He raises his right arm, pushing his navy sweater sleeve to his elbow—revealing his red snake tattoo. The ink seems to push further than where he stops his sleeve. She didn't notice it during her first stake out when he walked around half naked. The lines are delicate, the scales intricate on top of one another. "This is Vidar. Put away your gun or I'll have him take it away from you."

Vidar's tail vibrates following Warren's threat, it's golden stare piercing hers. Willow's jaw is slack, her brows furrowed as she takes a few steps backwards and inches her gun back to the holster on her hip. The snake adjusts, lowering its tail and bellies away, disappearing into the shadows of the trees where it came from.

Warren saunters toward the slumped figure, picking it up with ease. Willow's eyebrows raise, waiting for a response from him. "I need more words. What is–Vidar? You *control* him? How?"

The stalker's remains drape over Warren's shoulder like a potato sack. His lifeless arms sway with each turn Warren takes. Warren turns his arm so she can view the tattoo again. "Very astute conclusion. He's a basilisk."

"Basilisk? Shouldn't–" she pauses. *Is it a dumb question to ask?* "Shouldn't we have turned to stone by looking at it?"

Warren's eyebrow quirks. "He has that capability, yes. But I didn't want this man to have an easy death." His features darken. "You would have been in the crossfire as well. Restriction works better."

"So, he can just turn it off?"

"Basilisks have another thin layer of skin between their eyelids and eyes that they can use to shield that power from taking place. Vidar does such when I command, but I don't recommend risking it with a Basilisk in the wild if you were to ever come across one." He moves, walking back inside the back door leading to the morgue. The thought of running into one of those things in the wild gives her goosebumps. *What else is Warren capable of?*

"Wait, where are you going?" she questions as she follows him through the doorway.

"What does it look like I'm doing? I'm removing a dead body from the middle of a public parking lot," he grumbles. "You need a towel."

"Sure, but I mean what are you going to do with him? We can't just get rid of it. Someone will be searching for him–"

"No. No one will look for him. Unfortunately for his case, I was here. I will make use of his body." Warren leads the two of them back into the chilling morgue and the hair on her arms stands.

"I could have taken him. Seems a bit like overkill," she huffs as she follows behind him through the halls, crossing her arms over her chest to warm herself.

"You were mere seconds from death," he notes, tossing the man onto an empty table. The newest victim lays on the steel surface next to it, a white sheet draped over her.

It's true. The life in her veins pulsed like a flicker, one moment away from snuffing out. She's never felt anything like it. The reminder of her own weakness makes her grimace. "Well, if he didn't have control over that water I would have taken him."

Warren nods. "I can't disagree. You're lucky he was new to using the power."

"How could you tell?" she asks. The stalker flinched at every sound, presenting himself like a scared cat. But the behavior resembled that of someone on a high.

"He showed us as much. It took him a bit to create that small amount of water. Not to mention the twitching. If I had to guess, someone or *something* granted him the ability. Either through magic, or a magical drug or potion."

That would track with her previous thoughts. A magical drug? This is way out of her wheelhouse.

"So now what? Will you burn him to hide the fact he was here? What if Sam catches you?" Her fingers fidget with her necklace as she moves. "You just…killed him." She croaks. Warren should be arrested. He just murdered someone. Or–something?

"Sam most often works the funerals and deaths by natural causes. His wife's parents are currently sick, so his attendance is going to be sporadic. It works to our advantage this way. And yes, I killed him. He was in the act of killing you and then would have taken our evidence. I will do my examination on both the victim, and our stalker here to see what I can find. If anything, he'll be a nice snack." He grins and his canines flash.

"Snack? He's dead…you're going to drink after a dead person?" A wave of revulsion washes over body from head to toe.

A sharp, cold laugh exits his breath. "Death is a matter of perspective. You'd rather I take the living for my meals? Will you offer up your neck instead?"

She shivers and steps back, narrowing her scowl.

He lets out a breathy chuckle. "That's what I thought."

She pats her jean pockets. Relief lets her settle as she pinches the small rectangular outline against her pocket. "Next time, a heads up would be preferred. I'm not a fan of snakes. Call me when you're done with the bodies, and we can regroup."

Warren's hands go up in a wave, bending down so his teeth meet the stalker's neck. She averts her gaze, picking up the pace to head back to the station.

*

Black acrylic nails clack against the keyboard.

"Hey, Sunny. How's it going?" It's the same question Willow asks every time she sees her.

"Another day closer to death, Willow. Just another day," Sunny responds. If only Sunny knew how right she was. Death may linger closer for some if she can't figure out what's happening in town.

Willow navigates through the corridors; her footsteps echo on the tiled floor until she meets the detectives' main office. Inside, the team gathers, already deep in discussion about the newest victim. Her stomach knots. *Lying to protect them is okay.* As long as everyone is safe and Willow and Warren can catch the entity responsible for this, it'll be fine, right?

Milo looks up first, meeting Willow, his expression grim. "Another murder, huh?"

"Unfortunately." She attempts to keep the urgency out of her response.

"It looks like some of Nadia's group are working on the documentation from the scene, so it shouldn't be long until we have that," Milo states.

Willow nods. Restaging a crime scene, firstly, is illegal. However, with Warren's assurance that it's the only way to keep her team at arm's length, she refrained from protesting and let him proceed. "Blackwood's working on the most recent victim."

"Were you able to get the casino's footage?" Jasmine asks.

Damn. Willow hoped she could watch it alone first.

"Oh right! Thanks to Jasmine, I have this." The flash drive reflects the fluorescent lights as Willow spins it between her fingers.

The team gathers, pulling their chairs closer to the television that sits upon a rolling cart. Jasmine fidgets with wires in the back to make it flicker on. Misty Pines is a growing town—most would think that with the economy booming, local businesses and departments would have more funding allocated to advanced technology. Wrong. The television flashes on, the frozen camera of the casino main floor present.

A puzzled expression lifts across Willow's face. "Seriously? They only gave me one camera's worth of footage?"

"Shockingly, they only have one camera and it's this one. Unless of course, they are hiding the rest," Jasmine adds.

"That doesn't make any sense. It's a newly built casino. You would imagine that they'd have dozens of cameras, right?" Willow quizzically asks the group.

"Yeah, I mean, if we didn't already think something fishy was happening at the Golden Wolf, this confirms that something's up. What do you think? Money laundering? Drugs?" Milo asks.

"Maybe. Let's see what limited view we can see with this." Willow presses play and leans forward.

The hum of the television draws their focus in. The customers on screen are the size of ants, she's barely able to make out facial features as the grainy muted colors flicker on the screen. The angle of the camera focuses on the center of the room where most of the tables sit, but the edges of the entrance to the room remain blurred, allowing them to note small shapes of individuals— but no details. The casino bustles with activity as patrons socialize, dealers work at their tables, and bright wheels spin.

"There." Willow points, spotting the first victim, Jonathan Davies, as he walks into the casino with the timestamp of eight thirty-five at night. At least, she thinks it's him. He carries a lack of confidence as he walks around, browsing at some of the tables until he sits at one near the center of the room.

"It's hard to tell with this blurry camera, but I think he's at the blackjack table," Leo speaks up.

Willow's gaze flickers to him, before returning to the screen. "You're familiar with blackjack?"

Leo nods. "Growing up, my family didn't have a lot. So, my grandpa taught me how to play cards to keep me busy. I'm actually pretty good, not to toot my own horn or nothin'."

"Of course you are," Milo scoffs. "You've also been watching too many western classics."

Willow ignores Milo and presses play. Jonathan engages in conversation with the dealer before placing a bet. Due to the camera angle and constant noise, their conversations aren't audible. Jonathan leans forward, sitting on the very edge of his seat as his left leg bounces against the metal bar at the foot of his chair.

"Pause it there," Willow instructs.

Jasmine freezes the frame as a muscular male walks and takes a seat next to Jonathan. The man's identity remains unrecognizable due to the angle of the camera, the only details worth noting are his olive skin and sable hair. He runs his fingers through his hair, exhibiting more confidence compared to Jonathan.

"Potential suspect?" Milo asks.

"Not necessarily. I just wanted to take the scene in for a second, making sure we don't miss anything. And there's no way to get a better look at their faces?" Willow asks, directing her question to Jasmine as she scoops a handful of popcorn pieces into her mouth.

Jasmine shakes her head. "It's the only angle we have. And coincidentally no real sound."

"Keep going," Willow commands.

The two men talk back and forth as the dealer takes rounds passing out the cards. Jonathan shifts in his chair, and the screen flickers. In an instant, Jonathan and the man are gone from the game–the two of them walking in opposite directions.

"What just happened? Go back!" she demands.

Jasmine rewinds twenty seconds and slows down the video. The timestamp glitches, jumping forward where they were previously.

Jasmine's shoulders pull back, her neck muscles strained. "We just jumped forward about eighteen minutes."

"What are the chances we can get proof that it was done maliciously and not technical difficulties?" Milo hesitates to ask.

"I'd say the chances are slim," Willow responds. *Not to mention how long it'd take to get the rest of the missing content.* She bites the inside of her cheek. It's unfortunate for the case, but it may play to her advantage at keeping the rest of her team at a distance. It's less information that could hurt them in the mix. Unfortunately, it may be beneficial for Warren to review this too. Perhaps he can see something she can't. Willow exhales, throwing her head back and rubbing her temple.

"We obviously need to go back! Willow, I can join you." Milo's resentment mixes with eagerness.

Willow shakes her head. "Not yet. Jasmine, download this to your files so that we can watch this without the drive. I will take it home to keep reviewing. I also need more information from Jonathan's phone. Any weird text messages, phone calls, deleted apps, anything that feels off. I don't think we have enough evidence for a full search warrant of the casino yet, but we can try?" She takes another breath. "Let's see what's discovered on the newest female victim. Leo, watch the rest of the footage leading up to this point.

Dunn, start gathering all you can on the newest crime scene. If you can, figure out her identity before Warren and then when you know, call me. I'll be working on the same thing, but from home. I need concentration."

"I guess if you're the Chief's favorite you can do whatever you want," Milo mutters under his breath in a huff.

Willow whips her head back to Milo. "Excuse me?"

"She's earned her title here, Mil. Don't be so butt hurt. If we don't respect our own department's authority, who will?" Leo interjects, attempting to smooth over the tension.

Her ears ring, heat flooding her skin. "I don't need your respect. I need you to do your damn job, which includes doing what I say. We have a murderer to catch," Willow seethes, snapping around to stride away.

CHAPTER 21

SYMBOL OF PROTECTION

Rain pelts Willow's face; the droplets cascade down her cheeks as she stares up into the sky. She takes her time walking to the cafe, not bothering to use an umbrella. The sound of rain has always been comforting. It reminds her of home. When Willow and Kai got stuck inside on rainy days, Kai would allow her to watch him play video games. Shooting zombies didn't bring her any pleasure or entertainment, but she tolerated it since it brought him joy. Even back then she'd give anything to spend time with him. He must have been able to tell, because after a few rounds he would get off and ask her to play Candyland together.

The physical feeling of the rain hitting her skin grounds her. The business of these cases, the knowledge of the supernatural–the tension she's been holding under her skin loosens, like the rain attempts to wash her worries away. Unfortunately, it doesn't work that way.

The copper bells clatter against the glass door as Willow pushes the cafe doors. Nadia sits at their usual table. A soft glow brightens Willow's expression as she approaches, finding her regular order of a cappuccino with extra cinnamon steaming in the empty spot across from Nadia. The near movement catches Nadia's attention.

"You look like you could use a break." Nadia pushes the coffee closer to Willow.

"No rest for the wicked," Willow laughs. The heat against her lips balances the chill of the rain drying on her skin. "Thanks for this," she continues.

"You got it." Nadia beams as she reaches into her bag, pulling out several folders stuffed with items of various shapes and sizes. "Here's everything from the scene. It took me a while to develop the entire collection since I couldn't do it in the office. Photos, notes, the works." The folders are heavy in Willow's grip.

Due to the graphic content, Willow moves them under the table to view the photographs. The brief snippets of photo visible are just as disturbing as she remembered. "You did a great job," Willow says, glancing at Nadia. "I know it isn't easy doing this."

Nadia's features harden, a countenance Willow rarely sees on her optimistic friend. "It wasn't." Nadia's chocolate eyes gaze into Willow's. "But I knew it had to be done. For the case and for you, no matter what you keep from me." Willow expected contempt, but only senses disappointment. *It's worse.*

Dull numbness sets in the more Willow's teeth gnaw on the inside of her cheek. The two of them sip their coffee in silence for a moment, each lost in their own thoughts. Eventually, Nadia breaks the silence.

"Is tall, pale, and handsome helping you get any breakthroughs with the case?" Nadia places her coffee mug back on the slanted table, careful not to spill. "Any updates on the first victim?"

"I don't know if I'd call them breakthroughs, but we are moving along slowly. I guess moving in general is better than not at all?" The inflection of her question strikes as though she's trying to convince herself. Her leg bounces. "We have reason to believe that the male victim encountered someone at the casino of suspicion, but we are at a wall right now with it. That's my next hurdle."

"I like the fact you didn't retort on the handsome comment. So, the two of you are moving, *slowly*?" Nadia's eyebrows quirk.

"No, Nadia. The case is moving slowly. There's not an *us*." Willow clicks her tongue. "We are moving at our own pace, in parallel directions until he completes his job, and then we will move opposite ways." There's no point in commenting on his looks. Objectively speaking, Warren is attractive. Very attractive, and *deadly*.

"Well, that's weird. I didn't realize parallel directions include spending time together and being taken care of when you're sick? You don't get sick. And when you do, you ignore it and continue on like the psychopath you are!" She accuses.

Willow's leg bounces faster. "It was a freak coincidence!" Her lips form a line. "I couldn't wait anymore. I ran to pick up his notes on the victim. I got sick while I was there. I…" she hesitates, her brain spins to come up with a believable lie, "I couldn't keep my puke down. I fainted from being dehydrated…I think." Her attention drifts to her coffee, tracking the foam as it bubbles.

Nadia gasps. "Are you serious? You let yourself get that bad again? And what about that?" She points to stitches on her neck, which have fallen out at this point, but the fresh scar remains.

Her nose crinkles. "It wasn't like last time. When I passed out, I fell and hit the corner of a table. He stitched me up. It was cheaper than going to the hospital. I'm fine, I swear."

Nadia holds out her pinky. Willow's shoulders slump in defeat, hooking her pinky around hers. *The first pinky promise she has lied on.* A sick churn grips her belly.

"So, you two aren't a thing?" Nadia presses again.

"I swear if you ask me that one more time, you'll never see me again," Willow snips. A storm bristles beneath her skin at the accusation.

"Great! So, what about Gideon?" Nadia perks up, an obvious bias of preference toward Gideon. It's understandable. He's more likeable than Warren.

"I don't really have the time for entertaining the thought of dating."

"You have time to sit with me here for coffee?" Nadia challenges.

"Firstly, this is work related. Secondly, yes because if I don't make time you will show up to my house demanding time so really, I don't have any other options. Thirdly, I've known you for years. There're people dying that count on me to solve their murders. No dating."

"Will, just one double date? I think things between me and Al are becoming more serious. He'd love to know you like I do." Nadia glows, full of hope.

"That's great to hear! He can know me after I catch a murderer." She takes another gulp of her drink, wiping the froth off of her top lip. Nadia's mouth turns downward. "I'm not ruling it out. Just, give me some time. I've got you and Gideon both hounding me and it's becoming irritating."

A text pings from Willow's cell. She taps the illuminated screen.

"Hey Willow, it's Gideon! I just finished my jog around town and passed the station and thought about you. Got any fun plans this weekend?"

What impeccable timing.

"You've only ever dated the dangerous, bad boy types! Give a golden retriever man a chance. I could tell by the way Gideon talked about you that he's into you. Which, I won't lie, made me a tad jealous, but Aldaric has more than made up for that." A bright blush heats her face.

Willow's eyebrows raise. "Oh, has he? You confess to your priest about that?" A playful grin pulls at Willow's mouth.

"Of course I have! Shut your mouth." Nadia fidgets in her chair.

Willow savors the moments she can catch Nadia off guard. Her phone buzzes again. This time, it's a text from Warren.

"I'm finishing up here. Head over when you finish your hot milk."

She whips her head around the cafe, searching for snakes or God knows what else he can control or do to keep tabs on her.

"Everything okay?" Nadia questions, noticing her shift in mood.

"Sorry, I have to run. Warren's almost done with the autopsy." Willow chugs the rest of what remains of her coffee and gathers the evidence folders Nadia provided.

Nadia's features soften, her voice subdued. "That was quick. But I get it. Keep me posted. Be safe."

"Always."

*

The sterile smell of antiseptic and faint odor of formaldehyde permeates the air and Willow's face scrunches while she rubs Vicks Vaporrub under her nose. A trick she learned from her brother. Vivid memories of Kai coming home from his first crime scene–an elderly hermit who passed away of natural causes, but it took weeks to discover he had passed.

Kai threw up on the gentleman's reader's digest collection. Another officer gave him the tip, and when he came home, he emptied his pockets of five jars of the rub. It takes someone with a strong stomach to have the career of a mortician. Brutal crime scenes, bodily fluid, gore, she could handle. The smells that accompany it–harder to deal with.

The female victim's chest splits wide open as two large pieces of steel equipment peel the ribcage back, her heart missing from the cavity. Metal bowls rest on the side cart, arranged with purpose containing other pieces of tissue or organs. Warren glances up as she enters. "You're here." He sets aside his tools and removes his gloves. "I was just wrapping up." He stands, taking off his white coat and draping it across the stool.

She nods. "What did you find? My team is working on getting her identity, it shouldn't be long since we know she lives in town." He gestures for her to come closer, pointing to the autopsy report spread across the side table. She hesitates at first but eventually joins his side. To her surprise, his handwriting is neat and legible, notes with facts and questions beside them litter the pages. Willow's gaze drifts to the woman's remains. She looks different under the fluorescent light. Imperfections stand out and discoloration creeps across the entire front of her figure.

"As you may recall, she was found collapsed downward in a praying position. There was no external bleeding on the scene or visible signs of a struggle," Warren starts.

"I'd say there are more signs of struggle now," she retorts. Splotches of reddish-purple bubble in different areas of the victim's face, a large amount present on her forehead.

"No, not necessarily. I believe you are referring to the discoloration of her skin. Although it can present like bruises, this is actually a part of livor mortis. The color shows where the blood accumulated within the blood vessels due to gravity. She was kneeling, head down, arms extended with her palms together. Look," he points to her forehead, then moves to reveal her forearms, "almost her entire front side of her body has this. It's from gravity and where the blood pooled from the pose she was placed in."

The entirety of her forearm shines a bright shade of pink, noticeably pinker than the rest of her undertone. "So, what's the cause of death then? There's no way she wasn't murdered given how she was found."

Warren leans against the table and crosses his arms. "Short answer, heart attack."

"What's the long answer?" She tilts her head.

"Long answer, I can't tell what happened to her. There were traces of semen in her system, but no sign of force. A rape kit came back negative. There is no sign of physical trauma. The only indicator I found was evidence of a heart attack."

Willow's legs move on their own, pacing the room. "That doesn't make any sense. She's a healthy young woman, isn't she?"

"That is correct. Her brain, lungs, all her organs appear to have been in great shape. Heart attacks are even less common in females." His expression remains neutral.

"What are you saying? What happened to her then?" Willow questions. *Why can't he give her a straight answer?*

"Did you interact with this woman often?"

"I wouldn't say very often, no. There were just a few occasions that we ran near each other at the gym. Maybe a few awkward smiles of acknowledgement. Why?"

"Is there anything you notice out of the ordinary about her?"

He's leading her to an answer. She turns her attention back to the deceased. Just like the first time she observed her, the first thing that stands out is all the various discolorations. Her chest splayed open for display. A peaceful expression found her in death. Now that she's closer, she seems thinner than she remembers?

"Now that I look, her under eyes are more sunken in. It's hard to tell with all the discoloration." She glances up from the victim to find Warren brandishing a sly grin.

"Indeed. To put it simply, I think she was *drained of life* without leaving a mark other than stress on her heart. I speculate that's how she died. I, however, cannot put that on the autopsy report. So, it will be a heart attack."

Willow frowns, absorbing the information. "What kind of supernatural creature drains life from the living? Other than you, of course," she jabs.

"*Funny.* Vampires don't directly drain life, it's blood. They are two different things. As far as what creature does this, I will have to continue to do research on it. There are thousands of legends, and there is a lot of uncertainty around this. With the goons we've seen following you, we will need to be more careful, for your sake." Warren adjusts the black round-rimmed glasses on the bridge of his nose.

"My sake? I don't need you to worry about me. Worry about yourself." She scowls.

"I cannot die, sweetheart. I need you to help me find this thing– so yes, I need you to stay alive." His lips press into a thin, brittle line, barely holding his frustration.

"You can't die?" Her eyes bulge, ignoring the new pet name.

"I cannot. Trust me, I've tried," he responds, adjusting his position and turning away from her to busy his hands. *He regrets telling her.*

"You've tried?" Willow murmurs.

For the first time since meeting him, she feels sympathy toward him. What life experiences has he encountered to make him so angry? And so– sad? When she thinks about it, she can't imagine a world without death. A lot of people would love nothing more than to live forever. Willow couldn't say the same. It seems her and Warren both share the sentiment.

"I don't need any pity," he responds with a harsh, bitter edge. She struck a nerve.

"Are all vampires immortal?" she asks, dumbfounded by the thought.

"No. Most of them can be killed by piercing the heart, decapitation, or being burned alive."

"Then—why can't you?" she asks.

His shoulders stiffen. "That's none of your concern."

"Sorry, I didn't mean to pry." Her lips draw into a frown.

Warren turns toward her, searching her face. The eye contact makes Willow uncomfortable, and she averts her gaze back to the body.

"What did you discover from the footage you were given?" He changes the subject.

"That there's a whole eighteen minutes missing on the video, which I'm sure just so happened to be a glitch." The white of her knuckles glow in her tightened fist. "And then that's it. Jonathan's gone. He spoke with someone, but with the angle of the camera, we couldn't see their faces."

"Interesting. There is not much here in the office that I can use to help, but I will watch the video when we get home this afternoon," he says.

"When *we* get home?" Her forehead wrinkles.

"You are not safe alone. You've been almost killed. *Twice*. Granted, the first time you interrupted me, but still. Someone or something has obviously taken a liking to you. Worst comes to worst, you can be bait and it'll lead them to my domain."

"I don't remember asking for your protection," she says as a matter of fact.

"And I don't remember caring if you asked. And frankly I'm tired of having this conversation." Warren's jaw clenches.

She bites her tongue, and for some reason unknown to her, a ping of dejection lands like a stone in her gut.

A sigh escapes his mouth. "Listen, as I've told you before, I'm not the villain here. You can accept my help; it will not make you any less strong of a woman to allow me to aid you." He presses his point with a calm, unyielding edge.

"You don't know me well enough to speak to me like that." Willow shakes her head, physically trying to shake off any emotion her brain wills her to feel. "I—just don't understand why you even need me. You are more than capable of doing this by yourself. And now I'm in the middle of all of this, being followed by vampire-ghost-magic people, I can't even sleep in my own bed—" she trails off, the frustration building.

Warren places a hand on the side of her shoulder and squeezes it in a soothing grip, pulling her mind from the beginning of her spiral.

"Take a breath," he pauses as Willow gauges the level of comfort she has with him laying a hand on her, "I am strong, but as we've discovered, this is bigger than me alone. For us to both get what we want, we will have a greater chance of succeeding with your mind as well. Whether I like it or not, I do need you." He pauses. "I also suspect you may have more ties to the otherworldly than you realize."

"What have you been hiding from me?" her accusation comes wrapped in caution. The brief comfort of his touch is slammed out by her walls being thrown back up. In several conversations he has danced around answers.

Warren's chin tilts, moving his hand away from her shoulder. "What do you know about that necklace of yours?"

Her hand shoots for the necklace and twirls it in between her fingertips. "I–my brother gave it to me before he passed. He always wore it, but he gave it to me. I was having–a hard time. He thought it would cheer me up."

Through a swollen eye, Willow stares at the chipped wooden floor of her room. Her knuckles are covered in bloodied scratches, her limbs begin to ache as the adrenaline rush fades. Her internal thoughts are muffled by the external screaming between her parents, arguing over where they each went wrong with her.

"You don't start a fight you can't finish, especially not against one of my lieutenant's sons, Willow!" Mr. Rhodes barks, his mood sour from being called to come pick her up in the middle of a workday, despite her mother already being at home and available.

"What were you thinking?" his voice booms throughout the house.

Willow's silence is deafening.

"Honey, let's let her reflect on her mistakes. Go back to work, and we can discuss her punishment after she has considered how her actions impact others." Mrs. Rhodes chimes in, comforting her husband.

He storms out of the room, not looking back. Mrs. Rhodes gives Willow a scowl of disappointment as she follows Mr. Rhodes out of her room, the door slamming shut. Her vanity mirror shakes, knocking off several polaroids of her and Kai, and another of her and Nadia out of the frame. Willow sniffles, trying not to cry too loudly for her parents to hear. They can't know. It only makes them more angry.

Her bedroom door creaks back open, her sniffles come to a halt as she wipes her cheeks and nose. The cloth against the wetness on her cheeks rubs them raw, but she ignores the pain. Familiar cobalt orbs peer from the crack in the door. She forces a smile, dropping it immediately. A fake invitation in.

"Hey there," Kai's masculine voice whispers. He peers behind his shoulder before creeping into the room, twisting the doorknob, and closing the door without a sound. Willow nods in his direction. Kai saunters to her bed, sitting beside her on top of her frilly pink, ruffled comforter. "So, uh…what happened today?"

She sniffles, keeping her neck craned to the floor. "There's no way you didn't hear Dad. I'm sure the whole town heard him yell."

"That's not what I asked."

She sighs. "Brandon Stevens was calling this new kid names. He got in his face and teased him. The kid tried so hard not to cry. I told him to knock it off and he took it as a challenge. He got in my face—so I pushed him away. He tried to push me back so I took a swing at him before he could. The new kid ran away crying to get help and before you know it," she shrugs and points to her blackened eye.

Kai nods, processing the story. "Man, I'd hate to see what Brandon looks like if all you got was this shiner."

His comment tugs a grin to her lips before she can stop it. He rubs the back of his neck, his fingers grabbing the chain of his silver necklace. He glances down at it in thought before unclasping it from the back. "I know this may not be your thing as much as the rest of the family, but it's always made me feel protected and at peace. I want you to have it. If not forever, just a while to help."

She lifts a brow. "I can't just take your necklace; you've worn this ever since Grandfather gave it to you."

"Think of it as a loaner then. Grandfather would have been fine with that."

"I'm not sure about that. I was never the favorite, this was meant for you."
She pushes his hand away with the necklace in it.

He offers her an impassive look. "Listen, just take the damn necklace to appease me, alright?"

"Are you alright?" Warren asks, taking suspicious blinks.

"Why?" A slight panic seeps through her tone. "What makes you say that?"

His expression twists, wrestling with doubt. "I speculate that there is some sort of magical ward placed on that necklace. I can't say for sure what type surrounds it without research."

Her stare holds on the silver cross necklace in between her fingers. "You're just now saying something about this?" She chokes on her anger. *Magic has potentially been wrapped around her neck the entire time?*

"You can leave it on. This is just an assumption, but I don't think it was intended to bring harm. You've had it on for how many years? A decade almost?" He delivers the words in a flat, hollow cadence.

"A little over a decade," her jaw shifts.

"My hypothesis is that whoever gave that to your brother, or your brother himself, had access to magic and needed this for something." Warren leans forward, extending his fingers to pull the cross pendant out of Willow's grasp to inspect it.

She draws back, but his grasp is stronger, keeping her in place while he gets a closer look at her necklace. The proximity makes her breath catch, the smell of eucalyptus and sandalwood fills her nose. His scent is oddly clean, despite his profession. His fingers brush against her skin as he lifts the cross pendant.

"There's without a doubt something warded on this," he says, his resonance low and almost intimate as his breath touches her skin. "But I can't know more without further examination and research, if you will allow me, that is. With a human eye it's almost impossible to see, but there are tiny carvings etched into the design, creating a spell."

Willow swallows hard, her words come out as a whisper, "I don't see how my brother would know or have access to magic. Do you think it's helping me? Or could it help us with what we're searching for?"

"Perhaps," Warren replies, his eyes locking onto hers. "Let me look into this." The intensity of his stare and the closeness of their bodies makes Willow's pulse quicken. Warren's gaze, dark and probing, brims with curiosity and a shadowy something she can't unravel.

"Warren–" Sam pushes the steel door to the morgue open.

Warren instantly drops her necklace and takes a step back. Willow's face tightens and her ears burn.

"Yes?" Warren leans against the table coolly, seemingly unbothered by the interruption. He coaxes a soft, reluctant smile to life.

"I apologize, I didn't mean to interrupt." Sam hesitates to come inside the room further.

"No interruption, we were just finishing up discussing the victim's cause of death," Willow adds without hesitation. *What was that?* The inner voice shrieks inside her mind, bouncing off her skull. She clears her throat before proceeding, "Based on the staging of the victim, and the lingerie she was found in, the killer's motivation must be sexually driven. Since she had a heart attack, it could have been potentially induced by whomever she was having sex with?" The openness they once had slips away as Sam continues into the room.

Warren nods. "Semen can live inside the body for up to five days. There is a sliver of a chance the killer isn't the one who produced the semen found inside her. So, take that into consideration for your investigation as well, Detective," Warren adds.

Sam glances at the remains on the table. "That would make sense."

"But then someone posed the victim after her death, for whatever reason," she sighs as all the details of the case whirl in her mind.

The table scoots several inches back as Warren pushes off, standing straight. "Detective Rhodes, this is all my findings. I will have it all in a written report and have that to you in the next two days."

Sam drapes the white cloth over the entirety of her figure.

"Got it. Thank you for the information. Sam," she directs her attention to him and grins, "it was nice seeing you again. It's been a bit."

"And you as well, Willow."

Chapter 22
THOUGHTS OF A PESSIMIST

Willow's ash brown hair whips around in a frenzy as she drives. The brisk wind is a weak attempt to refocus and energize herself. An invisible, crushing weight sits behind her temple. A level of exhaustion she has never reached before consumes her. Another day of being unable to remember the last time she slept. *What day is it?* They're all starting to blur together. Fingers tremble as she dials Nadia's cell. The phone rings for a few beeps before she picks up.

"Hey, everything okay?"

"Yes? Why wouldn't it be?"

"Oh. You just never call unless something bad happens, or for work, or I guess for both now," Nadia trails off.

"Yeah, I'm sorry about that," Willow pauses, "I think this case has just been more difficult than I realized. In more ways than one." Defeat presses onto her vocal chords.

"Why don't you talk to the Chief about taking a step away? Maybe let Milo take the lead? I was shocked that the Chief put you on this."

"Ouch," Willow winces.

"No! Not because you aren't capable! You are the most capable! You know, just because of Kai. Please know I didn't mean it like that!"

A sad laugh escaped from Willow's pursed lips. "I know, don't worry. But I need this. It's just–something I gotta get through on my own, you know?"

"I get it," Nadia sighs. "So, what do I owe the pleasure of getting a call from you?"

"Oh, right," she almost forgot why she called, "I wanted to tell you before you found out, and I swear on my life Nadia, I don't want to hear any snide remarks. But I wanted to let you know that I won't be at the house for a while. I have a bug infestation and will have people coming to spray, but it'll be a bit before they will let me back in."

"Why would I–"

"And I'm staying with Warren until I'm able to come back home," Willow adds, spitting the words out as fast as she can.

Radio silence ripples on the other end of the phone. "As friends, *got it*?" Willow's pitch raises an octave.

"I didn't say anything at all."

"Good. I will still have my phone and my own room," she emphasizes. "So, if you need me, you know how to reach me."

"Mmhm," Nadia hums.

Willow can practically see the *I told you so* grin plastered on her face from behind the phone.

"Anyway, that's it. Just wanted to update you before you came banging on a bug infested door with no one there."

"Well, I appreciate the heads up. I'm looking forward to weekly updates, yes?" Nadia's response almost feels like a threat.

"There will be nothing to update you on other than the case, but I will do that." Her tone remains neutral, unwilling to throw Nadia the bone she keeps searching for.

"Sure thing. Stay safe. Love you, Will!"

Willow simpers. "Right back at you. Talk later."

The phone screen blackens as the call ends, timing perfectly as Willow parks in her gravel driveway. She takes a moment to stare at her home. The small, red brick cottage stands still. In this moment she realizes how fast paced she has lived for the last decade, failing to stop and take in the moment. Acknowledging she's alive.

Pessimistic thoughts of not returning back here cross her mind, making her to wonder if she has wasted most of her life in pursuit of something unattainable. A cold embrace wraps around her ankle. A petite jade and black snake wraps around the visible skin above her sock. She shrieks, kicking her foot out of instinct. The snake lands a few feet away but slithers back to her.

She jumps back, staying on the balls of her feet, ready to run at any moment. She glances around the perimeter of her home—finding no one.

"Are you with Warren?" she whispers. If the trees could talk, they would call her crazy. *Wait. If trees could talk, maybe at this point she is crazy.* The snake slithers into the shape of a heart before unfolding, holding her gaze. "Can I not have a moment to myself?" she groans. The snake circles itself in front of her, then slithers to lay on her porch. "I'm just packing, get off my ass." She scoffs as she steps past the snake. Her footsteps quicken as she moves by, not trusting it or *him.*

The familiar underwhelming scent of fresh laundry and soil greets her as she enters her home. Willow floats through the rooms, as if dancing through the air as she waters her plants. "You guys better not die on me while I'm gone," she whispers to them as she pours water over the potted soil. She pulls the curtains in the kitchen and living room open, allowing more streams of light to enter the home. "Hopefully this will help."

After scrambling to locate Kai's case files, stuffing her duffel bag of clothes, chargers, and her favorite childhood blanket, she's ready to leave. The front door has to slam three times to get it in the right spot to lock.

Her phone buzzes.

Gideon:

"Listen, this may be too forward…but I can't stop thinking about you. I'd love to take you out to coffee or dinner. If you're not interested, I understand, you don't have to respond. But I wouldn't do myself justice if I didn't try."

It's been so long. The urge to feel normal, *or hell,* even stable pulls at her. Butterflies flutter in her stomach.

"Hi. Sorry, I'm awful at communication. I'll need to check my calendar. I'll regroup with you soon."

It'll buy her some time to think.

CHAPTER 23

HEAVY METAL AND TOMATO SOUP

B y the time she reaches Warren's secluded residence, dusk begins to set over the trees. The soft glow of the outdoor lights illuminates the porch as she approaches with her large army green duffel bag slung over her shoulder, her movements slow and staggered. Her tennis shoes scrape against the brick with each step she takes up the porch. Her knuckles strike the door with a thud. She leans down to peer through the windowpane in the center of the door. There's no movement on the other side from what she can tell. Another knock. *Thud thud.* Still no response.

She huffs, the weight of her duffel bag irritating her. For a chance, she reaches out to turn the knob and to her surprise, it opens.

"Hello?" Willow calls out as she drops the duffel bag onto the hardwood floors. The silence envelopes her, broken only by the distant, rhythmic thrum of heavy metal music. She doesn't receive a response. She pushes further into the home, inspecting her surroundings closer than she did the first time she stayed here, *against her will.*

Following the sound of the music, she makes her way through the home. Gold framed canvases hang in careful arrangement along the hall. One painting is a serene lake, with a long-boarded dock that stretches into it. Beams of tiny light peer through the cloudy sky behind the lake. The second painting further along on the left side of the hall is an abstract piece but resembles the backside of a naked woman. She has yet to discover a single photo of Warren, family, or friends.

Music seeps through the single solid black door ajar at the end of the hallway. Beyond it, she finds a set of stairs leading into a basement. The music thrums louder as she descends, the creaking of the wooden steps fade beneath the guitar's jagged riffs. She doesn't mind the genre of music, but the sheer volume is deafening by the time she reaches the bottom of the stairs. Even with vampire hearing, he may have not heard her come in. At the bottom of the steps, she finds herself in a spacious home gym. Darkness engulfs the entire room with all black walls, and black flooring mats. A fully mirrored wall catches her off guard—her own reflection staring back, the dark circles beneath her lash line shouting louder than she can bear. The thoughts spin in her mind, unable to string a coherent idea as the music blares from above. Rows of grandiose speakers in the rafters of the ceiling vibrate the hair on top of her head.

The whites of her eyes peek around the corner, finding Warren lying on a bench and doing chest presses. His focus remains on the heavy bar in his clutches. Her brows shoot as high as her forehead allows, viewing the four stacks of large plates on both sides of the bar. The vintage sleeveless t-shirt Warren wears leaves his red snake tattoo on full display, his muscles flexing with each press of the bar. His long hair is tied back, but a few strands escape, falling across his forehead. The white stripe of hair cascades around his jaw.

For a moment, Willow watches, captivated by his strength. The muscles are a perk too, though she would never admit it aloud. Warren gives one more push before re-racking the weights and sitting up. He angles away from her as he grabs his phone, and the music dies mid-note.

Through the mirror, Willow studies him. Strong hands grasp the hem of his shirt, lifting it up to wipe sweat from his brows, revealing a toned stomach. A happy trail of hair leads below his waistline of his sweatpants.

"I'd like to tell you to pull up a chair to get comfortable while you undress me with your eyes, but that was my last set of the night." A smirk ghosts Warren's lips as he glances over his shoulder.

Her open mouth slams shut. A glare pulls her brows forward as she thinks of a response that wouldn't inflate his ego. Instead, she finds herself taking a sharp swivel to walk back up the stairs without a word.

Like lightning, a white streak flashes past her and stills at the step just ahead of her. Warren gazes down at her, his mouth pulled into a grin. "No response?"

There's the ego. Now that she thinks about it, there may be no way to deflate it. She pushes past him to walk back into his living room. Her shoulder checks him in the chest, barely moving him an inch. "I knocked, you couldn't hear me, so I let myself in. We have world saving to tend to, if you haven't forgotten."

"Oh, no I heard you. I wanted to see if you would let yourself in or not. I can't work with a pushover when treachery is imminent."

"You thought even for a second I was a pushover?" she deadpans.

He smirks, walking around the kitchen island and cranks the knobs on the stove. "Of course not. It's just fun seeing you get riled up." From the cabinets below he pulls out two different cooking pots. "Please, sit down and rest for a moment."

"What are you doing? We have things to do." The tapping of her foot clicks against the wooden floor.

"When was the last time you had anything to eat?" he asks.

The corner of her mouth pulls into a slight frown, unable to recall the answer.

"Right. You cannot be of use if you're dead. Sit. I am making food," he demands, his posture straightening as he speaks.

"Fine," she bites back begrudgingly, plopping down on the leather couch in the living room. The seat doesn't give, her hip cracks from the abrupt movement. "Do you ever sit on this thing?" she complains, kicking off her shoes and throwing them by the front door to pull her feet onto the couch. Willow wiggles and shifts as she tries to get comfortable.

"Can't say that I do. I mainly stick to the library, gym, and bedroom."

"What's the point of having all this," she motions her arms to the entire living room space, "if you don't even use it? What do you even need a bedroom for? Do vampires even sleep?"

"There's plenty of other things to do in a bedroom besides sleep." Amusement flickers at the corner of his mouth, but his focus remains pinned to the ingredients he's chopping.

Her lips purse flat and she pulls out her phone to scroll through the group message from her colleagues. There are several GIFS from Leo, Milo butts in with unimportant facts about said GIFS, and no text at all from Jasmine. Leo and Milo are essentially talking to themselves at this point. She thinks for a second before typing in the chat.

Jasmine, can you check on Brian from the casino and see if he has any background? He's a floor manager.

Within a minute Jasmine responds, "*Yep. Will do after I get confirmation on this female victim's dental records so we can have an identification. Should be soon.*"

An instant chime from Milo sends in, "*Oh, too good to respond to us Jasmine?*"

Jasmine likes the message, which makes laughter spill from Willow's lips before she can stop it.

The noise catches the attention of Warren as he stirs the biggest pot present on the stove eye. The corners of his lips lift with amusement. "I don't think I've ever heard you laugh."

She fiddles with her shirt sleeves

"It's one of my coworkers. She's the type of person who's really quiet, but when she talks, she's hilarious without trying. Especially at the expense of Milo." Thinking about it again makes her giggle. She pulls her water bottle to her lips.

"Milo? Is that the fellow who's in love with you but you won't give him the time of day?"

Her eyebrows lift with shock, almost spitting out her water. She stifles a choke. "What? No? Who told you that?" She shifts on the seat again and picks at the loose string that has begun to come off the side of her pants leg.

"Just through the lily vine."

Her brow raises. "You mean the grape vine? Lilies don't have vines," her head tilts, "either way, no. Everything is professional."

"Right," his voice drips with sarcasm.

Willow isn't sure of how much time has passed, the silence and stillness is a welcomed rest. The warmth from the kitchen acts as a lullaby, her eyelids yearn to close.

Warren takes the pot off the stove and turns off the burner. Dishes clink inside the sink. "Come, eat."

"What is it?" she asks as she takes a deep inhale. The aroma of basil and onions makes her mouth water. Willow stands with forced effort, dragging herself to the marble island.

"Tomato soup. Eat," he pushes a bowl he just poured across the counter to her. A single serving steams from the bowl.

"Are you not having any?"

"I have no use for human food. I'll satiate myself later, don't fret."

Her eyebrows scrunch together. "Stay away from my neck." she threatens.

"I already told you; I do not drink from the living if I can help it." His features soften before hardening once more.

She picks her bowl and spoon off the table and heads toward the couch.

"Fine, I'll eat. But we multitask. Let's get to work." She sits on the floor by his coffee table and pulls the flash drive and laptop out of her bag.

"I have perfectly fine dining chairs," Warren says under his breath, following her like a shadow; grabbing the round rimmed glasses off the counter and placing them on his face. He snatches the laptop out of her grasp. The screen powers on and illuminates his focused expression, navigating with ease to the video.

"Yeah, that's fine. I didn't need my laptop anyway," she sneers.

"You and your team have already assessed this. It's my turn."

Willow can see the reflection of the footage from his glasses, not bothering to look at the laptop. She observes his expressions, analyzing him to find any flicker of recognition.

"What a sorry excuse for security footage," he mutters. Somehow, the pixels on the screen of her laptop are even worse than the old school television in the office. Warren leans forward as the mysterious casino Casanova struts into frame. "Hm."

"Friend of yours?" Willow's eyebrow quirks.

"I am not the killer, but you should still treat me as a suspect," he gives a large audible exhale and whispers under his breath, "it'll keep you safer that way." He continues, "Not a friend, but I want to say this man seems familiar somehow. Ultimately, you're right. With the edits on this video, it is useless. However, it's good to have confirmed that something unnatural is occurring at the casino. Have you learned anything from your team on the female victim?"

"No," she glances down at her phone. "Not yet. The killings are very different. It feels like different killers. Different motives. But with all the creatures, the supernatural, whatever they are, I feel like I should throw everything out on what I've been taught." She rubs her temple with one hand, the other subconsciously swings her necklace back and forth on the silver chain. "They are waiting for the dental records from the deceased. I'm assuming you didn't pull those so it would take them longer to get her identification and buy us time?" He nods.

The tension in Warren's jaw prepares her for anxiety. "Do you trust me?"

"No." She grimaces.

"Good. I'm taking you on a quick trip in the morning. It's time to visit your family."

CHAPTER 24

FAMILY REUNION

After hours of arguing and having to drag Willow out of the house, her silence has been all consuming. The lining of her stomach quivers, then tightens, lined with lead as the heaviness causes her entire body to sink deeper into the passenger seat. The rising sunlight dances between the trees, casting fleeting shadows across Willow's face as she stares out the window.

"There's no use in pouting. I've told you, it's a quick trip," he says as he scratches the stubble on his cheek.

"You expect me to happily go along with this with no explanation or details from you? You may have done some research into my family, but I promise you—*you don't know them*," bitterness slices through her words, "there's no reason for us to visit them. We might not even be let in, so it's a waste of time," she sighs, defeat dampens her breath.

The trees become familiar as Warren pulls into the semi-secluded estate of the Rhodes family. As always, the pristine landscape reveals the middle-class home, as though every blade of grass was cut by hand. The white-washed brick is pure, not a splash of any other color or imperfection, just how Mrs. Rhodes liked to have things.

The tire swing that Kai screwed into the tree many years ago sways with the wind, creaking. Flashes of her childhood race into Willow's mind. Her heart aches, as though the million Band-Aids that had been covering it were ripped off all at once.

Warren parks the car. "Listen, all I need you to do is to walk me inside the home. We'll browse, take a quick peek at your former stuffed animal collection, then be on our way." His stab at a lighthearted joke fell flat with

Willow's blank stare. His long fingers extend, cupping her chin upward to face him. Her breath catches in her throat, flinching at his touch.

"Look at me," he murmurs. "You said you'd do whatever it takes to solve this. Are you still in?"

Damn him. She nods, then swallows as she focuses on his dilated pupils. He releases her chin and grasps the door handle. "Excellent. Now, after you." In a flash, he's on the other side of her door, opening it for her to step out.

The air from Willow's lungs stutters as the two of them walk up the front steps of what she used to call home. She finds herself touching her chin where traces of Warren's fingers lingered.

Warren gives her a nod before ringing the doorbell. Shuffling followed by a cough echo from inside and her throat rubs together like sandpaper. Her mother peers from behind the window and hesitates before unlocking each of the bolts on the door. *Click. Shuffle, click click. Click, Thud.* After unlocking the four bolts, the door creaks open.

Mrs. Rhodes nose crinkles as though she stepped in dog shit with bare feet. "What are you doing here?" Disgust curls around her words as her hardened features shoot daggers at Willow.

Time reverts; Willow's two feet tall and three years old again. A lump catches in her throat. "I—"

"Good morning, Mrs. Rhodes. It's a pleasure to meet you! I've heard such wonderful things about you from Detective Rhodes here," Warren interrupts, extending his hand forward for a handshake.

"And who are you? What are you doing on my property?" Her disdain trails to the unfamiliar man in front of her, keeping herself sheltered behind the door.

"I apologize; I got ahead of myself. My name is Daniel. I am new to the Misty Pines police force. Rhodes has been showing me the ropes and I have always respected former Chief Rhodes, and the excellent police work Officer Kai did. I asked if I could meet Chief Rhodes, and she agreed. Is now a good time? I just want to thank him for his service and his dedication to our city—maybe even ask him some questions on how I can become a better officer!" The grin on his facial features mimic that of a puppy, a stark contrast of his typical personality. *Maybe in another life he was an actor.*

Willow stifles the grimace her face wishes to make. Somehow, this version of himself doesn't suit him as well as the grumpy old man.

Willow tries to keep her expression neutral and clears her throat. "Is Dad around?"

Mrs. Rhodes's attention shifts back and forth between the two before settling on Willow. "He's not in. He went fishing. A call would be a good first step, wouldn't you think?"

"Mrs. Rhodes, this is my fault. I was so excited training, and I wanted so much to meet him, and even you! I pushed too much; I apologize for being so unprofessional. I just want to be the best officer I can." His body language shifts, sulking almost. "My little sister is a paramedic too, so our families have a lot of similarities."

Willow shoots him a sideways glance. *How much does he know about her family? It's been many years since her mother was a paramedic.* The blue in Warren's iris pulses as he stares at Willow's mother.

Mrs. Rhodes's lips tighten. "Robert loves talking about his glory days. He'll be sad he missed you. Kai was an excellent officer. The best of the best. No one could ever replace him," she sighs and swallows, "under normal circumstances I wouldn't even entertain this for a second. But I can tell you care. I haven't touched his room since the day he died. I couldn't," she chokes back. "Would you like to see? That's all I can offer, Robert fishes for hours."

A sympathetic mask glazes over her expression. A look that Willow had seen her give Kai thousands of times for every half assed apology he would piece together.

Warren lights up with quiet joy. "I would love nothing more."

Mrs. Rhodes's attention turns to Willow. "You may show your protege Kai's room. Do not touch anything. While you're here, take the box of your belongings that's on the floor of your old room. I've been meaning to donate them, but if you're here that would be more convenient for me." Her words leave an acrid aftertaste in Willow's mouth. "Daniel, would you like some tea? I can put some on the stove."

"That sounds lovely, Mrs. Rhodes," Warren responds with a gentle nod, guiding Willow forward to follow her mother into the house.

Willow can't be sure, but she could swear his eyes pulsed burgundy for a split second as Mrs. Rhodes turned around.

The house is a photograph stuck in time, everything from the tacky off-yellow wallpaper to the beige carpet remains preserved from her childhood. Mothballs and sanded wood tickle the inside of her nose. Robert Rhodes must have taken up woodworking as a spare hobby in his retirement, which would make sense. He isn't the type to rest and stay idle.

Mrs. Rhodes disappears into the kitchen, leaving Warren and Willow in the hall. "Second door on the right," Willow says in a hushed whisper to Warren.

Within a second, he's gone. Her steps are covered in molasses. It's been over a decade, being in this home, seeing his things. When she envisioned this day in her mind over and over, she thought it would be easier than this—or that it would never happen. In her mind, she wouldn't come back here until her parents died. The hair on her arms raises as she makes it to the doorway. The same doorway that has pencil marks etched into the side, marking Kai's and Willow's height progression as they aged. Though Willow's height stopped being tracked when she was five. The last entry for Kai was the day he graduated high school.

As she enters the threshold of the room, she discovers Warren glancing over the bookshelf. Most of Kai's books were historical fiction, utopian, or autobiographies. Willow never understood the appeal of it. Warren grabs two magazines from behind Kai's books, revealing two busty, scantily dressed women on the covers.

"A man of taste, I see."

"Surely you didn't want to come all this way to look at my dead brother's nudey magazines?" she snips, looking anywhere but the print in his hand.

He places the magazines back in their original spot, his fingers dancing along the spines of the other books as he searches through. "Of course not, I'm a classy man," he pauses, "the real thing is much more preferred."

"God, please stop talking."

The vintage wooden chest sitting at the foot of Kai's bed catches Warren's attention. "Hm," he says out loud as he tucks his loose strand of hair behind his ear and bends down.

A thin layer of dust puffs in the air as the lid creaks open. Clothes bulge from the top, all from the eighties that more than likely haven't seen daylight since they were placed within the box.

His touch dances around the lining of the trunk. "What are you looking for?" Willow asks him. The length of her fingernails scratches the side of her arms as she continues to monitor the doorframe to Kai's room. "We need to hurry," she adds in a whisper.

"That is precisely what I am doing," he mutters with a flick of his wrist, a wooden compartment on the outside of the chest pops open. "There you are." He grins as the two of them move closer.

"What's–" Willow trails off as Warren pulls out a faded leather-bound book and a dull blue dagger. "How did you know where to find this? What is this stuff?" she interrogates.

"This is unexpected." A frown pulls at the corners of his lips during his pause. Intricate lines and curves of what appears to be a forgotten language are etched into the surface of the blade. He places the book in the waistline of his pants, careful to use his white striped button up to conceal it as he untucks his shirt.

"What is all of this? Why did Kai have this? How did you know where to find this?" Her pulse quickens.

"To answer your question, a small trace of magical aura. Here, conceal it in your ankle sheath." He extends the dagger toward her.

Her gaze tightens. "How did you know I had that?" she asks as she snatches the blade from him. As her fingertips touch the handle, the serrated edge of the blade turns into an electric blue light, glowing. "Uh–"

"Well, that's new." His eyebrows lift. "I'd say this visit has proven useful. We have a lot to research." Warren grins.

"Why is it glowing?" she yells in a hushed whisper.

A few rooms over Mrs. Rhodes yells, "Daniel, do you like sugar in your tea?"

"Yes, please. I'd love some sugar!" he calls out from the room.

"Why would you get sugar? We need to figure out what's happening!" She panics, holding the illuminated blade.

"I intend to figure that out. I don't plan on staying long enough to drink it anyway. Let's get out of here so we can discuss this more without prying eyes," he whispers.

Before Willow could speak, he wraps his muscular arms around her, enveloping her within his shadow. Within a blink, they are back outside near Warren's car. Her thoughts are scattered, like leaves in a storm, impossible to gather or focus. She reaches out for balance, grabbing hold of the closest thing to her–Warren's arm.

"The first time traveling at vampiric speed can induce vertigo. I should have warned. You should settle in a minute." He doesn't move, allowing her to regain her balance against him.

Willow groans. "A heads up would have been nice. I've snuck out of this house more times than I can count, I could have walked myself." Her grasp loosens as the spinning earth slows. She can at least make it into the car herself. The doors slam behind her as they enter the car and Warren backs away from the house, not giving pause.

"I believe this has been a very fruitful journey," Warren says.

"Easy for you to say, *Daniel*," she rolls her eyes, "I have so many questions." The blade continues to glow as it dances in between her fingers. "We're just leaving without saying anything?" Guilt makes her stomach swirl.

Warren's eyebrow quirks. "Do you actually care enough to say goodbye to that woman?"

Her mouth opens to protest, just to fall short. "No. Nevermind." The inner child that never healed attempts to peek through again. Willow stuffs her back in the mental prison she created decades ago.

"Family doesn't treat each other that way," he mutters.

She ignores it. There's not a single part of her that wishes to discuss her family any further. Let alone with *him*.

Warren continues. "I'll have to consult with a couple of acquaintances of mine. I'm not well versed in magical runes. I can only identify basic magic users and items, unfortunately." He grabs his chin as his arm rests on the window to his door, watching the road but with obvious racing thoughts.

"That's what these markings are?"

"I believe so. It's an old language."

"Why would my brother have this? Why a hidden compartment? Could it belong to someone else?" Her mind spins as she tries to recall childhood memories.

"In time, we will find out," he says, his response cautious as if handling her with oven mitts.

"In the meantime, take off that necklace. I am going to need it for my research."

She clutches it into her chest. "I thought you said it's safe?"

"That was before we found all of this." He gestures to the items taken from Kai's room.

She crosses her leg in the seat and her fingers rub against the cross one last time before she removes its silver chain from her neck.

CHAPTER 25
CARDIO TECHNIQUES

S he trudges through the police station entrance, her shoulders slumped and exhaustion lining her face. The oppressive weight of visiting her family home lingers like a shadow over her, leaving her drained emotionally and physically. Her heart aches from the strained memories and cold reception she received, but none of it came as a surprise. The lack of sleep has given her plenty of hours to replay the rejection in her head repeatedly. The pure disgust of being in her mother's presence.

The familiarity of her surroundings offers her comfort. Dragging her limbs, she lowers herself into the chair, its old frame groans under her. As she shifts through the piles of paperwork on her desk, Jasmine and Milo approach her; Jasmine holds a manila folder with a somber expression.

"You look like shit," Milo states, placing a steaming cup in front of her.

"Thanks. New information?" She blazes past his comment, bringing the coffee to her lips.

"We've got an I.D. on the female victim from the park," Jasmine speaks.

Willow's fatigue is momentarily forgotten as she takes the folder with a weary nod. Her fingers tremble as she opens it, revealing pages of the details of the victim's identity.

"It's confirmed for us through dental records. Amelia Rogers, twenty-five years old, new elementary school teacher at Wood Grove."

The breath catches in her throat as Willow reads about Amelia's life—a life that had barely begun, ended with violence. Twenty-five? She had her whole life ahead of her. She's a member of the church, Willow notes. *Why her?*

Old photos that Jasmine must have found off social media are printed. Amelia grins ear to ear next to friends in almost every photo. She studies the pictures, her heart heavy with the realization that this isn't just a case to solve–it's a tragedy that touched her life in a way she hadn't expected. A snapshot into what Willow's life could have been.

"I recognized her the minute I saw her, and I didn't interact with her other than simply exercising next to her. I'm sure this will impact the community deeply. The first victim wasn't a local but still shook everything up. This," she pauses and takes a deep breath, "this will cause chaos."

"Leo's on his way to break it to the family," Milo responds.

She nods. "What about the press? Has the Chief been looped in?"

Jasmine speaks up, "I met with him this morning. He said he would handle them. It was only a matter of time before they came anyway."

"Do we have her phone records? Or location? A phone wasn't found on the scene, but I don't know anyone today without one."

"I'm waiting to get clearance, but I imagine once the family knows, the process will speed up. Leo also knows to ask if they have her cell as well."

"Got it. Dunn, join Leo. The two of you need to tag team interviewing the family, coworkers, friends, anyone at all who had a connection to Amelia. Specifically ask questions regarding her dating history. If she had met with someone the night of the murder, surely someone close to her would have knowledge of where she was going, or something to give us a clue of where to look next," Willow adds.

"What will you be doing?" Milo questions, his tone borderline accusatory.

"I'm focusing on the casino, we still have the first murder to also deal with, don't forget. Will that be a problem?" she challenges him. The tension in the air makes Jasmine shift; she clasps her hands together and glues her focus to the floor.

"No problem, it just seems like we are doing a lot of grunt work and you're just getting to enjoy yourself at a casino. Or with that new mortician," Milo bites back.

Willow's jaw clenches. "I don't enjoy any part of any murder that has happened in our city, nor do I enjoy those committing murder running around free without punishment. As far as the mortician goes, he's a colleague who helps us, so you'd be wise not to piss him off. Or your *Detective Sergeant*. Got it?" Her words seethe as she holds back the volume she wishes to shout into Milo's face.

Throwing out her title is something she always hated, but she doesn't have the time for dysfunction in the ranks. Why can't they trust that she's doing everything in her power to lead them and protect them? It's not like they're bored. She's at least giving them something to do within the case.

"Understood." Milo's lips tighten as he wheels around and walks out the door, not sparing either of them another glance, cursing under his breath.

Jasmine bites her bottom lip. An audible exhale pushes through Willow's clenched teeth, "It's going to be a long day."

*

The back of Willow's chair presses as far back as it can recline. Words bleed together, her eyes bleary from staring at case files and the computer screen for hours. The late hour and the cold glow of the desk lamp makes her feel even more drained. She rubs her temples, trying to press the headache away. Every light is off, except hers that remains flickering. The bulb glows hot, begging to be turned off. As her time in law enforcement has dragged on, her colleagues have learned to not argue with her and let her work until she can't anymore. It's been a while since she's stayed a prolonged period in the office anyway. "Ten at night?" Willow mutters to herself after checking the clock.

She should head back to Warren's for a break, but there's so much to catch up on. A quick workout will help clear her mind, and if not, it'll at least tire her muscles enough to ease her closer to rest. She grabs the extra gym bag she keeps under her desk and flips the light off before exiting the station. The cool night air hits her cheeks as she walks to the gym. The city street is quiet and the occasional street light flickers as tiny insects wander aimlessly, waiting for the next flash.

Arriving at the gym, she pushes open the doors to be greeted by the low hum of the fluorescent lights and the soft thump of bass from the music playing over the speakers. Only a few dedicated late-night patrons scatter across different machines and weights. As fast as her groaning muscles can, Willow changes into her workout clothes, a simple gray crop top and leggings, tossing the remainder of her things into her locker.

Why did she think twenty minutes of HIIT cardio would be a good idea? Sweat trickles down her brow, dripping off the tip of her nose. The hatred Willow has for cardio matches that of her disposition toward clowns. And she *loathes* clowns. Unfortunately, it's necessary for members of law enforcement to continue to train. At any time, one of them may have to travel on foot pursuit, and no one wants to be the officer out of shape letting the suspect run free. After her sprint, she pauses, allowing herself a rest break. Next, some weights.

The closer she approaches the free weights; Willow catches a glimpse of a familiar silhouette. Gideon leans into a sitting position on a bench nearby. Fitted workout gear clings to him, tracing each powerful muscle underneath. His blonde hair glows more icy than normal under the fluorescent light. A sly grin spreads across his face as their eyes meet.

"Well, isn't it my lucky day? I didn't expect to see you here at this hour." His voice lures her to come closer.

Willow offers him a tired smile, hovering at a nearby weight rack. "Needed a break from work to clear my mind. What're you doing here so late? Are you working?"

"I worked my shift earlier this morning. Now I'm just getting in a late-night workout," he says with a casual shrug. "Though, if you need a personal trainer, I don't mind clocking back in for you." He grins and the attention makes her cheeks flush. The conversation feels like she's charging her battery, gaining more energy by the second.

She pauses for a second. "Well, I could use a spotter. Would you mind?"

His head tilts curiously at her. "I'd love nothing more. Show me what you've got." He moves out of the way as Willow scoots by him. As she passes, the scent of scorched bark and cherries envelopes her.

"You smell amazing," she says without thinking. The edge of her canine teeth clamps down on her tongue, mentally scolding herself. "Sorry, that's inappropriate, I'm not sure why I said that out loud."

A dark smirk curls the edge of his lips. "I'm glad you think so, and here I was thinking I would just smell like sweaty socks," he jokes as he presses in behind her as she gets in front of the squat bar. He extends his forearms under her armpits, nodding to give the go ahead when she's ready to begin her squats.

Willow sucks in a breath and forces it out, trying to steady herself. It's been a while since she lifted, and Gideon's presence makes her heart beat faster than normal. She plants her legs shoulder-width apart, feet firmly grounded as she prepares for the lift, watching herself in the mirror in front of the rack. She lowers herself into the squat, her muscles tense and strain as the barbell rests pressing down on her shoulders. With ease, Willow stands. She lowers herself again for another repetition.

Gideon's gaze is unwavering, his focus on her from behind. "Nice and easy," he encourages.

Willow grits through her teeth as she pushes up from the squat. She can feel his breath on the back of her neck, sending a shiver down her spine, causing her to falter in her strength back up. As Gideon sees the struggle, he places his arms under hers, his chest cradles her back as he gives her assistance to rerack the weight.

His grin is both approving and teasing, a subtle lift of his lips as he says, "I'm very impressed, you're much stronger than you look."

Willow's cheeks flush from the exertion and his comment. "Thanks for the help, I'm a little out of shape strength wise."

"Time for cardio now?"

"I actually started with cardio, so that's probably all I've got left." She glances around at the other weights to determine her next lift.

"Such a shame," he murmurs. "I'd love to help you with cardio sometime. I have a few–interesting techniques I think you'd enjoy." *Oh, there's no doubt about that.* As she turns, she meets his stare–inches from her. Her stomach flips. "But not without dinner first, of course. My treat?" He runs his fingers through the sweat covered, blonde waves. He drinks in the shape of her, slow and deliberate, as her skin flushes with heat.

"I think," she hesitates, "I'd like that. You're nothing but persistent, aren't you?" she teases to distract from her heart palpitations.

"Any man would be a fool to not be interested in you, Willow. Shall I pick you up tomorrow night?"

"I–I'm actually staying with a friend right now while my home gets treated for termites. I will probably just leave from work though, so how about picking me up from the station?" The inner voice screaming from her mind tells her to reject him, don't get close. But admiring Gideon at this moment, she can't seem to pull away. It's a taste of normalcy outside of murder and the supernatural–and she's craving it. *Him.*

"I'll pick you up from the station at seven." His hand extends, brushing her hair behind her ear, trailing his fingers down her cheek and neck. "I can't wait. Be safe tonight." He leaves her with a short kiss on the cheek, burning with heat.

"See you then." She blurts before turning to leave with hurried strides, not daring to twist back around for a second glance.

The cold air pulls her back into alertness. Her fingers interlock, resting on top of her head as she walks toward the direction of the station to pick up her car. Butterflies flutter at her core. Racing thoughts slow as her empty hands remind her of the gym bag she left in the locker room. The next time she visits she'll have to get her belongings.

"I need a cold shower," she mutters to the silent trees, kicking snapped sticks off the ground.

*

Aged paper and leather fills her senses as she steps into Warren's library. The whisper of turning pages and Warren's muted murmur drift from the far corner, barely there. The room is in disarray. Literature lays open on the floor and tables, blank pages are scattered and covered with scribbles and symbols unknown to her. Warren hunches over a stack of books on the floor, his brow furrowed in concentration as he scrawls notes down.

"You've been busy." She sweeps over the chaotic scene.

He doesn't look up. "You could say that. I've been trying to piece together information on this necklace and reading through your brother's things. I had to meet with some others to get their opinions on some symbols, but I think I'm getting closer."

"I thought we weren't supposed to bring others into this?" she asks with her arms crossed. *He was pissed when she brought Nadia into the second crime scene.*

"I didn't give any details on anything. Unlike your human friend, witches and ghouls don't ask too many questions. Therefore, it's a gain on our end."

"You know witches and ghouls? They're here in town?" Willow's eyebrows raise.

"There's more than just witches and ghouls. But that's a worry for another day. Come here." He holds out his hand; her silver chained necklace dangles in between his fingers, glinting in the dim light.

"That's just what I need. A worry for another day." She takes the necklace, recoiling as her fingers brush against his.

"From here on out, wear this at all times." A firm edge delivers his words, yet there's a hint of something almost gentle in his eyes.

"Why? What's so special about it now? It won't kill me?" she asks as she slips the necklace back around her neck, not questioning it. Honestly, going this long without it has felt wrong. It has become a part of her.

He leans back, stretching his arms as he rises to meet her. "This is more than just some pretty accessory and fond memory. It has wards placed on it, meant to protect you from certain types of magic just as we thought.

However, I have yet to discover its limits of protection, and against what entity. It doesn't protect you from vampires, at least."

"How do you know that for sure?"

Time stands still. One moment she's standing, the next she's face down, bent over the arm of Warren's couch. Both of her wrists are held together by Warren who only uses one arm, chuckling. She shifts to struggle against him to free herself, but her movement is pointless. Like trying to wrestle against a brick wall.

"Point made, now get off me," she says through a clenched jaw.

He releases her arms, allowing her to lean upright once more. "Like I said, no protection from vampires. But it will do you well to always keep it on."

She scoffs, "This was the first time I've taken it off since Kai gave it to me. No problems there. What do you think it does?" She studies it, trying to find the carvings etched into it. It's no use, the only thing she can see is the polished silver.

"I'm making an educated guess here, but my hypothesis is that it can warn you of danger. My second theory is that it can prevent compulsion."

"Is that what you used on my mother?" There's no hostility in the words. It's a genuine question. There's no way she would have allowed them inside—unless it was beyond her control.

"Yes. I don't use it often, and before you ask, I have not used it on you. And I don't plan on it." Something fragile passes over him and he avoids her entirely. A tangible weight hangs in the room. For some reason, that thought never crossed her mind.

Interesting reaction. "Did you understand or find anything in the book left in his chest?" She changes the subject.

"I'm having to decipher most of it. It appears he created his own code to write things down and keep it safe. I did learn one word, but it doesn't look great for us."

"And what would that be?"

"Demons." A frown tugs at his lip from the neutral expression he has been trying to hold.

Willow nods and begins to pace in the circle. "Demons. Got it. Okay, great," her words run together. "Do you think it's too late for me to get baptized?"

Warren's eyebrows raise. "I know that's a joke, but probably not a bad idea for you to consider."

She tilts her head, surprised at his response. "Are you religious?"

"That's a complicated question," he states.

"Well, I'd be interested to hear a complicated answer," she retorts, wanting to pry somewhat into his personal life.

"I believe I am, or rather that I have to be. My existence calls to question everything we know about life and death. I was cursed with this," he gestures to himself and then he flashes his fangs, "and among my hundreds of years of life I have met and heard of countless other creatures that should be impossible."

"So, why do you feel like you have to be?" she asks, confused on what point he was trying to make.

"My whole existence is against God. I have met demons. Demons exist. If demons exist, wouldn't God? It is something I have gone over again and again, and I'm not sure I'll ever know. But it's something I know that I must believe in. And if God does all things good, then whatever has cursed me to live this life is not of God and I have no choice but to obliterate it from the surface of the Earth." His demeanor shifts—hardened, dark, and unreadable.

"Is that what your goal is? To kill what turned you into a vampire?" The thought had crossed her mind before, but it never felt like the right time to ask.

"Amongst other things." He straightens his shoulders and shifts his jaw from side to side, unclenching it. "Speaking of our goal, we need to start training. You're nowhere near ready for any type of combat."

"Excuse you, I'm in great shape!" she scoffs.

"I didn't say you weren't in excellent shape. I said you aren't ready for combat. You can take down an aggressive drunk off the street, not a vampire. And *especially* not a demon, if that is in fact, what we are dealing with." He crosses his arms waiting for her retort.

"Fine," she bit back, "when do we start?"

"Now."

CHAPTER 26

MUST BE FATE

Darkness welcomes Willow and Warren into the weight room. Bleach and rubber reeks throughout the basement and Willow's nose scrunches. *Has he been cleaning down here?*

A lone bookshelf presses against the wall, filled with books and vintage statement pieces. An old typewriter catches her eye. It's odd to have a bookshelf located in a weight room. Her head tilts, inspecting it. Warren's hand touches the book spines, landing on *Interview with the Vampire*. He removes the novel, but it stops halfway—a loud click echoes. *How fitting.* Creaking, the shelf pops open, revealing a hidden passage. He gestures for her to enter.

With hesitant steps, she crosses the threshold. Faint light gleams within the darkness, allowing her to make out slight details of the room. The padded black floors continue in. Dark ebony shelves packed with books and trinkets line the walls. A stainless-steel deep freezer stands alone in a corner.

"What is this?"

As Willow finishes her question, from the shadows a figure steps into the pale beam. Sage green portals glow from the darkness, burrowing into Willow. Her steps falter, and she stumbles backward.

"Detective, this is Verena," he gestures between them, "she will be training you in hand to hand combat."

Willow's eyebrows quirk, her gaze doesn't leave the tall, muscular woman before her. "I thought you would be the one training me?"

"I'll test you to see if Verena has effectively trained you. I have other matters to tend to. You will be spending a few hours training every day for the indefinite future."

Verena studies Willow up and down. Willow slouches, feeling trapped under her scrutiny.

"It'll be a pleasure training you, Willow." A sweetly sinister leer pulls at the corners of her mouth, fangs extended, making Willow shiver. Her threateningly sharp jawline is accentuated by her short, sleek, dark brunette bob that lays just above her shoulders. If you combined every attractive female assassin into one person, it would be a spitting image of Verena.

"Will she kill me?" Willow whispers to Warren.

"Tempting, but no. War here made me make a pact that you will remain alive and with minimal injury." Disappointment rings through Verena's retort.

War? Is that a nickname? "Minimal injury. *Lovely.*"

"Verena will be on her *best* behavior," his neutral tone belies the danger simmering beneath, "I assure you." His eyes narrow on Verena as she flaunts a flirtatious smirk. Willow stiffens and turns, unable to meet either of their eye contact.

"I'm always on my best behavior. You know that." Verena moves closer towards Warren. *They seem awfully close.*

He side steps her, circling back to Willow. "Training starts now. Remember this is life or death when the time comes, so give it your all. Show her what you've got."

"I never give anything less than all my effort," Willow says, annoyed at the suggestion. "Maybe leave one of your snakes here to keep an eye out?" she whispers.

Verena giggles, stretching her arms overhead.

"Every inch of this home is always under my watch. Just focus on your training," he adds as he walks back toward the bookshelf entrance to leave.

Every inch? "Wait, you can see everything in the house all the time? Not when I shower, right?"

He peeks from the door frame with only his head visible, a smirk dancing on his face. "That's a conversation for another day. Enjoy." He winks as he leaves, turning on the overhead light as a final gesture.

A cool rush of wind blows Willow's hair back before she can turn around. The shot of air sucks every ounce of moisture from her corneas, forcing her eyelids to beat fast. Her eyesight returns, meeting Verena inches away from her face. Willow flinches, her heart stuttering from the shock.

"Jesus!" Willow exclaims.

"Let's begin. To start, your reflexes are incredibly, and humanly, slow," Verena states, crossing her arms and waiting for Willow.

"Probably because I am one!" Willow snaps.

Verena's condescending words send Willow's blood pressure soaring. The two of them shuffle to the center of the room, away from the larger objects lining the walls. With the lights on, she notices training dummies scattered in various spots on the padded floor. Mysterious hues of fuchsia and blues shimmer on the shelves, the liquid dancing in the glass bottles it sits in. On the opposite wall next to the deep freezer, rows of weapons form a threatening barrier. Any weapon Willow could name is on the wall. Guns, mallets, knives, axes, bows and arrows–the works. It's like his own mini armory.

"First things first, you need to learn the basics. Supernatural creatures are completely different from humans. You'll need to be fast, but for what you'll lack in speed you will have to make up for in intelligence and adaptability." Verena's irises glimmer like the edge of a blade, sharp and deadly. Though a beautiful shade of green, there's a dullness to them. The countenance of someone who's witnessed a lot of death. Very similar to Warren's, and the one Willow sees in the mirror every morning.

Verena demonstrates a few basic stances and techniques; her movements are precise and powerful as she demonstrates on the dummy. "This is a basic defensive stance. Your feet should be shoulder-width apart, knees slightly bent so you don't pass out. Balance is important." Willow mimics her stance, trying to match Verena's form. "Okay, now show me what you've got," Verena adds, readying herself for Willow to attack her.

"I taught self-defense in the academy. I don't see how this is any different." Willow takes a readying breath before shifting her weight from left to right, hoping to keep Verena guessing on which way she would come before putting all the strength she can muster into her punch. Just as her fist is about to connect with Verena's jaw, a flash of darkness blurs–then a sharp pressure builds in her lower back. A shriek leaves Willow's mouth.

"Not bad. If you are trying to die immediately," Verena whispers in her ear from behind, moving her sharp fingernails from Willow's back.

The balls of Willow's feet stay moving, keeping a small circle while she scans the room for the female vampire. Soft footsteps tap against the floor, but Willow cannot physically see her. It isn't until a heavy hand cracks against her neck that she discovers Verena. At this moment, it's too late. The pain radiates through her spine, causing Willow's limbs to draw up and slam against the floor. First, spots sprinkle through her vision. Then as fast as Verena, it tunnels–blackening completely as Willow loses consciousness.

All the breath from Willow's lungs is sucked out as frigid water pours over her limp body, the temperature so low it feels scalding against her skin. She gasps, searching for air.

"Get up," Verena commands. Each leg straddles over Willow's torso as she sneers.

"In combat, you need to think about your opponent's weaknesses. Each entity, creature, and person can have different vulnerabilities–some may be strong but slow, others fast but not durable. Vampires for example, a stake to the heart will kill us. But it specifically has to be ash wood."

The fog in her vision clears, bringing everything into sudden, vivid view. Willow doubles over, hands on her knees, drenched in freezing water. In between breaths she rasps, "A stake? I thought Warren couldn't die. Also good to know– in case I need to kill you."

Verena's brow furrows with a lift of amusement. "As if you could get close enough to me to stake me." She pauses, hands on her hips. "Warren's a different story. Now, get in a defensive stance. You aren't done with me yet."

"What happened to him? He's a vampire, right? What makes him so different from you?" Willow presses. Seizing the only opportunity she may have, since Warren won't divulge any information himself. *Though, he may be listening in on their conversation.* Her legs wobble as she stands.

Verena's mouth twitches as she draws her fists back in a fighting stance. "It's not surprising he hasn't told you. He doesn't talk about it much. Hell, I barely know the details." She shifts her weight to her left foot, pressing forward and extending her right leg right into Willow's exposed abdomen. Willow's too slow to block, as the kick sends her sliding to the edge of the room. The friction between her shoes and floor vibrates her entire body and a groan echoes through the room. Admitting defeat isn't in Willow's vocabulary. She hobbles back to face Verena, who smirks.

"Warren wasn't turned into a vampire like most are–which is by being bitten and ingesting vampire blood, or by being born of two vampires. From what I know, he received a curse. He somehow pissed off the wrong old hag, and she cursed him. To live forever as the undead, craving blood, and to watch everyone he's ever loved die."

For a reason unknown to Willow, her heart aches. Verena doesn't give

Willow the chance to process this new information, slapping her with an open hand across the face. Lava churns in Willow's veins.

"Pay attention," she hisses, circling Willow.

The hours that pass feel like both minutes and days at the same time. Willow's senses are shocked after receiving one stunning blow after another. Perhaps it wasn't the best idea to train with a vampire right after working out at the gym. The image of Gideon's smirk fades in and out of her mind.

Verena's movements are slowing, though probably not due to fatigue. *Is it possible she feels sorry for her?* The thought infuriates Willow, yet the agony building in her muscles pleas for her not to complain. Verena stops using her vampiric speed to bolt around the room, but instead stays close—wailing her left fist, right fist, and then a heavy kick to Willow's obliques. The kick sends Willow five feet backward, but she remains standing. Barely.

"Are you *trying* to kill me?" Willow groans, attempting to contain the bile rising into her esophagus.

Verena's stare could cut glass and she closes the gap between them, pressing in further. "You need to trust me. It's for your own good." Her knuckles connect with the right side of Willow's jaw. A deafening crack rings in Willow's ear.

Willow spits on the floor, blood and saliva weave together. The next punch Verena sends isn't as fast, allowing Willow to dodge it. "I don't trust you! I don't know you! I barely trust Warren." She backs away, her chest heaving. The right side of her jaw swells; the muscles throb but grow progressively number.

"You should trust him." The fingernails on Verena's digits extend into sharp claws. Almost as though it senses the rage within Verena, a western rattlesnake slithers out from behind an axe mounted to the wall. Its tail rattles in the air, warning her. Verena sneers at it.

"What about demons? What's their vulnerability?" she asks in between dodging Verena's fist, changing the subject.

"It depends on the demon. I know for some low-level demons, holy water can hurt, but not kill them." Verena flashes a step away, watching Willow. "You're picking this up decently enough. You're slow, but not bad for a human." She smirks, tucking a strand of hair behind her pointed ears.

A headache builds, pressure pressing against the walls of Willow's skull. "Thanks, I guess."

Warren interrupts by stepping into the doorway, heavy claps echoing in the training space. "That's enough for today. Verena and I will discuss your progress." Willow doesn't need to be told twice.

"Yes, *Masters*," she huffs through staggered breaths. Her fingers find an imaginary skirt, dipping into a curtsey while tossing her vision as far back into her skull as possible. There's an awkward air of waiting. Willow can take a hint, she's no longer welcome. A hot shower calls her name anyway.

The two vampires don't wait long after Willow's exit to address her performance.

"She's got potential." Verena whispers under a hushed breath. "But she'll need to be pushed harder if she wants any chance of survival against whatever you have going on, if it's as big as you believe it is. You really think she's of any use?"

"I have no doubt she will rise to the challenge," he boasts.

It isn't her intention to eavesdrop, but she isn't going to pretend she didn't hear this snippet of conversation. An exhausted smile slips onto her lips hearing his praise. The rattlesnake from earlier slithers beside her, peering up at her—as though checking to ensure she heard.

*

Willow's knees shake as she enters the station. Despite her efforts of slathering concealer on, the discoloration penetrates through. It's unknown if they're dark circles, or a shiner from her training—but either way she's running out of energy to care. Officers move about, a low hum of activity present in the building. It's surprising, given how most of the day shift should have already left by now.

Even Sunny is gone for the day, Willow notes, walking past the empty desk. Not even one of her teammates are in sight. A sigh of relief flows through her mouth, grateful to sit at her desk for a moment of peace while she waits on Gideon to pick her up.

She eases herself onto the chair, sweeping her maroon silk dress to the side, allowing her leg to go between the slit at the bottom to sit more comfortably. She doesn't dress in formal wear often, and on the occasions she does, she remembers why. The dress constricts to her muscles, displaying more of her curves, it's suffocating and unnatural; her hands shift over her arms, a nervous habit returning. It took hours of convincing herself to go. Several internal conversations and arguments with herself almost drove her to cancel. But the thought of taking a couple hours away to eat some delicious food and stare at a handsome trainer won her over. *Just free food,* she convinces herself.

"Woah." Milo stops in his tracks.

She chews at the inside of her jaw and crosses her arms. "What?" *The attention makes her want to crawl under a rock.*

"You look–nice." Milo's gentle cadence falters. He's scared to compliment her now? He flirts with her all the time.

Her eyebrows scrunch close together. "Thank you?"

A dry scrape rasps in his throat, coarse like sandpaper. It's painfully obvious he's struggling to keep his eyes above her neck. "Glad you're here, did you listen to the recorded conversation that Bennett and I had with Amelia's roommate?"

Her posture straightens. "No, I wasn't aware you sent that. When? What happened?"

The corner of Milo's mouth pulls downward. "Over a day ago. I hadn't heard from you and tried calling but you didn't answer. It's all in the drive for you to access. The roommate ended up telling us that Amelia had been dumped by her longtime boyfriend recently and started seeing men off of dating apps. Jasmine's working on getting the data from the apps of hers, but we still haven't located Amelia's phone. Bennett's working on tracking down the ex-boyfriend for questioning and getting a statement."

Willow nods as she listens. "Great. Good call." From the corner of her eye she catches a glimpse of Gideon getting out of his car. Willow jumps up and straightens her dress. "Let me know what you find out," she says to Milo as she gathers her bag and starts toward the front exit.

"Are you not helping with the investigation today?"

Willow turns back to Milo, who is regathering he gaze away from her exposed legs. Her mouth tightens in a hard line. "I stayed up late last night reviewing the autopsies and crime scene photos, so I will work again later tonight. Call me again if anything comes up or you need me, I'll make sure my phone is charged, and the ringer's on." Her hand lifts in a clumsy gesture to Milo.

Disappointment sets across Milo's face as Gideon approaches the doors.

Willow can't help but beam a smile as Gideon opens the door for her. There's something different about him this evening. Is he taller? His brown dress shoes clack against the floor. He straightens the maroon tie around his neck. The corners of his mouth quirk up, raking over every part of her.

"Unintentional matching? Must be fate," he chuckles. "Shall we?" He extends his arm for her to take.

She nods, taking his arm in her hand.

CHAPTER 27

RAINCHECK

Classical Italian music settles in the background. There's a rustic charm about the place with its wooden tables, soft candlelight, and a gentle aroma of garlic and fresh baked bread wafting through the air. It's the first time in a while that Willow has been out of Misty Pines, *let alone a date*. The hostess guides the two of them to a secluded table at the back of the house by a window, which offers a view of the quaint street outside. Gideon pulls out Willow's chair with a charming smile as she sits.

"You are stunning as ever, Willow. I must say, this place is lucky to see such a beautiful guest." The frozen glaciers in his irises invite her in, captivating her attention.

She finds it easy to get lost in them. The black fitted suit and maroon patterned tie against his pale skin and blonde hair accentuates his features. Compared to his typical gym attire, this ensemble almost makes her want to swoon. *Almost. Stay focused, there's plenty more work that needs to be done.*

"Thank you. I suppose you have a talent for picking out restaurants. It smells delicious in here." She pulls the top of her dress up her chest further. *Is she being awkward?* She pushes her shoulders back, realizing her posture was that of a shrimp.

"I'd like to think I have good taste in many things." He leans forward, his gaze fixed on Willow with curiosity. "Tell me more about yourself. What do you do for fun when you're not fighting crime?"

Willow takes a sip of the water on the table, glancing over the menu. It's limited in size, and each item costs over thirty dollars per person. She winces at the price. "Unfortunately, most of my time is taken up by work.

But I do enjoy reading when I can and going to the gym for a stress reliever." As they chat, a young waitress approaches their table. Her ringlet auburn curls are pushed back with a cloth headband. On her white blouse, the name tag reads 'Ella'.

"Good afternoon. My name's Ella and I'll be your server this evening. Can I start you two off with something to drink?" Ella welcomes, her rosy cheeks lifting.

"We will have a glass of your best red wine," Gideon answers for both of them, catching Willow off guard.

A spark of recognition lights Ella's features. "Wait, you're a personal trainer, right? I went to your yoga class a couple weeks ago! You helped me with my flexibility."

"Oh, yes! It's good to see you again, Ella. Will you return for another class soon?" he asks her.

Willow leans back in her chair and observes the two of them.

"Of course! I didn't expect to see you out here. I figured you'd be too busy with all your classes to leave town! I still can't believe you teach in Misty Pines. I've been following you on social media for forever!" Ella gushes.

"Well, I like to mix things up. My brothers and I are trying to get out and travel more, once they all are in town to visit, that is. Besides, it's always nice to support local small businesses and see familiar faces. I wanted to explore a little bit with my lovely date."

A blush dusts across Ella's face, attempting to hide her excitement. "It's great to see you. I'll get that wine for you both and then I can take your order when you're ready." She rushes off toward the kitchen, as she walks away, she glances back at Gideon.

Willow's eyebrows raise. "You sure are a local celebrity, huh?"

"Is that jealousy I detect?" His eyebrows wiggle.

Her head tilts to one side and nostrils flare with a twitch. "I don't get jealous. There're too many other things for me to be preoccupied with. Plus, you're here on a date with me, *not Ella*." Willow crosses one leg over the other, showcasing her muscular legs through the slit of her dress. He was much more charming the other night.

"I don't like to brag, but I have a pretty large following on social media. I'm able to train people online and some of my videos have done really well. So, I guess you could call me a local celebrity." He grins. "If it makes you feel any better, I don't recognize her at all."

Willow didn't know about that side of him. That's the point of dates, she guesses. Insecurity bubbles within her. There's no way she's the only one he's showing interest in. Not with the level of attention an influencer gets. The number of women flocking to him in his classes? *Wait, why is this upsetting to her?*

Gideon reaches across the table, tilting her chin to look at him–as though he senses her thoughts. "You're the only one I want to be with this evening, Willow."

She clears her throat. "Well–you're in luck then. Just for tonight."

"We will see about that," he teases.

*

The sunset tries to peek through the gray clouds, the dark sky fading into a sepia tone. A warm glow from the streetlights blends in with the sky. Gideon holds the wooden door open as Willow exits. The evening drapes itself in a peaceful calm, with a gentle hum of conversation and distant laughter spilling from the restaurant. Their fingers lightly brush against each other every other step they take back towards his car.

"Did I manage to make the night memorable?" he asks.

"The pasta carbonara was impeccable. You definitely made it *interesting*," she responds, remaining neutral. She did enjoy the night. Gideon's presence is warm, and every word that comes out of his mouth burns with passion.

"Interesting? That's not exactly a glowing review." He fakes offense.

"It's a start. I'll need a bit more to go on before fully deciding," she teases, leaning against his closed passenger side door.

The look he gives her tells Willow everything she already was thinking. He knows what he's doing. His presence presses in, confident and calm. "As you know, I'm a man of persistence. I can handle a challenge."

Her heart races. He searches her face, as though trying to read her mind. His eyes trail lower to her chest, then back up.

"Are you enjoying the view?" She decides to call him out, a smirk plays on her lips.

"What do you think?" he whispers, tucking a strand of her hair behind her ear and leaning closer. The only thing she can focus on is the fullness of his lips, parting.

Gideon gently places his hand on her cheek and leans in; crashing together in a tender kiss. Willow's eyebrows raise as she leans into him, furthering the kiss. He pushes back and her exposed back arches against the cold exterior of the car. A shiver runs down her spine. His mouth consumes her, wanting more— claiming her. She grabs a hold of his tie, loosening it in the process. He grins against her mouth in response. Her necklace sits on her hot skin, yearning for more of his touch. The sides of her dress hike up, resting on her hips where Gideon's hands trail, until finding rest on her ass. She doesn't object.

"Is that Willow?" Hearing her name causes her to pull away, heavily out of breath. Her fingers grasp the bunched material at her hips, pulling her dress down back to a respectable length. Gideon's gaze remains on her, a sultry smirk playing at his now tender lips. In the distance, Nadia waves in sharp, hurried sweeps. Behind her, Aldaric follows, simply happy to be there. *Nadia?*

"I'd love to continue this," Gideon whispers in her ear before pulling away to readjust his tie and belt. His breath caresses her skin and Willow's cheeks flush; a tight-lipped gesture is all she can muster for a response.

"I would have never thought I would run into you outside of town!" Nadia suffocates Willow in a big bear hug, swaying her from side to side. "Oh!" she exclaims, ogling at the man beside her. "Willow, you remember Aldaric!"

Aldaric glances at Gideon before stepping forward to shake Willow's hand. "Good to see you again, Willow." His stance rigid as he checks his watch.

"Sorry, this is Gideon, my–" Willow trails off as she gestures to Gideon who tilts his head with a devious smirk, before extending a hand to Aldaric.

"Her date for the evening," he finishes her sentence. "It's a pleasure to meet you."

"Likewise," Aldaric gives him a quick handshake, "Nadia, we best get going. I made reservations for a special table and menu at this place. We shouldn't be late. We will have to plan a trip in the near future." Aldaric waves as he pulls the sleeve of Nadia's jacket to grasp for her hand.

"We should! You both enjoy the rest of your evening," Nadia winks at Willow, and mouths, *"I'll call you later."*

Willow flashes them a grin, waving as the two of them enter the restaurant she and Gideon just left. An uncomfortable tension lingers as the two of them are alone again.

"Care for a second drink? Maybe at my place?" His lilt is honey. But right now, she isn't in the mood for sweets.

"Actually, could I take a raincheck on that? I left the station in a hurry and need to check on some things before I finish for the night–I'm sorry." She bites her lip.

Gideon's playful smirk falters. "Of course. Married to the job, I know. I eagerly await for your raincheck."

"Definitely."

CHAPTER 28

MONSTER

She lied. She isn't going to finish anything up at the office. Everything she can do can be done from her room. There's a small twist in her stomach at the thought. *Is that guilt? Is it from leaving things abruptly? Or for kissing Gideon in general?* Her stomach is tied in knots as she drags her feet up the brick stairs of Warren's home. The glow of the full moon breaks through the clouds, beams of moonlight shining a path to the home.

Classical music echoes through the halls, greeting her with its sweet melody. Her shoulders shrink. She had been hoping he wouldn't be in the house by the time she returned this evening. In her hand she carries her heels, unable to walk in them any further.

The sound of the sweeping symphony leads her to the library, where she discovers Warren leaning back with a wine glass in one hand, and a leather-bound book in the other, as he reads. His fingers grip the glass tightly. The room bathes in the warm glow of a few strategically placed lamps and candles, casting long shadows that dance along the walls. The moonlight streams through the glass windows.

Warren glances up from the journal, and his eyes narrow on her, his tension apparent. "You're back later than expected." His composure is fractured, the air surrounding him strained. The glint in his eye holds an intense, feral light to it. His movements are sharp and impatient, turning his head in her direction and tapping his foot against the floor in a fast tempo.

Something isn't right. She tries to remain cool, her breathing slowing. "Yeah, I just had to catch up on some things. You look like you're in the middle of something, I didn't mean to interrupt. I just kinda followed the music to see–" She trails off and begins to back away. "I'll just be going."

"I'm always in the middle of something. I am particularly more on edge tonight, however," he says through a strained confession, before taking another swig from his glass.

"Are you–alright?" She hesitates.

His focus flickers to the window, then back to her with stiff shoulders. "It's a full moon. This time of the lunar cycle tends to make things–more vivid."

She moves closer, looking to the moon. The moonlight casts a silvery glow on her maroon dress. A reflection of herself mirrors off the glass window of the library, moonlight illuminating her profile, making her appear almost ethereal. Warren follows her movement.

"What's the occasion?" his words are bitter, staring at the slit in her dress.

Her pulse quickens; uncertainty fills the air. It's suffocating. She takes a pause to respond. "I had a dinner date. Nothing crazy." *Keep cool.*

Warren's gaze hardens, his fingers tighten around the glass. "Nice, was it?" In a flash he's inches away from her, startling her as she staggers back. "Did he enjoy the evening as much as you did?" he asks, dragging his thumb against the side of her mouth. When he removes it, she can see lipstick remaining.

She drags her fingers across her mouth, hoping to erase the makeup left behind. She didn't wear makeup often; she thought the lipstick would have stayed in place better.

"It was just a date?" she says almost like a question, her fear making her second guess everything she wants to say.

"Just a date?" he asks. He leans forward; his gaze never wavers, but presses further in. The moonlight catches the sharp angles of his features, highlighting the tension in his expression.

"That's what I said, wasn't it? What's gotten into you?" she asks, the muscles in her shoulders tightening.

His eye twitches at her question. White hot knuckles bring the glass to his lips, chugging the remaining blood in the cup. Warren's tongue licks the drops that linger on the corner of his mouth.

"You need to go to your room," he commands.

A haze of confusion settles over her. "What–" she begins before he cuts her off as he appears behind her in an instant, his arm wrapping around her and his hand covering her mouth to keep her from talking. The heels from her hold thump against the floor as she releases them.

He whispers in her ear from behind, his breath tickling her neck, "I am seconds away from ripping your delicious throat out–or stripping you naked. Do as I say and go to your room, Detective. *Please.*" He rasps, as though he's fighting every instinct in his body.

Goosebumps litter over every inch of her skin.

"If you don't, I'll show you just what kind of monster I am," his breath comes in hard pulls.

She nods as he lets her go, nudging her forward. She picks up the pace and bolts to her room; her breathing shakes. In the distance, glass shatters and a guttural yell blares from Warren. The frenzy lasts for hours until the noise dies down. Willow falls asleep with a chair propped up under the door and her gun underneath her pillow.

*

When she wakes, Warren's nowhere to be found. Several statues and glass vases in the library are shattered. *How can she return to his home? Would he kill her for refusing to return?*

Fatigue clings to her like a second skin, damp and inescapable. Java sloshes over the rim of the mug she clutches. With a white-knuckled grip, she weaves through the office desks to make it back to hers.

Awareness tightens across her shoulders, noticing her colleagues glancing at her with uneasy expressions. Their whispers fade as she approaches. *What's their problem?* Her lips tighten as she pushes forward and sets up at her desk for the day. Just as she's about to open her laptop, Chief Hastings steps out of his door, his expression hardened. He beckons Willow over with a curt nod.

"A moment of your time, please," he says to Willow.

She nods, her heart sinking as she follows him. The blinds are drawn in his office, and the harsh fluorescent light fills the room. The Chief gestures for her to sit.

"What's this about, sir?" She takes a seat. A cold sweat forms along her brow. *It can't be good.*

The Chief sighs, "Willow, I've been meaning to talk to you about your recent performance and frankly, just your overall well-being."

"My performance? The team's doing great. I thought–"

"Have you even listened to the interviews from Dunn and Bennett from the other day?"

Willow is radio silent. She completely forgot. How could she have forgotten? *Oh, Warren almost ripped her throat out.*

"Your team has had minimal guidance from you. You've been coming in late, or not in the office at all. Which is fine, if you're out investigating but you've had Dunn and Bennett doing that part. Your focus seems off. This isn't just about the case; I'm worried about you. You aren't taking care of yourself." The corner of the Chief's lips pulls downward.

She shifts in her seat, swallowing a lump beginning to form in her throat. "I'm—just tired. There's a lot on my plate right now, but I need to solve this case. And I will," she says with determination.

"I understand, Willow. You know that I do. But you need to also take care of yourself. And that's why," he hesitates, "I'm putting you on paid leave for the time being. You need to rest, recover, and snap yourself back to where you need to be."

The words don't land right away, they hover. Unreal, as if she had misheard. "Leave? I don't need to leave. I'm fine! I'll start being in the office every day, I'll go to interviews with Milo and Leo. I'm snapped back in right now, sir!" Her tone reaches a higher pitch with each word as panic tries to consume her.

The Chief shakes his head. "It's not a debate. It's a formal decision for your own well-being and the well-being of the team. We'll handle things here. Take this time to sort yourself out."

Willow sits in silence.

"Will I be fired?" she asks in a soft sigh, attempting to hold back the tears that yearn to flow.

"Not at all. You're a valuable asset to this squad. I think these new murders are stirring something in you that you may have forgotten about," he adds, his look softening upon Willow.

A single tear breaks through and rolls down her cheek silently. She nods, rises, and walks out of the office without a word. Chief Hastings lets out a sigh, rubbing the back of his neck.

After every shove of a personal belonging, Willow adds anything she may need from case files into her bag behind it. She avoids eye contact from her colleagues who share whispers.

She glances up, Leo approaches with softness and sadness written across his drooping brow. "You okay?" he asks, maintaining a couple feet in between them and shifting from one side to the other.

Her lips quirk up as fast as they fall. "No. But I'll try to manage," she forces herself to say.

Willow doesn't know why, but her legs move on their own, closing the gap between them, wrapping him into a hug. This catches Leo off guard as he stands there, patting her arms with his.

"If you need me, just call," she whispers in his ear before releasing him from her forced hug. They share a knowing nod before she turns away to walk to the exit.

A deep voice calls her name before she has time to open the exit to the station. "Rhodes! Wait!" Milo slows his jog, stopping a few feet away from her. Willow freezes, her grip tightening on her bag strap as she blinks at him.

"What do you want?" Her nostrils flare.

"I just– wanted to let you know that if you need anything you can talk to me." He searches her face, as if trying to gauge how she had taken the conversation with the Chief.

Frustration coils inside her chest, hot and tight, until it springs free. "Why, out of everyone, would I talk to you, Dunn? I *know* you talked to him."

Milo flinches at her accusation, his tight features falling as he tries to explain. "No, that's not what I meant to do! I just–"

Willow cuts him off, "You just thought I would be better being completely kicked off the case? Away from work? The job I busted my ass to move up and grow in?"

"That's not what I wanted! You haven't been yourself lately." His body shrinks, pleading with desperation.

"You didn't think to bring any of your concerns to me first? These are the biggest cases I will probably ever see in my life."

His shoulders sink. "I–care about you. I knew you wouldn't listen to me. I couldn't watch you crash and burn. Please know that my intentions weren't malicious."

Willow's anger subsides like a wave receding back into the ocean, replaced by hurt and betrayal. "I can't have this conversation right now." She shakes her head. Her phone vibrates in her hand. A text from Warren fills her home screen. *I'll be away during the peak of the full moon. Don't look for me.*

"I'm sorry, Willow," Milo says after a brief, quiet breath.

"Yeah, me too." The doors are heavier than normal. *Maybe they're also saddened by her leave.*

Rain drenches her from head to toe, as if the sky cries for her disappointment. Droplets pelt her skin, masking the tears of frustration that struggle to break free.

The tightness in her face releases with each raindrop. The chill of the rain and wind mix, causing goosebumps to pepper her skin. She steels herself. *She'll be damned if this will stop her from solving the cases.*

CHAPTER 29

HIDDEN IDENTITY

Though her heart races, her body carries the many sleepless nights she's suffered. Typically, the fourth cup of coffee would have energized her more by now, but maybe she's developed a tolerance to such high levels of caffeine. She takes a sip, finding the coffee cold. *What day is it?* The moisture from her eyeballs have been wrung out like a wet towel.

Crime scene photos are scattered around the floor of Warren's guest room. Photos of Kai, Jonathan, and Amelia. Her chest hunches over, a hand covering her mouth as she stares holes into the photographs.

Guilt renders her frozen as the conversation with the Chief replays in her mind. She's been distracted, not giving all her attention to the case. Her attention has been selfish, lacking the devotion to lead her team. The photos in front of her remind her of this. This is much bigger than Kai. *He would be disappointed in her.* Disappointed that she's let the grief consume her as deeply as it has. She bites her bottom lip.

The motives behind each kill are visibly different from the other. Jonathan's life ended with brutality, total violence. The killer's intention of causing pain is evident by the mutilation of the victim after death. The casino's involved somehow. On the other hand, Amelia's killer displays sexually driven motivation. It could have been played off as a freak accident—if they didn't stage her body. *Now that she's off the case, she no longer has access to Jasmine for retrieving Amelia's last known purchase.* She groans. Her fingernails scratch underneath her hairline.

They hadn't discussed the possibility that a demon has been forcing someone else to commit these murders. *Is that plausible? Two different killers under control of a demon and that's why they have different motives? What are demons's motives?* She doesn't know anything about other creatures. *Why does she have to immediately jump to demons?* It could be another vampire. As adamant as she believed it in the beginning, there's no way Warren's the culprit. No matter how much she wishes it was the case. The possibilities are endless at this point.

Jasmine hasn't revoked her access to the work email yet. Willow's anxiety eases as the cursor hovers over the audio recording titled *Roommate Interview - Stephanie Williamson.*

Milo clears his throat, amping up to turn on his charm. "Please state your full name for the recording."

"Stephanie Williamson," a female's lifeless voice echoes.

"We understand this is difficult. Take your time in answering, but we do have some questions for you. Can you please start by telling us your relationship to Amelia Rogers?"

"She is—was my roommate." A sniffle breaks the pause in speaking.

"Is there anyone you can think of that would want to bring harm to Amelia?" Leo asks.

"We know this is hard, but you'll have to vocalize your response please," Milo adds.

"Sorry. No. I don't know anyone who would want to kill her. She was loved by everyone. And the way she was left to be found—"

Stephanie's weeping makes Willow wince from the sheer volume; the sadness is suffocating. The crying stops to cut back into normal conversation. Milo and Leo must have paused the recording to give her some time to compose herself.

"What was Amelia's dating history like?" Milo asks.

"She got out of a really serious relationship not too long ago. They met in college but when she moved here, she said it had become too difficult to do long distance, and she had no plans of moving. I think she used dating apps. She was always giggling and on the phone when she walked around the apartment. She wouldn't give me details since none of them were serious, but I can count at least three different men picking her up to take her out to dinner in the last few months."

"Can you give us a description of what these men looked like?" Leo asks.

"Sure. To the best of my ability," Stephanie retorts through a stuffy nose.

The sound of the floor creaking breaks her focus. Her index finger readily pushes the pause button, not wanting to lose her spot in the recording. Warren stands poised in the opened doorway; his presence veiled in silence.

"Have you slept since I left?" he asks as he stares down at her on the floor.

She assesses his stance, analyzing if he's a threat or not. She knows with only her limited training with Verena, she couldn't take him.

His rigid figure softens, slumping forward. "I–apologize for my behavior the other night."

Willow searches the floor, looking for something that doesn't exist.

"Are you aware of the superstition of werewolves changing on the full moon?" he asks.

She nods with a tight expression.

"Well, there's some truth to that. However, it isn't just werewolves, it's most supernatural creatures and they're all affected differently. Vampires become full of blood lust, werewolves shift, sirens sing their songs, witches concoct their potions for optimal effectiveness, the list goes on. It does not excuse my behavior, but that's a reason for it." He clears his throat and pulls on the collar of his shirt.

"So, you won't rip my throat out or strip me naked while I sleep?" She deadpans.

He winces. "No."

Photographs of the mutilated bodies stare back at her, reminding her of her failures. "I was put on mandatory leave today and taken off the cases."

"I heard," he meets her words with quiet compassion.

She doesn't react. She isn't even surprised. *Of course he heard.* He's everywhere all the time.

"Realistically, this will keep your friends safer, which I know is what you want."

"Sure, but now I don't have access to new evidence or tech support. And, if we even live after all of this is said and done, my career's probably over." Her head hangs.

"Not necessarily," he says, moving into the room and sitting on the guestroom bed. "It's just leave. You're still employed. I have connections, plus I believe we have a direction with your brother's journal."

"What did you discover?" Her enthusiasm perks up, almost forgetting about the journal to begin with.

"It has taken me a little bit to decipher the code to read it. I've made some good progress, but I'll have to continue my research with the help of my acquaintances." He sits on the edge of the bed, leaning back on both of his hands behind his back, gauging Willow's reaction.

"Are these friends that will kill me?" she asks with a wandering gaze.

"Any *friend* of mine would not be so stupid as to try," he threatens, leaning forward, closer to her. The way he phrases it causes her to meet his gaze.

Warren pulls the top layer of his hair into a knot, letting the rest of it fall past his shoulders. The tips of his pointed ears emerge where his hair parts. "I made some tea. Get properly dressed. We are going on a short trip to see a friend." He stands, gliding over and around the photos of the victims that lay in his path and exits the guest room, pulling the door shut behind him.

Willow releases a sharp exhale, twisting her back each side until it cracks. "Alright," she mutters as she stands to change out of her sleepwear. The energy to fight back is gone.

*

Her lashes flutter when Warren's car comes to a stop. A gentle firmness supports her head and neck as she presses against it; the warm earthy scent relaxes the tension in her shoulders. Warren's shoulder. She bolts upright, removing herself from his proximity. He eyes her from the driver's seat. Pressure builds, constricting in on all sides of her head and neck. Her index and middle finger circles the side of her temple. "Sorry," she mutters.

"I'm shocked you slept; you started to make me doubt that humans need sleep to survive."

She shrugs, still feeling the ache of neck pain. "Surviving and thriving are two different things. Where are we?"

"Our friend's home, that she has so graciously let us visit."

The two of them step out of Warren's car and walk up the gravel driveway to approach a secluded, Victorian home. Gargoyles loom with power atop the fence posts, welcoming visitors, or trespassers, upon entering. "*Our* friend, you said?"

"Of course I'm your friend!" a familiar feminine accent echoes as Sunny steps through the front door and onto the porch, Malcolm trailing behind her with a sluggish pace.

"You're shitting me," Willow murmurs in unbelief, her mouth parted. Sunny grins ear to ear.

Warren bows toward Sunny. A coy expression spreads across his features. She's been acquaintances with a vampire for years now, and she never knew. *And somehow—she's been completely safe the entire time.*

"Surprise?" She wraps Willow in an embrace. It clicks. It's all connected– how Warren has been able to keep up with Willow at the station and get tips on crime before detectives can respond.

"You're a mole?" Willow asks Sunny through a struggled breath, consumed within her embrace.

Sunny releases her, disgust twisting her features. "I am no such thing! I owed Warren a favor, so I've just been making sure he's in the loop of what's going on. It's not like he's the villain here."

"That we know of," Willow mutters.

"You know good and well that if you truly thought it was him you wouldn't be here right now. You'd already be dead."

"Our kind gets a lot of bad misconceptions thrown around; however, we are still dangerous by nature. If I could promise you anything, you've at least found the best kind of vampires you can surround yourself with, being a human that is," Malcolm interjects the conversation. His hard hands massage the back of his own neck. *Is he embarrassed?*

Willow can't argue with that. Warren, despite his sour puss mood, has been extremely protective and generous. Sunny and Malcolm have been nothing but kind and welcoming toward Willow. "You've been a vampire this entire time?"

Sunny takes a bow. "At your service." A black cat appears out of thin air as it circles around Malcolm's legs.

Willow jumps, startled by the feline's sudden appearance. Malcolm smiles, extending his arm to scratch its head. For the first time, Willow sees Sunny not in business casual attire. She has sleep shorts and an oversized t-shirt on, the sleeves rolled up to cuff around her armpit. A tattoo of a purple lily with greenery extends down her forearm.

"What's your power?" Willow asks, inspecting the tattoo.

Sunny glances at Warren with an unreadable expression on her face. His jaw ticks. "You know about these? I can control plants. It's not nearly as powerful as Warren's, but very useful."

Movement shifts from the corner of her eye, redirecting her attention to the rose bushes on either side of the columns connecting to the porch. The rose bush grows, thorny vines winding in circles up the column. Warren watches the roses glide to the roof, amusement lifts his tight features.

"Enough chitchat out here, please come inside," Sunny extends an invitation with grace, opening her front door for Willow and Warren to enter.

"Malcolm and I will be in shortly," Warren responds.

Sunny shoots them with a glare of suspicion, but she presses inside, pulling Willow to follow behind her. As they enter the threshold, the black cat circles in between Sunny's legs. Warm herbs and honey bake through the home. The emerald walls are covered with vintage antique trinkets and framed art.

"Can you please get out of my way?" Sunny's southern twang gives the impression she's being polite, but the twitch of her eyelid betrays her tone as she stares at the cat encircling her feet.

Willow swears she watches the cat's bottom wiggle, as though taunting her, before strutting away toward another room.

"What's its name?" The onyx feline blinks away without a trace. "That thing isn't a cat—is it?"

String lights line the hallway, guiding their path through the home. "Oh, Binx? No, that little rascal isn't a cat. She's our familiar."

"And what exactly…is that?" Willow hesitates to ask, not wanting to sound stupid.

Sunny turns. "Oh, right. She's a fey spirit. Typically, witches have them. She acts as a protector for Malcom and me," her eyes narrow in the direction the cat disappeared, "however, she only bonded with Malcom, so I'm chopped liver. She keeps me safe since I'm mated with Malcom, but she still aggravates the daylight out of me. If you need to use the bathroom, it's this door on the left," Sunny adds. The room is dim but filled with plants overflowing on the bathroom sink, which remind her of her own home.

"Mates? Is that a real thing? Not just in the books?" The idea piques Willow's interest.

Sunny's brow quirks, a knowing smirk tugging on her mouth. "What kind of books are you reading?" Color blooms across Willow's cheeks. "They are real," Sunny continues, tracing her fingers along the empty sections of the wall. "Most supernatural creatures have some sort of mating bond within our DNA. Each one is different, I'm sure."

Willow's hand tucks itself into her jean pockets. "How did you know that Malcolm was your mate?"

The living room opens up, comfortable and full. Several blankets are thrown over the couch and in a basket. An assortment of pillows, ranging in different designs yet all the same neutral color pallet lay scattered along the couch.

"We were at a mutual friend's party. Vampires like us often get together during the full moon and share the safe blood we've found, that way we aren't ravenous on a poor human bystander. I bumped into him accidentally, and he offered me a drink. When our bare fingers touched, *boom*. It felt like a tug at first. Then when our eyes met, time itself stopped. And within an instant, we both just—knew. Just as humans need air to breathe, vampires need blood to survive. And well, Malcolm is my mate and the only person I'll ever need again."

Willow's mind can't comprehend that kind of love. Her parents definitely didn't have that type of love. At best they were roommates who tolerated each other after Willow's birth. She chews on the bottom of her lip. The thought of a mate sounds so sweet. There's no worrying about the what ifs. "What do you mean by vampires like you all?" Willow asks.

"Vampires who don't feed on live humans. Most of us never asked for this kind of life, especially Warren. If we can keep control of our humanity and awareness, vampires like us force ourselves to restrain from feeding on humans. It takes a lot of discipline."

She never believed Warren when he claimed to only drink from the dead. *Hearing it from Sunny—has she been too harsh on him?* As soon as the two of them plop down onto the linen couch, Warren and Malcolm rejoin them in the living room. She's unable to read Malcolm's expression, but Warren's is that of agitation. But, what's new?

"I know you gave me a brief run down, but can you give me the details for what you need assistance with?" Sunny asks, directing her attention to Warren as he takes a seat on the various antiquated chairs.

Her hips shift from side to side as she crosses her legs in the chair.

Warren pulls out Kai's notebook from his leather satchel, handing it to Sunny. "I have deciphered half of this, however there are several runes embedded in the code that are throwing me off. Can you see if you recognize any of them?" His expression tightens as he watches Sunny flip through several pages of the journal.

"What's the purposes of runes? I've heard the term, but I've never actually known what they do. Is it just another language? Magic?" Willow probes.

Without looking up from the journal, Sunny responds, "Yes and no. They are a form of communication, but also a means for contacting other planes of existence. There's many different interpretations of runes and their meanings." She scrutinizes each single page.

Her fingers stop flipping, her mouth falling slack. "*Perthros*," she whispers.

Warren inclines forward in his chair, a spark in his gaze.

"This symbol," Sunny continues, pointing at the symbol resembling half of an hourglass on its side, which is circled in red ink. "It's used to represent the deepest level of the core of our being. Some say that it points to our destiny, some say that it refers to death, or a renewal in the spirit. It isn't used often unless someone means business."

"Very ominous and terrifying," Willow retorts.

Sunny's brows furrow. "I can't read the rest of that junk, so that's all I can really help with…but either way you spin it, it's bad."

Warren's face tightens. "I was afraid of that."

"I know this isn't what you want to hear, but you may have to go to The Pitt," Sunny adds.

Warren rubs the side of his temple, then moves to his jaw.

She continues, "If anyone will know what this is, it's Eryx."

"Who's Eryx?" Willow probes. Warren scowls at the name as it leaves her lips but remains silent. "What's a pit?" she presses.

"He's a nasty guy," Malcolm adds. An unspoken conversation happens between the three of them, leaving Willow shunned. There's something about this Eryx guy that they won't discuss.

"He's the leader of a coven in town. Except he's evil to his core. The rumor is that he made a pact with a demon to get multiple powers and now he's an expert in blood magic. If anyone's going to have more extensive knowledge about this, it would be him, unfortunately." Sunny sighs and continues, "The Pitt is his underground fight club, essentially. But with creatures of all kinds. Some join in for fun and provide entertainment, others fight to prove they are worthy of a trade." A frown tugs at the bottom of her lips.

"And a coven is–" Willow frowns, uncomfortable at admitting her own ignorance.

"A coven is a hoard of vampires all turned by the same person that gather with shared beliefs. Typically, it's those of sinister nature. It's also a term for a hoard of witches or warlocks," Malcolm responds.

Willow sinks back into her chair and nods. It appears there are many things she didn't know about her hometown. "Can I look at my brother's journal, please?"

Sunny extends her tattooed arm forward, handing Willow the used leather-bound book.

Hieroglyphics and randomized English letters are scattered against the paper. It's the scribbles of a mad man; she doesn't even recognize the handwriting.

"Warren, are you sure this is my brother's? I don't even recognize this. His handwriting was bad, but not *this bad*."

"Go to the inside of the front cover," he responds, his gaze unfocused.

As she flips to the front inside cover, on the inside is inscribed *Proprietas Kai Rhodes.* "Proprietas? Property, I'm guessing?" She frowns. The wishful thoughts of it originating from someone else, gone.

"Indeed," he groans, bending his neck side to side, cracking multiple vertebrae loud enough for the room to hear.

Willow continues to skim through the book, wishing to be of help to them in the middle of it all. In the bottom of the page, there's a rune that resembles the shape of the letter 'F' that catches her attention. *Where has she seen this before?*

Sunny stands up to stretch, and the black cat floats through the air, stepping on invisible clouds until it perches on her shoulder. "Will you be assisting us? Escorting us to The Pitt?" Willow asks.

"Hell no," she scoffs, followed by a chuckle. "This is the extent of the help I can and *want* to give in this situation. My favor has already been cashed in."

Warren nods in agreement. Without a word, he leaves the room, leaving Sunny, Malcolm, and Willow by themselves. Sunny's shoulders shrug, but the way she drums her fingers against her leg tells Willow just how anxious she is.

Outside they discover Warren leaning against a pillar, smoking a cigarette. Light rain falls from the blue gray sky, creating a pitter patter against the gutters of the Victorian home. The smoke mixes within the air, dancing around each droplet that falls. Warren's gaze is unfixed.

"Smoking's bad for you, you know," Sunny teases, cutting the tension.

"Add it to the list," his tone cuts with dry amusement, taking another drag. "What is it going to do? Kill me?"

The clouds shift with reluctant motion. With each movement, small beams of sunlight crack through the clouds, as if someone shone a flashlight through a cheese grater. An abnormal formation weaves in the sky. During the summer, she and Kai would lay in the backyard, telling each other what the other thought the clouds resembled. They would come up with the craziest ideas. This cloud looks like a swing set, she smiles to herself.

A lightbulb within her mind flashes and her head whips over to Warren. "I need you to take me back to the park, now."

CHAPTER 30

BRUISED EGO

Warren is silent but watchful as their feet sink into the wet earth. Fog hovers in the air, laying an eerie blanket of mystery over the playground. Willow's fingers brush the ground, retracing every detail of Amelia's crime scene. A gust of wind blows her hair, fanning it in front of her face and obscuring her vision for half a second. Warren leans against a nearby tree, skimming through Kai's journal while glancing upward from time to time to observe Willow. His lack of interest is disappointing, stirring a sense of doubt within her.

She sighs. The wooden planks of the playground set are ridged beneath her fingers as she walks in between the various pieces, trailing her touch along either side of the equipment. The first question they still don't have answers to: why did they bring the victim to the playground? Teachers frequent playgrounds to let the younger children burn off some energy. Was it to get close to her workplace and belittle her after death? The pose feels personal. Her teeth nibble at her fingernail. The team said she's involved in church. Degrading her beliefs? Had they inspected the entire playground top to bottom? She can't remember fully but knows there were no notes left by her team.

There are no traces of a struggle within the twenty-foot radius from the crime scene. Had there been any concern, she would have spotted it. She shrinks in, ducking her head under the wooden beams of the main structure. Typically, this area remains reserved for smaller children, but the spray painted wood and squashed cigarette butts prove it's a favorite hideaway for teens. Etchings and graffiti plaster one of the wooden bases. *Christy loves*

Brad, School Suxs, Jesus loves you amongst other memories carved into the wood. There's amusement in reading comments from others, frozen in time until the wood is eaten away. They continue to the pinnacle of the underside. Newly exposed wood, still a light shade of brown, slashes into the playset. She narrows her eyes and crawls closer. The letters B and P, however, instead of the rounded edges of them, are sharp, jagged points. *Could they be?*

"Warren!" she yells. "Come here!"

Warren takes his time, not using his speed to get there. He sinks low enough to glance down at her. "Are you taking notes of all the names so you can report them for damaging property?" She believes it's a joke, but his face shows no level of amusement.

"Look at this newer addition to the graffiti."

A groan escapes him as he bends down, crawling under to meet her. His gaze meets the carving, tilting his head with interest.

"These are runes, right? Not the initials B.P.?"

"Those are in fact, runes of some kind," he responds, biting his bottom lip as he searches around them, investigating for other clues.

She watches him as he focuses. His hand reaches into his back pocket, pulling his phone out to take a couple pictures.

"Seems like your gut instinct was right. I apologize for doubting you." He nods, an apologetic look sweeps over his face, sending an uneasy flutter through her chest. "How did you know to come back and check here?"

A great question. It would sound crazy to say, *a cloud reminded me of a childhood memory and my gut told me I needed to search the playground.* "Intuition? I haven't been much help lately, I'm glad I can contribute somehow." She scratches her nose and scooches back. Out of the corner of her eye she notes a fleeting smirk playing on Warren's face.

"Nonsense. This is the best lead we've had since finding your brother's journal. I need to do some more digging at cracking the cypher in the book, as well as finding out more about these runes and their different meanings. I can't be sure if it is referencing a name, or representing something like Sunny mentioned earlier." His fingers trace the etching in the wood, moving with the grooves of the carvings. As her shoulder knocks against his, it's like hitting an arm against the corner of a table.

"Sorry–excuse me," she mumbles as she escapes the confined play area, dusting off her clothes and stretching her stiff muscles.

Warren emerges after her, his expression vacant. "There's more work to be done. I have some errands to run, but I will drop you off with Verena for your continued training." He glances at his watch.

Her eyebrow raises. "Where are you going?"

His expression remains unreadable. "I have some things that need to be taken care of," he says, his tone making it clear that he isn't going to elaborate.

It's best she doesn't press further. "Alright, let's get going," she says with a defeated sigh.

Willow can't help but steal glances at him as he drives down the road. *She can't shake the feeling that he's keeping something from her.*

"Don't fret, Detective," Warren says, breaking the silence as though he senses her unease. "Verena will make sure you're as prepared as you can be."

She analyzes the split ends of her hair. "I'm not worried about that."

His head tilts. "And what are you worried about?"

"What in all of these scenarios am I not worried about?" A nervous laugh escapes her lips. "This all feels much bigger than the two of us, no offense. And I don't fully trust you. I know you're keeping something from me. Which, by the way, I don't appreciate."

"You want to know more about my history, yes?" His attention flickers from the road, meeting her gaze.

"That's a great start," Willow agrees, leaning forward in the passenger seat.

"A long time ago, in my youth, I lost my parents to cholera. I essentially raised myself." He pauses. There's a shift inside Willow, as though his pain is weaving into her own. "As a young adult, I matured faster than most my age due to my circumstances. I fell in love. Or—so I thought." Warren's eyebrows furrow.

Moving without a thought her hand seeks his shoulder, offering comfort before retreating, unsure.

"To this day, I'm still not quite sure what she was. She lured me in. I lost myself in pure admiration. Once I confessed my feelings, she fed on me. She kept going. And going. And going. As I drifted into what I thought was death, she whispered ominous mumblings of words I had never experienced before. I woke up, alone and stripped naked in a body I no longer recognized. An insatiable hunger riddled from within me." Warren stills, as if he is holding his breath from a memory he can't outrun.

"I—can't imagine how shocking that must have been. I'm sorry, Warren," Willow says almost in a whisper. She can feel the unspoken weight in between his words. There's no pity, but instead, a shared stillness, recognition. It's as though she's seeing the true him for the first time, in this moment.

"I've done a lot of horrendous things in my lifetime. I will probably do some more. My mentor saved me. He taught me how to live *humanly* as an inhuman can, I suppose. I owe him my life. My number one priority is to find a cure to my condition. For myself, and for others like me who want to live, but as a human until they die." The car comes to a halt in his driveway. He tears his eyes away, meeting Willow's.

She searches his features for any sign of lies or contempt. There's nothing but desolation and determination. Before she can form her response, he speaks once more.

"I tell you this in hopes that you will learn to trust me. We may have different reasons for ending this, but I'm just as dedicated as you. I hope one day you can learn that you can rely on others like I did." His confession is soft as he looks to his glass home. "Verena is inside. Her anger will only grow if you keep her waiting much longer."

A frown pulls at Willow's lips. As she exits the car, a nagging feeling tugs at her. She turns back to Warren. "I hope that I can be the one to help you find your cure..." The door slams behind her.

*

Willow's back presses against the wall as she pants heavily on the floor, her muscles screaming for a break. Verena, however, appears tireless. They are running on four hours of training, with little rest. She's moments away from collapsing. Her fingers interlock behind her head, and her chest heaves as she takes deep breaths while Verena circles the room. Beads of sweat run down her forehead, over her exposed abdomen and her black sports bra is soaked. Verena prowls over to one of the weapon shelves in Warren's hidden training room, studying each object with care before she selects a knife. In the dim light, the blade flashes, wrapped in purple and black leather that seems to absorb the shadows.

"Stand up," Verena commands. "We are going to kick it up a notch."

Willow pushes herself to her feet, knees wobbling as she stands. "What's with the knife?" She studies the blade, her expression guarded.

Darkness unfurls in Verena's face. "It would be unrealistic to believe anyone you encounter would only fight you with bare hands." She twists the blade in her hand; her attention focused on the knife. "Let's see how your defense skills are with a magical blade."

Before Willow can process what's happening, Verena lunges forward. Willow tries her best to dodge her swipes, her legs moving on instinct at this point. Sweat trails into the corners of her eyes, the salt burning enough to blur her vision. Despite her fatigue, she manages to avoid the blade several times, but Verena's relentless. Verena's irises blaze with vivid light as she summons another large knife out of thin air, appearing in her other hand.

In a swift motion, Verena catches Willow's side, slicing it an inch. Willow hisses in pain, clutching her side where crimson trickles down her exposed stomach. The wound sends a sudden sting, causing her to take deep inhaled gasps for breaths. A cold sensation spreads from the cut, radiating in every direction, and Willow feels her limbs growing stiff and heavy.

"What–what did you do?" Willow gasps, her voice trembling as her body grows immobile.

Verena flashes the knife with the purple and black handle. "A paralytic toxin from a basilisk. Don't worry, this knife contains the toxin in its most basic, mild form. However, the paralysis still works." She smirks, watching fear ripple through Willow's features.

Willow's heart races as she wills her legs to move. Her mind screams to fight back, but her physical form refuses. Unable to obey.

"Terrifying, isn't it? To be trapped within your own body?" Verena cocks her head to the side, circling Willow like a vulture.

In her mind, an audible voice whispers to Willow, "*Breathe. Release.*"

The presence stirs within her, calming the panic attempting to rise by the second. She closes her eyes and focuses on the pumping of her heart. It beats in slow pulses. She visualizes with every breath, a suction bulb removing the toxin out of her blood stream bit by bit. In middle school, this technique worked to calm her in the middle of a panic attack. However, a reaction to basilisk venom differs *slightly* from a panic attack at age twelve.

"That's *more* than enough training, Verena." Warren hisses, re-entering the room.

"You don't have enough faith in her, War." Verena motions him to take a closer look at Willow.

Inch by inch, Willow's extremities tingle. The sensation spreads through her fingertips and toes, eventually meeting in the center of her body at her heart. Willow's frozen fists loosen. Warren's weight shifts as he watches her fight off the basilisk toxin. Minutes feel like hours, but gradually Willow regains control, collapsing into Warren's arms. She blinks awake, lids still drooping, meeting Verena's stare.

Willow's voice is gravel. "You're a real bitch; you know that right?"

Verena lets out an unexpected cackle and shrugs. "You're one crazy human! In a real fight, you don't get warnings. Way to overcome and adapt!" She flashes a toothy grin, showcasing her fangs. "You should go get that cleaned up, so we don't start a frenzy in the house, hm?" Verena's heavy hand slaps Warren across the back.

Glancing down to her side, Willow finds Warren's hands wrapping around her waist. Blood covers his palm, and droplets run down her own leg. Warren keeps his focus on Verena. The muscles on the side of his neck bulges, drawing tight within his nape.

"Let go, I need to get cleaned up," Willow says, struggling to stand.

"Verena, you're dismissed. I'll summon you when we need you again." Warren's words are bitter.

Verena's mouth twitches before her expression returns to irritation. "Au revoir." She blows a kiss before vanishing.

The corners of the open flesh on Willow's side sting, the pain radiating through her extremities the further she moves to stand. His brows knit together as he watches her pitiful attempt.

"I apologize I didn't return sooner." He digs a first aid kit out of a cluttered shelf.

"Why do you have a first aid kit down here? Can't you heal yourself?" she asks him.

"Over time I can heal, but I heal quicker with blood. I put this down here for you once you started training."

"Oh," guilt tugs at her, "thanks."

"Here, sit down. You shouldn't need any stitches, but we should probably use glue for precaution." He rummages through his premade kit, searching for something.

She follows his instructions, sitting down against the shelf, allowing her frame to soften. It's easier to relax with Verena gone. Blood spatters against the training mat. It seems she bled more than she realized during their fight.

"Hold this." He lays the kit in her lap as he bends down to work on her exposed sides.

Various atypical items stuff themselves inside the first aid container.

There are several preserved rabbits' feet toward the bottom of the bag under a couple boxes of Band-Aids, making her mouth curl. *The poor bunnies. She doesn't even want to know its use.* A corked vial catches her attention; a shimmering blue liquid swirls within. The letters E and C are scrawled on a piece of tape that wraps around the top of it.

"What's this?"

Warren's eyes flicker to the vial and back down as he finishes bandaging her left side. "Energy and clarity potion. Sunny makes them."

"Potion? Like a witch?" She examines the tube in quiet inquiry.

"You didn't deduce from her home that she's a witch?"

Her eyebrows raise. "No, the grand reveal of my colleague being a vampire distracted me from considering she could also be a witch too?"

He nods. "An excellent witch," he corrects. "Her ability helps her render plant life for the healing potions she makes, but it seems to take her a while to get them made. That one is sort of like a magical shot of adrenaline, but it heals you slowly."

Energy and healing? She pops the lid off the vial and downs it, a tingling sensation spreading down her throat. Irritation tightens his expression, his jaw set and a lowered brow. "I only had that one. That's why I was bandaging you."

Her flesh grows warm from within, almost like tiny hugs against her skin. She shrugs in response. "This way I can keep training. It seems like I could use all the help I can get."

"For someone who doesn't trust me, you're either brave or stupid for drinking a vague potion from my basement. Let's just hope that Sunny's newest batch is almost ready." He trails off as he visibly restrains his frustration.

For the first time in weeks, Willow's spirit lifts. Any fatigue her muscles had, has dissipated. There's a sense of freedom, as though she just broke out of a decade of confinement. Even slight movement feels fifty percent faster. The fog swirling within her mind lifts, as a sharp sense of clarity washes through the room.

Warren stands, tilting his head as he observes her. "Did it help more than you realized it would?"

"I don't remember the last time I felt this—aware? Energized?" She's at a loss of words on how to verbalize the new sensation.

"Great. Ready for round two then?" he asks her as he walks over to the mat, awaiting her response. He tosses his black tweed jacket off into a corner, rolling his sleeves to rest at the bend of his elbow.

"Shouldn't I rest a minute since I've been going at it for hours now?"

She hesitates. *What will happen once it wears off? Will it be double painful? Cause her to go into hibernation?* There's no time for sleep.

"I would have given you that advice two minutes ago before you drank that, but now you're fine to continue. Actually, you may even feel better than if you started a fresh new day." The crack of his knuckles pop in a sequence as he stretches his neck side to side. This all feels very pointless, but she's still going to put her best effort forward.

"Before we begin, I do have something I want to give you," he adds, reaching into his waistband, pulling a familiar dagger out. "I know you can't use magic, but you can still have access to magical weapons to help you level the playing field." He extends the handle to Willow, pinching the blade between his fingers.

"Is this—"

"It's the dagger we found in Kai's belongings, yes," he interrupts.

The blade emits a soft blue glow as she takes it in her hand. It's been hiding in her nightstand. A part of her wanted to forget it existed. It's proof of Kai's involvement in things she doesn't understand. She doesn't want to think about how she may not have known her brother as well as she thought. A tingling warmth stirs within her, the effects of the potion finalizing. Warren keeps his focus on her. There's a gleam in his eye that makes her heart race.

"Ready?" His smooth voice carries an edge of challenge. A dagger of his own glimmers in his hand.

Willow nods. Her fist tightens around the handle of her blade, the blue tint reflecting off the right side of her silhouette. The leather grip feels cool and familiar and the magic it holds hums beneath the surface.

Without warning, Warren moves, a blur of speed and strength that takes her breath away. He isn't holding back at this moment, and Willow knows it. She barely has time to raise her dagger before he is on her, his movements fluid and precise. The first clash of metal on metal rings through the room as Willow parries his strike. Her arms shake with the force of it, but she holds her ground, pushing back with everything she has.

"Good," Warren murmurs, though not letting up. He presses forward; their blades dance as he tests her reflexes and speed. "You're faster. A bit stronger, too."

Her teeth grind against each other as she focuses on each movement and strike. The dagger in her hand seems to pulse with energy, amplifying her strength and sharpening her senses. She can feel the weight of Warren's gaze on her, assessing her every move. He comes at her again, and this time, she sidesteps, using his momentum against him. The tip of her knife grazes his side, just enough to cut through his shirt. He hisses, a flash of approval in his eyes.

"Impressive," he says, a smirk tugs at his lips. "But can you keep up?" He tosses his weapon, clinking against the floor.

Willow sheaths the dagger by her ankle, feeling her stomach hollow at the vulnerability of removing her weapon. Verena trains, typically, in hand-to-hand combat. Willow's surprised at how well she adjusted to using a weapon. Warren intensifies his attacks, moving faster, and striking harder with open hands. She struggles to keep up, forced to play defense, using her forearms for blocking.

In a blink, Warren disappears, becoming one with the shadows of the room. Her heart quickens. He's pulling out all the stops. Her stare darts from one corner to the next, willing him to appear.

One of the first lessons Verena worked with her on involved homing in on her other senses. *It's not reliable to only trust eyesight.* Her eyelids close and the soundwaves of the room heighten. A soft step taps in front of her–her lids burst open. In a swift move, Warren tackles her. He pins her against the ground, one hand around her wrists, the other at her side as he holds her in place.

His warm breath caresses against her ear as he speaks, low and challenging. "You've improved drastically. Not quite where you need to be, but color me impressed."

Her chest heaves with exertion, her pulse steadily climbing as she meets his gaze. There's an unfamiliar fire hidden in the depths of his stare. Pride mixed with something–darker. Seconds pass and neither of them move. Dilated pupils roam her face, lingering on the cupid's bow of her lips. Adrenaline courses through her veins, and the air between them tightens. An invisible, irresistible pull tugs her toward him. Her breath catches in her throat as she closes the distance between them. Their lips, inches apart. A spark of clarity cuts through his gaze. His expression hardens as he pulls away, loosening her wrists from his grasp and standing to his feet. The pit of her stomach sinks.

"Enough training for today. Get some rest. We will continue the investigation tomorrow afternoon and return to The Golden Wolf."

There's no second glance in his exit, leaving her to sit on the blood-spattered floor, humiliated. *Ouch.* The cuticles of her thumbs bleed as she picks the skin around her nails. The redness trickles onto the floor.

The sting of his rejection cuts deeper than she cares to admit. *Why did she do that?* With her hands resting on her knees, she gathers her legs, pulling them to her chest. The effects of the healing potion are nearing the end of its cycle. The exhaustion hits her all at once, leaving her muscles aching. The soreness feels like someone's inside her, pulling her muscles in different directions at the same time.

The bandages on her side are stained; bright red seeps through the white cotton in sporadic patterns. Upon removal, the once open wound has fresh skin. Dried blood flakes on the exterior of her skin. Her breathing shakes as she tries to push down the embarrassment and focus on something else– *anything else.* But it's no use. For now, all she can do is sit here in the empty room, nursing her bruised ego and aching muscles. All while she stares at Kai's dagger that lays across the room, unsure how she will be able to look at Warren again.

CHAPTER 31

HIDING IN PLAIN SIGHT

The memory foam of the bed swallows Willow deeper, the comforter wrapping her within a cocoon. The weight from her muscles pulls her further in as sleep overtakes her.

She finds herself in an endless room filled with miles of treasure— stacks of bills, gold coins, jewels, and poker chips glitter under a dim, flickering light. Like a dragon's hoard. The wealth surrounds her, but it feels suffocating, not liberating. The room closes in, as if the walls themselves were made of greed, pressing in on her from all sides, wanting more of her. Her breathing staggers as she stumbles forward, pushing through the coins at her feet.

Her steps are hesitant and slow. A broad desk anchors the corner. Gideon leans against it, waiting for her. A slow burn spreads in her chest. His eyes are half-lidded, watching her intently. He extends his hand out to her and pulls her into him, against his chest.

Desire and fear swirl inside her, two competing forces. His fingers tip her chin up, forcing her to meet his gaze.

"You're unlike the others. A forbidden fruit in the garden of Eden. You make it hard to resist," Gideon murmurs in her ear, sending shivers down her spine.

She doesn't respond, but simply leans into him, their lips crashing into one another. Her shape melts into his, carnal desire fusing with attention and affection as his hands roam her curves. In between shifting, documents fly off the desk— being smothered by their bodies.

The papers are stacks of scattered files and photographs. Photographs of Kai, his torso mutilated, blood soaking through his clothing, his face devoid of life, laying on the very top piles of paper. She pulls away from Gideon, and he disappears in an instant. An ache in her heart thrums against her ribs. As she reaches for one of the papers, it crumbles to dust in her grasp, dissolving into the air.

The room glitches as the shadows around her slither and rise from the ground, covering the money and forming tall, dark figures looming over her. They have no faces, only hollow voids where eyes should be. The shadows move closer, their presence heavy, chilling her bones. Shadows root her feet into the ground, keeping her from moving. Just as the darkness is about to envelop her, bright flashes of light erupt from nowhere, cutting through the midnight like blades.

The light clashes with the shadows, creating a chaotic battle of dark and light. The room flames with intense energy, the forces colliding with such power that the ground beneath her trembles. There's no sound, but the clashes send tremors of movement through her body.

Willow is caught in the middle, unable to move, the flashes of light blinding her, while the shadows pull her from beneath, trying to drag her down. Faint whispers, unintelligible but insistent, crawl up her neck into her ears, desperate to tell her a secret. But the words get drowned out by the clashing forces, lost in the chaos. Warren emerges from a new flash of light, bolting to Willow. The light surrounding him burns the shadows which hold her feet in place. Warmth follows him as he takes hold of her hand.

"Trust me," he says.

The shadows darken, but in turn, the light beams even brighter, until it all becomes too much. The room implodes, engulfed by the blinding light, her mind reeling from the overwhelming sensations.

With a gasp, Willow jolts awake, her heart thumps against her ribcage. Her pulse thrums in her throat and sweat runs down her cheek as she gulps for a steady breath.

"Willow, can you hear me?" Warren blurts.

Her confusion spreads as she takes in her surroundings. The guest room bed in Warren's home is humid, the sheets damp with sweat. Warren's touch rests on her shoulder, giving it a quiet shake. A dream. It felt–so real.

She can't speak, but she nods.

Warren relaxes, his shoulders slump down and he removes his hand from her. "Just a dream?"

"Nightmare," she manages to get out. She wipes her brow with her forearm.

"I could hear moaning from the other room, then other unknown noises. I wasn't quite sure what was going on," he adds.

Her mind replays the part of her dream with Gideon, and warmth floods her cheeks. "It wasn't all bad, not until the end at least." She retells most of the dream, leaving out the part about making out with Gideon, retelling the sequence to Warren. Her sentence trails off, unable to look at him directly.

He scratches his stubble. "That is quite the dream." The sun peeks through the window, bathing the room in a warm glow. "You've slept long enough, it's almost sunset. Get dressed, we are going to The Golden Wolf."

She blinks, stunned as she grabs her phone from the nightstand. Sure enough, it's late afternoon the next day. She panics, feeling a rush of guilt for sleeping so late. "Remind me not to drink potions from Sunny," she murmurs, blaming the elixir for causing her to crash out.

"Maybe next time ask before you take. Hm?" he responds with a snark, closing the door behind him to give her privacy.

As the door closes, she mimics his tone. Her mouth puckers, mocking his words.

"Vampire hearing, Detective," he calls from the other side of the door.

"Good!" she bites back, shimmying a black skirt over her hips. A mixed sense of nerves tighten in her stomach as her hand twists the doorknob.

*

The couple sitting beside Willow at the bar clinks their glasses together in celebration of something Willow can't hear and frankly doesn't care about. Her head swivels, searching for Warren, who sits at one of the many game tables. *Is that blackjack?* She squints. Five other players sit with him, their expressions vary. One woman at the table is hammered, her posture slouched, cheeks flushed, and she cackles at every spoken word. The man sitting directly beside her, presumably who she came here with, has one hand around her waist for support, and a pissed off scowl advertising *my wife is a sloppy drunk and I'm pissed about it.* Warren's expression remains neutral, as always. A constant poker face. She takes a slow sip, letting the rich, dark wine coat her tongue before swallowing.

The other three men at the table have creases on their foreheads and one bounces his leg with restless jitters. Warren's by far the most confident looking player. The two of them are supposed to be snooping, but it seems like he's trying to win some cash. She gulps the red wine, the bitterness mirroring the thoughts churning in her head.

"Pretty thirsty, huh? Would you like another glass?" the curly, redhead bartender asks, breaking her trance from her people watching.

Willow peers down at her glass, which is almost empty. "Sure, why not? Thanks," she responds, downing the remaining wine.

The bartender grins, pouring more. The wine sloshes back and forth, the liquid kissing the lip of the glass. Her eyebrows lift.

"The bottle had a little extra left, so I figured I'd give you the rest. Consider it your lucky day," the bartender notes.

Willow nods. "I don't have much of those anymore, so I'll take it." She throws down a twenty-dollar bill and moves from her chair, ready to scope out more of the casino floor.

She sways between slot machines, watching the wheels spin and the lights flash. It may just be the alcohol, but the jingles all flow together in a sweet melody, making Willow hum along with it. A familiar profile catches her eye in the distance. The hazy surroundings focus as her head leans forward, leering to confirm the man's identity. Clad in a sleek designer three-piece charcoal suit, his composed presence demands attention in the chaotic environment. *Aldaric.* His features are stunning, his thick beard perfectly lined, drawing attention to his strong jawline.

As if he could feel her stare burning through him, he turns, his expression briefly mirrors her surprise before he recovers, flashing her a dazzling smile. "Fancy seeing you here," his words come with a teasing ease, taking a few steps closer. "Taking a break from solving crime to win big?"

She manages a forced laugh. "Something like that. What about you? I didn't expect to see you here tonight! Is Nadia here as well?" Her balance wavers. *Damn alcohol.*

"No, Nadia's at my home resting. She said she had a long day, so she wanted to play with my dog and sleep," he shrugs. "I'm just checking in on some business. This place always has something interesting going on." His attention shifts around the room before returning to her, a hint of curiosity in his gaze. "And you? What brings you here?"

Willow hesitates. "Just– trying to unwind a bit." The wine finds its way to her lips once more.

Before he can respond, his phone rings. His brows furrow at the screen. "Sorry, I have to take this." Regret seeps into his apology. "We'll catch up later!" Without waiting for her response, he steps away, his phone already to his ear and volume low as he speaks into it.

Willow's head swirls as the multicolored lights flash from a nearby winner. She groans as a headache pierces the left side of her skull. *She's such a lightweight. Is it time to leave yet? Or at least snoop around some more?* Willow joins a small group of onlookers gathered at Warren's table to watch them play.

Warren slides another chip forward, his movements smooth and unhurried. His head tilts to the right and eyes tighten. Does he hear something? As she reaches his side, Warren whispers while studying his cards. "We've overstayed our welcome. We are about to have visitors if we do not leave."

Her breath catches; she analyzes the area, not noticing a change in anyone's behavior or anyone rushing to approach them. "What do we do?" she whispers back.

His lips curl into a small, amused smile. "We leave. Quietly."

"I fold," he announces to the table, rising with a slow stretch and gathering the remaining chips in his pants pockets. To the casual observer, it would seem as though he wanted to cash out after a lucky streak. He takes her hand, guiding her through the crowd, weaving between tables and players.

Glancing down, she can't help but trace over their hands. His engulfs hers, warm and steady. *Which now that she thinks about it, shouldn't his skin be cold?* Her head pounds with the sudden movement. The sensation of being watched burns in the back of her skull.

The moment they push through the Golden Wolf's doors, they break into a brisk pace, cutting through the throng of people waiting outside. The neon lights of the casino reflect off the wet pavement as Warren leads them around a corner and into the familiar narrow alley where she first discovered his vampire identity. Where despite his nature, he decided to save her.

"Why are we stopping so close?" she yells through a whisper, her head whipping back and forth, up and down the alley.

Warren lifts his head, pointing his ear toward the entrance. He pushes Willow against the brick exterior of the alley, caging her in with his arms. She freezes.

"Follow along," he commands in a whisper.

Before she can ask what's happening, he presses his hips against hers, his lips capturing hers in a sudden, heated kiss. For a moment, Willow is too stunned to react. The kiss is fierce, urgent, and tinged with a raw depth that takes her by surprise. His hands slide to her waist, pulling her closer as if they had been there the entire time, lost in each other. She can feel the coolness of the wall against her back and the warmth of his chest pressing against hers. Even with the alcohol, her spine stiffens unsure of how she should react.

Footsteps grow louder. *Oh.* They are hiding in plain sight, disguised as a couple in a moment of passion in an alley. Her eyelids close, allowing herself to get lost in it, simply to play the part he so wishes her to do. Her chest aches. As he feels her relax into him, he deepens the kiss, his lips moving against hers with a controlled intensity.

His fingers brush against the base of her neck, sending a shiver down her back. His lips are soft, and hungry. *Tender.* The stubble along his jaw rubs against her cheeks, causing warmth to flow to them. Her tongue dances against his, toeing the line of getting close to his pronounced fangs. The thrill of it makes her core vibrate with electricity. *This is a ploy—a necessary act. Yet...she needs more.* Her body responds instinctively to his touch.

The footsteps of the men trailing them slow as they approach the entrance of the alleyway. Their voices are muffled; she isn't sure if it's due to them whispering, or if she's too overstimulated by Warren's mouth to care about what she hears. He pulls away from the kiss, a softened, silent ache lingers across his features—then his attention jerks to the rustling nearby.

"Do you fucking mind?" His bark comes out gruff and gravelly, a rough echo of its usual smoothness.

Willow shifts against the wall, caving in as the awkwardness sets in. Warren doesn't wait for an answer—his focus snaps back to her, and he captures her mouth with another kiss.

She focuses on the shocking tenderness of his lips, attempting to block out the fact that strangers who want them dead are watching them make out. *This is humiliating.* As her mind wanders, Warren's touch brings her back, caressing her lower back. All thoughts, other than his skin on hers, exit her mind.

"*Oh, shit. Sorry,*" the unfamiliar voice mutters.

The footsteps continue further past them, fading into the distance.

Warren pulls back once again, his forehead resting on hers. They both continue to breathe hard, the air between them buzzing with adrenaline. There's a quiet fire in his gaze as it meets hers, probing the ocean-blue stillness of her irises.

"They're gone," he mutters.

She nods and swallows deeply, her heart pounding from the narrow escape. The skin where Warren touched her tingles, leaving her skin sensitive and feeling vulnerable. All her emotions swirl together like soup. *She can't pinpoint it, but it isn't a bad feeling. For the most part.* The embarrassment from the other night, however, she could do without. Her expression deadens.

"Sorry, I had to think fast," he murmurs, though his face is neutral, something flickers in his eyes—regret? He speaks as though he needs an immediate excuse, and given her personality, that's an intelligent assumption, but somehow this hits her in the gut.

She swallows. "Well, it worked I guess." She pushes off the wall, shoulder checking him.

He allows his shoulder to give with her shove. "Yes, it did."

They stand there a moment, the tension palpable, waiting for the other to make a move first, before Warren steps back. "We need to keep moving." Seriousness settles back into his stress. "We're not out of danger yet."

CHAPTER 32

THE PITT

"Are you thinking that this Eryx guy's behind all of this?" Willow asks, slurping Warren's homemade spaghetti. After the two of them left the alley, nothing but silence hung in the air. No conversation about the kiss they shared. Typically, Willow would resort to anger and be straightforward with him, but for some reason in this scenario, she'd rather pretend it never happened. *Self-preservation, perhaps?*

Warren winces, watching the spaghetti sauce splatter all over the side of her mouth and the counter. Sensing his disdain, she slides a napkin over the mess, cleaning it off. One thing she's learned since moving in is that he's an excellent cook and will never let her sleep without having at least one meal. Now that she thinks of it, she should probably go to her house soon to check on the place.

"Hard to tell at this point, but he will be able to answer some of our unsolved questions. I overheard several workers at the Golden Wolf last night use him by name when speaking to each other about picking up supplies. But I'm afraid this won't be an easy task. I hoped it wouldn't come to this." A frown tugs at his lips.

It's not often she sees concern from Warren, which makes her stomach ache. "Sunny mentioned he's skilled in blood magic?"

Warren rubs his neck. "Yes. He's a manipulator that works closely with the shadows. Luckily for us, however, he's a businessman and has boundaries in place he would like to uphold. If we come with money, we have a good chance he will give us the information we request. If we catch him in a good mood, that is."

Her eyebrows raise. "The money I make is barely enough to pay for my mortgage and utilities. Will this money come from your funds?"

"Of course," he scoffs.

She says between chewing, "Right, I forgot that all vampires are filthy rich." She didn't know anything about his wealth, but the home she currently sits in, while eating homemade pasta noodles and sauce is enough to show the difference in their tax bracket.

He rolls his eyes. "If you've been alive for over two-hundred years and you aren't wealthy, you're not doing it correctly." Fair point.

Her shoulders shrug in agreement. Satiated and swollen, Willow stretches in her seat. Warren isn't looking at anything in particular, his expression distant and hollow.

"What is it that you aren't saying?" Willow asks.

His brow furrows. "I'd much rather leave you here while I visit The Pitt for more information–"

"There's no way you're going without me; I have put my life on the line–" she interrupts, but he talks over her again.

"If you'd let me finish my sentence... Unfortunately, you will have to accompany me. Or at least another human."

"Another human?" Her brows knit.

"I could always seduce another participant and have their memories altered–but that sounds more of a hassle than just having you tag along."

Willow's jaw clenches.

"Don't pout." There's a spark of mischief in his lilt, far more lighthearted than before. "The Pitt requires each creature to bring their own life source, so to speak. And as I require blood, I must bring a human." A muscle ticks in his cheek, quickly suppressed.

"Fine. I guess I should get ready. I'll bring my dagger." Irritation pricks at her.

"Yes. Also, put on your nicest outfit. We must give them the best show we've got."

*

"Whatever happens down here, remember it's to gather information and keep us alive," Warren states.

How has she never noticed this before? Just below The Black Pine Tavern, a set of stairs descend from outside. The air grows thicker the further the two traverse down the narrow stairway, draped in murky light, leading to The

Pitt. Sweat, iron, and booze nip her nose. A wooden door etched with obscure symbols of lines and contorted shapes, creaks open– revealing a sprawling underground club and arena.

"How is it possible that this exists, and the locals never run into it? Or other creatures?" she asks.

"Blood magic. Eryx created it. There's a glamour effect masking it from anyone other than supernatural creatures, or those who use magic." Warren's hand finds the small of her back, guiding her forward. "The supernatural survives on being hidden, it's something we thrive at. There are other doorways around the world leading to The Pitt. It's not technically located in Misty Pines, but one of the entry doors is located here."

Through the threshold, they are met with a gruff man with a permanent scowl plastered on his face. *Could he be considered a man?* The burnt orange scales across his skin are in the process of shedding. Each of his yellow eyeballs blink individually, watching them as the green vertical slit narrows on the two of them. Willow's breathing speeds up.

"State your name."

"Warren Blackwood," Warren states. The chatter of the nearest room hushes, all attention draws to them.

Whispers ripple through the sea of threatening individuals–some creatures she's only ever read about in fantasy novels. The lizard traces Warren up and down, familiarity and skepticism lingering on his expression, though he lets them pass.

A sea of gazes floods the couple upon entry. *It's clear from their reactions that Warren's presence demands respect— or perhaps fear.* Warren draws Willow in, tucking her against his hip with quiet strength. Several onlookers avert their gaze, resuming previous conversations. Her arm helixes around Warren's; her attention is held hostage by a group of several gorgeous women, wearing little to nothing, dancing on a platform stage. They're surrounded by hoards of men. Creatures? Both, it seems.

Her eyes bulge. It's nothing like she envisioned. Electronic dance music hums in a rhythmic beat. One performer glides forward, teal scales shimmering along both sides of her body. Another stands tall, her scarlet skin striking beneath a shade of lipstick even deeper in red—could she be a demon? The last sways gently, lost in what seems like a trance. Bite marks litter her neck, arms, and the inside of her thighs. Blood oozes down her exposed skin. *She's human.* Willow's muscles flex; her mouth curls.

Warren's gaze flickers to hers, pulling her close.

"Now's not the time to act brave, Willow." His lips almost touch her ear. A delicious shiver trails down the curve of her back. His mouth shifts to her neck, his teeth grazing the top of her skin, scratching it enough for her to feel, but not enough to make her bleed. She freezes. "Remember what I said before we came down here," he murmurs before pulling away from her neck.

Her stiffened spine decompresses. *Okay, okay. Breathe.* She clears her throat but doesn't bother to hide the contempt in her tone. "*Right.* Lead the way."

A metallic odor mixed with various liquor and men's cologne hovers like fog. The atmosphere of The Pitt is contradictory. On one hand, it's one level up from being a dump, yet on the other hand, almost every being in attendance is in a suit and tie, or extravagant dress. If the bartender put a drink down too fast on the bar, it would probably collapse from how rotted it is. A towering, rusty, chain-link fence blocks off a large chunk of the right side of the area, creating a cage. Two human-like creatures wail each other into a pulp within the confinements of the cage. Dog-like snouts protrude on both of their faces, snarling and growling after every punch they throw. Throngs of boisterous patrons chant with excitement for their choice of the winner, encouraging them to hit harder. *If they hit any harder than they already are…they may die.* Willow clings to Warren's shoulder.

"If you try getting any closer to me, you'd be up my ass," he mutters.

"Listen, I read books with characters like this, but being face to face with them—" She pauses as a beautiful siren man walks by them. Scales glitter with hues of indigo and aqua, smiling with sharp teeth at the two of them. "*It's much different than my books. And maybe, unfortunately, a little less hot than what I read,*" she whispers.

Warren's eyes roll, but he doesn't push her away. His thumb traces against the exposed skin of her lower back.

The tension is heightened as a long-limbed silhouette detaches from the shadows beyond the cage. Shadows carry it through the air, heading directly toward Warren and Willow.

Warren stiffens, pulling his shoulders back. Willow adjusts accordingly, following his lead.

"I cannot believe my shadows! To have the one and only, Warren Blackwood, in our presence!" the man exclaims, his announcement echoes throughout the underground chamber as he closes in on the two of them. *He's humanoid—that's for sure. Definitely not a regular human.*

Whispers continue amongst the mass of beings within The Pitt. Willow dares to look at the unknown man, finding his stare already on her. Or at least she thinks he is? The more she focuses, she notices a thick layer of white film coating the irises. His lips twist into a predatory smirk, revealing his pure white fangs. *Ah, another vampire. Of course.* An aura of malevolence sends a shiver down Willow's spine.

"What brings you here, *old friend?*" His words corrode like acid. *Old friend?*

"I'm here for information, Eryx. And I'm willing to pay for it."

"Information you seek? How dull. You know, you've always been so—transactional." He pauses. "But you've piqued my interest. It must be something interesting if you're desperate enough to be here." Eryx circles them like prey, his gaze flicking to Willow with dark curiosity before returning back to Warren. "I have plenty of information. But what is the fun in simply handing it over for some cash when I'm dealing with you?"

Warren's eyes narrow. "What do you want?"

His grin widens, an eerie excitement lighting up his features. Soft tendrils of shadow flicker off Eryx's figure. "A fight. Right here, right now, in the pit. If you can manage to put a single scratch on me, I'll answer any questions you want. No money necessary, for a friend of course." The crowd stirs at Eryx's challenge, anticipation spreading through the arena. Willow's heart pounds in her chest as she glances at Warren, wondering if he will take the bait. *Just who is this guy?*

"And if I don't manage to land a scratch?"

Eryx's cloudy orbs vibrate, shifting to Willow. "Your pretty little blood bank is mine," he hums.

Her throat drops into her stomach as an invisible heaviness surrounds her.

Warren's nostrils flare, but without hesitation he responds, "Deal." *DEAL?*

Eryx lets out a hearty chuckle, the shadows dance with excitement. "Excellent! It's been far too long since I've had a worthy opponent." Addressing the crowd, his arms raise high, a gesture that elicits roars of approval. "Tonight, you will witness a fight for the ages!"

The werewolves flash their teeth, spitting in the face of the guard yanking them out of the cage, hauling them away. Eryx removes his black jacket and matching black dress shirt, revealing his exposed pale skin–except it's completely scarred and covered in tattoos. The ink varies in shapes and swirls, unfamiliar writing, and even somewhat familiar runes. His skin absorbs the light around him, casting shadows that dance and flicker as though it's also alive. He places his burgundy pocket square on top of his folded shirts. Willow and Warren follow suit; it isn't until they reach the cage that Warren drops Willow's hand.

"Please don't lose," she whispers.

"I wouldn't dare," he responds, winking and following Eryx's lead of removing his shirt. *In any other circumstance, she may have enjoyed watching this. Maybe.*

Eryx and Warren enter the cage, hungry for violence. Shadows pull the cold metal bars behind them, shutting them in. The crowd falls into a hushed silence; smoky shadows whirl around Eryx, floating in all directions, taunting Warren.

Warren's muscular form coils with lethal intent.

An older, balding man from the entrance of the cage shouts, "Alright you bastards, here's a fight to remember!" He stumbles around the horde with a wicked grin, attempting to hype up the crowd. "Mr. Eryx has claimed his rules. All Mr. Blackwood needs to do is put a scratch on him! There will be five minutes on the clock to ensure that no funny business is pulled against Mr. Eryx. Other than that, this is our normal no rules fight. Everything goes! May the wickedest man win!" The crowd whistles with cheer.

Willow's shoulders rise as she pulls her arms close, feeling as though she's under a microscope. Chilling, bone cutting stares rake her over. *Warren better make this quick.*

Without warning, Eryx darts forward, moving with agility that defies his size. Warren's ready, but Eryx is faster, his movements just a blur as he slips past Warren's initial attempts to strike. Shadows cling to Eryx, swirling around him like a living shield. The crowd murmurs in awe as Eryx continues to dodge Warren's blows with ease, taunting him with every missed strike.

"You've lost your spark, old friend," Eryx sneers, his voice dripping with mockery. "Or perhaps it's a special human's distraction that's making you weak." He flicks his gaze toward Willow, a cruel sneer buries into her. "You have always been soft. Maybe when I take her for myself you can grow into the powerful vampire you were supposed to be."

A low, menacing growl escapes Warren's throat, his fangs bare in fury. Within seconds, his speed increases drastically. He moves with the fluid grace of a predator, snake like. Willow can no longer keep up with their movements; they are clashing dark flashes.

Eryx's laughter echoes throughout the cage. "Oh, have I found a sore spot? She is one who can take care of herself, I've noticed. Maybe not at this moment, but it's there, isn't it?" he speaks almost in code, looking in Willow's direction.

Willow's eyebrows furrow. Kai's necklace grows hot, alerting her. When Willow catches a glimpse of Warren, there's a familiar glaze across his features. *Strategy.*

Just as Eryx ducks from another strike, one of Warren's snakes, nearly invisible in the chaos, slithers from the shadows and strikes with lightning speed.

The serpent's fangs sink into Eryx's ankle, causing him to stagger, glaring down at the snake, a dark laugh bubbles up from his chest. "Venom? What a cheap shot," he kicks his leg, sending the snake flying back to Warren.

He catches the snake, its white scales curling around his forearm. Warren's eyes flash victorious as Eryx's leg buckles, the venom must be taking its effect. He doesn't collapse or show any sign of fear. Instead, he laughs again, a deep, resonant sound that carries through the arena. "Congratulations, Warren," he says, the amusement never leaving his voice. "A deal is a deal, even if it was your *pet* that landed a scratch."

"No rule against it." Warren shrugs.

The ghostly sheen over Eryx's vision didn't soften the sharp line of his mouth.

There are mixed responses from the crowd. Some want to clap, but seem frightened of Eryx's response, the others are too intoxicated to care and explode in cheer. Several men groan with disappointment, throwing cash to another man stuffing a burlap sack full of earnings. With a slight limp, Eryx gestures for Warren to follow. "Come," he says as he approaches Willow. "You've earned your information. Let's discuss this in private."

CHAPTER 33

RHODES FAMILY SECRET

The sensation in Willow's fingers grows numb the tighter Warren grasps her wrist. Creatures of all kinds survey them as they weave through The Pitt. Cyclops, vampires, hairy mid-transitioning werewolves–she can barely keep up. Narrow midnight silhouettes shift and swirl, grabbing Eryx's shirt and dressing him while in transit. Warren's shirt is on but unbuttoned; he hasn't dropped her hand since exiting the cage. The closeness soothes her in a way she doesn't expect. Eryx takes them to the bar but passes behind the counter. Past the bartender, a single rusted, metal door creaks open with the help of Eryx's blacken spirits. A dark entry greets them, a thin light in the distance shines overhead.

This must be part of the magic Warren mentioned. The layout of the underground club and the additional room up these stairs doesn't make sense to fit under the tavern. Old leather and mothballs permeate through the room upon entering, the style of it nothing like she pictured. Where Eryx exudes malevolent energy, she expected nothing but darkness. This room glows with light, every surface is pure white. Ironically, a downward facing pentagram is branded into the hardwood itself, Willow winces as she steps into it.

"Welcome to my humble abode." Eryx grins, spinning toward them. "Please, have a seat. Let's talk." He motions to the chairs in front of the marble fireplace.

"We are fine standing. We don't plan on being here long," Warren responds, not moving them an inch.

"Very well, suit yourself." His brows quirk in amusement, sitting in the biggest leather chair. "I'm very impressed with your fighting skills. It seems you've mastered using your enhancement power well." Eryx smirks. A cloudy gaze travels down Warren's arm, where his tattoo would be, if it wasn't covered by the sleeve of his shirt.

"There's no need to flatter me when we both know you let me win that fight, for whatever reason that may be." Warren bites. *Is that true?*

A pull of amusement creeps into a grin. "I don't know what you mean," Eryx says innocently. "Now, let's get down to business. What information are you inquiring for?"

"There have been two murders in this town recently, as I'm sure you're knowledgeable of," Warren begins. Eryx's excitement flattens. "We were hoping to learn more about what you have heard about the murders, and also if you would take a look at this to see if you had any insight to this."

Anxiety grips Willow the second Kai's journal touches Eryx's hand. *She already had her doubts being here and she didn't know this man. This journal has so much in it, and they are slapping it directly into the hands of a man who's known for being the most sinister vampire in town.* Eryx tilts his head with interest as he flips through the pages. Willow watches every move he makes.

"This sounds like a two-part request," Eryx says, skimming the worn pages of the journal. It seems he doesn't have any trouble with his vision, despite the cloudiness of the white hue that stretches across both irises.

"We hypothesize that they are both related to the same issue at hand, therefore, it is a single request for information," Warren retorts.

For a split second she feels Eryx's gaze on her. Warren steps forward, shifting on his feet to stand in front of Willow. Irritation nips at her heels; she can't defend herself. Maybe if she keeps quiet, they will forget she's there. That always worked for her growing up– before the bullies started getting physical. Except for once, she has someone standing up and protecting her. Warren's her shield.

"Neither I, nor any coven member of *mine* committed such crimes. We don't get caught. The victims were no one of importance to us, so we haven't had any interest in who did it," Eryx says.

Eryx stops on a single page in the journal. His tattooed hand snakes down the surface, feeling every inch of it. Willow peeks her head over Warren's shoulder to try to see more.

"What interesting family history you have, love." Eryx tilts his head, looking past Warren, to Willow.

Her mouth pulls to form a line. *What does that mean?* Warren puffs out his chest. Eryx smirks.

"Now, now, Casanova, I'm a man of my word."

Eryx's hand stops in one spot, his finger pointing to a cluster of symbols, runes, and letters that Willow can't make out from the distance she stands at. Not that she would understand them anyway. "*Sui desiderium*," he speaks as he passes the journal back to Warren.

"Care to elaborate?" Warren asks.

"Selfish desire," Eryx says as a matter of fact.

In an instant, Eryx transports beside Willow, catching her off guard as she gasps at his proximity. Warren bares his fangs. Shadows lick her skin; the chill makes her shiver. "Willow, is it?" he asks her.

She holds her chin up to him, refusing to show fear, but her curiosity overpowers whatever fear she does have. "What makes you think that's my name?"

"That journal you have in your possession does, my love. It's interesting that you don't seem to know your heritage."

"Heritage?" She asks. Warren drills holes into Eryx with his glare.

"A family of slayers, it appears. From what I gather, the tradition skipped over certain generations but brought back by the owner of the journal. You must not have gotten the family memo," he teases.

A cold twist of clarity winds through her. The hidden daggers, journal, the warded protection necklace. *He—knew about it all? He died hunting something, not someone.* His torso, shredded to pieces. The killer isn't human. Her hand flies to her mouth, covering it to hide her reaction but failing miserably. Tears of frustration flood her eyes, but she refuses to let them fall. Instead, they build, pooling into a dam, blurring her vision. *"You knew all of this and didn't tell me?"* Her voice comes out a whisper as she pins her gaze on Warren.

"I have my reasons, and now you'd do best to remember what we discussed prior to this afternoon and why we are here," he snaps.

She isn't sure why, but it hurts her pride. Her face flushes, embarrassment setting in as she awkwardly stands there between two asshole vampires after being scolded like a disobedient puppy. The emotional whiplash wrecks her concentration; a small stream of teardrops fall.

"Very interesting." Eryx watches the two of them. "You know, I have a couple of associates that work for me who have heard whisperings of someone crazier than even I, who is attempting to summon one of the top seven most powerful demons in the underworld."

"Top seven? What would someone want with one of them? Why release them?" Warren's voice changes from furious, to now frantic.

Eryx shrugs, the shadows curling around his bicep, moving up his arm and rolling around the base of his neck where his pale white hair ends. "One could assume power. Who doesn't want more power?" He brandishes his fangs. "Imagine what would happen, if someone was able to take control and wield that power? Go up against God Himself?" Eryx circles them once more. "I believe it to just be a rumor. It would take years to summon one of the seven," he adds.

Warren stands still, his features twisted as if he's witnessed something horrible. Willow remains quiet, unsure of what's happening.

"Pity, I think I broke him," Eryx whispers behind Willow, his breath serpentines down her neck.

This snaps Warren out of his trance and he pulls her away from Eryx. "I appreciate your information. We are leaving now."

"Are you sure? I'm feeling generous tonight. I'll give you more information if you'd really like it. All that I ask for in return is a small sip from your blood bank," Eryx adds, sauntering closer to them.

Willow's skin goes cold.

"I don't share," Warren hisses in response, wrapping his arm around her waist.

"If either of you," he trails Willow up and down, "changes your mind, you know where to find me." Eryx turns and walks back to the leather chair, and waves his fingers at the two of them, almost as a taunt.

The two of them make for the exit, running into a young blonde at the top of the staircase.

"Excuse me." Her half-lidded gaze blinks, adjusting her shirt to show more cleavage. She pushes through the two of them, joining Eryx on the chair by straddling him.

Willow averts her stare, continuing down the stairs. A gentle pressure squeezes her hips, lifting her. Within a blink–Willow and Warren are back outside the entrance to The Pitt. Willow continues walking forward as Warren grabs her wrist.

"Hey–" he starts before she cuts him off, yanking her wrist back.

"Don't you *hey* me! You've known I come from a family of," she lowers her voice into a whisper, "*slayers* and you didn't think to tell me first?" Her lips draw back in a snarl.

"I planned on telling you once I had all the information. That journal still isn't fully deciphered, but with his help, I have more guidance on the rest. Your brother was an intelligent hunter, so it hasn't been easy to get through. It wasn't the right time."

"That's not your information to keep!" she yells. Quietness consumes the street, other than the muffled conversations and off-key karaoke bellowing from the tavern. "You've been keeping this from me, letting me walk around clueless. When would have been the right time, Warren? After more people die? What if there's something within me that I can activate to help us?"

Warren turns toward the direction of the bar, the fluorescent blue light illuminating his profile. "You weren't ready."

"Not ready?" Willow's frustration spews like a firehose. "You don't get to decide that! You don't get to decide if I'm ready or not!"

"I didn't tell you because I didn't want you to lose focus. There has been a lot going on. Your family's history…it seems to be complicated, and it wouldn't have helped you then."

"Well, what about now? Do you think this has helped now, by not telling me?" She throws her hands in the air, her breath coming in sharp, angry bursts. "You've been playing me this whole time! I don't even know what else you aren't telling me. I never even wanted to be here!" Uncontrollable tears flow. "I've never been so scared in my life. It's an exhausting feeling– like I am always seconds away from death at any moment. The only thing I've ever wanted since high school was to find my brother's killer. And something that changes things drastically, you kept from me." Her voice trembles, unable to finish her thoughts as she finally vocalizes feelings she's had for a decade, pent up inside her, waiting to escape.

Warren takes a step closer; his voice lowers but does not lose intensity. "You are not a toy. You are not something to play with. I'm trying to protect you."

She scoffs through the tears, "Protect me? I just—I just started feeling like it was safe to trust you. Started to believe that you could help me and watch out for me. I don't know what to do!" It's been a while since she's cried. "And while we're at it, what about that kiss in the alley? Are we just going to ignore that?" *Time to lay it all out there at this point.*

Warren's jaw tightens, and for a moment only silence fills the gap between them. When he does respond, words catch, heavy with regret. "I made a call. Maybe it wasn't the right one, but I thought it was best. I never intended to hurt you or cause you not to trust me. I won't apologize for trying to keep you safe," he sighs, rubbing his fingers along the side of his stubbly jaw. "The kiss was–a distraction. And it worked."

Her eyes narrow. "A distraction? That's all?"

"That's all. It kept you safe. My choice of not revealing your family history also kept you safe, for the time being that is." A knife to her gut.

"This isn't about you keeping me safe. It's how you decided what was best for me, without considering my feelings or simply asking me." She wipes her face with rigor, not caring about smearing the makeup.

"You're right. I did make the decision without consulting you. I won't lie and say I regret my reasons, but–I regret that it hurt you." His fist unfurls.

The admission softens something in Willow, but it doesn't lessen the anger. Tears sting like wet fire. Mascara streaks across her dress from where she wipes her hands off. A gurgle bubbles from her stomach, but she kicks back the nausea. "No more secrets. I'm just as much in this as you are. I'm an adult and we can discuss these things, *got it?*"

Warren nods. "No more secrets." Without another word, they continue down the street, the silence between them heavy.

*

Crickets chirp and the night mist thickens. It's been a while since Willow visited Kai's grave. She didn't want to say something out of anger to Warren, so she told him to move ahead. That she'd be late and not to follow her. In Willow's high school and police academy days, she visited his grave every week–sometimes more than once.

"Sorry it's been a while, brother," she whispers, her fingers trailing against the top of the tombstone. Sobs escape her lungs as she buckles to her knees. *How is she going to do this?*

"Willow, are you okay?" Gideon's voice breaks through the cries.

She didn't even hear footsteps. Hopping to her feet, she rubs her nose and clears her throat.

"W-what are you doing here?" she stutters.

"I saw you walking from the bar, I was going to call you over, but you seemed pretty angry–"

Oh. He saw her yelling at Warren. "That–that was nothing. I'm fine. You must have heard me venting to a coworker. I've been–stressed. I'm fine." She presses her lips together, attempting to act cheerful.

He frowns, approaching her side. "You don't have to lie." Kai's grave sits and watches them. "I've never liked that guy. I get a bad feeling about him."

Her brow furrows. "About Warren?"

"That mortician, right? From the coffee shop? Yeah. Not a fan." *If only Gideon knew.* "Was he a relative?" Gideon finally asks, reading the headstone.

"My brother," she whispers.

"I'm very sorry for your loss. I can't imagine losing a sibling." Strong arms wrap around her, embracing her in a heavy hug. The weight of her body collapses into his, wrapping her arms around his waist. She chokes back the cries that try to escape. Lips kiss the top of her head.

"Thank you," she manages to say. "This is—nice." She pulls away to meet his stare. His fingers move in an instinctive gesture of comfort, wiping a tear, and holding her face in one hand.

She cradles his hand against her cheek, snuggling into it. His head moves down. Her calm is shattered by a kiss–punishing and angry, catching her off guard.

She withdraws, tightening her lips. "What was—was that? Sorry–I can't. Not here." Her mind flutters.

Gideon pulls away, shaking his head in sharp movements. "I'm so sorry– I don't know why I did that."

"It's okay, I'm sorry if I gave mixed signals. My mind's–scattered to say the least," she stumbles through her apology.

He nods. "You're sure you're okay? You can stay at my place tonight."

"I'll be okay, I swear."

He nods. "Well on that note, I'll get back to my run. I had to make sure you were safe. Again, very, *deeply* sorry. Call me if you need anything? And maybe I can take you on another date to make up for this?"

"I'll make sure to let you know. Thanks, Gideon." Her smile falters as his back turns, waving in the distance.

CHAPTER 34

IDENTITY REVEALED

Four messages, and still no response from Nadia. A heavy breath exhales through Willow's nose. *This is what she gets for never being the one to put more effort into their friendship.* Nadia has always been the one to carry the weight of it. After the spat with Warren, then the awkward encounter with Gideon—she only wanted Nadia. Her text to Nadia sent late into the night; she could still be asleep. She hasn't heard Warren this morning, but she's sure he's lurking somewhere, waiting for her to come out of her room. They're supposed to review footage and go back to the casino later tonight.

When she returned to Warren's home, the energy to change into pajamas left her. *Is this disgusting? Perhaps. But as of now, she doesn't have the mental capacity to care.* As she stretches, a sharp edge scratches her breast from under the dress.

She winces with a shocked gasp, yanking the top of the dress away from her chest. A black matte card falls, fluttering to the floor. Her eyebrows furrow. She doesn't recall getting anyone's card, let alone placing it there. An unknown number is printed on one side, the other has a single name–Eryx. Her mouth crinkles. *When did he do that? It sure as hell wasn't her that placed it there.*

The thought of trashing it comes to her mind, but she can't bring herself to. For some unfortunate reason, she may need it. *In the nightstand drawer the card goes.*

A scalding hot shower and a fresh change of clothes later, she exits her room. Droplets of water fall off her damp hair, splashing on her oversized thrifted sweatshirt. The sweet sound of Warren's violin travels down the hallway, a small surge of hope lifts her spirits. Warren faces away from her, his left fingers moving along the violin as the right hand pulls the bow in delicate motions–creating a tender composition from the library. Instead of saying anything, she sits down on one of the leather chairs, waiting for him to finish.

He turns, not pausing his song. "Are you ready to go over everything we have one more time?" He finishes his last note, removing the violin from under his chin and places it back in the case that rests on the coffee table.

"Yeah." She avoids his gaze, still bitter from the night before.

The software to access the police station's database is locked down, since she's on leave, but thankfully she saved all the evidence onto the computer itself. *Highly inappropriate and borderline misconduct, but that's the least of her issues at this point.*

The shuffling of papers and occasional click of the laptop's trackpad interrupts the silence hanging in the air. Willow's thoughts drift as she revisits each crime scene through the evidence, her notes scrawled in the margins of the photographs. Observing them now, she realizes most of it is chicken scratch. *It's a miracle she can read it.*

After several hours, the pictures blur together. Standing, she arches her back, rolling her shoulders to ease the tension. Warren glances at her before turning his attention back to the laptop. Flickering camera footage from the Golden Wolf plays on the monitor. Despite her irritation toward him, she moves closer to view the screen sitting in his lap. *They are missing something, other than the obvious missing time from the video itself.*

Jonathan is tense, his body language tight and restricted, almost paranoid the way his head swivels every time he sits at a new table. He adjusts his shirt periodically. The suave man joins him, and chats for a brief few minutes before the edited footage skips ahead, and everyone at the table is gone. *That man.*

"Rewind it," she demands, not having the patience with Warren to ask nicely.

He doesn't argue, rewinding the clip. This time, she focuses on the man in black who visits the table. The way he hovers near Jonathan, close but not too close, like a shadow following its source. The footage is too blurry to make out exact facial details, but the longer she focuses, the more a familiar sensation gnaws at the edge of her memory. *Could it be?* Her heart sinks, willing her theory to not be true.

"It's been *Aldaric*–this whole time. That's him." Her breathing kicking in short, quick breaths. Any anger she had toward Warren has now dissipated. "It's him! I saw him there when we were at the casino last. We spoke briefly, and he seemed–surprised to see me." Willow trails off. She still hasn't had a reply from Nadia. Granted, it's early in the day and typically Nadia will sleep in as long as she can, so maybe that's the case? Her stomach churns.

"Are you sure?" he asks, though his tone suggests he already knows the answer.

"I mean–I think? Is this even possible? Nadia hasn't answered my texts. She's not safe! We need to get him! What if–" He cuts her off before she can spiral.

"Listen. We need more information. If we kill the wrong guy, a guy that happens to be dating your best friend, that has more of an impact than I'm willing to let happen if we are wrong," he says with quiet control, his demeanor helping Willow to adjust her own as her breathing slows back down.

"What about Nadia?" She waits for his reassurance, maybe even a comforting embrace—or hell, a squeeze of her hand. But it never comes.

"This stays between us," he repeats, firmly. "I will start an investigation into him. If what Eryx said is true, in what he has been hearing, we are likely dealing with a high-level demon, or one of the Princes of Hell. Eryx likes to talk in hints and riddles."

"What is a Prince of Hell?" It obviously sounds like bad news.

"They are the physical embodiment of each cardinal sin. The strongest demons to live and rule over Hell. There are seven." Warren's fingers tap against his thigh.

Pressure builds behind Willow's eye sockets and her fingers pinch the bridge of her nose. *A Xanax could really help right about now. The overwhelming feeling of impending doom isn't treating her well.* Standing from his chair, Warren places a hand on her shoulder. She flinches at first, then his touch goes ignored as her mind wanders. There's so much rage built up, but she doesn't know which outlet to send it. Warren? Aldaric? Supernatural creatures in general? Milo for being the reason she's on leave? Herself for not being a better friend to those around her?

Herself. She's the reason to blame. She knows it. She can't do this alone anymore. Warren's fingers squeeze her shoulder, only halfway taking her mind off the self-pity she sinks into. A scowl finds her lips, and her shoulder jerks away from his touch. Warren pulls his hand away, nibbling on his lower lip.

"The timing is poor, but tomorrow is the full moon. I'll need to be locked away in my room or gone these next two days." A silent battle shows in the way his jaw locks and brow tenses. He sighs as he motions over to several stacks of books on his desk. "I've managed to find some old texts that may help us with our research in the Princes of Hell, demons, and summoning these powerful entities. It will be enough to keep you busy for the next two to three days until we can go to the Golden Wolf."

"It's a full moon already? We have to wait for it to pass in order to go to the casino? What if more bodies start appearing? Isn't time of the essence?" she questions.

"Yes, we have to wait. You are no match by yourself, and I cannot properly operate until it is over. It may seem silly to you but take note that I am restraining myself right now and it isn't even at its peak yet. This isn't a scenario I take lightly." He regards her with caution. "I'm protecting you and everyone else. You're smart enough to know that I can't afford to be around anyone during this time."

"I can't just sit around doing *nothing*." Her jaw clenches, anger seething beneath her skin.

"You won't be, you'll be doing research on my behalf. You're a big girl and I'm sure you will figure it out," he snips, pushing his hair back.

Her eye twitches and lips tighten. "Fine," she hisses. "Put the material in a stack somewhere in here and I'll start when I get back. I'll be back within a couple hours." She turns on her heels, not leaving any room for argument.

"Where are you going?" he yells.

She ignores him, grabbing her keys, and leaves with the sound of the door slamming behind her, which reverberates through the house for good measure. The cold air stabs through her clenched teeth as she walks aimlessly toward downtown, but it does nothing to cool the anger bubbling inside her. *She knows Warren can't just turn off his instincts, but it doesn't make it any less frustrating when they are on the edge of understanding what's happening in this town.*

She pulls out her phone, wanting to grasp for any inch of connection she can get from another person. *"Hi, are you free? I could use a distraction."* *Is she doing this out of spite? Maybe.*

The sound of windchimes against the back of the door at the coffee shops ring, playing their melody to alert the staff that a new customer has arrived. Gideon responds to her; the ding draws her attention back to her phone and away from the glass case of pastries.

"I'd love nothing more than to give you a distraction, sweet Willow. Unfortunately, tonight's no good. Can we take a raincheck for another night, with something a bit more exciting?"

Even the way he flirts through text gives Willow butterflies, though it's short lived. Once again, she's left with emptiness. Guilt coils within her, battling with the part of her that sees Gideon as a weapon to be used against Warren. He doesn't deserve that. She can't help but also feel self-pity, knowing she's the reason she feels so alone. A black coffee and blueberry muffin sing to her from behind the counter as a familiar voice interrupts her inner thoughts.

"Willow?" Milo hesitates at the entrance before approaching. "Hey. Didn't expect to see you here," he greets, his wave forced and awkward.

Great. After swallowing the saliva pooling in the back of her throat she speaks. "Just grabbing some caffeine to help get me through the night. How have you been? How's the team? I've been meaning to reach out," she pauses to search for the right words, "but I didn't want to cross any boundaries. Or get fired for obstruction of justice or tampering with evidence," she halfway jokes. *She's already committed those.*

Her shoulders slouch forward. *She has been trying to keep herself busy so she wouldn't have to acknowledge her feelings about missing her job, or even to her surprise– her colleagues.*

Milo stuffs his hands into his jacket pockets. "I'm still sorry, you know. Everyone misses you. It's just not the same." He avoids making eye contact.

"Order for Willow?" A petite female barista calls, placing the coffee and muffin on the counter.

"Thanks." Willow responds. Her and Milo stand in uncomfortable silence for a moment before Milo breaks the tension.

"Look, this case has been tough on everyone. We're stuck, if that makes you feel any better." He stares at his shoes. It does make her feel better. Not because her team's failing, but because that means hopefully, they are safer than she'll be.

She frowns, feeling his disappointment. "You guys are going to catch the person responsible for this." Her heart aches at her lie. Sleep deprivation drags his fraternity boy features into resembling an overworked line cook. The bags under his eyes are fully packed, ready for a vacation—a feeling she knows all too well. "You should get some rest; you don't look too hot right now."

"But I look hot other times?" He cracks a lopsided grin before it fades, running his calloused fingers through his unkempt hair. She can't help but return the smile.

"I'll catch you later, Dunn. Seriously, get some sleep and start fresh." She pushes forward, walking past him to leave the shop.

"I will when you take your own advice." His eyebrows raise in a challenge. Willow pays him no attention and throws her hand up in the air.

Clouds cover the town and a soft sprinkle of raindrops drips against the ground. Willow holds her palm out for the rain, admiring the beauty of nature. The thunder rattling in the distance offers relief. Lighter gray clouds pass by the darker ones, escaping the town to head to the next. The dark, charcoal clouds remain in place, conglomerating into one looming, onyx nebula.

The rain hits Willow's phone screen, blurring the words under the water. A green bubble notification magnifies under the raindrops. *Nadia.* She unlocks her phone in a sweeping motion.

"Hey, Will. Sorry I've been MIA. I've been working like crazy and in my free time I'm either sleeping, or with Aldaric, so I've been a bit busy! I'm going back to sleep since I stayed out working an hour away at 3 this morning. Lunch soon? Love you."

Willow exhales an audible sigh of relief. At least Nadia's safe. For now. Nothing in her text signals a red flag. She feels herself hardening as she thinks about the battle ahead, nervousness, anxiousness, but mostly anger mixes within her. Time to dig into the research. Her hand brings the red coffee cup to her mouth, chugging half of it to prepare for another all-nighter of studying.

CHAPTER 35

THE PRINCE OF GREED

Not long ago, Willow once eagerly awaited the night. The stars would peer through the mist, twinkling down at her, giving her hope that her dedication to Kai's case would come with a resolution, justice. That maybe where he is now is better than here. As she sits at Warren's vintage wooden desk in the library, looking out the window, she finds her chest tight. The full moon burns bright, and in turn, brings out the most carnal desires of already evil creatures. *Well, mostly evil creatures.* Warren, despite his dryness, isn't all that bad in the big scheme of things.

Her fingertips rub against the embossed paper of the tomes Warren left for her to study. *Has he already read these? She doesn't know much about what he does when he disappears.* Warren does a surprisingly good job at being even keeled, not revealing what information he does or doesn't know. The first book she picks up is an older, black faded leather-bound journal. Scents of coffee grounds, metal, and wood flip through each page, reminding her of playing with Kai in her grandfather's work shed. He would mainly carve wood and create trinkets out of empty coffee cans, calling it "work". *Though, now Willow knows he did much more than woodworking to keep busy.*

The ideology of demons stretches across a multitude of religions. In many of these, demons are considered to be fallen angels. They have similar characteristics such as immortality, spirituality, and various immunities. Unlike God, demons are not all knowing. Each has a different knowledge base specific to it. It's said that these fallen angels serve the Devil, alluring people into destructive behavior, false teachings, and encouraging separation from God. They thrive from temptation. Feed off it, until they have corrupted a person beyond comprehension.

A heap of the books she skims through are arranged in a tidy stack. There are various journals in a language or code she's unfamiliar with. An entire world of the unknown– sitting at her fingertips. It feels as though she's lived a thousand lives just these last few months. Willow pulls a scarlet journal from the next in line in the pile. *The Seven Princes of Hell* is scrawled in gold cursive on the front, written in English. Her neck cranes further down to read. The initials *M.R.* are scrawled inside the cover. The handwriting of the journal is delicate, and oddly familiar.

"Of all the fallen angels, the seven strongest demons reign over Hell. The Seven Princes of Hell each have many names, though they represent each individual sin of the seven deadly sins.

Lucifer, the Prince of Pride.

Beelzebub, the Prince of Envy.

Satan, the Prince of Wrath.

Abaddon, the Prince of Sloth.

Asmodeus, the Prince of Lust

Belphegor, the Prince of Gluttony.

Mammon, the Prince of Greed."

Greed. Her breath wavers.

"Selfish desires," Eryx says.

Speaking in riddles. Willow's frantic, flipping through to find the section on greed. One hand picks the skin of her lips while the other holds the page ready to turn.

"Before his fall from grace, Mammon was obsessed with the bounty of treasures that are limitless in the heavens–particularly gold. After following Lucifer's suggestion of using the treasure found for his own personal gain, Mammon created his fall from heaven, becoming consumed with obtaining riches. The Devil pronounced him to be among the Seven Princes to rule over Hell. Mammon is the prince who personifies the sin of greed, wealth, and prosperity."

The text is broken up with a drawing of a man–gold skin, with money-green eyes that pierce right through her, sitting on a golden throne with endless treasure covered in blood behind him.

"Mammon's greatest weakness lies within his unquenchable thirst for more. Mammon can be trapped by the very riches he covets. Though as long as humanity holds greed within their hearts, Mammon cannot be killed. Banishment or sealing away the princes is the only way to rid them on our worldly plane of existence. To complete the banishment, one would need a skilled sorcerer or witch,

cursed binding rope, and the proper spell of banishment to hold back an entity of such power. It is incredibly draining."

The last entry is short.

"Over the course of decades, many have tried to summon the princes, each for various reasons. Summoning a prince takes an exponential amount of time, as well as excruciating pain for a sacrifice. Before a sacrifice is made, the summoner must make contact with the prince to strike a deal. At the completion of the ritual, a pact shall be made, and then time passes to allow the prince to travel from hell and ascend into our plane. May peace find the summoner's soul, for there is no turning back."

This is what they've been searching for! She grins down at the journal. *This has got to be what Eryx was hinting at!* Surely Warren hasn't read this yet or else they would've already acted. The journal slams shut, leaving her ring finger lodged between the pages so she wouldn't lose her spot, rushing to Warren's room.

Her wrist twists the doorknob to his room, only halfway expecting him to be there. "Warren? I found–" The sight before her rips the words from her throat.

Heavy, corroded chains strap to each of Warren's wrists, pulling him against his bedroom wall. His chest heaves through a torn shirt, exposing skin glistening with sweat as he struggles against the restraints. The whites of his eyes are black–his irises glowing a bright crimson with bloodthirsty hunger. The sharpness of his fully extended fangs could cut her just by looking at them.

The full moon's light streams in through the window, peering through scattered clouds in the sky, casting an ethereal glow on his iridescent skin. The room smells of sweat and blood, a metallic taste permeating the air. His head snaps up at the sound of the door opening. The sight of her makes him turn halfway, clinging closer to the chains tethered to the wall. *Every fiber of her being screams at her to run.* But she doesn't. She can only stare. *He's– mesmerizing.*

He snarls, his voice a low, restrained growl, "Leave. *Now!*"

"I found something that can help us. We–we need to act quickly." *This can't wait.*

His eyes flicker between the person he knows her to be and the uncontrollable desires coursing through his veins. His body shakes, straining against the chains, muscles bulge as he tries to stay in his spot. For a brief, terrifying moment, the chains hold.

Then, with a deafening *crack*, they shatter, scattering against the floor.

Warren lunges forward, faster than her mind can register. A supernatural hunger radiates from crimson orbs, seeping into hers. She stumbles back, but he doesn't go for her throat. His control–while hanging by a frail thread–holds enough that he doesn't touch her. Instead, he yanks open the lid to a nearby cooler, grabbing several blood bags from within the ice.

He rips them open, drains them in quick pulls, never looking away from her. The moment feels intimate. Fear mixing with–desire. Every muscle flexes, struggling against his natural impulses. Three more empty bags are tossed onto the floor. The tension in the room is palpable. The glowing glare dims, but his once crazed features shift into something darker–more primal. He steps closer, the air between them thick with something unspoken, a dangerous tension she wasn't expecting.

"Willow–" His voice is low, husky, causing her spine to straighten.

This is the first time he's used her first name to address her. The room feels too small, the space between them too intimate. She should step back. She knows that. The way he watches her, gaze trailing along her silhouette, makes her forget how to breathe. There's hunger in it—soft, deep, dangerous, she can't look away. His fingertips brush her cheek, then down her neck, hovering over her pulse point. Her breath hitches. The warmth of his touch makes her stomach tighten.

"I warned you," he murmurs, his voice smooth but with a dangerous edge, like velvet with an open flame under it. "You shouldn't have come in here. Why can't you just be obedient and listen when I tell you to do something?" His jaw clenches. "Your heart is *pounding*."

His hand lingers on her neck, thumb tracing the line of her jaw. Her heart pounds, as though it sings to him. *The logical part of her brain screams at her to pull away, wanting her to regret her decisions. But she doesn't move. She can't. She should be scared, but she isn't.*

Warren leans in, his lips brushing against her ear. "I don't like that look you're giving me."

A flush creeps over her skin as his words settle over her. The intoxicating scent of him mingles in the air and she finds herself leaning into his touch. Her mind's at war with her body, like two magnets of the same side pushing against each other. But Warren's magnet is the perfect charge for hers. His hand finds the small of her back, pulling her closer until their bodies are nearly touching. His lips hover over hers, the heat between them palpable, crackling like fire.

Warren's dangerous. Crossing this line can change everything–but at this moment, she doesn't want to stop. She has been stifling these feelings for a while now. It's becoming harder for her to maintain the facade. His other hand tangles in her hair, pulling her head back just enough to expose her neck.

"Do I frighten you, *Willow?*"

"Not anymore," she breathes. *A truth.*

"Tell me to stop," a quiet plea slips out—unsteady and yearning as his lips hover near her skin.

She doesn't say a word.

His warm breath ghosts over her skin, sending a shiver down her spine. With a sudden shift, he closes the space between them. The cruel ravishment of his mouth crashes against hers with a hunger that sends shockwaves through her core. This should have been their first kiss. It feels–*right.* Willow gasps against his lips and her hands find his shoulders for stability as he presses her against the wall beside his bed. She groans.

He pulls away, eyes half-lidded, muttering to himself, "*I–shouldn't.*"

It's too late for Willow. She needs this. "You should," she whispers, trailing a hand down his sculpted chest.

The inky depth of his stare pulls her in, unable to resist. He doesn't argue, finding her lips once more.

His hands roam over her flesh, fingers tracing the curve of her waist. There's a firm gentleness to his touch, a simmering urgency that makes her ache for more. Her breath hitches as his lips leave hers, trailing a slow, deliberate path down her neck. Where she expected sharp fangs to pierce, his soft, reverent mouth drags kisses. Fangs lightly graze her throat–lingering without breaking skin.

"You're playing with fire," she whispers, breathless as she threads her fingers through his long hair, black and white tangling between them.

A low chuckle rumbles in his chest as he leans into her. "I'm not the only one." A firm hand squeezes her ass.

His touch slides around her hips, sweeping her weightlessly into his arms, taking her to the bed. Her legs wrap around his waist, pressing against his as they stumble together, the world around them paused. He hovers above her for a moment, the air between them charged. His body, full of desire and painful restraint. "I wish you weren't so stubborn," he breathes.

"No, you don't," she whispers back, eyeing his happy trail that disappears below his pants.

He sighs, "*No. I don't.*"

Her fingers hook around his belt loop, pulling him toward her. Following suit, he takes the bottom of her shirt and pulls it over her head. She cooperates; the chilling air hits her chest. The weight of his form against hers is intoxicating, grounding her in the moment as he kisses her again–slower this time, more deliberate as his tongue dances with hers. Instinctively, she arches into his touch, yearning for the friction.

His arms wrap under her, unlatching her lacy bra and tossing it off to the side. She thrusts her hips off the bed, helping him to remove her pants. Their movements grow frantic as clothes are discarded carelessly on the floor, the barrier between them dissolving with each heated kiss, every touch sending them spiraling deeper into the moment. Insecurity tries pulling at her. *She's so…exposed.* Warren pulls her chin up to meet his piercing stare.

"Dangerously *beautiful*," His voice comes out in a husky whisper. The words melt her worries away. He reclaims her lips.

Her fingers run over the sides of his torso, feeling every muscle flex. The prolonged anticipation is almost unbearable. Willow's body responds as if she had been waiting for this moment since they met. *And maybe she had.* The intensity of his gaze makes her heart skip a beat.

"I'm strong," he winces as though in pain. "But if I go any further, I'm afraid I won't be able to stop." He's slow to remove his pants, waiting for her to change her mind.

"You don't have to–" she rasps.

His pants hit the floor and the entirety of her face flushes at the sight. The urge to touch him grows. He drinks her in, desire simmering beneath the surface. *Hunger.* Any inclination of hesitation he had–gone. And her advances say the same. Her hand extends to him, running up his thigh, rubbing the length of him. A groan escapes his lips. In a blink, they are on the bed, Willow straddling his stomach.

"I'm in control of this, we–we do this my way," he growls in between kisses, his fangs poking from his parted lips.

She nods. *Anything he wants.*

"*Good,*" he praises.

She can't hide her reaction to his words. Aching for him. With ease, she backs up. Her fingers wrap around his length as she eases herself onto him. A moan escapes her and the room disappears. A sense of completeness fills her as she begins to rock her hips. His head lulls against the bed, his mouth parted. Using his chest for stability, her fingers roam over each muscle. She leans forward, bringing her raw lips to his neck. He stiffens. It doesn't stop her, as her tongue traces circles against his neck.

"I want you to know–how hard it is to restrain myself with you." His hips buck under her, craving the movement as much as she is.

"Don't hold back," she shutters, not caring what the words mean as she moans.

He pulls away, with a gentle force he leads her to look at him. *Really look at him.* "Don't say things you do not mean, Willow. I won't have you be so careless." She isn't sure how to decipher that–but at this moment, she doesn't care. *This feeling—she never wants it to end.* In an instant, she's under him, the bed soft beneath her. He thrusts harder, licking her earlobe, his teeth grazing her. Willow can't hold back her cries of delight.

The roughness of his hand moves recklessly to her slender neck. The hand rests there, no real pressure behind his grip–only a reminder of his control. The darkness of his desires travels to her breasts, trailing his tongue down her chest and in patterns across her nipple. The sensation floods her, too much all at once.

Their bodies move in perfect harmony, each touch and sound driving her closer to the edge. The room fills with the hums of their breathing, their bodies entwined. Willow's mind is a blur of sensation, her hips completely in sync with his as the pressure inside her builds, coiling tighter and tighter until she can't hold back any longer. She matches his urgency with her own unsatiated needs. With a final, gasping breath, Willow shatters as the pleasure washes over her in waves of ecstasy, trembling beneath his muscular form. Abandoning herself to him.

He follows her over the edge, his own release shaking him as he buries his face into her neck. His jaw unhinges; his teeth grip a section of her throat–but he restrains himself. Retracting them back he lets out a loud, audible moan.

A moment passes and neither of them move. Laying on his chest, they breathe in sync within the quiet stillness of the room. Her heartbeat thrums against his. The exertion finds Willow, pulling her into a sleep. The last thing she feels is his lips pressing into her forehead, a whisper of warmth as the world falls away.

CHAPTER 36

AFFINITY FOR MAGIC

The heather gray bamboo bed sheets affix to the side of her cheek, sticking to her drool. Her hand bats at the sheet, while she winces with irritation, and it falls beside her head. The vaulted ceiling of Warren's bedroom stares back at her. In a deep stretch, she expands her chest with her arms overhead. As the bedsheet falls, cold air hits her exposed breasts. Her arms rush to shield her front, her hands enclosing under each of her armpits as they search for any glimmer of warmth.

She blinks in rapid succession, adjusting to rid the sleep lingering in them. As the light enters the large window, she notices the wear and tear from the chains that were pulled against the wall, blood spatter along it. Blood bags are ripped in half and thrown all over the room. The image of Warren willingly chained against the wall flashes in her mind, causing her to frown. *Where is he?* As she shifts in the bed, her hand touches a slightly crumbled, then flattened piece of paper.

The note reads, *I'm sorry. Prepare to make a trip to the Golden Wolf when I return. -W.*

Warren's phone lies on the foot of the bed. She sighs, bringing her knees to her chest, wrapping her arms around them.

*

The morning drags on as she distracts herself by snacking and rereading old notes, but the boredom settles in like a fog. Willow flips through the collection of books in Warren's library, not focusing on any of the words. His absence feels heavier than she expected. Thoughts run rampant, while her hands busy themselves. She doesn't regret what they did last night. But she can't help but feel that he regrets it, based on his abrupt exit. She sighs, tossing the book in her hand to the coffee table. This information has been reviewed what feels like a thousand times.

The same answer remains: nothing new has been discovered, the demon of greed is running loose, and the world could be ending as we know it. *Greed.* She didn't get the chance to tell Warren. A blush heats her cheeks.

For a moment, she considers calling Jasmine. She would say it's just to check in on her and how she's doing, but selfishly, it wouldn't be the reason for her call. Willow knows Jasmine would also never break command by giving her additional information while out. That's one of Jasmine's many great character traits, however a negative one for Willow in this exact moment. Asking her to search anyone in particular would also lead them to the demon itself, which is what she wants to protect her team from. Based on Willow's conversation with Milo, they haven't had any luck moving the case along. She suspects that if any additional evidence was located, it comes from Jasmine obtaining search warrants for the victims' phones.

Is Nadia still safe? Could Aldaric be the Prince of Greed? He killed Johnathan for something that happened at the casino? It's so strange, he seemed like an average guy. Well, a very handsome and rich, average guy. Nadia has been kept alive this long, so perhaps they have it all wrong?

Willow pulls out her phone.

How have you been? Want to grab dinner soon? Send.

Willow's fingers scroll through her contacts, hovering over Sunny's name. There's a chance Sunny has heard of something in the office. Even if she can't help, it may be a welcomed distraction. She dials Sunny's number, leaning back into the couch as she waits. On the third ring, Sunny picks up.

"Hey, Willow," Sunny's warm and calming voice comes through, "what's up?"

"Hi," Willow replies without urgency. "I was wondering–are you working today? If not, could I come over? Maybe you can teach me some magic?" She speeds over the last question. *Oh.* "Wait, are you still in bloodthirsty killer mode?"

Sunny cackles on the other end of the phone. "Oh, child. You must have seen Warren last night." Willow's cheek burns against the phone pressing against her ear. "I'm pretty hungry, but Malcolm's keeping us both well fed with our stocked supplies. The peak is gone for the most part. I will say, it affects each vampire differently, but since Warren was cursed it takes a hold of him a bit more severely than us. Come on over! I'm not sure I'll be able to teach you much, but we can have a conversation about that." The call ends.

Her lips lift in a soft expression, a trace of relief setting in. The drive to Sunny's is peaceful as she watches the sky shift from the full gray of an overcast to a deeper, threatening shade of slate. The clouds roll in thick and low, the edges tinged with a promise of rain. By the time she pulls into Sunny's driveway, the air picks up, sending the wind chimes on the porch into a soft, erratic melody as they clink against the pillars. Thick raindrops pelt the bridge of Willow's nose as she jogs to the home. Sunny answers the door almost immediately, her oversized sweater hanging below her knees. Her curls sweep back into a loose clip, keeping them out of her face as she welcomes Willow with tender joy.

"Just in time," Sunny says, stepping aside to let Willow in as the wind kicks up. "Barely missed the storm."

The warmth of the room wraps around her like a blanket. Her bones settle. The scent of dried herbs and incense fills the air, and the cozy glow of candles scattered throughout the room makes the space feel magical. The two of them plop onto her plush couch as the rain taps against the windows.

"So," Sunny observes her with mild interest, taking a sip of blood from an opalescent, crystal cup, "you mentioned wanting to learn magic? What brought this on?"

"With everything going on, I need to be more useful. No matter how hard I train, I will never size up to a supernatural creature," her brows draw downward in a frown, "I *think* I can manage staying alive. But if I'm going to be any help at all, I need to be more defensive. That's where I was hoping you'd come in to help." She gulps.

Sunny raises an eyebrow. "I get it. Magic isn't exactly a quick, easy fix though. It's not just about learning spells. It's about what you're connected to. Some people are born with a natural affinity to it— whether it's the elements, shadows, healing, or something else entirely. You've gotta have that spark. Being a human, I can't promise that you'll have any."

Willow's stomach sinks, her hope dimming.

"But," Sunny continues, "there are things you can learn that don't require an innate magical gift. Potions, for example. There's a science to it, a craft. You combine natural remedies and herbs with the right words over it, and you can make something powerful. Healing potions for example."

Willow perks up. "That'd be better than nothing. I'd love to learn if you're willing to teach it to me."

An infectious grin spreads from ear to ear as Sunny stands, motioning for Willow to follow her. "Let's see if you've got a knack for it. We'll start small. I'll teach you how to make a basic healing potion–nothing too intense since we want it done quickly. Most of it's about getting the right ingredients and knowing the incantation to activate their magical properties. If you can manage this, *maybe* then we can tackle exploring more."

The rain pelts the side of the kitchen window that opens right above her sink, overlooking the garden in their side yard. The tops of vegetables sticking out of the ground sway with the wind and rain. Candles are lit and laid out in groups around the kitchen from the counters to bookshelves against the wall, and on her dining table. No overhead lights are on in the house, Willow notices. *This home is a dream. Do all vampires own beautiful homes?*

"Did Warren tell you about my family history?" Willow browses through various liquids Sunny has sat out on her kitchen counter.

"He didn't need to tell me. The Rhodes name is very well known for vampires that are local." Sunny washes her hands, scrubbing under her black nail polish.

"I don't–I didn't follow in that path, I hope you know. But I'm hoping it means I can have more of an affinity to the magic, like you said," Willow reassures her. "I do have another question, though."

"Hun, the thought of you staking me has never crossed my mind," she cackles, drawing the attention of Binx, who struts into the room. "But go ahead, shoot."

"When Warren and I visited The Pitt…Eryx passive aggressively referred to Warren as *friend*. What's the history there?" Her hand picks up a black vial with pure white marbles sitting at the bottom.

Sunny dries her hands on a emerald green hand towel, her expression that of concern. "It's not really my story to tell," she sighs. "But I can tell you that they grew up together. Close enough that at one time, they'd call each other, brother."

Willow's hand slips and the black tube smashes against the floor. The liquid spews in every direction and the white marbles bounce off the hardwood floor. Binx bolts in pursuit. "Sunny! I am *so* sorry!" She rushes to grab a towel.

"Wait! Don't let the liquid touch your hand!" Sunny cries. Willow freezes in place. "Don't worry, I can clean it." With a flick of her finger, towels appear out of thin air, wiping the mysterious liquid up in small circles. "Unluck liquid hex," she states. "That's the absolute *last* thing you need right now." Sunny stifles a pathetic laugh. "Anyway–Are you ready?" Sunny says, spinning to the collection of ingredients.

Willow nods, ready to try her hand at magic.

Sunny guides her through the process with patience and care, explaining each step as they work side by side in the warm, herb-scented kitchen. Together, they mix dried lavender, crushed sage, and a touch of valerian root with a blue vial of enchanted water. Sunny moves like a ballerina, dancing back and forth while demonstrating the correct ratios, and reciting a soft incantation to activate the potion's minor healing properties. The muscles in Willow's hand cramp from jotting down notes in rapid flow.

By the time they finish, the bowl glows a light green hue, the magic imbued within subtly pulsing with life. The radiance of the magic sings a song of beauty, but with each passing pulse, exhaustion clings to Willow like a weight.

"That's pretty much it! You did well today. How about we relax for a little bit and decompress? Would you like some tea?"

"Please. I think I could use some. For some reason, I feel kinda tired all of a sudden."

"It seems so simple, doesn't it? But it wears you down, especially if it isn't something you do often, or have an affinity for. Being a human, it makes it even more difficult. I'm surprised you've done what you have. Great job!" Sunny slaps Willow on the shoulder, causing her to stumble forward. "Sorry! Why don't you go sit on the couch? I'll fetch Malcolm and have him make us some of his tea while we catch up."

With a nod of her head, she continues through the plants and candles into the living room. She's much too tired to argue. The give of the couch swallows her, allowing her to sink into the seat. Her eyelids flutter, batting to stay open.

"Good evening, Willow. I've been told you have requested my special tea–" Malcolm and Sunny pause, believing Willow had succumbed to sleep. Her breathing is soft and steady, her body curling into the cushions, and her face peaceful, despite the long day.

"Let's let her sleep," Sunny whispers to Malcolm.

Willow doesn't have the energy to open her eyes.

Sunny drapes a blanket over Willow, tucking it in around her and stepping back.

"Hey, I'm sure you're tied up, no pun intended, but I wanted you to know if you didn't already, Willow's at my place," Sunny says in a low voice. *She must have called someone, hearing Sunny's conversation spark out of nowhere.*

There's a pause on the other end before Sunny responds. "I'm just going to let her stay tonight. She's wiped out. It's no trouble at all. She'll be safe here. See you then." Sunny hangs up. Rain continues to fall, breaking up the silence of the night.

"She'll figure it out," Sunny murmurs. "But it's going to take some time."

The more Willow fights, the less she wins as sleep washes over her.

*

The aroma and sound of sizzling bacon pulls Willow from her slumber, the popping of the grease echoing around her. A deep voice hums a sweet melody in the kitchen, accompanied by a *SMASH* of glass hitting the floor. Willow jolts upright.

"Not my Pyrex set! You don't even eat, get away from my glassware!" Sunny yells in a whisper. Shadows dance in the kitchen, and the black cat scurries into the living room. The lanky feline sways in a circle, eyeing Willow as it notices she's awake. Cats intrigue her. *Even though this cat isn't really a cat, right? Can it talk?*

As though she read her mind, Binx poofs into her lap, startling her. "Gah–don't scare me like that!"

Malcolm peeks his head down the hallway after hearing Willow's voice. "Good morning! We have breakfast almost ready if you'd like to join us at the table. Sunbun has moved her plants so there's room for us to eat," he teases.

Over the sound of cracking eggs Willow barely hears Sunny say, "Hush your mouth, don't let my babies hear you say that. They love their spots on the table."

Binx poof out of sight, allowing Willow to stand to her feet. Her appetite increases the further she moves into the kitchen; the savory aroma of breakfast food makes her mouth water. A plate full of bacon, scrambled eggs with cheese on top, a glass of orange juice, and a pitcher of burgundy blood spreads out on the wooden kitchen table.

"I hope you slept well and have an appetite!" Sunny grins. "All this food's for you!"

"Did you guys wake up extra thirsty?" She inspects the pitcher of their drink of choice on the counter.

"We're always hungry, but we needed a little extra for–"

"Me." Warren glides in from the back door with silence. He tucks the white strand of hair behind his ear and the sight of him makes her pulse skip.

"When you fell asleep, I let Warren know that you were here. You know, in case he came home and realized you weren't there, so he didn't think that you ran away or were killed or whatever." Sunny's lips draw in a line. *A micro expression of guilt.*

Warren doesn't have anything to add, pouring his drink into a Disney glass set Sunny sat out for them. The scowl of Donald Duck splays across Warren's cup. After taking a large gulp and licking the blood dripping down the corner of his mouth, he studies the container. "Cute," he mutters.

"Shut up, they're thrifted. I'm allowed to like things," Sunny says defensively, taking a seat next to Malcolm at the table. Malcolm holds Sunny's hand, giving it a squeeze.

"Go ahead and eat, Willow. When you're finished, we need to leave to plan our mission for what you've discovered and how to kill it," Warren says. He avoids eye contact, rubbing his nape.

Willow picks at her fingernails. "Did you read any of the texts you gave me before you locked yourself away?" Willow strikes up the courage to speak to him directly.

"No, that's why I gave them to you. I only recently acquired them, so I assumed it would be able to keep you busy while I waited out the blood lust." He flits his gaze away from her.

She gulps her orange juice down while eating a sliver of bacon, speaking in between bites. "We can't kill it. Do you remember what Eryx said? Selfish desire? After reading, I think we are dealing with one of the Princes of Hell. *Greed.*" The air in the room thickens. "The only way to defeat it is to banish it from our plane of existence or seal them away, both of which would require a skilled witch or sorcerer."

Warren's shifts with sudden interest, though his gaze averts hers. "That's what you discovered last night," he states. *Correct. The sole reason she ever considered interrupting him during his blood lust.* It appears neither of them were able to ignore the pull of the moon.

"Yes," Willow directs herself toward Sunny, "I know you said you won't get involved any more than what you've already done–but you wouldn't be willing to go back on that statement would you?"

Fingers twitch at Sunny's side. "I'm sorry, but I can't help. I may dabble within the witch world, but I'm not skilled enough to deal with a Prince of Hell–if that's what's going on here."

"No, but I can," Malcolm interjects.

Warren's mouth pulls into a tight line. An ache etches into the lines of his forehead.

Sunny frowns. "Mal, you can't do that. Do you know what kind of things a demon can do? Let alone a *Prince of literal Hell?* There's no promise you'd survive. You can't," she begins to ramble.

Malcolm's hand squeezes his wife's hand tighter.

"You know they need our help. Listen, this is bigger than all of us and if I can help keep this world, evil or not, around a little longer for you to live in, I will do anything within my power for you, my love." Gentle hands caress Sunny's cheeks as tears sprinkle her jawline. The reality of what could come is soul crushing–literally, if they lose that is. Willow can feel it as much, even in the air. *Luckily, if Willow were to die, she doesn't have anyone like Sunny has Malcolm.* The bitterness stings.

"I'll do everything in my power to make sure he gets to come home to you, Sunny," Willow chokes, water glistening behind her lashes. *Damn sympathy tears.*

"We both will," Warren corrects her. "We wouldn't ask if it wasn't detrimental, but this is something that could change the world as we know it. If he or another sorcerer doesn't help, none of us will come back."

"Or worse, you'll be the only person living among the demons," Sunny stares at a flickering light overhead. *That's right—Warren can't die.*

"It won't come to that, because with Malcolm's help we will rid Greed of this world." Willow snaps, her irritation becoming increasingly higher at the thought. *Something took her brother. A killer free.* Justice fans the flames of her internal fury.

Malcolm beams. "Right. You two create a plan, Warren—call me when everything's laid out and we can go over my part. In the meantime, I want to spend as much time with my Sunshine as I can." He kisses her on the temple, his dreads falling, tickling her cheek as he pulls away.

A brief, mournful lift pulls at Warren's lips. "Absolutely. I'll call you soon. You two enjoy your evening," he turns, catching a glimpse of Willow over his shoulder as he opens their back door, "when you're done I'll be in the car."

*

The quietness is suffocating. It's taken her almost the entire drive to work up the nerve to speak. She clears her throat. "So–" she starts, ready to put down all the disclaimers that it wasn't anything serious, things happen, but she doesn't get the chance to.

"I apologize for my chains breaking. I shouldn't have been stupid enough to not know my own strength, especially with how old they are. I should have joined Verena like I typically do. What happened last night won't happen again. It was too close of a call." The haste of his speech causes him to borderline ramble. Verena's name stings like poison.

"I see," is all that manages to escape. She squints, hoping that tightening them will keep her from crying. This is the most she's cried since Kai died. *When did she grow so soft? Or rather–when did she allow herself to show the tenderness she's worked so hard to stuff inside?*

"Now that the worst is over for my restrictions, I will start formulating a plan with Malcolm. We will take our time, researching everything before jumping in. We'll need blueprints of the casino, the staff list, and backup plans in case all hell breaks loose."

"That sounds too time consuming. What about Nadia? She's practically a captive. She needs us to act fast." She says through a clenched jaw. There's no time to worry about her bruised pride.

"If she's managed this long, she's still safe. If we go in without a developed plan, they will sniff us out and then she'd really be in trouble. The more meticulous we are with this plan, the better. Understood?" he questions, sounding like a drill sergeant. This version of Warren gives her whiplash.

"Understood." Her jaw tightens. She manages to drive to Warren's home without crying, parking the car in his driveway. Warren gets out and only turns around when he realizes she isn't following him.

"Are you going to sit in your car all day?" he speaks through the rolled down passenger window. Sharp wind cuts through the gap—the fire brimming from her core neutralizes the numbing chill of the air against her exposed skin.

"I'm running to my home for a minute. I need more clothes and to water my plants. I'm sure most of them are dead by now. Don't you or your little snake friends follow me, or I'll shoot them. I need some air." The window rolls up, not waiting for his response. In the rearview mirror she watches Warren eye the car as she exits down the driveway once more.

CHAPTER 37

BLOOD PACT

Leaves crunch under the weight of Willow's feet as she paces her front yard. *She should arrive any minute now.* The wind howls, rustling the tree branches overhead. A heavier gust of wind blows Willow's hair back. Verena leans against the nearest tree, picking underneath one of her fingernails with disinterest.

"Thank you for coming," Willow starts.

"What's this all about?" Verena's arms cross, her shoulders angle away.

Willow exhales. *She doesn't want to ask. There's nothing she would love more than to figure it out on her own. But—she's simply not capable. Not with what they are going up against.* "I need your help," she pauses, "and I'd like you to not tell Warren. Not yet, at least."

Verena's eyebrows raise, growing with interest. "Oh? Help with what?"

"I would like for you to come with me to the casino to investigate. Warren's taking too long, and my best friend has been hooking up with a Prince of Hell."

Verena's tightened lips loosen, mouth agape. "Well that just sounds thrilling in my opinion."

"This is serious! I need to go there tonight! And while I'm all for making plans, Warren is dragging this on when Nadia's life may be on the line. I don't want her to become victim number three." The corner of Willow's lips pulls down.

"And what do I get out of this? Do you understand the wrath of fury I'd get from Warren if I did this and didn't tell him? I may as well be dead." Verena zeroes in on Willow.

"He will never have to know. I need protection in case things go south. It's only for observation to see what else we can learn. And if something goes awry, call him for backup."

"Hmph. I dunno, that's still not very appealing." Verena struts away, in slow steps.

"Wait! Fine! I'll–I'll let you drink from me." She pleas with a twisted face. The words escape her mouth before considering the implications of this new deal.

The longest layer of Verena's bob swishes, as her neck whips around. "That's what I'm talking about! You have yourself a deal. I'll gather my things in preparation. We shall meet tonight. Don't forget your weapons." She blows Willow a kiss before vanishing.

*

Hollow knocking of Willow's fists thump against the familiar rotted door. A loud grunt groans from behind the entrance. The door cracks, one single yellow and green spotted eye glaring at her from the other side. She gulps, tightening her fists. "I'm here to request a meeting with Eryx. Let him know that Warren Blackwood's human would like to see him. That should suffice." She hopes that would be more than enough for entrance. There's no time to waste. *Should she have consulted with Verena before coming here? Yeah, probably. Too late now, though.*

The mustard-colored eye narrows on her. "Stay here," the creature wheezes before slamming the door in her face. The rain has been holding off, but the clouds are ever present, blocking most of the sun so all that bleak overcast remains, casting a hazy violet over the sky. Crows caw as they fly overhead; the sound is unnerving.

A couple thuds echo behind the entry. The door opens, revealing the overweight lizard man. "You've been granted access to a meeting. Boss says you know where to find him." His blubbery figure shifts to the side, motioning for her to go inside.

She nods, following the sticky bar floor, quickening her pace. The stairway up to Eryx's room is draped in darkness, except a faint glow that brightens at the top with each small step she takes. As she reaches the top, a dark silhouette leans against the doorframe.

"It must be my lucky day," Eryx says in a low voice.

She struts past him, shoulders back and chin held high. He doesn't move, allowing her to shoulder check him, turning his body to follow hers.

"I know Warren doesn't know you're here." Amusement lingers on his grin. "You must either be stupid or have unmitigated gall."

She exhales, "Probably both." Her knees quiver.

Shadows circle his arms with excitement as he watches her, pacing back and forth in the room. "So, what is it you would like to discuss? I imagine it must be important if you came here, at the tail end of a full moon, and you didn't bring your guard dog." *Shit.* She completely forgot. The muscles in her neck tighten. "I can sense your fear," he whispers, from behind her. "I can see it coursing through your pretty veins."

"How can you see if you're blind?" The question slips before she can filter her thoughts. The ivory of his clouded irises rake over her.

"I knew I'd like you. They told me I would." His fangs rest against his lip, curling into a sinister smirk.

"They?" The presence of another figure takes up space in the room, but Willow sees no one.

"The shadows." He revolves around her from behind.

She expects warmth, but frigid ice presses against her back at his touch. She doesn't dare to move.

"What is it you would ask of me my dear?" His breath tickles the back of her neck, inhaling her scent. "Are you wearing garlic?" His laughter blurts out, sharp and wild. The sight makes her uneasy as he halts under her gaze.

A blush dusts her cheeks. *It was foolish for her to try rubbing garlic on her before coming here. How's she supposed to know it wouldn't work?*

"You'd do well to study vampires if you're going to continue fraternizing with us. Using garlic to thwart vampires is more of a myth than we are." He leans against the chair as he plays with his black belt, loosening it from his waist.

"I came to ask for your help–help in defeating the Prince of Hell, Greed. Well, that's who we believe it is at least. Warren's too prideful to ask, but I'm not." She pushes through, trying not to focus on his lingering attention to her hips.

"I'm impressed you picked up on my clue. But sorry, sweets. I don't get in the middle of demon business. Not even if it affects the world," he adds, as if reading her mind for her next outburst. Her shoulders slump. "However–I dabble in many businesses, as you may guess. I have a large collection of magical weapons and items that you may deem useful in whatever you have planned." Her ears perk up.

"I'll take anything that you'll let me," she says, almost pleading.

"And what shall I get in return?" He unbuttons the top three buttons on his black dress shirt, his platinum blonde chest hair and tattoos peering back at her from his exposed skin.

She picks at her nails. "What would a man who has everything want?"

His hand combs through his sleek hair, tucking one strand behind his ear. "It would be so easy to ask for your body," he finishes unbuttoning his dress shirt, leaving it open to showcase his sculpted chest, "but I will wait for you to come to me. It'll be so much more enjoyable that way. Instead, I have a deal for you. One of which would also benefit you. It seems there has been a young blonde cop running around snooping on my business, which is causing certain operations to slow. I cannot have this. Instead of killing him, which would be easier and *preferred*, I ask that you step in and get him off my tracks. Think of this as immunity for me to continue to conduct my business, and in exchange, I will allow you to pick an item or two from my collection," he purrs.

She winces. The bar is within Leo's beat. "Fine. I'll take your deal." The decision settles in her chest—solid and final.

He grins. "Let's make it official, shall we?" A black blade conjures out of thin air, landing in Eryx's palm. The blade slices the tip of his middle finger, a small amount of blood pools to the surface. He extends the knife toward her.

"This won't turn me into a vampire, will it? If that's the case, I refuse." The thought causes bile to bubble in the back of her throat. If there's anything she's learned over the last few months, being inhuman is severely overrated.

"You've got a lot to learn my dear," he flashes his fangs in a toothy grin, "no, this will not turn you. You've got to be near death, or dead, and ingest vampire blood to be turned. Warren's an exception, not a rule." He winks.

She chews on her bottom lip as she mimics the same motions, pricking her middle finger enough to make scarlet draw. Eryx holds up his hand, palm facing her. She follows suit, unsure of what's happening. Their middle fingers touch first, cut on cut. A soft pulse of warmth radiates from her fingertip before his wound knits itself shut. His fingers interlock with hers as he brings her hand to his mouth, kissing her knuckles sweetly.

"The deal is sealed."

She yanks her hand back, inspecting her fingertip. A small amount of blood pools as she closes her fist. "What did I just do?" she hesitates to ask.

"Ensure you will keep your promise." A knowing grin lifts. He sticks his middle finger in his mouth, tasting the remainder of her essence. "Delicious." He shudders. "Follow me, I shall show you my collection. However, I expect you to keep this our little secret."

The stairs creak beneath her feet as she follows him back down to the main level of the underground hideout. "Warren will find out when I use whatever said item I take, so he will know eventually." The guilt sits as a hollow ache in her stomach. Shame weighs her down from going behind Warren's back. *But this needs to happen–for Nadia. And it's not like she's keeping it from him for forever.*

"I expect no less, but I meant he doesn't need to know about the rest of my–collection."

She clears her throat. "How do you and Warren know each other?"

Eryx's chin tilts upward. "It's not surprising he doesn't talk about it. Many, many, moons ago, we were both found by our Mentor. He tried teaching us how to live, assimilate into the human world we once knew. Warren became the obvious, favorite pupil. Our Mentor and I had–a disagreement. I tried convincing Warren to leave and come with me, but he refused. It's been decades since I saw him last, until recently that is." His hand trails along the walls, as though marking his territory with his shadows. "But we are two different people, searching for two polar opposite things."

Polar opposite? "So, you're–searching for immortality?" Willow swallows.

"Indeed." He smiles, but it stops at his lips.

The shadows float from Eryx to a doorway, illuminating the hidden door with darkness, if such a thing could occur. The fluorescent lights flicker before finding a steady hum of electricity, brightening the entirety of the room. Over twenty-five rows of industrial shelves fill the room. The essence of cedar and dust swirl in the stuffy air. The sheer volume jaw dropping, both out of concern and twisted interest.

"How am I supposed to know what to look for?"

"Are you drawn to any of the items?" he asks, leaning nonchalantly against a shelf.

She deadpans, "I'm not going to let you swindle me in our deal. I need something that's useful in banishment, or at the very least, dealing with demons. Surely you know your own inventory."

He smirks. "Yes and no. I was simply…curious. Some of these items of course have been identified. Yet, there are some others who remain a mystery. I have a group of changelings who conduct the experiments to test these items, but the last group had their organs purified into liquid, so I am currently searching for more." The shape of horror blooms where her words fail her. He laughs, "As long as you don't go to the very back left shelves, you'll be relatively safe."

"*Lovely*," she retorts, trailing in between the shelving closest to the door. Various items line the shelves–vases, jewelry, art. A golden tube catches her eye as it lays singled out from the other clusters of items on the ledge. She presses a fingertip against it, testing the safety, discovering it's– a tube of lipstick? A muddy mauve color lives under the top.

"Fascinating." He moves closer to her, plucking the lipstick from her hand. She resists the urge to make a joke about how it's not his shade. "Charmed lipstick. Apply this to your lips and the individual you kiss next will be under your command, no fighting it either. The downside is the charm only works for a limited use."

Her eyebrows raise. This can be a very useful item; however she isn't confident she can sway Aldaric to kiss her. "How will I know when the time runs out?"

He tilts his head, gazing at the tube in his hold. "I've been told that the lipstick will turn black, when out of magic."

The thought of it is intriguing to say the least. Olden trinkets and children's toys on the nearby shelves seem appealing, but none scream useful. Plus, she doesn't have the time to ask Eryx what every creepy item he owns does. "I'll take it," she peels the lipstick back from his hands, "do you have anything else specifically for demons, banishment, or sealing?"

He closes his eyes for a moment. Movement from beneath his eyelids shakes, and the shadows vibrate around his arms before dissipating as he opens his milky orbs. "There's one item that's embedded with magic similar to my own, if you think you can handle it."

"Why couldn't I handle it?"

His expression tells her she should know the answer. "Blood magic has a mind of its own. The shadows–have their own desires. Desires much stronger than the wielder." He turns away from her, trailing his blacked-out fingers along each shelf. At this point, it's harder to tell the difference between his shadows or a tattoo. They appear one in the same.

A million different questions run through her mind she wishes to ask him. Though, there's no time. The air sharpens around her, a strange vulnerability creeps in. She decides against pressing any further, unsure of where the conversation would take them. Eryx seems different from how

Sunny and Warren described him. Dangerous and crazed, all the same. But there's a nagging curiosity in the back of Willow's mind. *Maybe another time.*

His shadows come to life once more as his hand hovers over an emerald, hand bound book. The edges of the pages are irregular, faded yellow and brown. "Ah, yes." He exhales, clutching it in his hand. "This book can help you answer most questions you may seek."

"About demons?" Her head tilts.

"About anything, my sweet," he purrs, extending the book to her. "Use this with your own discretion. With each use, you shall hear from the shadows that live in the book. Every answer will come with a price. That's all I can divulge but do know that this is one of my best items. When you're done using it, please return it. It shall be sold for a pretty penny one day."

A shockwave of electricity hums through her as she takes the book. The muscles in her legs quiver as she struggles to stay standing.

"I told you; the shadows are strong," he adds, observing her reaction.

She regains her composure. "I can handle it. Uh—thank you. I hope this is all I'll need. I'll take care of the patrolling officer." She nods.

"Very well. I shall escort you out." He bows and takes charge in leading them to the exit. Before they reach the door, he pauses, a shadow drifting back to him carrying a cylindrical object. He tosses it to Willow. "Add this to your collection. Think of it as a gift for the start of a beautiful relationship together." He grins.

"This isn't a relationship, it's business." Her eyebrows furrow. "What's this?" She twists the cream cylinder around. A wick sits inside. "A candle?"

"Oh, it's much more than a candle," his head swivels, surveying The Pitt, "it's getting late. We can discuss the candle another time. More guests will arrive soon, so I must get properly dressed." He winks, opening the door himself for her to exit.

Guilt sits heavy at the bottom of her stomach, palms sweaty. She swallows hard, nodding at Eryx. "I appreciate your time."

"I look forward to giving you more than just my time." His shadows crawl, circling her neck then brushing against her lips. He smirks as he closes the door between them.

CHAPTER 38

FOOLISH RESCUE

The frigid air cuts through Willow's dress; every hair stands from her skin. She grasps at the bottom of her navy gown, pulling the hem down her leg for warmth. The ruching collects at her left side, accentuating her muscular curves, tightening her concealed firearm around her thigh. The discreet bulletproof plate under her dress presses against her chest, still hidden despite the plunging neckline.

Verena is unphased by the chilling air, even with more of her skin exposed. The black bodycon dress she wears molds to her figure, making her look like the lethal weapon she is. Its high neck mimics that of a turtleneck, but it's sleeveless. The sides of the dress are crisscross straps, as the front and back dangle in one single piece of black fabric. *It must be nice not having to wear holsters, since she's a living weapon herself.*

"Are you ready?" Willow asks.

Verena scoffs. "Of course. I'll keep my distance. Maybe get a drink or two while I'm at it, win some money, who knows what the night will entail?" She winks.

"Alright. Let's do this."

"Willow?" Gideon calls from behind, walking closer to the entrance of the casino. *Shit.* "Gideon! Hi." She simpers, her cheeks burning from how wide grin pulls. Verena's eyebrows lift.

He approaches the two women. "Out for another night of investigating? Oh, I'm sorry. Is this a friend of yours?"

Verena chimes in, a forced smile lifting her cheeks. "We just met, actually. I couldn't help but admire her dress! It's cute, right? Anyway, I'll definitely be getting that dress in another color. Thanks for the tip! Have a great night!" she cheers, leaving the two of them alone outside, entering the building. *If anyone could cheat a polygraph with ease, it'd be Verena.*

"I forgot how easy it is for girls to make friends if it involves fashion," Gideon laughs.

"That's true. Just wait. Everyone's friends when you're drunk in the women's bathroom," a nervous laugh escapes her.

"Well, I wanted to stop by to try my luck tonight. I'd love to have you join me if you're free? Maybe you're my lucky charm." She can't really say no.

"I'd love to. I'd like to get a drink first, if that's okay?"

"Absolutely! It's a date." He winks, extending his arm for her to hold onto.

Willow's fingers are restless, tapping against her crossbody strap, hugging it into her chest. Knots twist and turn in her stomach, as if searching for an escape in the labyrinth of her gut. With a roll of her shoulders, she attempts to rid her mannerisms of their nerves. *She belongs here,* the lie repeats like a soundtrack in her mind. *We're just here for observations.* But the unsettling feeling in the air tells her otherwise. Cigar and cigarette smoke taint the air. The bridge of her nose crinkles, unable to mask the disgust. A large bachelor party takes up most of the slot machines, their drunken bodies swaying, voices carrying across the casino as they lose more money than they intended.

Brian's back is turned, but Willow recognizes his oily hair immediately. She averts her gaze and presses forward, pulling Gideon behind her. Hopefully, the drastic change of her appearance can keep herself from being identified by the ones searching for her. Curly waves are styled into a messy updo; brown and cream eyeshadow sweeps over her eyelids, bringing attention to her bright blue eyes. The mauve lipstick coats her lips, accentuating her cupid's bow. It's nothing outrageous, but more than she's used to.

It's a tight squeeze in between a group of gentlemen, but Willow manages to find a vacant seat near the bar. Behind the bar, she notes a cluster of workers in all black, shuffling with exhaustion. Most of the men carry lofty crates. Each box has a worker on one side, lifting together as they inch toward the stairway, careful of the transition from the floor to the steps. *Heavy and fragile items, it seems. Illegal material, perhaps? What if—what if Ace is actually Greed and it's not Aldaric? Is it a mistake coming here?*

"Can you get me an old fashioned? I'm going to run to the bathroom and then get some chips if that's okay with you?" Gideon's words melt like honey, only catching the sweet soothing sound. If he asked to repeat back what he said, she'd look like a fool. The way he tilts his head as he speaks, his grin–all enticing. She nods, unable to string a sentence. "I'll be back." He kisses her cheek before heading away.

The bartender finds Willow shortly after. "Yes, one old fashioned and then I'll have–"

A flirty giggle chimes through the broken chatter of the bar. Willow's head snaps in the direction of the familiar sound– a tether forms in between the crowd, finding Nadia, who serves another customer a drink. Willow stands, leaving the bartender confused. Unlike the rest of the workers, Nadia's dressed in a glamorous floor length, golden gown. Slits are on either side of her leg, showing off her olive skin. Golden jewelry adorns every extremity and each ear. She's dressed like a walking Oscars award. Nadia's cheerful demeanor switches within an instant; locking eyes with Willow. Confident hands tremble, fingers unsure whether to fight or flee. The tray she holds tilts, almost crashing onto the couple she's serving. With an awkward apologetic nod, Nadia breaks away, taking faltering steps toward Willow.

"What are you doing here?" The dimples in her cheek sink deeper the wider Nadia grins, but the dimness in her normally bright smile tell Willow all she needs to know.

"Are you okay?" Willow pulls Nadia into an embrace, scanning the nearby patrons.

"Everything's great! Just working for some extra cash! Death has been slow lately," she laughs, but it comes out like a squawk.

Willow's mouth pulls into a tight-lipped line. "We both know that's a lie," she grabs Nadia's hand and squeezes, "I'm going to get you out of here. Let's go."

Tears swell, Nadia's lip quivers, no words forming. A firm hand clasps down on Nadia's shoulder. Willow follows the length of the arm, crashing into Aldaric.

"Willow, what a pleasure to see you again!" he exclaims, turning to grab two premade bubbly drinks from a lanky man in black, footsteps away. Once the drinks leave the tray, the worker makes for an abrupt exit. "Nadia, you shouldn't be serving, you should be celebrating with me. Here! Drinks on me! Today is a special day, after all."

Willow's neck tightens, struggling to swallow. "What's the occasion?" *Playing along is the only option she has.* Her jaw ticks. Across the room in full view, Verena sits in another man's lap, kissing his neck. *Damnit, Verena!* Gideon's nowhere in sight, not that he can help in this situation. Willow gives a nod of thanks, her grip wavers before accepting the drink. Nadia's smile fades as she takes the glass.

"It's my birthday today, and we are all celebrating! Aren't we—*friends?*" Aldaric's attention circles the area. Everyone in the nearby radius cheers with applause, toasting their drinks in the air. Willow's a gazelle who just stepped foot into the lion's den.

Out of habit, Willow's jittery hands snake through her hair, tussling a few strands out of her updo. Nadia looks like a deer caught in headlights, full of terror but a crazed smile plastered across her cheeks as she sips the drink.

"It's—it's delicious," Nadia stammers. Microscopic bubbles rise to the top of Willow's drink. Through her clenched jaw, she follows suit, allowing the tiniest sip to reach her. Her tastebuds dance as the sweetness hits her tongue. Notes of floral with a hint of—honey?

"Only the best money can buy." Aldaric's head tilts back, his gaze following down his nose.

Assessing her. A pause, and his head swivels around the tables. "Is Gideon here with you?"

"He was, he just ran to the bathroom, so he'll return soon." Her fingers tighten around her drink. "I'm yure I, he—" she stops.

The tip of her tongue tingles, growing numb. She reaches for her mouth— feeling nothing. Nothing but gibberish flows from her throat. First, her extremities grow numb. Every instinct flares awake as Nadia's eyes streak white—rolling into the back of her skull. Before Nadia can fall, Aldaric catches her within his arms. A rush of illusion pulses around him, a brief flicker of demonic features fading back into Aldaric's perfect jawline. White hot pain melts inside her brain. Willow's line of vision blurs from the outside in. The last thing she sees is Aldaric carrying Nadia away, before Willow's head smashes against the ground, knocking her completely unconscious.

CHAPTER 39

AGONY

The skin around Willow's wrists shrieks in agony, rubbing against ice cold shackles. The room spins. Dry air capsulates in her throat, sandpaper scratches in her vocal chords as she strains to make a sound. Pungent fumes of urine and metal clash, bringing nausea bubbling into her esophagus. She slams her eyes shut, willing the urge to vomit away. The sound of her groans echoes off the walls of her containment.

It takes several attempts for her sight to adjust to the light of the room. A single fluorescent light flickers overhead, ready to go dark at any moment. The feet are the first thing she notices, laying in front of her on a black stained, twin sized mattress. Both of their wrists are bound behind them with rope. The gold dress they wear ushers a flood of memories, reminding Willow of how she got here. Nadia's feet dangle off the side of the mattress, barefoot. Willow's legs collapse as she tries to stand. The strength hasn't returned yet. Pain shoots up her arms; she winces as she leans forward as the chains allow.

"*Nadia*," she rasps, her voice low and barely audible. The sandpaper of her throat rubs together.

"Nadia," she says more clearly. No movement. Willow's brain pounds against her skull.

Each of her wrists are in a separate shackle. A rusted, metal chain extends from each, leading to a bolt in the wall. The chain pulls taut as she moves her arms, but there's no sign of being released. If she needed to, there's enough slack to move closer to the wall, but not enough to go any further toward the middle of the room where Nadia lays. The blood flow returns with the extension of her legs. Her black heels cause her feet to ache. The cold concrete floor presses against her skin, her dress raising up a few inches, revealing empty holsters.

"Damn," she groans. *But wait. She still has her shoes.* Willow pulls her legs back into a crisscross, taking slow movements to ensure she doesn't pass out from moving too fast. With her heel resting on the opposite knee, her jaw unhinges, clamping her teeth down on her shoe. *Luckily for her, she's always been flexible.* She pulls, removing the high heel from her foot and holding it in her mouth. Barely, she is just able to extend her neck, allowing her restrained hands to grip the shoe.

Here goes nothing. Rearing back as much as she can, she attempts to throw her shoe.

With a clap, the shoe smacks against the side of her head. The point of the heel makes a direct impact with the hollow of her cheek. Nadia winces, opening her jaw for movement. *She's alive.* Willow's heart steadies.

"Nadia, please wake up. Open your eyes." Nadia's torso shifts back and forth, groaning with each slight movement. Her thick eyebrows scrunch together, almost touching. "Nadia, wake up!" Willow snaps in a hushed whisper.

She moans against the mattress, curling her legs to her chest in the fetal position.

"Nadia, can you hear me? I need you to open your eyes," Willow says, unshaken.

Nadia's eyelids slit open as her head lolls to the side. "Oh God," she chokes, hyperventilating, "God, please. I've strayed so far. Get us out of here," she screams at the top of her lungs, her bound hands shaking, clasped together.

"Stop! Don't draw attention, we need to get out of here!" Willow snaps. A lump of guilt rises as Nadia's features collapse, wet lines streaking her cheeks. "I'm here with you, do you hear me? We are going to get out of here if it's the last thing I do. Tell me everything you know," she adds. "Is he–not human?" A question she can no longer ignore. Bile sizzles from her throat. Had she told Nadia from the beginning—would she be in this situation now?

"He–" she chokes, holding back a sob, "was so wonderful. Charming, influential, everything he did was so lavish. I–" she wipes her nose into the bend of her arm, "was so wrong. It was blinding. I wanted him to love me. I'd be anything he wanted me to be. I let him have anything he wanted. He fed off that. Off me. And all that's left–is *nothing.* I'm nothing without him. Will, I–need him."

"I never want to hear you say that ever again, do you hear me?" The volume in her voice carries louder than intended. "You're everything and more, you don't need him." The skin around her delicate eyes burn, holding back the tears welling up within her own. "All my life you've forced your friendship on me against my will, and I never knew, until this moment, how much I needed that, your friendship. *You.* Now snap out of this, and get up, we are getting out of here."

A heaviness lives in her stare. Nadia's lips quiver as she sniffles, her chest fluttering in and out as she stifles her cries.

Both of their throats close as the sound of thudding footsteps come from outside the room. *They're too late.*

CHAPTER 40

BETRAYAL

A strong silhouette outlined by the light of the hallway enters the room. The muscular hand flips the light switch, illuminating Willow and Nadia's holding area. Aldaric stands in the doorway, peering down at the two women bound and chained on the floor with a smirk of amusement.

"Aldaric–You sick bastard!" Willow yells. Her outburst causes him to chuckle.

"Aldaric. Mammon. Avarice. Ace. *Greed*. I have been called many names," he says flippantly, meeting Nadia in the center of the room and kicking the filthy mattress she lays on. *He's Ace.*

A roach scurries from under the bed. An expression of desperation consumes Nadia, both terrified and needing approval. Nadia forces herself to sit upright in his presence.

Aldaric's hand cups her cheek. "You're merely a casualty of war, my dear. A shame. There isn't much else for me to take. Though, it was fun while it lasted." His hand drops, brushing against her skin and leaving Nadia yearning for more.

His gaze darts to Willow. "You should've just left it alone, Detective. You could've survived longer. You have so much potential there. Potential for me to *take*," he huffs, nostrils flaring. "And now I can't have it. Things aren't ready yet."

She swears he grows taller with every word he speaks.

"I'll take everything you own–starting with that pitiful excuse for a house you call *home* by turning it into an Airbnb for all these losers flocking to this town for tourism. Their pockets will bleed dry, right into my horde.

I'll take the lives of everyone you love, making you watch as their souls become my playthings. Then, I will give you to my brother, who will end your life. But in exchange for your physical body, your soul will forever be mine. And this, foolish human, is what happens when you are greedy and go against Greed itself." Darkness unfurls, devilish features flickering across his human persona. Piercing onyx black holes, rows of sharp jagged teeth–soul sucking fear drains the air from her lungs. "And to come alone, nonetheless. How truly arrogant you are." He hisses. But she wasn't alone. Unless Verena never saw her get taken.

Quick footsteps patter outside the room. A short, balding man in black approaches. He can barely see out of the massive black eye he's sporting. "Sir, I'm sorry to–interrupt." He hesitates; a vein pops from his forehead. He doesn't spare a glance at either of the girls on the floor. Aldaric's brow lowers as the man whispers in his ear.

"I'll return soon. There's business to take care of. If there's one thing I won't tolerate, it's cheaters. But don't fret, I won't take long," he snaps, turning on his heels.

The short man lingers behind him, leaving the lights on as they exit. Nadia's silent tears fall from her cheeks as she stares into nothingness. Willow's necklace burns against her chest.

The light gives Willow more to work with. Industrial shelves stack against the left corner of the room, closest to the door. All of Willow's weapons and her bag sit upon cardboard boxes near the shelving. Gallons of bleach line the bottom shelf. Nadia takes deep breaths, rocking herself back and forth in the fetal position, her movements sloppy.

"Nadia, I need you to snap out of it. This place," Willow's head moves in a rapid circle, motioning for the room they're trapped in, "have you been here before? What is this?"

"N–no. I–I've only," she clears her throat and blinks, "seen them take people down. I'm so sorry. What have I done?" Nadia's eyelids slowly close. "Will, I—*sleep*."

"No, Nadia! Stay awake!"

Nadia's head hits the mattress, bouncing from the impact. The gold dress shimmers as her chest rises and falls with each inhale and exhale. Willow's head drops, both in relief and exhaustion. *Nadia had more to drink than Willow did, so it may take longer for her to regain full consciousness. They both will need all the energy they can muster to escape.*

Under the mattress Nadia lays on, markings are carved into the floor–

spiraling in a circle from the middle of the room, all the way to the doorway. With her head still down, she traces the markings on the floor. She can't quite identify what she's seeing, but some of the symbols seem familiar. Are these runes? Spells? She chews the inside of her cheek. Either way, it reeks of disaster. The edges of the carvings are jagged.

It reminds her of the times her and Kai snuck out of school and wandered through the trees along a hidden path back to their home. They would jump on every larger fallen tree limb, hearing the snap echo through the woods. One of the last times they did this, in their favorite tree outside of their home, Kai carved their initials into the wood with his favorite dagger. *The same one that glowed blue when Willow first held it not too long ago.*

As memories flood back into Willow's mind, a sense of warmth washes over her. Her eyelids grow heavy, as she closes them and loses consciousness once again.

*

The room groans, ushering her awake. Air shoots in her nose, a deep inhale clearing her senses as she lifts her head to scan the environment. How long has she been out? Nadia sits awake, her attention drawn toward the entrance. Blonde hair peeks from the doorframe. The soft features of Gideon's face peek from behind the doorway, his dilated pupils wide as he locks eyes with Willow. There's no hesitation. Gideon bolts for Willow, analyzing the chains, her wrists, and to Nadia on the mattress on the floor.

A choke of relief expels from Willow's lungs. "How did you find me? I've never been happier to see you," she rattles back, choking down tears of relief.

"Are you hurt?" He holds her wrists, examining the shackles. "I just finished grabbing the chips when I saw you being carried away by a staff member. Oh, gorgeous, your poor face." He winces, running his fingers over a tender spot on her forehead. "When I asked what happened to another one, they told me to leave. I had to sneak back in. I waited until they went back upstairs to come back down." The pad of his thumb rubs against her wrists, gently massaging them. "Who did this to you?" Gideon seethes.

"Find a key or a cutter! We don't have time. Get Nadia's bindings undone first, then mine. I think she needs medical attention!" Words pour from her mouth like a waterfall.

Nadia's barely present, lost behind a half shut stare.

His eyebrows scrunch together, "By the looks of it, both of you do!" he responds with a tinge of bitterness. He hesitates to leave Willow's side but gets up and begins to fidget with Nadia's bindings.

"Listen, you may not agree– but we need to call Warren. He can help, he needs to know where I am–" Instinctively she pulls forward, searing the iron further into her skin.

Peace pours over Nadia's worn expression. Her fingers interlock, clasping together. No sound leaves her mouth, but her lips work fast. *Is she– who is she talking to?* Gideon halts, leaving the bindings halfway undone.

Heavy footsteps from above grow louder, getting closer. The idea of freedom was a distraction, causing Willow to lose focus of her surroundings. "Gideon, run!" Willow whispers. Gideon hops to his feet.

Aldaric walks into the room; his eyes narrow on Gideon.

"Did you do this to her?" Gideon bit, his chest expands outward.

"And what if I did?" Aldaric teases.

"How dare you place her luscious skin in these shackles? You know I prefer leather!"

Willow's brows pull together in a frown. Whatever she ingested is causing her to hallucinate.

"I told you, brother. Her body is yours. You must understand, I had no other choice. She's a fighter as you know." Aldaric's arrogance is all consuming.

Willow's jaw goes slack. A faint dusty pink aura glows around Gideon's skin. As he turns, an indescribable hue of red inhabits his iris'. A sudden coldness hits her, rushing through her core.

"How is she supposed to fully feel the things I intend to do to her? I thought you were more skilled than to resort to *drugging* her! I can smell it in her veins!"

Brother. Willow chokes, hyperventilating, which draws Gideon's attention back to her. "Hi, sweetheart. What a shame the gig is up, I was really looking forward to our date." Gideon winks at her, his tongue lightly flicking against his canine teeth.

Aldaric's eyes roll in exaggeration. "I don't know, give her water or something. She should come off it within the hour." He waves flippantly in the air.

Betrayal plunges into Willow's stomach, ripping through her like a knife. Every inch of her skin that Gideon touched burns. *Betrayed. Used. How could she have been so stupid?* Completely blind to him. Silent tears stream down her cheeks, burning through her gritted teeth. She lets her head fall.

"Now, now." Gideon clicks his tongue, tipping Willow's chin up to meet his stare. "Don't ruin that pretty face with tears. We still have much ahead for you and I." He squats, crouching to Willow's level. The heat of his skin burns next to hers. She can't move. Fear has her in its grasp. Gideon's tongue trails up her cheek, licking the tears from her face. The desire to touch him eats at her. *It's all his influence. These are not my feelings.* The need continues to build within her core. *What is wrong with me?* Her lip quivers. Without warning, Gideon whips his head to Nadia.

"I heard murmurs of a prayer, you know." Gideon surveys Nadia with disgust, directing his comment to Aldaric whose arms are crossed.

His eye twitches. "I thought we discussed this, Nadia? How many times do we have to have this conversation?" An irritated sigh breathes through his nose.

Nadia shuts her eyes again, muttering under her breath. Though Willow can't make out the words, it's obvious by Aldaric and Gideon's reaction that they understand what she's saying. Gideon shrinks inward, his upper lip curls. Aldaric's mouth forms into a snarl as his rigid frame saunters to the center of the room. Nadia's arms shake, fingers still clasped together.

"Nadia, stop! Don't–lay a hand on her!" Willow stutters. A sting of pain shoots up her wrists. "*Nadia, get up and run!*"

Stillness takes hold of Nadia as her prayers end. Her gaze lifts to Willow's, a gentle ache behind the smile that lifts. "Death may have brought us together, but it could never tear our friendship apart. Do you understand? This is His way. It has and will always be this way. Please don't cry, Will–"

"Wait!" Willow shrieks.

Nadia's lips part again, but before she can speak, gold flares through her skin like lightening.

Every vein glows as the gold creeps across her skin. A blood curdling scream gurgles from Nadia's throat. All the muscles in her figure constrict as her body convulses. Gold crawls up her neck, spills across her face, then floods her hollowed sockets— burning with an inhuman golden light, no longer hers. Crimson follows the gold luster, running down her cheeks like tears.

"*Please stop!*" Willow cries, screaming at the top of her lungs over Nadia's. She struggles against the chains, sloshing skin from her wrists but unable to break free. The two men watch Nadia with extreme pleasure.

"If you have decided you're against me, I will take what I want." Aldaric's hand rams into Nadia's back.

"Take me instead!" Willow shrills. *"Please–No!"* She can't do this.

Gideon bends down beside Willow, forcefully grabbing her cheeks to watch Nadia struggle.

The sound of bones snapping pierce the air. Aldaric's hand punctures through her chest, with her golden and bloody heart oozing in the palm of his hand–slow pulses that halt. The golden radiation fades as her lifeless form falls limp like a rag doll onto the stained mattress. Willow's throat closes before she releases a guttural scream. White hot, scalding flames burn from her necklace against her chest. Greed studies the once pulsing heart in his hand. Gideon stands, beaming at his brother.

"What a fragile thing, the human heart. And to think, you all give it so easily–*tsk.*" His fist tightens around the heart until it pops like a balloon. "Plenty more of these to be found. Makes them not as valuable. Not as pretty either," he adds.

Willow vomits, unable to stop herself. She chokes through tears, spitting the rest of bile from her mouth. Mascara and eyeliner are smeared, running down her cheeks in the pattern of her cries.

"Have your little fun," Greed says to Gideon. A slow, wicked grin curls at his lips, meant for her and her alone. "I expect our agreed upon deal to be fulfilled when you are finished." All traces of humor drain from Greed's expression.

"You sure you don't want to join? Or stay and watch?" Gideon teases with a sultry voice.

"Don't be so barbaric. I've got better things to do. Ring me when you're finished, and we'll clean this place up. Since this one is law enforcement, we will have to do better at disposing of the body than the other two," Greed responds.

The other two. Images of Amelia flash into Willow's mind. The lingerie. The position. The–*lust.* Two killers, with two different motives. One of greed, the other of lust. The whole time, Willow has had the enemy right under her. And against her. Her skin throbs. *Willow's his second.*

As though he senses her realization he turns to her. "Please don't get jealous, Willow. You know that what we have is special! Nothing as of right now, will ever top the feelings I have for you." His long eyelashes bat at her. "Amber meant nothing to me. Really, she had no passion. *Very* vanilla. Even with my glamor, she was pretty bland. That's not really my type. But you," he squats down, tilting his head at her, his eyes the color of cherry blossom petals, hypnotizingly beautiful, "I know exactly what you're capable of. And who you are. And that, my dear, is *thrilling*."

"*Amelia*," she whispers, keeping her head hung.

"Who?" Gideon asks, inches away from her.

"Her name was Amelia. Not Amber," Willow speaks through gritted teeth, then spits in Gideon's face.

Gideon's tongue flicks over the edges of his mouth, licking the saliva. "Now, now. Let's save that energy for a little later, shall we?" A heavy pressure rains down the back of her neck, drawing her vision into instant black.

Endless miles of pitch-black stretch as far as the eye can see. Every angle visible—nothing but darkness. A soft hum rings through the air.

"Hello?" Willow speaks. No echo, no movement, nothing. All that remains is the hum.

The shadow is enveloping, as though she can feel herself shrinking into nothingness. A drop of water hits the floor. Or at least what she imagines is the floor. Obsidian above leaves no traces of clouds, rain, or sky. As her chin tilts up, water rolls down her cheek, down her chin, and falls below her neck. Her hands move to her face. Running tears coat her jaw, leaving them cold. She didn't realize she was crying. A loneliness far beyond what she's ever experienced in her life, so far, carves a hole in her heart.

For the first time in many years, she prays with clasped hands and shaky knees. "I–I don't know what I'm doing. Can you hear me?" Sandpaper rubs in her throat, and it shakes as she forces herself not to cry. "God? I don't even know if I'm alive. Is this Hell? I just—no, I need—to save the people I care about," her lip quivers, "I don't have much left anymore."

Her head hangs, staring at her barely visible extremities in the darkness. Under her, a few miles away, a bright light streams upward. An orb, leaving a trail of luminescence in its wake. It levitates faster, stopping short of a few inches from Willow. She backs up instinctively.

She studies it, moving her head around to view it from each side. There's no visible structure to this ball of light. It is nothing, but light. "If this is how I die, just please hurry and do it."

"Be strong and courageous. Do not be frightened, and do not be dismayed, for your God is with you wherever you go." A thundering voice fills her mind.

Frantically, she searches the void of onyx surrounding her. There's no way this is happening. Is this death?

"You are not dead, my child. Not yet." The voice rings in her mind once again.

"What is this? What are you? Where am I?" Her blood runs cold.

"You called out for me, did you not?"

Her silence pierces the air, the low hum almost deafening. This cannot be real. She must be dreaming.

"You are unconscious. There is still work that must be done to defeat the evil that's ascended." Her shoulders slump forward, feeling numb. "Who—are you?"

"Why do you ask a question you already know the answer to?" The gentle voice wraps around her, like a warm blanket fresh from the dryer.

Uncertainty. Guilt. A flood of emotions rushes through her. A magnetic pull draws her attention to the light. It should be blinding, but it isn't. It's inviting. Nowhere near the kind of inviting Gideon was. This yearning feels more—parental, nurturing even. A feeling Willow hasn't experienced in over a decade.

"I must leave," the voice echoes. Panic sets on the subconscious projection of her face. "Fear not. You already possess the gifts, tools, and resources to reign victorious. Remember that. Not even the kiss of death will separate you from me." The light circles her, leaving a kiss of warmth against her temple before shooting overhead, a trail of glittering light left in its path. Weightlessness covers her feet. Darkness crawls up her legs. Like plunging into an ice bath, it consumes her, knocking the breath from her lungs.

CHAPTER 41

LUST

The air constricts, leaving Willow gasping for her breath. Short, quick inhales wake her. The back of her neck twinges in pain, a stiffening ache encompassing her muscle with each movement she makes. The disorientation evaporates, leaving a stronger sense of clarity than she had before. Goosebumps run along her flesh. Her focus trails down, she finds herself in a cherry red lingerie set. *It's nothing she owns.* A sneer scorches her face. Rope binds her wrists together, but her legs are free.

Attempting to stand, her legs wobble under her own weight, collapsing inward. The drugs are still making their way out of her system. Adrenaline pushes her survival instincts flowing through her veins, scavenging her surroundings. Searching for any means of escape. Multiple black stains seep into the wooden floor. An ironed bar bed frame holds a king size mattress in the back of the room. Scarlet silk duvet covers draw attention to the corner, while a black leather sitting chair faces the bed. A pair of black leather straps lay at the foot of the bed. The most unsettling part of the room isn't the built-in bookshelf of torture devices, but how the other three walls, and ceiling are covered in mirrors.

The room shimmers, as though covered in a veil of mist. There are candles lit in unorganized clusters around the room. Her neck aches, remembering Gideons touch. *How long had she been knocked out? Surely by now Verena has gotten Warren involved, right?*

"I will say, my only regret is I couldn't put you in the chains first myself." Gideon appears, leaning against the bedpost at the foot of the bed. "That's why I had to rearrange the scenery. Figured I'd put you in something more comfortable too." He winks. "Don't worry though, I didn't pull any funny business undressing you. I want you to *remember* what I do to you before your last breath leaves your lips." A sinister, lustful smirk curves with dark intent. She doesn't respond. A rebuttal is exactly what he wants.

His fingers dance around his dress shirt, unbuttoning one button at a time. His exposed skin shimmers in the veil of mist covering the room. Conflicting thoughts battle against each other in Willow's mind–one who's entranced with his beauty and body, the other full of disgust and shame knowing what he is. Gideon's skin radiates perfection, as though he's an ancient Greek carving. *There's no denying it. The deadly sin of Lust.* Someone managed to free two of the Princes of Hell. *She should have read more into the other Princes.* The corners of her mouth tug down.

He picks her up by the rope bound around her hands. With ease, he lifts her, hooking the rope around an iron wrought chain that descends from the break in mirrors along the ceiling. Willow barely stands on her tiptoes, the sockets in her shoulders screaming from being stretched overhead. The pads of his fingers sweep over her curves, igniting heat from her core. Her breathing hitches, fear freezing the foul remarks she wishes to spew.

"You know, lust and greed often get confused. Because I want you entirely, but not the same way Greed does." Gideon caresses her, fingers trailing along her cheek and down her bare neck. "Physical items can be easily destroyed. Forgotten about as time goes on. Passion and desire? Pure pleasure? Now that is something that can be replicated over and *over again.* Remembered forever." His hand finds its way around her neck, running over her scalp as he takes a fist full of hair and yanks, causing her to shriek in pain. The strength behind his grip eases, but he keeps her hair entwined with his fingers.

"Don't worry, I won't put you in too much pain all at once. You've already passed out a couple times today. I'll make sure this lasts. Luckily for you, I have excellent stamina." He winks, biting his lip with a smirk. His expression alone makes Willow's toes curl, both in attraction and terror.

"It's amazing, right? How much lust can confuse the body? You hate that you're drawn to me." With a flick of his finger, he cuts the lingerie top off, leaving her chest exposed.

She flinches. "Please, stop," she begs in defeat.

"I love hearing you beg," he whispers in her ear.

She winces. Her reaction causes him to frown.

"Am I no longer enough now that you see through me? Let me see, I think I know what you'd rather see." The glittering mist swirls around his skull. When the mist dissipates, Gideon's face is no longer his own, but instead–Warren's. A softer version of Warren. "This is it, right? Mr. Tall, brooding, vampire asshole?"

Her jaw clenches.

"Figured so. Tell me, what does he possess that I do not?" Gideon circles Willow, his nose brushing against the back of her head, inhaling her scent. Her sweat filled, bloodied, fear riddled scent. "How is it that the possessive *blood sucker* can touch you places and I could not?" He snarls, eyes dropping to her chest and lingering on the cross necklace. "I'm sure this has something to do with it, the cheeky bastard."

He leans in, pressing a feverish kiss into her collarbone, avoiding contact with the necklace. She freezes, unable to move. The sensation in her arms grows numb. *She's going to die here.* His forehead rests against hers, focusing on her lips. *You already possess the gifts, tools, and resources to reign victorious.* The voice echoes in her mind. A tug pulls her forward. Her lips part, responding to Gideon's advances.

"I knew you'd come around, sweetheart. This can be enjoyable for you too, if you let it." He closes the space between them and presses his mouth to hers—hungry and unrelenting.

She gives in, holding her breath. A magnetic pink spark of electricity zaps between their lips as he pulls away. The façade of Warren's features fall, replaced by Gideon's twisted face.

"You tricky witch, what have you gotten yourself into?" He tilts his head, licking the remaining lipstick he smeared off her mouth. The lipstick from Eryx she put on before coming to the casino. *Whether it be a freak accident or holy intervention, she will be singing praises of thanks later.*

Let's hope this works. "Banish yourself from this plane and do not return," she hisses.

Laughter erupts from his throat. "You are more fiend than I thought," he sneers, complimenting her as cobalt magic glows at his wrists and feet. "You may have outwitted me, but I will never disappear. I'll be behind every phone. Computer. Magazine. Show. Every perverted thought anyone has, it will keep me here. I'll return again. And when I do, I will have something extra special for you, *Heir of Ash.*"

Various shades of blue illuminating light dance throughout the mist, exploding as if the magic itself cheers. Just like that, Gideon is gone. She sweeps the room, breath quickening and panic rising. *Is this real? Did she really do it?* Mist continues shimmering against the candlelight and she's still tied up. The hook above her creaks, swaying with each tiny movement, every breath.

She struggles against the rope, pushing off what little ground her foot touches, yet all she can muster is to sway in circles. The feeling in her arms is gone, but her fingers can still move. *That's a good sign at least.* She forces herself to focus, slowing her breathing. Flexing her fingers, she tests the give of the knots. Tight, but not impossible. Gideon's biggest mistake was underestimating her. With deliberate movements, she twists her wrists, trying to widen the loop just enough to slip free. The maneuver grants microscopic feeling back into her hands, the rope scraping against her skin. She bites back a cry. Acknowledging the pain is a luxury she can't afford.

The weight of her head falls, searching the floor for anything that could give her an edge. There's a ridge in the wood, giving her just enough leverage to push up, relieving a portion of the pressure on her wrists.

Footsteps thud from behind the door. Desperation surges through her veins like fire. Twisting her wrists harder, the rope loosens ever so slightly. Sweat drops down her brow, stinging her eyes.

Come on, come on.

With a final, forceful tug, her right hand slips free. The blood rushes back into it as it hangs down, a strange warming tingle pulsing through the entire arm. She gasps, not waiting to celebrate. The freed hand shakes vigorously as she opens and closes her fist for the sensations to return. Using the slack in the rope, she frees her other hand. The arm hangs like dead weight at her side. The pounding of moving feet grows louder.

She careens to the cabinets near the torture wall. There's no sign of her belongings. *I'll take everything you own.* Willow remembers the words Greed threatened. All that remains in the drawers are Gideon's wardrobe. She rummages through the clothes, snatches a folded white dress shirt, and slips it on, leaving the buttons undone as she tries to cover herself. She buries her nose in the bend of her elbow to keep the mist out of her lungs. *It's probably too late now.*

Her arms feel like socks full of sand, swinging around the room as she pushes the tools off shelving. Her heart races. There are three black, wooden doors, each missing a doorknob to leave. The door closest to the wall of torture instruments has a single keyhole where a doorknob would be. A guttural scream of frustration rips from her throat. She grabs anything and everything she can touch, craving nothing but destruction. A lamp shatters, glass shards scatter against the floor causing rainbow reflections from the mist to project against the wall.

Next, she slams a ceramic vase to the ground. The silence during the aftermath breaks by the creaking of a door. Gideon enters the room. Willow stumbles back, her bare feet crushing the broken glass deeper into her exposed soles. She's numb to the pain. "How are you here? I got rid of you!" she screams.

He grins, but his icy stare widens with confusion. "I've come to get you," he begins before Willow dashes to the instrument wall, grabbing a wooden bat. Crusted, bloodied nails are hammered into the top.

"*Stay the hell away from me!*" She runs forward to the steel hook, pushing it forward, missing Gideon's skull by inches. She draws the baseball bat back, winding up her swing.

Aldaric side steps Gideon, his expression calm but with furrowed brows. His hand moves to cover his nose and mouth. "Hold your position. Let me." An incantation mutters through his lips. The shimmery mist parts, swirling into a tornado-like vacuum into his hand. Aldaric's irises glow lavender. As the mist dissipates, a dry burn soaks into her vision.

The palm of her hand digs into her eye sockets. Blinks come fast as she twists, steeling herself for the attack. When she turns, Warren and Malcolm stand before her–their shoulders stiff, lips pursed. Warren tears the baseball bat hovering inches from his skull, out of Willow's clutch. His palm grasps the bat. Several nails puncture it and exit the other side, but he doesn't wince. Warren must notice the flicker of recognition in her eyes. "Willow, who are you looking at?"

"Wha–are–are you real?" Her body is a rock, stiff in a defensive stance. The air in her throat constricts.

Malcolm speaks before Warren can reply, "You're safe. What you see now is real. I dispelled the glamor in the room." His words falter, each syllable heavy with a quiet, reluctant ache.

Willow releases the handle of the bat as Warren pulls the nails out of his palm, allowing it to fall to the ground.

Without hesitation, Warren grabs her by the shoulders, shaking her. "What the hell were you thinking? You could have gotten yourself killed!" He bares his teeth before pulling her into his chest, cradling the back of her head. "*I'm so glad you're okay,*" he whispers.

Her lip quivers. As hard as she tries, she fails. Her tears burst like a dam. "I'm so sorry," a sob chokes in her throat, "*Nadia–*" Warren glances at

Malcolm, who grimaces, reacting to Willow's own pain. Willow shakes in between trying to catch her breath.

"What do we do? How do we get out of here? Where are we?" she rambles. "I'm so sorry I didn't wait or let you know what I had planned." She burrows her face into Warren's chest as shame consumes her. If she had just listened, Nadia may still be here. The sweater vest he wears soaks up her tears.

"Verena made us aware. Let's regroup on that thought after we're out of here. Most importantly, you have been found, and we are getting out of here. But first, we need to find Aldaric," Warren says.

Malcolm nods his head as he circles the room, not touching anything but taking mental note of everything. As Willow's tremors slow, Warren releases her from his stiff embrace.

"Someone managed to summon Lust as well. It wasn't just Greed. It was–" a lump forms in her throat, "Gideon."

His eye twitches; a micro expression of a snarl raises his lip. "I'm unfortunately not surprised." He joins Malcolm in studying the room, surveying the doors without knobs.

She sniffles, her jaw tightens, taking a deep inhale and exhales. "I banished him. Gideon won't return. Not for a while at least. I think."

He glances over his shoulder back to her. "And how exactly did you do that?" he asks, sounding skeptical of her capabilities, which strikes a nerve with her.

It may be best to omit some of the truth. "I was able to acquire a magical item and used it to command his banishment. I wasn't sure it worked when I saw you come in–you were Gideon...and Aldaric. But he was livid. I watched him disappear into another plane. It definitely worked."

"And where *exactly* did you discover a magical item?"

"That's beside the point. Listen, he's gone. But Greed's still out there. He said he had plans for me after Gideon finished with me. He has all my things. My clothes, weapons," she pauses, "he has Nadia somewhere. I need them back. *Her back.*" Rage keeps her tears contained in a cage. A cage she will have to reopen once there's a promise of safety. A promise needing to see through until the end—for Nadia.

The disposition on Warren's face that says he isn't ready to end this conversation, but he will put a pin in it for now. Great, if they make it out of here alive, she has that to look forward to.

Malcolm slides in between the two of them, cutting the tension as he pulls out a glass bottle filled with a similar blue color as the potion she had gotten from Warren after being poisoned by Verena. A cork seals the bottle, twin wraps around the neck of the bottle. A lavender sticky note sticks to the side of the glass as Willow takes it in hand, turning it over.

Don't die. -Sunny

A sorrowful laugh escapes her breath. Without being directed, Willow pops open the cork and gulps the potion down. The familiar warmth finds its way down her throat, sending small pulses of energy through her body. But this one feels–different. The warmth lingers, coursing through her veins, dulling the pain, but not completely eradicating it.

"This is it," he murmurs, his voice apprehensive. Malcolm kneels in front of one of the doors, his finger tracing the area where the doorknob should be. Inside his leather jacket, he pulls out a vial of dark liquid, and another vial with a single shard of an obsidian gem. "Be on alert. I'm going to open the door, I hope."

Warren steps in front of Willow. Every muscle in his body is tense, coiled like the predators he controls–ready to strike. "Stay behind me." His voice low and firm.

She doesn't argue, the eerie silence that fills the room making her stomach twist. Her nails dig into the palm of her hand, the pressure keeping her grounded.

Malcolm chants, the obsidian shard glowing faintly between his fingers. Golden runes appear in a spiral on the door, pulsing with Malcolm's every word. The temperature in the room drops, and a low rumble reverberates throughout the ground under them. The runes crackle and spark, the golden color turns into a sickly green. The wood groans as if it's alive, warping unnaturally.

"That's not supposed to happen," Malcolm bites, his chant faltering.

"What do you mean that's not supposed to happen?" Warren snaps, his stance shifting.

The air grows heavier, weighing down on Willow's chest. Echoes of whispers ring inside her ear, and her hand shoots to cover them, but the insidious voices grow louder.

"Whatever you're doing, finish it!" she shouts through the voices. The louder they grow, the easier it is to understand. They call out her name. *Willow. Willow. Heir of Ash. Imagine the things you could do with the power we hold. All the revenge you could exact, with no consequences. All the things you could achieve. The loved ones you could bring back.*

A touch silences the voices. Warren tips her chin with his fingers. "Are you okay?"

She shakes her head. "I—I'll be fine."

He studies her features, as though searching for a lie, before he removes his hand. "Get ready," he says, stepping forward.

Malcolm pours the dark liquid onto the door, and the shard blazes with a light so bright she's forced to shield her eyes. The door groans one final time before swinging inward with a deafening crack, revealing a yawning darkness that pulses. The walls watch them, as though they are alive. A tunnel of darkness stands before them. An iridescent light illuminates further down, a beacon in the dark. Warren leads the group ahead. Malcolm follows suit, glancing back to Willow and nodding his head. Her bare feet freeze against the icy tile floor. The emerald light turns fluorescent as they approach.

"Welcome," a voice rumbles from the darkness, smooth and cold, sending a chill down Willow's spine, "I've been waiting for your arrival."

CHAPTER 42

IT'S WAR

The disembodied voice reverberates through the room and flashing white light stuns Willow's senses. Her jaw goes slack as her vision comes to. White marble covers every surface, from the floor to the ceiling. Golden grout and flecks sprinkle a pop of shimmer throughout the tiling. Warren's dress shoes clack against the floor, echoing through the pristine room. A hall of riches.

A diamond encrusted chandelier sways from the ceiling above. Rising pillars line the perimeter, ranging in various sizes and heights. Luxurious items rest on the velvet pillows atop each column. Ancient artifacts, extravagant paintings, and precious gems sparkle as though freshly polished. This place mimics a museum. A red carpet runs directly through the middle of the room, ending at a set of steps. At the top, a golden throne. Beside the throne, a stone platform sits out of place. Willow's steps falter as her breath sucks into her throat.

After a moment of hesitation, she moves. Malcolm extends his hand, attempting to grasp her wrist. His fingers make contact, but Willow snatches her hand before he can take grasp. Warren's arm swings in front of Malcolm, shaking his head as the two let Willow trudge forward. Her nails dig into her palm enough to draw blood.

Nadia's corpse lays on the stone platform by the throne, posed as though she's ready for a casket. Delicate hands lay on top of each other, resting on her stomach. The gold sequin dress is dull, dried blood crusting over large patches of the material. The liquified gold has hardened, running down her face like a golden trail of tears. But Nadia's expression is peaceful. No longer in pain.

The echoing of slow-paced claps circulate the room. "The audacity you people have. Making yourself right at home, aren't you?" Greed's brutal voice lingers in between the claps. Amber spheres emerge from the shadows. He doesn't acknowledge at any of them. Instead, he scavenges the room, attention lingering on each of his possessions displayed before shifting to the next, ensuring that each item is accounted for.

"I believe you have some of our things. *Her* things," Warren challenges.

Willow is frozen by Nadia's side. She tilts her head to the side, keeping the vampires in her line of sight. There's no time for grief. But she's also not in the position to make a hasty move.

"Everything in this room belongs to me, including *you*. There's no leaving." Greed's eyelids droop and a twisted grin pulls at the corners of his mouth. His fingers echo with a thundering snap.

Heavy footsteps thud from the darkness as a figure enters the room. Malcolm shifts. A tank of a man with a thick, muscular frame rolls up his sleeves. A ragged scar slashes across his face from the right of his temple, over his eye, and past the bridge of his nose. Behind him, a lanky man ticks in rapid motion to stand at his side. The way he moves sends Willow's heartbeat wild. The men stand in place, waiting for a command.

Her discomfort lures Greed's attention, giving Willow an unamused glance. "It was foolish for Nadia to speak such blasphemy. Disgusting she would sacrifice herself in that way. I suppose I did her a favor. Not like humans are good for anything else," he hisses. The smirk on his face tells Willow he's trying to rile her up. *And it's working.*

"*Sacrifice*," Malcolm whispers to Warren. Warren's posture straightens.

"I don't sense Asmodeus. Did you manage to dispose of him for the time being?" His arms idle by his side, fingers stretching out like claws.

"He didn't get to enjoy much fun, unfortunately for him," Willow's voice shakes, betraying her attempt at composure as her knuckles turn white in her fist.

Greed sneers. "That's what happens when you play with your food. He was always the softest on humans out of all of us. I guess we see who the superior Sin is, don't we?"

CLANK

The sound echoes from behind Warren and Malcolm. The two men turn their head to the sound, grins wavering. Malcolm and Warren don't move. Their expressions are unreadable. Within seconds, a lifeless body flies through the hallway entrance, sailing past Warren and Malcolm. A muscular, female ogre lands mangled a few feet away from Willow. The ogre's neck twists in a complete circle, blood gushing down her neck. Greed's lackeys' eyes widen before they narrow on the figure in the shadows.

"Nice of you to join," Warren scoffs. His attention never wavers from Willow.

Verena's tongue traces her lips, wiping the blood from her chin as she struts behind Malcolm and Warren. She adjusts the black straps of her waist holster. "That's a funny way of saying thank you?"

Her heels clack against the tile. She moves at a measured pace, more than likely on purpose to draw attention to herself. Willow grips the table, afraid to move even an inch. She feels an invisible clasp around her heart, impending doom drawing near. Verena glances around the room, propping her arm on Warren's shoulder.

Willow wouldn't call Verena a friend by any means, but she recognizes her expression from their countless hours of training. *She's about to win.* It's a level of focus and expression that Warren mimics as well. *And Willow couldn't be happier to see her.* Instead of waiting for a command, Greed's men approach Verena with arrogant, false confidence. There's a ping of pity, deep *deep* down inside Willow for the men.

"Carla always underestimated other women, it was one of her weaknesses," the scarred man spits at Verena.

The shifty slender man follows behind him by several steps, glancing at the ogre on the floor. "Don't worry, we'll finish what she didn't." His bloodshot eyeballs spin in the hallow sockets unnaturally. Is this one even living?

Verena peers up at the man with a shimmer in her eye. "So, you're saying you're smart enough to *not* underestimate a woman?"

The larger man shakes with laughter. "Women shouldn't underestimate other women. Men are in a different league. There's nothing to estimate. You have no chance."

Willow's ping of pity dissipates.

Verena's tongue licks the front of her teeth. Malcolm and Warren wince.

"Foolish," Verena whispers as she takes a single step forward, effortlessly plunging a hidden blade that emerged from her elbow deep into the man's gut. If Willow blinked, she would have missed it.

The man's hand shoots to his side as the blood pools around his hand, coating each digit within seconds. "You bitch!" He staggers forward as his free hand reaches for a gun at his hip.

"Catch!" Malcolm shouts, his palms shimmer, aiming one at the man and the other at Willow. An amethyst glow envelopes the man's gun as it levitates out of the holster and flings its way at Willow. She grasps the grip; her trigger finger hovers–ready to shoot.

Verena smirks. "I guess you and Carla have some things in common?"

The slender man's gaze shifts to Willow, sitting like a duck. A thick gulp of saliva coats her windpipes. *She could try to shoot, but based on his movements, he can avoid the shot with ease.* He twitches, arms contorting as she steps forward. Before he can travel any further, a flash of white stalks him from behind.

"Going somewhere?" Warren growls in the lanky man's ear before sinking his fangs into his throat. In a single motion, he rips his esophagus out. Blood sprays from the gorged wound. He lets the carcass fall. "Get your head out of your ass! Now's not the time to choke! Got it?" Warren hisses, a streak of blood spatters against his face, dripping from his brow.

She blinks away her shock before checking the gun. Only five rounds loaded. Better make them count.

"Imbeciles!" Greed's voice booms throughout the room. Verena slices the bigger man's head clean off his shoulders, tumbling onto the floor as it bounces like a dropped marble.

Greed's figure lifts off the ground, hovering inches away from the ceiling. Turning his palms outward, pools of liquid gold pour from them. A gold waterfall flows freely from his palms. As the gold hits the floor, instead of splashing, it springs back up, forming solid gold, expressionless soldiers. The soldiers march in unison, their footsteps creating a thundering wave. Greed hovers, watching with amusement.

Warren groans, his shoulders slumping before they perk back up as if giving himself a mental pep talk. All three of them dash to the soldiers, colors of black, white, and red clash against the gold, as they attack with lightning speed.

Willow's allies fight valiantly while she cowers behind the body of her dead friend. A gentle tug of her sleeve makes her head turn, to find no one there. Her gaze drifts. In her line of sight on one of the pillars, rests Kai's dagger. Willow turns back to Nadia. "I'll be right back," she whispers before ducking behind the nearby marble pillar, crawling her way to retrieve what is rightfully hers.

A soldier meets her, blocking her from the pillar with the dagger. It doesn't have a face. The features are smoothed over, light indents place where the shapes of the eyes, mouth, and nose would be. *There's no time to think.* Willow reaches forward to grapple the figure. She tries leveraging her weight to bring it to the ground, but the weight of a gold soldier is about as much as one would expect. It's immovable. The golden warrior head butts her, a gash bursting across her left eyebrow. Her grip wavers, but she clamps down again. Blood rushes down her cheeks as she squints through her left eye, relying on the right for full vision.

How does someone defeat gold?

"Willow, move!" Malcolm shouts.

Without hesitation she pushes off the soldier, grabbing Kai's dagger from the platform in the process and moves behind cover. The dagger glows the familiar blue within her hand. A wall of flames engulfs the area within a straight line as the gold soldier bubbles. *Heat. Heat will melt gold.*

The metal creature hobbles toward Willow, slower this time as its feet sink into the floor, a liquid gold path trailing behind with every step. Willow screams, wincing in the flame, lunging forward, striking the gold with her dagger. The weapon sinks into it, bubbling more until it bursts, popping into a puddle on the tile. The fire roars, the liquid sizzling like magma.

The marble pillar offers relief against the burns on her back as she catches her gasping breath. Her fingers wipe the blood from her eye. The sound of glass smashing and marble cracking drowns out the room. With a final breath, she peers her head around the pillar. Malcolm crouches beside the stone platform with Nadia. What was once an army, lays as a pool of liquid gold. Warren and Verena engage with Greed, cautious to not make any false moves. They don't even know what he's capable of.

Willow makes eye contact with Malcolm as he motions for her to come closer. The tattered sleeve of her shirt wipes the blood and sweat mixture from her brow as she sprints toward the throne, thankful that Warren and Verena move fast enough to keep the Prince of Hell preoccupied. *That's all they're doing–keeping him busy.*

"Draw this exactly as it shows on the ground. Use the blood from your hands and face," Malcolm commands, removing a spellbook from his leather jacket interior. Chants spew from his mouth. Nerves twist in her stomach. Her fingers tremble. She can't afford to mess this up. Her fate lies in these vampires' hands. Pushing through as instructed, she matches the runes and pattern to the one in his book. It circles itself, creating a spiral of fragments of shapes and foreign words. Similar, but different from the pattern found in the basement of the casino. A hazy lavender flares from Malcolm's orbits as he switches pages.

The clanks of weapons and fists clashing pause as Greed lands a punch into Verena's abdomen, sending her flying into a shelf of items. She shrieks. The shelf breaks in half, Greed's belongings shattering against the floor. Tumbling shelves and rubble crush Verena. Warren pauses, standing back on the ground, calculating his next move while he catches his breath.

"Look at what you've done!" Greed growls.

"*Alligatura*—" Malcolm repeats in the moment of silence.

The demon prince's lips curling back in a snarl as a guttural shriek escapes. He knows exactly what Malcolm is trying to accomplish. Aldaric's handsome features twist, frame contorting. The bones in his jaw break, cracking in reconstruction. His olive skin turns peridot, like a bad bruise. The skeletal frame is no longer human. His eye sockets are black bottomless pits, and his silhouette has doubled in size, an almost ogre-like form. His mouth foams with multiple rows of protruding teeth, as he screams, leaping in the direction of Malcolm and Willow.

"Damnit," Warren exclaims.

Both of his palms slam onto the floor, a thick cloud of smoke infiltrating the room, swallowing Greed whole.

Greed's thick arms swing, wafting the smoke away. Vidar wastes no time, striking from the haze, knocking the prince back. The basilisk's body constricts around Greed's large frame. Willow's grip on Kai's dagger tightens, readying to defend at whatever cost.

"*Et hoc tibi obligo*," Malcolm utters his last words, extending his hand to touch Nadia's. "This is what she wanted. With her sacrifice as the conduit, we can win." His lips tighten, as his other hand tosses a rope at Willow, turning away. Nadia's remains levitate off the table.

"No! *Wait!*" Willow cries.

CHAPTER 43

SEE YOU IN HELL

Violet magic illuminates from Malcolm's extremities, snatching Willow's bloody hand in his.

Warren attempts to slice Greed's thick skin with a sword he picks off the ground. The slash closes within seconds. Vidar constricts tighter. Its jaw unhinges, but before it can clamp onto him, the demon's arms break free with a bellowing yell– throwing the basilisk into Warren. He wails in pain as his back slams against the wall, rubble collapsing from the impact. Dust permeates the room, blocking Willow's view.

"Warren!" Willow screams. She pulls toward him, but Malcolm's grip keeps her in place.

"Don't break our link!" Malcolm thunders.

In a few leaps, Greed closes the distance. His meaty claws clasp around Willow's waist, causing her to shriek. Her wounds scream with fiery agony. He pulls, but Willow's body hesitates to move as Malcolm keeps them planted. Malcolm's flesh is now rock.

"Enjoy hell." An inhuman gurgle explodes from Greed's demonic mouth, followed by a sinister cackle.

"*I'll see you there!*" Willow screams, using the dagger in her free hand to plunge deep into his eye, glowing cobalt blue.

Greed growls, saliva stringing from tooth to tooth, blowing toward her with his exclamation. A black hole stretches from within the damaged eye of Greed.

Malcolm yells, "*Expello!* Now Willow!"

The runes of blood flash on the floor. The light travels from the floor, flowing into Malcolm's eyes, then his hands. Warmth runs through Willow's grip as the radiating energy blazes into her, transferring into the prince. She drops the dagger. Using her free hand, she yanks the binding rope tied loosely around her waist and wraps it around Greed's wrist. The rope can only reach one wrist. That's all she must have needed. Scarlet chains materialize from Malcolm's palm, spiraling around his arm, over and around Willow's, and then strapping across Greed's body. The prince drops Willow. At first, the chain acts like a seat belt stretching over each shoulder—then each side blasts to the ground, bolting into the blood runes.

The prince squints down, finding his foot within the spiraling symbols. A final chain wraps around his neck like a collar, slowly inching into the floor. It's as though someone is cranking the chains by hand to the ground. His grip loosens on Willow as she falls on her feet to the ground. Greed struggles against the force pulling him down, finding Willow's horrified gaze.

"I will find you again, *traitor*. He will not be pleased that you turned out this way," he growls against the floor, twisting with all his might.

As his disfigured cheek presses against the runes, the circle splits—becoming a bottomless portal. The chains heave into the threshold, rattling until Greed's bulbous form is consumed within it. It seals, flashing a magenta light before fading and cutting off his roar.

Malcolm releases Willow, quickly smearing the blood so it no longer resembles the previous symbols. With a heavy exhale he collapses on his back, panting with a staggered breath. The hardened rock of his exterior crumbles, revealing the smooth ebony skin underneath.

"Is—it done? Is he gone?" she rasps.

Malcolm groans, tilting his head toward her. "We did it." He coughs, spitting blood off to the side.

"Oh, God," she panics, reaching to check for injury.

"Overdid it a bit, I'm afraid. Need—rest." He gives a dismissive wave, allowing his lids to shut.

Vidar regains his consciousness, its tail sliding, causing large chunks of marble ceiling and wall to tumble to the ground. Willow's legs are heavy as she stumbles to stand. Where's Warren? The adrenaline numbs her feet as she limps to the wreckage, stomping on shattered glass. The stench of the smoke stings her nose. She discovers Vidar first, his scales heaving as though he's struggling to breathe. On the other side, Verena holds her side, bent over as she sits on a pile of debris. A scowl plasters her face, kicking a chunk of marble from her path. It flies across the room. She coughs, expelling marble dust from her lungs.

Verena notices her stare. "I'm fine, thanks," she groans.

Willow runs to Verena, wrapping her in a tight embrace.

"Woah," Verena grunts. Her already battered body stiffens even more. In awkward motions, she pats Willow on the back.

"Thank you for not leaving me. And getting help," Willow whispers.

Verena's shoulders fall, leaning into the hug but not reciprocating. "Well, I would have been dead if I hadn't." A grin ghosts Willow's lips.

Beyond Verena, a scarlet snake holds its head high, in defense. She releases Verena from her grasp.

Warren.

Willow's breath hitches at the sight–Warren pinned beneath a jagged slab of concrete; his legs twisted unnaturally. Willow bolts toward him, ignoring her open wounds screaming in anguish. Raven hair spills over his face, lashes resting against his skin. Vidar sidewinds, following her close enough to be her shadow. His hefty tail slaps some of the rocks out of the way, clearing a path for her. Her fingers hover below his nose, feeling for breath.

"Warren! Can you hear me? Hello?" She shakes his shoulders.

He winces, moaning in pain. Eyes closed; his hands feel the boulders crushing his legs.

"Don't move! I'll get us help," she stands, only to halt under Warren's grip around her ankle.

"*Stop,*" he rasps. "No need." He pulls in deep, ragged gasps. "Give me a second."

Warren's sight fixates on Vidar. Without a word, the basilisk knocks the concrete off Warren's legs. The tibia and fibula bones protrude from his legs, piercing the skin, while his ankles are flattened. Warren clenches his jaw. "*Fabulous,*" he huffs. Within minutes, the bones suck back into his skin. They reset themselves with no stent needed. His ankles twist into place, coupled with popping and the sound of grinding. The gaping holes from the protrusions close–as if they never existed.

Willow's jaw falls slack. Warren's mouth wrenches as though he's tolerating an incredible amount of pain. She reaches for him, hoping to offer some semblance of comfort.

"Why–"

"I can't die." He stares at his healing body.

She remains silent, not sure what the right response would even be. The external injuries heal. *How much internal damage did that fight do?*

"Boo, freaking-hoo. *I can't die, it's so tragic,*" Verena pipes up, mocking him with a tinge of anger. "Get out of here with that. We all were almost turned to gold statues, and fucking banished a Prince of Hell!" She throws a baseball sized chunk of concrete at Warren. He doesn't bother dodging it, lost in thought as it breaks against his head. "We need to get the hell out of here before your little friends show up." She directs her attention to Willow. "Oh, also. After this, don't expect anything from me for at least another decade. And our deal still stands." Verena spits her own blood onto the floor, wiping her mouth with her wrist.

"Deal?" Warren questions, slowly raising to his feet. Willow offers her hand for assistance. He ignores it. "I'm fine."

Her shoulders shrink in.

"Thank you though," he adds, making eye contact with her. They share a glimmer of unspoken sorrow.

"In exchange for Verena's help," Willow begins.

Verena's eyes go wide, indirectly telling her to shut her mouth. Her lips clamp shut.

"In exchange for her help, *what?*" Warren's scowl burns on the vampire assassin.

Willow gulps. "*She can have some of my blood,*" the words come as a whisper.

"Absolutely not. For more reasons than one," his lips pull back in a disappointed snarl at Verena, "your reward is that I haven't staked you," he hisses.

"We can discuss this later, we need to get the hell out of here," Verena spits.

"Malcolm! Are you okay over there? Blink twice if you're still alive," Warren's shout echoes across the remaining marble.

"Been better," he rasps, from his position on the floor.

The dust settles, revealing more of the room. Nothing but pure destruction. Pools of gold have turned to black tar; every item of Greed's melt into thick sludge. The throne melts, forming a pool around the stone platform surrounding Nadia–whose body is untouched. The torturous gold that streaked Nadia's cheeks is replaced with watery tears. A single daffodil lays under her hands.

Life does not consist in an abundance of possessions. Willow recalls this phrase from a memory of her childhood. She cannot remember the context, or why the words come to her.

CHAPTER 44
CHERRY ON TOP

The chilling drizzle of rain patters against the ambulance. Flashing lights of police cars and the neon sign light the exterior of the casino parking lot. Firefighters reel their hoses back to the truck after extensive use of extinguishing the flames from the building. Willow sits as the paramedic splashes antiseptic on the bottoms of her feet, stinging to her core. She draws her feet back and groans through clenched teeth.

Thankfully, Willow had the forethought to grab her dress and belongings from the basement before being rushed outside for medical care. It kept her from having to explain her previous indecency. Warren and Verena took Malcolm to Sunny's for recovery. Verena demanded Willow to come with them, but she couldn't leave without helping clean up the mess they helped cause. Or without Nadia. Mainly without Nadia.

She winces each time the paramedic wipes the lacerations on her arms. "You don't know when to quit, do you?" Milo approaches, his rain jacket hood up, covering most of his head.

"If I had a dollar for every time I've heard that." She jests through the pain, her expression clouded. That phrase, each time spoken, has changed her life drastically.

He inspects her wounds. "You put up quite the fight, didn't you?"

"I wouldn't expect anything less," a familiar deep voice cuts in from behind Milo. Chief Hastings clasps his hand on Milo's shoulder, shaking him roughly. Willow straightens her posture.

"At ease, Rhodes. I'm so glad you're okay." His hard exterior wavers.

She forces a smile back at him, only to turn away when she feels tears beginning to form.

"Willow!" Leo cheers, jogging from a parked unmarked police car. "I heard you saved a ton of people in there!" He points to the casino. "And you helped catch one of the biggest underground smugglers in northern Oregon? All while on leave? You just couldn't save any of the fun for us!" Leo teases.

So, they were smuggling. Two birds with one stone, she supposes. "It didn't happen the way it sounds–" she begins, worried what the evidence will show.

"You're a hero," Milo interrupts her. "Don't dismiss yourself of that." His stare hardens.

"I don't even remember what happened," she mutters.

The paramedic shifts in front of her, taking a flashlight and holding up a finger in front of her to follow. "You have signs of a concussion, so memory loss can be expected depending on how severe it is."

The casino doors open, drawing the group's attention. Brian, the floor manager, trudges with his hands handcuffed behind his back, escorted by an officer. *The cherry on top.*

"You saved many lives tonight. Sometimes it's being at the right place at the right time. If you weren't there, there would've been dozens of more casualties. We may have lost some lives, but many more were saved." The Chief affirms Milo's previous statement. Her lips quiver.

Willow clears her throat, coughing. "What exactly happened?"

"Those idiots must have hired rookie chemists. Their drug lab exploded, and the place caught on fire. Like the Chief said. Right place, right time." Leo shakes his head. "I didn't realize you gambled!"

She scrutinizes the neon sign of the Golden Wolf. Heavy smoke surrounds the building. She didn't think much of it due to the nature of this city, but it's much more than mist. *How badly did Malcolm's flames damage this place?*

"I'm glad you texted me when you did. Leo was already out patrolling near the area, so we were able to get here fast and call the fire department," Milo adds.

Her eyebrows draw together. "I texted you?"

Milo pulls his phone out of his jacket pocket. "Sure did." He shows her the message.

Golden Wolf fire. Come now. She didn't send that.

Her mouth twists to one side. "Hm, I guess I did." She coughs again. There's a silence between the group as no one knows what to say.

"You're done. I recommend bed rest for a week. Stay away from screens and have someone monitor you periodically while you sleep for the first two nights," the paramedic states, packing his equipment back into a first aid kit, taking it with him to the next person who sits on the sidewalk waiting to receive help.

The surrounding streets are cordoned off by caution tape. Several journalists and cameramen are scattered around the tape, yelling questions in hopes someone stupid enough answers–ready to spin the story in the direction they've already decided is the truth.

"You heard the man, get some rest. Do you need someone to drop you off at home?" the Chief asks.

She shakes her head. "No, thanks. I just–need a bit. I'll call for someone if I need it."

Milo and Leo exchange a skeptical glance.

"Understood. We'll be on our way then." He motions for the rest of the guys to leave. "Rhodes, one last thing."

She peers up from the ground.

"Your leave is released. I expect to see you back in the office promptly. When you have medical clearance, that is. But take your time, okay?"

Joy floods her face, which makes him stifle a chuckle. "Yes, sir."

CHAPTER 45

ASCENSION

Three weeks later

W illow stands still. Detached. Saddening deja vu.

Her hands are firmly clasped, the leather of her winter gloves squeaking as the priest delivers a solemn eulogy. His voice carries through the large gathering, but Willow barely registers the words. Her attention lands on the mourners–Nadia's family, her colleagues, others who had whispered about her in life, but now shed tears for her in death. *She would have been so pleased with how many have come to celebrate the life she lived.*

Nadia's sleekly polished wooden coffin rests above the open grave, waiting to be lowered beneath the dirt. Her plot is a few feet away from her grandparents, whom she loved dearly. Growing up, her grandparents would take her and Willow to the next town to the only mall within a fifty-mile radius. The two of them would giggle as cute boys passed by, glancing in their direction as they puffed out their chests. It was on one of those trips that Nadia found her favorite stuffed pink gorilla–Lorenzo. Only Willow knew of him, since most teenage girls refrain from sharing their stuffed animals after the age of eleven.

Lorenzo is tucked under Nadia's arms, held with comforting love as the lid to the casket closes. Nadia's father lays a bouquet of delicate ivory poppies on top as the casket lowers six feet underground. Nadia's mother weeps, the volume of her sobs stabbing into Willow's chest with every cry. Somberness clings to her father, a shell of the man he was before her passing. As though the life within him had been drained–*her life*. Mr. Valentine pulls his wife closer, gripping her within his rigid arms as other mourners join to toss flowers into the grave.

Willow hesitates, then crouches to pick a single white rose from the bouquet at her feet. She approaches the edge, her steps slow and filled with dread. *"I'm so sorry,"* she whispers, her voice cracking as she drops the rose onto the coffin. It lands, contrasting beautifully against the darker wood stain of the coffin. The wind picks up, carrying with it a sense of finality. The crowd disperses in waves. Willow lingers, gaze fixed upon the grave, unable to move.

"Blackwood did a good job." The Chief wraps an arm around Willow's shoulder, squeezing her into a side hug. Her thick, black winter coat bunches at the shoulder where his grip meets.

She nods. "She looked amazing as always."

The town's corruption has dwindled since the casino incident, but its shadow lingers like a bruise on Misty Pines. The casino, once the glittering pinnacle of backdoor deals and false hopes of riches, stands closed during further investigation, its neon lights dark. A victory, but it came at a very high cost. Nadia was a casualty of the fight. *The beginnings of a war.* Willow could sense this much. In the end, they determined that Jonathan's death was a result of getting caught cheating, then getting into it with the smugglers that ran the casino. Amelia's case remains unsolved, with all leads growing colder by the day. Another family with no closure.

Willow's weight shifts, frozen grass crunching beneath her Doc Martens. Another figure presses against her other side. She doesn't bother lifting her attention. Chief Hastings loosens his hold, nodding at Warren. The Chief grabs Willow's hand and gives it a brief press before releasing and walking away.

"How could she do it?" she mutters, asking the question that has been running in her mind for weeks.

"There are good people out in the world. Ones who would do anything for the people they care about. And even some who would do anything for those they don't even know," Warren replies, his tone steady. After a pause, he continues, "Some would say, individuals in your profession are those kinds of people."

That isn't something she ever considered. "Don't compare us. She was much better than I." Her head turns in a sharp, dismissive motion. She hasn't admitted it out loud, but the way her life stands—she's unsure she should even return to law enforcement. She can't bear the idea of losing anyone else.

"There's no comparison. It's something we will never understand. In all my years, I can tell you this—death is never easy. With every death you witness, a piece of you is changed forever," he swallows, "but everything is as it always should be. Even when it doesn't make sense now."

His words anger her, simply because she knows it's the truth. Death has single handedly ruined everything in her life. She hasn't been the same. None of it ever made sense. It never will. *The only thing that's been consistent is the pain.*

"I told you; I can turn her...if you wish," he offers with quiet reassurance.

"*No*," Willow spits. "She would never want that. I wouldn't want that." Silence stretches between them, thick and unmoving. She lets out a deep exhale. "I trust you." *It's something she should have told him sooner.*

"Where is this coming from?" he asks, brows drawn together.

"I shouldn't have acted hastily. I know I can't do this on my own. I thought asking for Verena's help would work, but I should have waited and acted with you and Malcolm as a team. I've...never had anyone I can rely on since Kai." Cracks spread throughout the iron guarded around her heart. "Thank you. For saving me, for everything." She avoids his gaze, speaking as though it's the last conversation she will have. That's her mentality moving forward. Every conversation *could* be her last.

"I will *always* protect you. Even against your will."

She turns, their eyes meeting. They share the same mask of determination reflected in one another. She wants so badly to ask him why. *Why protect her? Admittedly, she fears the verbalization of his answer.* Warren isn't giving up on their cause. Her purpose has changed, that's for certain. How can she selfishly focus on vengeance for Kai, when the world's at stake?

"Come, let's go." He nods in the direction away from the grave, guiding her by the shoulders.

The sun dips below the horizon, casting hues of crimson and shadow. Harsh winds scream through the trees in the woods of Misty Pines. Beneath the town, where even the light dares not to tread, others stir with anticipation. Five ancient names are clawed into the ruins, waiting to arise. Two have fallen—but it was never about them. It's all of them. The stars blink—the darkness claiming the beauty that once was. The night is a promise of one simple thing: they are coming. *They will ascend.*

ACKNOWLEDGEMENTS

I have so many thanks to give, because in truth—I am extremely blessed. I have such an amazing support system and group of people around me cheering me on. Thank you to my husband, Patrick, for encouraging me and being my first beta reader. Thank you for not holding it against me when I stayed up late writing instead of watching a show together. Alora and I are so lucky to have you. I love you.

Thank you to my family (both blood and in-laws), for loving me and encouraging this new journey for me. Special thanks to my brother-in-law, Alex, because without your push I would have never written this story.

To my beta readers—Emily, Robi, and Marigrace, your feedback has shaped my story into what it is today. I'm so thankful for your guidance and friendship.

To my Editor, Mallory Day, thank YOU for every ounce of praise and constructive criticism. Truly, I couldn't have written this story without your help.

Thank you to Vic and Lero of Lily Tea Art, for bringing my vision to life for my beautiful cover!! Working with you two has been a dream, and I couldn't be more thankful!

To my daughter, Alora, I pray that this encourages you to always chase your dreams and know that you're able to do hard things, and you shouldn't be afraid to put yourself out there. I will.

Dad, although you are gone, I really finished this for you. Now I can be published just like you. I love and miss you.

www.ingramcontent.com/pod-product-compliance
Lightning Source LLC
Chambersburg PA
CBHW071545110726
47908CB00007B/2007